HOMUNCULUS

ALSO BY JAMES P. BLAYLOCK
AND AVAILABLE FROM TITAN BOOKS

Lord Kelvin's Machine
The Aylesford Skull
The Aylesford Skull Limited Edition

TITAN BOOKS

Homunculus
Print edition ISBN: 9780857689825
E-book edition ISBN: 9780857689832

Published by Titan Books
A division of Titan Publishing Group Ltd
144 Southwark Street, London SE1 0UP

First edition: February 2013

1 3 5 7 9 10 8 6 4 2

A CIP catalogue record for this title is available from the British Library.

Printed and bound in the United States.

To Viki

And, this time,

To Tim Powers,
for scores of good ideas,
unending friendship, and good cheer.

To Serena Powers,
who deserves more than this humble volume.
William Hazlitt sends his apologies to
Jenny Bunn.

"What a delicate speculation it is, after drinking whole goblets of tea, and letting the fumes ascend into the brain, to sit considering what we shall have for supper—eggs and a rasher, a rabbit smothered in onions, or an excellent veal cutlet! Sancho in such a situation once fixed upon cow-heel; and his choice, though he could not help it, is not to be disparaged."

WILLIAM HAZLITT
"On Going a Journey"

"I should wish to quote more, for though we are mighty fine fellows nowadays, we cannot write like Hazlitt. And, talking of that, Hazlitt's essays would be a capital pocketbook on such a journey; so would a volume of Ashbless poems; and for *Tristram Shandy* I can pledge a fair experience."

ROBERT LOUIS STEVENSON
"Walking Tours"

PROLOGUE

LONDON 1870

Above the St. George's Channel clouds thick as shorn wool arched like a bent bow from Cardigan Bay round Strumble Head and Milford Haven, and hid the stars from Swansea and Cardiff. Beyond Bristol they grew scanty and scattered and were blown along a heavenly avenue that dropped down the sky toward the shadows of the Cotswold Hills and the rise of the River Thames, then away east toward Oxford and Maidenhead and London. Stars winked and vanished and the new moon slanted thin and silver below them, the billowed crescent sail of a dark ship, swept to windward of stellar islands on deep, sidereal tides.

And in the wake of the moon floated an oval shadow, tossed by the whims of wind, and canting southeast from Iceland across the North Atlantic, falling gradually toward Greater London.

Two hours yet before dawn, the wind blew in fits above Chelsea and the sky was clear as bottled water, the clouds well to the west and east over the invisible horizon. Leaves and dust and bits of paper whirled through the darkness, across Battersea Park and the pleasure boats serried along the Chelsea shore, round the tower of St. Luke's and into darkness. The wind, ignored by most of the sleeping city, was cursed at by a hunchbacked figure who drove a dogcart down the Chelsea Embankment toward Pimlico, a shabby vehicle with a tarpaulin tied across a humped and unnatural load.

He looked back over his shoulder. The end of the canvas flapped in the wind. It wouldn't do to have it fly loose, but time was precious. The city was stirring. The carts of ambitious costermongers and greengrocers already clattered along to market, and silent oyster boats sailed out of Chelsea Reach toward Billingsgate.

The man reined in his horse, clambered down onto the stones, and lashed the canvas tight. A putrid stench blew out from under it. The wind was from the northeast, at his back. Such was the price of science. He put a foot on the running board and then stopped in sudden dread, staring at an open-mouthed and wide-eyed man standing on the embankment ahead with a pushcart full of rags. The hunchback gave him a dark look, most of it lost in the night. But the ragpicker wasn't peering at him, he was staring skyward where, shadowing the tip of the moon overhead, hovered the dim silhouette of a great dirigible, a ribby gondola swinging beneath. Rhythmic humming filled the air, barely audible but utterly pervasive, as if it echoed off the dome of the night sky.

The hunchback leaped atop the seat, whipped his startled horse, and burst at a run past the stupefied ragpicker, knocking his barrow to bits against a stone abutment. With the wind and the hum of the blimp's propellers driving him along, the hunchback scoured round the swerve of Nine Elms Reach and disappeared into Westminster, the blimp drifting lower overhead, swinging in toward the West End.

* * *

Along Jermyn Street the houses were dark and the alleys empty. The wind banged at loose shutters and unlatched doors and battered the new wooden sign that hung before Captain Powers' Pipe Shop, yanking it loose finally in the early morning gray and throwing it end over end down Spode Street. The only light other than the dim glow of a pair of gaslamps shone from an attic window opposite, a window which, if seen from the interior of Captain Powers' shop, would have betrayed the existence of what appeared to be a prehistoric bird sporting the ridiculous rubber beak of a leering pterodactyl. Beyond it a spectacled face, half frowning, examined a rubber ape with apparent dissatisfaction. It wasn't the ape, however, that disturbed him; it was the wind. Something about the wind made him edgy, restless. There was too much noise on it, and the noises seemed to him to be portentous. Just when the cries of the windy night receded into regularity and faded from notice, some rustling thing – a leafy branch broken from a camphor tree in St. James' Square or a careering crumple of greasy newspaper – brushed at the windowpane, causing him to leap in sudden dread in spite of himself. It was too early to go to bed; the sun would chase him there soon enough. He stepped across to the window, threw open the casement, and shoved his head out into the night. There was something on the wind – the dry rustle of insect wings, the hum of bees… He couldn't quite name it. He glanced up at the starry sky, marveling at the absence of fog and at the ivory moon that hung in the heavens like a coathook, bright enough, despite its size, so that the ghosts of chimney pots and gables floated over the street. Closing the casement, he turned to his bench and the disassembled shell of a tiny engine, unaware of the fading of the insect hum and of the oval shadow that passed along on the pavement below, creeping toward Covent Garden.

It wasn't yet four, but costermongers of all persuasions clustered at the market, pushing and shoving among greengrocers, ragpickers, beggars, missionaries, and cats. Carts and wagons full of vegetables were crammed in together along three sides of the square, heaped with onions and cabbages, peas and celery. On the west side of the square sat boxes and baskets of potted plants and flowers – roses, verbena, heliotrope and fuchsia – all of it emitting a fragrance which momentarily called up memories, suspicions of places at odds with the clatter and throng that stretched away down Bow Street and Maiden Lane, lost almost at once among a hundred conflicting odors. Donkey carts and barrows choked the five streets leading away, and flower girls with bundles of sweet briar competed with apple women, shouting among the carts, the entire market flickering in the light of gaslamps and of a thousand candles thrust into potatoes and bottles and melted heaps of wax atop brake-locked cartwheels and low window sills, yellow light dancing and dying and flaring again in the wind.

A tall and age-ravaged missionary advertising himself as Shiloh, the Son of God, stood shivering in sackcloth and ashes, shouting admonitory phrases every few seconds as if it helped him keep warm. He thrust tracts into random faces, as oblivious to the curses and cuffs he was met with as the throng around him was oblivious to his jabber about apocalypse.

The moon, yellow and small, was sinking over Waterloo, and the stars were one by one winking out when the dirigible sailed above the market, then swept briefly out over the Victoria Embankment on its way toward Billingsgate and Petticoat Lane. For a few brief seconds, as the cry went round and thousands of faces peered skyward, the slat-sided gondola that swayed beneath the blimp was illuminated against the dying moon and the glow it cast on the clouds. A creaking and shuddering reached them on the wind, mingled with the hum of spinning propellers. Within the gondola, looking for all the world as if he were piloting the moon itself, was a rigid figure in a cocked hat, gripping the wheel, his legs planted widely as if set to counter an ocean swell. The wind tore at his tattered coat, whipping it out behind him and revealing the dark curve of a ribcage, empty of flesh, ivory moonlight glowing in the crescents of air between the bones. His wrists were manacled to the wheel, which itself was lashed to a strut between two glassless windows.

The gondola righted itself, the moon vanished beyond rooftops, and the dirigible had passed, humming inexorably along toward east London. For the missionary, the issuance of the blimp was an omen, the handwriting on the wall, an even surer sign of coming doom than would have been the appearance of a comet. Business picked up considerably, a round dozen converts having been reaped by the time the sun hoisted itself into the eastern sky.

It was with the dawn that the blimp was sighted over Billingsgate. The weathered gondola creaked in the wind like the hull of a ship tossing on slow swells, and its weird occupant, secured to the wooden shell of his strange swaying aerie like a barnacle to a wave-washed rock, stared sightlessly down on fishmongers' carts and bummarees and creeping handbarrows filled with baskets of shellfish and eels, the wind whirling the smell of it all east down Lower Thames Street, bathing the Custom House and the Tower in the odor of seaweed and salt spray and tidal flats. A squid seller, plucking off his cap and squinting into the dawn, shook his head sadly at the blimp's passing, touched two fingers to his forehead as if to salute the strange pilot, and turned back to hawking and rubbery, doleful-eyed occupants of his basket, three to the penny.

Petticoat Lane was far too active to much acknowledge the strange craft, which, illuminated by the sun now rather than the reflected light of the new moon, had lost something of its mystery and portent. Heads turned, people pointed, but the only man to take to his heels and run was a tweed-coated man of science. He had been haggling with a seller of gyroscopes and abandoned shoes about the coster's supposed knowledge of a crystal egg, spirited away from a curiosity shop near Seven Dials and rumored to be a window through which, if the egg were held just so in the sunlight, an observer with the right sort of eyesight could behold a butterfly-haunted landscape on the edges of a Martian city of pink stone, rising above a broad grassy lawn and winding placid canals. The gyroscope seller had shrugged. He could do little to help. To be sure, he'd heard rumors of its appearance somewhere in the West End, sold and resold for fabulous sums. Had the guv'nor that sort of sum? And a man of science needed a good gyroscope, after all, to demonstrate and study the laws of gravity, stability, balance, and spin. But Langdon St. Ives had shaken his head. He required no gyroscope; and yes, he did have certain sums, some little bit of which he'd gladly part with for real knowledge.

But the hum of the blimp and the shouts of the crowd brought him up short then, and in a trice he was pounding down Middlesex Street shouting for a hansom cab, and then craning his neck to peer up out of the cab window as it rattled away east, following the slow wake of the blimp out East India Dock Road, losing it finally as it rose on an updraft and was swallowed by a white bank of clouds that fell away toward Gravesend.

ONE
THE WEST END

On April 4 of the year 1875 – thirty-four centuries to the day since Elijah's flight away to the stars in the supposed flaming chariot, and well over eighty years after the questionable pronouncement that Joanna Southcote suffered from dropsy rather than from the immaculate conception of the new messiah – Langdon St. Ives stood in the rainy night in Leicester Square and tried without success to light a damp cigar. He looked away up Charing Cross Road, squinting under the brim of a soggy felt hat and watching for the approach of – someone. He wasn't sure who. He felt foolish in the top shoes and striped trousers he'd been obliged to wear to a dinner with the secretary of the Royal Academy of Sciences. In his own laboratory in Harrogate he wasn't required to posture about in stylish clothes. The cigar was beginning to become irritating, but it was the only one he had, and he was damned if he'd let it get the best of him. He alternately cursed the cigar and the drizzle. This last had been falling – hovering, rather – for hours, and it confounded St. Ives' wish that it either rain outright or give up the pretense and go home.

There was no room in the world of science for mediocrity, for half measures, for wet cigars. He finally pitched it over his shoulder into an alley, patted his overcoat to see if the packet beneath was still there, and had a look at his pocket watch. It was just shy of nine o'clock. The crumpled message in his hand, neatly blocked out in handwriting that smacked of the draftsman, promised a rendezvous at eight-thirty.

"Thank you, sir," came a startling voice from behind him. "But I don't smoke. Haven't in years." St. Ives spun round, nearly knocking into a gentleman under a newspaper who hurried along the cobbles. But it wasn't he who had spoken. Beyond, slouching out of the mouth of an alley, was a bent man with a frazzle of damp hair protruding from the perimeter of a wrecked Leibnitz cap. His extended hand held St. Ives' discarded cigar as if it were a fountain pen. "Makes me bilious," he was saying. "Vapors, it is. They say it's a thing a man gets used to, like shellfish or tripe. But they're wrong about it. Leastways they're wrong when it comes to old Bill Kraken. But you've got a dead good aim, sir, if I do say so myself. Struck me square in the chest. Had it been a snake or a newt, I'd have been a sorry Kraken. But it weren't. It were a cigar."

"Kraken!" cried St. Ives, genuinely astonished and taking the proffered cigar. "Owlesby's Kraken is it?"

"The very one, sir. It's been a while." And with that, Kraken peered behind him down the alley, the mysteries of which were hidden in impenetrable darkness and mist.

In Kraken's left hand was an oval pot with a swing handle, the pot swaddled in a length of cloth, as if Kraken carried the head of a Hindu. Around his neck was a small closed basket, which, St. Ives guessed, held salt, pepper, and vinegar. "A pea man, are you now?"

asked St. Ives, eyeing the pot. Standing in the night air had made him ravenous.

"Aye, sir," replied Kraken, shaking his head. "By night I am, usually up around Cheapside and Leadenhall. I'd offer you a pod, sir, but they've gone stone cold in the walk."

A door banged shut somewhere up the alley behind them, and Kraken cupped a hand to his ear to listen. There was another bang followed close on by a clap of thunder. People hurried past, huddled and scampering for cover as a wash of rain, granting St. Ives' wish, swept across the square. It was a despicable night, St. Ives decided. Some hot peas would have been nice. He nodded at Kraken and the two men hunched away, sloshing through puddles and rills and into the door of the Old Shades, just as the sky seemed to crack in half like a China plate and drop an ocean of rain in one enormous sheet. They stood in the doorway and watched.

"They say it rains like that every day down on the equator," said Kraken, pulling off his cap.

"Do they?" St. Ives hung his coat on a hook and unwound his muffler. "Any place special on the equator?"

"Along the whole bit of it," said Kraken. "It's a sort of belt, you see, that girds us round. Holds the whole heap together, if you follow me. It's complicated. We're spinning like a top, you know."

"That's right," said St. Ives, peering through the tobacco cloud toward the bar, where a fat man poked bangers with a fork. Lazy smoke curled up from the sausages and mingled with that of dozens of pipes and cigars. St. Ives was faint. Nothing sounded as good to him as bangers. Damn pea pods. He'd sell his soul for a banger, sell his spacecraft even, sitting four-fifths built in Harrogate.

"Now the earth ain't nothing but bits and pieces, you know, shoved in together." Kraken followed St. Ives along a trail of sausage smoke toward the bar, crossing his arms in front of his pot. "And think of what would come of it if you just set the whole mess aspin. Like a top, you know, as I said."

"Confusion," said St. Ives. "Utter confusion."

"That's the very thing. It would all go to smash. Fly to bits. Straightaway. Mountains would sail off. Oceans would disappear. Fish and such would shoot away into the sky like Chinese rockets. And what of you and me? What of us?"

"Bangers and mash for my friend and me," said St. Ives to the publican, who looked at Kraken's peapot with disfavor. "And two pints of Newcastle." The man's face was enormous, like the moon.

"What of us, is what I want to know. It's a little-known fact."

"What is?" asked St. Ives, watching the moon-faced man spearing up bangers, slowly and methodically with pudgy little fingers, almost sausages themselves.

"It's a little-known fact that the equator, you see, is a belt – not cowhide, mind you, but what the doctor called elemental twines. Them, with the latitudes, is what binds this earth of ours. It isn't as tight as it might be, though, which is good because of averting suffocation. The tides show this – thank you, sir; God bless you – when they go heaving off east and west, running up against these belts, so to speak. And lucky it is for us, sir, as I said, or the ocean would just slide off into the heavens. By God, sir, this is first-rate bangers, isn't it?"

St. Ives nodded, licking grease from his fingertips. He washed a mouthful of the dark sausage down with a draught of ale. "Got all this from Owlesby, did you?"

"Only bits, sir. I do some reading on my own. The lesser-known works, mostly."

"Whose?"

"Oh, I ain't particular, sir. Not Bill Kraken. All books is good books. And ideas, if you follow me, facts that is, are like beans in a bottle. There's only so many of them. The earth ain't but so many miles across. I aim to have a taste of them all, and science is where I launched out, so to speak."

"That's where I launched out too," said St. Ives. "I'll just have another pint. Join me?"

Kraken yanked a faceless pocket watch out of his coat and squinted at it before nodding. St. Ives winked and pushed away once more toward the bar. It was an hour yet before closing. A tramp in rags sidled from table to table, uncovering at each the stump of a recently severed thumb. A man in evening clothes lay on the floor, straight out on his side, his nose pressed against a wall, and three stools, occupied by his sodden young friends, propped him up there as if he were a corpse long gone in rigor mortis. There was an even cacophony of sounds, of laughter and clanking dishes and innumerable conversations punctuated at intervals by a loud, tubercular cough. More floor was covered by shoe soles and table legs than was bare, and that which was left over was scattered with sawdust and newspaper and scraps of food. St. Ives mashed the end of a banger beneath his heel as he edged past two tables full of singing men – seafaring men from the look of them.

Kraken appeared to be half asleep when minutes later St. Ives set the two pint glasses on the tabletop. The pleasant and solid clank of the full glasses seemed to revive him. Kraken set his peapot between his feet. "It's been a while, sir, hasn't it?"

"Fourteen years, is it?"

"Fifteen, sir. A month before the tragedy, it was. You wasn't much older'n a bug, if I ain't out of line to say so." He paused to drink off half the pint. "Them was troublesome times, sir. Troublesome times. I ain't told a soul about most of it. Can't. I've cheated myself of the hereafter; I can't afford Newgate."

"Surely nothing as bad as that…" began St. Ives, but he was cut short by Kraken, who waved broadly and shook his head, falling momentarily silent.

"There was the business of the carp," he said, looking over his shoulder as if he feared that a constable might at that moment be slipping up behind. "You don't remember it. But it was in the *Times,* and Scotland Yard even had a go at it. And come close, too, by God! There's a little what-do-you-call-it, a gland or something, full of elixir. I drove the wagon. Dead of night in midsummer, and hot as a pistol barrel. We got out of the aquarium with around a half-dozen, long as your arm, and Sebastian cut the beggars up not fifty feet down Baker Street, on the run but neat as a pin. We gave the carps to a beggar woman on Old Pye, and she sold the lot at Billingsgate. So good come of it in the end.

"But the carp affair was the least of it. I'm ashamed to say more. And it wouldn't be right to let on that Sebastian was behind the worst. Not by a sea mile. It was the other one. I've seen him more than once over the fence at Westminster Cemetery, and late at night too, him in a dogcart on the road and me and Tooey Short with spades in our hand. Tooey died in Horsemonger Lane Gaol, screaming mad, half his face scaled like a fish."

Kraken shuddered and drained his glass, falling silent and staring into the dregs as if he'd said enough – too much, perhaps.

"It was a loss when Sebastian died," said St. Ives. "I'd give something to know what became of his notebooks, let alone the rest of it."

Kraken blew his nose into his hand. Then he picked up his glass and held it up toward a gaslamp as if contemplating its empty state. St. Ives rose and set out after another round. The moon-faced publican poured two new pints, stopping in between to scoop up mashed potatoes with a blackened banger and shove it home, screwing up his face and smacking his lips. St. Ives winced. An hour earlier a hot banger had seemed paradisial, but four bangers later there was nothing more ghastly to contemplate. He carried the two glasses back to the table, musing on the mutability of appetite and noting through the open door that the rain had let off.

Kraken met him with a look of anticipation, and almost at once did way with half the ale, wiping the foam from his mouth with the sleeve of his shirt. St. Ives waited.

"No, sir," said Kraken finally. "It wasn't the notebooks I'm sorry for, I can tell you." Then he stopped.

"It wasn't?" asked St. Ives, curious.

"No, sir. Not the bleeding papers. Damn the papers. They're writ in blood. Every one. Good riddance, says I."

St. Ives nodded expansively, humoring him.

Kraken hunched over the table, waggling a finger at St. Ives, the little basket of condiments on his neck swaying beneath his face like the gondola of a half-deflated balloon. "It was that damn *thing*," whispered Kraken, "what I'd have killed."

"Thing?" St. Ives hunched forward himself.

"The thing in the box. I seen it lift the corpse of a dog off the floor and dance it on the ceiling. And there were more to it than that." Kraken spoke so low that St. Ives could barely hear him above the din. "Them bodies me and Tooey Short brought in. There was more than one of them as walked out on his own legs." Kraken paused for effect and sucked down the last half inch of ale, clunking the glass back down onto the oaken tabletop. "No, sir. I don't rue no papers. And if they'd asked me, I'd 'a' told them Nell was innocent as a China doll. I loved the young master, and I cry to think he left a baby son behind him, but by God the whole business wasn't natural, was it? And the filthy shame of it is that Nell didn't plug that damned doctor after she put one through her brother. That's what I regret, in a nut."

Kraken made as if to stand up, his speechifying over. But St. Ives, although shaken by bits of Kraken's tale, held his hand up to stop his leaving. "I have a note from Captain Powers," said St. Ives, proffering the crumpled missive to Kraken, "asking me to meet a man in Leicester Square at eight-thirty."

Kraken blinked at him a moment, then peered over his shoulder toward the door and squinted round the pub, cocking an ear. "Right ho," he said, sitting back down. He bent toward St. Ives once again. "I ran into the Captain's man, up in Covent Garden, at the market it was, three days back. And he mentioned the..." Kraken paused and winked voluminously at St. Ives.

"The machine?"

"Aye. That's the ticket. The machine. Now I don't claim to know where it is, you see, but I've heard tell of it. So the Captain put me onto you, as it were, and said that the two of us might be in a way to do business."

St. Ives nodded, pulse quickening. He patted his pockets absentmindedly and found a cigar. "Heard tell of it?" He struck a match and held it to the cigar end, puffing sharply. "From whom?"

"Kelso Drake," whispered Kraken. "Almost a month ago, it was. Maybe six weeks."

St. Ives sat back in surprise. "The millionaire?"

"That's a fact. From his very lips. I worked for him, you see, and overheard more than he intended – more than I wanted. A foul lot, them millionaires. Nothing but corruption. But they'll reap the bread of sorrow. Amen."

"That they will," said St. Ives. "But what about the machine – the ship?"

"In a brothel, maybe in the West End. That's all I know. He owns a dozen. A score. Brothels, I mean to say. There's nothing foul he don't have a hand in. He owns a soap factory out in Chingford. I can't tell you what it is they make soap out of. You'd go mad."

"A brothel that might be in the West End. That's all?"

"Every bit of it."

St. Ives studied the revelation. It wasn't worth much. Maybe nothing at all. "Still working for Drake?" he asked hopefully.

Kraken shook his head. "Got the sack. He was afraid of me. I wasn't like the rest." He sat up straight, giving St. Ives a stout look. "But I'm not above doing a bit of business among friends, am I? No, sir. I'm not. Not a bit of it." He watched St. Ives, who was lost in thought. "Not Bill Kraken. No, sir. When I set out to do a man a favor, across town, through the rain, mind you, why it's, 'keep your nose in front of your face. Let it rain!' That's my motto when I'm setting out on a job like this one."

St. Ives came to himself and translated Kraken's carrying on. He handed across two pound notes and shook his hand. "You've done me a service, my man. If this pans out there'll be more in it for you. Come along to the Captain's shop on Jermyn Street Thursday evening. There'll be a few of us meeting. If you can round up more information, you won't find me miserly."

"Aye, sir," said Kraken, rising and fetching up his peapot. He secured the cloths and tied them neatly about the lip of the pot. "I'll be there." He folded the two notes and slipped them into his shoe, then turned without another word and hurried out.

St. Ives' cigar wouldn't stay lit. He looked hard at it for a moment before recognizing it as the damp thing he'd pitched at

Kraken an hour and a half earlier. It seemed to be following him around. The man without the thumb loomed in toward him. St. Ives handed him a shilling and the cigar, found his coat on the rack, checked the inside pocket for his parcel – actually a sheaf of rolled paper – and set out into the night.

Powers' Pipe and Tobacco Shop lay at the corner of Jermyn and Spode, with long, mullioned windows along both the south and east walls so that a man – Captain Powers, for instance – might sit in the Morris chair behind the counter and, by rotating his head a few degrees, have a view of those coming and going along either street. On the night of the fourth of April, though, seeing much of anything through the utter darkness of the clouded and rainy night was unlikely. The thin glow cast by the two visible gaslamps, both on Jermyn Street, was negligible. And the light that shone from lit windows here and there along the street seemed to have an antipathy to flight, and hovered round its sources wary of the damp night.

Captain Powers would hear the sound of approaching feet on the pavement long before the traveler would appear in one of the two yellow circles of illuminated pavement, then disappear abruptly into the night, the footsteps clop-clopping away into silence.

The houses across the street were inhabited by the genteel, many of whom wandered into the pipe shop for a pouch of tobacco or a cigar. It would have been lean times for the Captain, however, if it hadn't been for his pension. He'd been at sea since he was twelve and had lost his right leg in a skirmish fifty miles below Alexandria, when his sloop sank in the Nile, blown to bits by desert thieves. He had saved a single tusk of a fortune in ivory, and twenty years later

William Keeble the toymaker had made him a leg of it, the best by far of any he'd worn. Not only did it fit without taking the skin off that little bit of leg he had left, but it was hollow and held a pint of liquor and two ounces of tobacco. In a pinch he could smoke the entire leg, could press a button at the tip and manipulate a hidden plate, the size of a half crown, which would slide back to reveal the bowl of a pipe. A tube ran up the inside of his pantleg and coat, and he could walk and smoke simultaneously. The Captain had only done so once, largely because of a sort of odd fascination with the idea of Keeble's having built it. The bewildered stares of passersby, however, had seemed to argue against the wisdom of revealing in public the wonderful nature of the thing. Captain Powers, grizzled from sea weather and stoic from thirty years of discipline before the mast, was a conservative at heart. Dignity was his byword. But friendship precluded him from letting on to Keeble that he had no real desire to be seen smoking a peg leg.

Keeble's house, in fact, sat opposite Powers' store. The Captain looked across the top of his companion's head at the lamp burning in the attic shop. Below was another room alight – the bedroom of Jack Owlesby; and on the left yet another, the bedroom, quite likely, either of Winnifred – Keeble's wife – or of Dorothy, the Keeble daughter, home for a fortnight now from finishing school.

His companion cleared his throat as if about to speak, so Captain Powers let his gaze fall from the window to his friend's face. It had the unmistakable look of nobility to it, of royalty, but it was the face of Theophilus Godall of the Bohemian Cigar Divan in Rupert Street, Soho, a face that at that moment was drawing on an old meerschaum pipe. Carved on either side of the bowl was the coat of arms of the royal family of Bohemia, a house long since scattered and flown from a fallen country. The pipe had had, no doubt, a vast and peculiar history before passing into the hands of Godall, and who knew what sort of adventures had befallen it since?

"I was with Colonel Geraldine," Godall was saying, "in Holborn. Incognito. It was late and the evening had proven fallow. All we'd accomplished was to have spent too much good money on bad champagne. We'd had a pointless discussion with a fellow who had a promising story about a suicidal herb merchant on Vauxhall Bridge Road. But the fellow – the second fellow, that is, the herb merchant – turned out to be already dead. Hanged himself these six months past with his own gaiters, and the first fellow turned out to be uninteresting. I wish I could say he meant well, but what he meant was to drink our champagne.

"Before he left, though, in came two of the most extraordinary men. Obviously bound for the workhouse but neither had any color to him. They had the skin of frog bellies. And they had no notion of where they were. Not the foggiest. They had a sort of dazed look about them, as if they'd been drugged, you might say. In fact that's what I thought straightaway. Geraldine spoke to the larger of the two, but the man didn't respond. Looked at him in perfect silence. Not insubordinately, mind you. There was none of that. There was simply no hint of real consciousness."

The Captain shook his head and tapped the ashes of his pipe into a brass bowl. He looked at the clock under the counter – nearly ten-thirty. The rain had slackened. He could see none at all falling across the illuminated glass of the streetlamp. Footsteps approached slowly, drawing up along Jermyn Street. They stopped altogether. Captain Powers winked at Theophilus Godall, who nodded slightly. The footsteps resumed, angling away across the road toward Keeble's house. It was just possible that it was Langdon St. Ives, come round to Keeble's to discuss his oxygenator box. But no, St. Ives would have stopped in if he'd seen a light. He'd have spoken to Kraken by now and be full of alien starships. This was someone else.

A hunched shadow appeared on the pavement opposite – the shadow of a hunchback, to be more exact – and hurried past the gaslamp into darkness, but the Captain was certain that he'd stopped beyond it. He had for five nights running. "There's your man across the road," said the Captain to Godall.

"Are you certain of it?"

"Aye. The hunchback. It's him all right. He'll hang round till I switch out the lights."

Godall nodded and resumed his story. "So Geraldine and I followed the two, halfway across town into Limehouse where they went into a pub called the Blood Pudding. We stayed long enough to see that it was full of such men. The two of us stood out like hippopotami. But I can't say we were noticed by any but him." And Godall shrugged back over his shoulder at the street. "He was a hunchback, anyway. And although I'm not familiar with this fellow Narbondo, it could conceivably have been he. He was eating live birds, unless I'm very much mistaken. The sight of it on top of champagne and kippers rather put us off the scent, if you follow me, and I'd have happily forgotten him completely if it weren't for your having got me onto this business of yours. Is he still there?"

The Captain nodded. He could just see the hunchback's shadow, still as a bush, cast across a bit of wall.

A new set of steps approached, accompanied by a merry bit of off-key whistling.

"Get your hat!" cried Captain Powers, standing up. He stepped across and turned down the lamp, plunging the room into darkness. There, striding purposefully up toward Keeble's door carrying his packet of papers was Langdon St. Ives, explorer and inventor.

In an instant the hunchback – Dr. Ignacio Narbondo – had vanished. Theophilus Godall leaped for the door, waved hastily at Captain Powers, and made away into the night, east on Jermyn toward Haymarket. Across the street, William Keeble threw back the door and admitted St. Ives, who squinted wonderingly at the dark, receding figure that had hurried from the suddenly darkened tobacco shop. He shrugged at Keeble. The Captain's doings were always a mystery. The two of them were swallowed up into the interior of Keeble's house.

The street was silent and wet, and the smell of rain on pavement hung in the air of the tobacco shop, reminding the Captain briefly of spindrift and fog. But in an instant it was gone, and the thin and tenuous shadow of the sea vanished with it. Captain Powers stood just so, contemplating, a lazy shaving of smoke rising in the darkness above his head. Godall had left his pipe in his haste. He'd be back for it in the morning; there was little doubt of that.

A sudden light knock sounded at the door, and the Captain jumped. He'd expected it, but the night was full of dread and the slow unraveling of plots. He stepped across and pulled open the heavy door, and there in the dim lamplight on the street stood a woman in a hooded cloak. She hurried past him into the room. Captain Powers closed the door.

St. Ives followed William Keeble up three flights of stairs and into the cluttered toyshop. Logs burned in an iron box, vented out into the night through a terra cotta chimney, and the fire was such that the room, although large, was warm and close, almost hot. But it was cheerful, given the night, and the heat served to evaporate some of the rainwater that dripped in past the slates of the roof. A tremendous and alien staghorn fern hung very near the fire, below the leaded window of the gable that led out onto the roof, and a stream of water, nothing more than a dribble, ran in along the edge of the ill-sealed casement and dripped from the sill into the mossy, decayed box that held the fern. Every minute or so, as if the rainwater pooled up until high enough to run out, a little waterfall would burst from the bottom of the planter and fall with the hiss of steam into the firebox.

Darkened roof rafters angled sharply away overhead, stabilized by several great joists that spanned the twenty-foot width of the shop and provided avenues along which tramped any number of mice, hauling bits of debris and working among the timbers like elves. Hanging from the joists were no end of marvels: winged beasts, carved dinosaurs, papier-mâché masks, odd paper kites and wooden rockets, the amazed and lopsided head of a rubber ape, an enormous glass orb filled with countless tiny carven people. The kites, painted with the visages of birds and deep-water fish, had hung among the rafters for years, and were half obscured by cobweb and dust amid the brown stains of dirty rainwater. Great shreds had been chewed away by mice and bugs to build homes among the hanging debris.

The red pine floor, however, was swept clean, and innumerable tools hung over two work benches, unordered but neat, brass and iron glinting dully in the light of a half-dozen wood and glass sconces. Coughing into his sleeve, Keeble cleared a score of mauve seashells and a kaleidoscope from the benchtop, then swept it clean with a horsehair brush, the handle of which was elegantly carved into the form of an elongated frog.

St. Ives admired it aloud.

"Like that do you?" asked Keeble.

"Quite," admitted St. Ives, an admirer of William Morris's philosophy concerning beauty and utility.

"Press its nose."

"Pardon me?"

"Its nose," said Keeble. "Press it. Give it a shove with your fingertip."

St. Ives dubiously obeyed, and the top of the frog's head, from nose to mid-spine, slid back into its body, revealing a long, silver tube. Keeble pulled it out, unscrewed a cap at the end, found two glasses wedged in behind a heap of wooden planes, and from the tube poured an equal share of liquor into each. St. Ives was astonished.

"So what have you got?" asked Keeble, draining his glass and hiding it away once again.

"The oxygenator. Finished, I believe. I'm counting on you for the rest. It's the last of the lot. The rest of the ship is ready. We'll launch it in May if the weather clears up." St. Ives unrolled his drawing onto the benchtop, and Keeble leaned over it, peering intently at the lines and figures through startlingly thick glasses.

"Helium, is it?"

"And chlorophyll. Powdered. There's an intake here and a spray mechanism and filter there. The clockworks sit in the base – a seven-day works should do it, at least for the first flight." St. Ives sipped at his glass and looked up at Keeble. "Birdlip's engine: could it be duplicated on this scale?"

Keeble pulled off his glasses and wiped them on a handkerchief. He shrugged. "Perpetual motion is a tricky business, you know – rather like separating an egg from its shell without altering the shape of either, and then suspending the two there, one a quivering, translucent ovoid, the other a seeming solid, side by side. It's not done in a day. And the whole thing is relative, isn't it? True perpetual motion is a dream, although a sage named Gustatorius claimed to have produced it alchemically in 1410 in the Balkans, for the purpose of continually turning the back lens of a kaleidoscope. A wonderful idea, but alchemists tend to be frivolous, taken on the whole. Birdlip's engine, though, is running down. I'm afraid his appearance this spring may be his last."

St. Ives glanced up sharply. "Are you?"

"Yes indeed. When it passed five years ago it was low, fearfully so, and far to the north of its passing in '65. So I've a suspicion that the engine is declining. The blimp may well drop into the sea, but I rather think it's tending toward Hampstead where it was launched. There's a homing element in the engine; that's what I think. A chance product of its design, not anything I intended."

St. Ives rubbed his chin, unwilling to let Keeble's revelation push him off his original course. "But can it be miniaturized? Birdlip has been up for fifteen years. In that time I can easily reach Mars, Saturn even, and return."

"Yes, in a word. Look at this." Keeble slid open a drawer and pulled out a wooden box. The joints were clearly visible, and the box was painted with symbols that appeared to be Egyptian hieroglyphs – walking birds and amphibians, eyeballs peering out of pyramids – but there was no sign of a hinge or a latch.

It immediately occurred to St. Ives that the box was a tamper-proof bottle of some sort, perhaps a tiny, self-contained still, and that he would be asked to poke the nose of a painted beast in order to reveal an amber pool of Scotch whisky. But Keeble set the box squarely atop the bench, spun it round forty-five degrees or so, and the lid of the box opened on its own.

St. Ives watched as the lid rose and then fell back. From out of the depths of the box rose a strangely authentic-looking miniature cayman alligator, its long, toothed snout opening and shutting rhythmically. Four little birds followed, one at each corner, and the cayman snapped up and devoured the birds one by one, then grinned, rolled its eyes, made a sound like a rusty hinge, and sank into its den. After a ten-second pause, up it rose again, followed by miraculously restored birds, fated to be devoured over and over again into infinity. Keeble shut the lid, rotated the box a few degrees farther along, and smiled at St. Ives. "It's taken me twelve years to perfect that, but it's quite as workable now as is Birdlip's engine. It's for Jack's birthday. He'll be eighteen soon – fifteen years he's been with us – and he's the only one, I fear, who sees these things with the right sort of eye."

"Twelve years it took?" St. Ives was disappointed.

"It could be done more quickly now," said Keeble, "but it's fearsomely expensive." He was silent for a moment while he put the box away in its drawer. "I've been approached, in fact, about the device – about the patent, actually."

"Approached?"

"By Kelso Drake. He seems to have dreams of propelling entire factories with perpetual motion devices. I haven't any idea how he got onto them in the first place."

"Kelso Drake!" cried St. Ives. He almost shouted, "Again!" but hesitated at the melodramatic sound of it and the moment passed. It was an odd coincidence, though, to be sure. First Kraken's suspicion of Drake's possessing the alien craft, and now this. But there could hardly be a connection. St. Ives pointed at the plans lying on the bench. "How long then, a month?"

"I should think so," said Keeble. "That should do nicely. How long are you in London?"

"Until this is accomplished. Hasbro stayed on in Harrogate. I've got rooms at the Bertasso in Pimlico."

Keeble, winking at St. Ives, began unscrewing the handle of a heavy chisel with an iron two inches wide. There was a bang at the casement overhead, as if it had been suddenly blown closed in the wind. Keeble dropped the chisel in surprise, the inevitable liquor within the handle flowing out over the drawing of the oxygenator device.

"Wind," said St. Ives, himself shaking from the sudden start. But just as he mouthed the word, a bolt of lightning lit the night sky, illuminating a shadowy face that peered in over the sill, and precipitating a wash of sudden, heavy rain.

Keeble cried out in horror and surprise. St. Ives jumped across to the tilted stepladder that led to the boxy little gable. There was a shout from above – a cry actually – and the sound of something scraping across the slates. St. Ives flung open the window in the face of the rain, and climbed out into the night, just as a head and shoulders disappeared over the edge of the roof.

"I've got him!" came a shout from below, the voice of Jack Owlesby, and St. Ives started toward it, thinking to follow the man down. But the slick roof would almost certainly land him in the road, and he could just as easily use the stairs as Keeble had done. As he clambered back in at the casement there was another shout and a creaking and snapping, followed by curses and the swish of tearing vegetation.

St. Ives bolted for the stairs, taking them two at a time, passing a bewildered Winnifred Keeble on the second-floor landing. Further cries drew him on toward the gaping front door and into the street where Keeble wrestled with the marauder, the two of them slogging through an ankle-deep puddle.

Lights flared on in Powers' shop, then abruptly winked out again, then back on. Windows slammed open along the street, and cries of "Pipe down!" and "Shut yer gob!" rang out, but none of them louder than Keeble's shouts of pain. He held his assailant round the chest, having grappled the man from behind as he attempted to flee, and the man stamped the toymaker's toe with the heel of his boot, unable to shake Keeble off.

St. Ives rushed at the pair through the rain, hollering for his friend to hold on, as the criminal – a garret thief, likely – pulled the both of them down the road. Captain Powers, just then, erupted from the mouth of the tobacco shop, stumping along on his peg leg and waving a pistol.

Just as St. Ives drew near, thinking to throw his coat over the thief's head, Keeble set him free and reeled away, hopping on one foot toward the curb. St. Ives' coat, flung like a gill net, fluttered into the mud of the roadway, and the man was gone, loping up Spode Street into the night. Captain Powers aimed his pistol at the man, but the range was too great for any but a chance hit, and the Captain wasn't one to be cavalier with his shooting. St. Ives dashed after the retreating figure, leaping onto the pavement in front of the pipe shop, then nearly colliding with a cloaked woman who appeared out of an adjacent alley, as if, perhaps, she'd come along the short cut from Piccadilly. St. Ives dodged into a wall, and his chase was at an end, the criminal disappearing utterly, his footfalls dying away. St. Ives turned to apologize to the woman, but there was nothing to see but the dark tweed of her cloak and hood, receding into the gloom along Jermyn. A gust of wind whistled along after her, rippling the surface of puddles beneath gaslamps. And on it, unseasonably cold, came the last quick scatter of pre-dawn raindrops.

TWO

THE TRISMEGISTUS CLUB

St. Ives had always felt at home in Captain Powers' shop, although he would have been in a hard way to say just how. His own home – the home of his childhood – hadn't resembled it in the slightest. His parents had prided themselves in being modern, and would brook no tobacco or liquor. His father had written a treatise on palsy, linking the disease to the consumption of meat, and for three years no meat crossed the threshold. It was a poison, an abomination, carrion – like eating broiled dirt, said his father. And tobacco: his father would shudder at the mention of the word. St. Ives could remember him standing atop a crate beneath a leafless oak, he couldn't say just where – St. James' Park, perhaps – shouting at an indifferent crowd about the evils of general intemperance.

His theories had declined from the scientific to the mystical and then into gibberish, and now he wrote papers still, sometimes in verse, from the confines of a comfortable, barred cellar in north Kent. St. Ives had decided by the time he was twelve that intemperance in the pleasures of the senses was, in the main, less ruinous than was intemperance along more abstract lines. Nothing, it seemed to him, was worth losing your sense of proportion and humor over, least of all a steak pie, a pint of ale, and a pipe of latakia.

All of which explained, perhaps, why the Captain's shop struck him so absolutely agreeably. From one angle it was admittedly close and dim, and there was no profit examining the upholstery on the several stuffed chairs and settee that were wedged together toward the rear of the shop. The springs which here and there protruded from rents in the upholstery and which carried on them tufts of horsehair and cotton wadding had, in their day, quite possibly been crowning examples of their type. And the Oriental carpets scattered about might have been worthy of a temple floor fifty or sixty years earlier.

Great pots of tobacco stood atop groaning shelves, now and then separated by a row of books, all tilted and stacked and quite apparently having nothing at all to do with tobacco, but being, it seemed to St. Ives, their own excuse – a very satisfactory thing. Everything worth anything, he told himself, was its own excuse. Three or four lids were askew on the tobacco canisters, which leaked an almost steamy perfume into the still air of the room.

William Keeble hunched over one, dangling his long fingers in at the mouth of the jar and pulling out a tangle of tobacco that glowed golden and black in the gaslight. He wiggled it into the bowl of his pipe, then peered in at it as if in wonder, working it over from as many angles as possible before setting it aflame. There was much in the gesturing to attract a man of science, and for a moment the poet within St. Ives grappled with the physicist, both of them clamoring for the floor.

St. Ives' study at Heidelberg under Helmholtz had brought him into contact for the first time with an opthalmoscope, and he could remember having peered through the wonderful instrument into the eye of an artistic fellow student, a man given to long walks in the forest and to gazing at idyllic landscapes. Just as the operation began, the man had seen through an unshuttered window the drooping branches of a flowering pear, and a little tidepool of gadgetry that ornamented the interior of his eye, suddenly enlivened at the sight, danced like leaves in a brief wind. For a frozen moment after St. Ives removed the instrument and before a blink sliced the picture neatly off, the pear blossoms and a sketch of cloud drift beyond were reflected in the lens of the man's eye. The conclusions St. Ives had drawn tended, he had to admit, toward the poetic, and were faintly at odds with the methods of scientific empiricism. But it was that suggestion of beauty and mystery which attracted him so overwhelmingly to the study of pure science and which – who could say? – compelled him to wander down the crooked avenues that might at last lead him to the stars.

The Captain's tobacco canisters – no two of them alike, and gathered from distant parts of the globe – reminded him, open as they were, of a candy shop. The feeling was altogether appropriate and accurate. His own pipe had gone dead. Here was the opportunity of having a go at some new mixture. He rose and peeked into a Delft jar containing "Old Bohemia."

"You won't be disappointed in that," came a voice from the door, and St. Ives looked up to see Theophilus Godall pulling off a greatcoat on the threshold. The street door slammed behind him, jerked shut by the wind. St. Ives nodded and tilted his head at the tobacco canister as if inviting Godall's commentary. There was something about the man, St. Ives decided, that gave him an air of worldliness and undefined expertise – something in the shape of his aquiline nose or in the forthrightness of his carriage.

"That was originally mixed by a queen of the royal house of Bohemia, who smoked a pipe at precisely midnight each evening, then drank off a draught of brandy and hot water in a swallow and retired. It has medicinal qualities that can't be disputed." St. Ives could see no way out of smoking a bowl. He began to regret his inability to do justice to the rest of the queen's example, then saw, out of the corner of his eye, Captain Powers emerge from the rear of his shop carrying a tray and bottles. Godall smiled cheerfully and shrugged.

Behind the Captain, cap in hand, plodded Bill Kraken, his hair a wonder of wind-whipped happenstance. Jack Owlesby bent in through the door behind Godall, bringing the number of people in the room to seven, including St. Ives' man Hasbro, who sat reading a copy of the *Peloponnesian Wars* and sipped meditatively at a glass of port.

The Captain stumped across to his Morris chair and sat down, waving haphazardly at the collection of bottles and glasses on the tray.

"Thank you, sir," said Kraken, bending over a bottle of Laphroaig. "I'll have a nip, sir, since you ask." He poured an inch of it into a glass, tossing it off with a grimace. He seemed to St. Ives to be in a bad way – pale, disheveled. Hunted was the word for it. St. Ives regarded him narrowly. Kraken's hand shook until, with a visible lurch, he shuddered from top to bottom, the liquor taking hold and supplying a steadying influence. Perhaps his pallid and quaking demeanor was a product of the absence of alcohol rather than of the presence of guilt or fear.

The Captain tapped on the countertop with his pipe bowl and the room fell silent. "I was inclined to believe, just like yourselves, that last Saturday night's intruder was a garret thief, but that's not the case."

"No?" asked St. Ives, startled by the abrupt revelation. He'd had such a suspicion himself. There was too much deviltry afoot for it all to be random – too many faces in windows, too many repeated names, too many common threads of mystery for him to suppose that they weren't part of some vast, complicated weft.

"That's right," said the Captain, putting a match to his pipe. He paused theatrically, squinting roundabout. "He was back this afternoon."

Keeble nodded. It had been the same man. Keeble couldn't have forgotten the back of the man's head, which is all of him he'd seen this time again. Winnifred had been at the museum, cataloguing books on lepidoptery. Jack and Dorothy, thank God, had been away at the flower market buying hothouse begonias. Keeble had been asleep an hour. He'd been dabbling at the engine, and had put the whole works – the plans, the little cayman device, notes – in a hole in the floor that no one, not another living soul, could sniff out. Then he'd given up the ghost at noon and welcomed the arrival of blinking Morpheus. A crash had brought him out of it. The casement window again. He was sure of it. Footfalls sounded. The cook, who was coming in through the back door with a chicken, was confronted by the thief, and slammed him in the face with the plucked bird before snatching at a carving knife. Keeble had rushed out in his nightshirt and, once again, pursued the man into the street. But dignity demanded he give up the chase. A man in a nightshirt, after all. It wasn't to be thought of. And his foot – it was barely healed from the last encounter.

"What was he after?" asked Godall, breaking into Keeble's narration. "You're certain it wasn't valuables?"

"He ran past any number of them," said Keeble, pouring himself a third glass of port. "He could have filled his pockets between the attic and the front door."

"So nothing was taken?" St. Ives put in.

"On the contrary. He stole the plans for a roof-mounted sausage cooker. I'd intended to try it out in the next electrical storm. There's something about a lightning storm that puts me immediately in mind of sausages. I can't explain it."

Godall, incredulous, plucked his pipe out of his mouth and squinted. "You're telling us he broke into the house to steal the plans for this fabulous sausage machine?"

"Not a bit of it. I rather believe he was after something else. He'd been at the floor with a prybar. He'd seen me slip the plans into the cache. I'm certain of it. But he couldn't get at them. I've a theory that he balanced the casement open with a stick so as to be able to shove out in a nonce. But the stick slipped, the casement banged home and latched, and in a panic he snatched up the nearest set of plans and ran for it, thinking to be out the back before I awoke. The cook surprised him."

"What can he do with these plans?" asked the Captain, tapping his pipe out against his ivory leg.

"Not a living thing," said Keeble.

Godall stood and peered out to where wind-whirled debris danced and flew along Jermyn Street in the night. "For my money Kelso Drake will market such a device within the month. Not for profit, mind you – there wouldn't be much profit in it – but as a lark, to thumb his nose at us. He was after the perpetual motion engine then?"

Keeble began to assent when a banging at the door cut him off. The Captain was out of his chair at once, his finger to his lips. There was no one beyond the seven of them whom they could trust, and no one, certainly, who had any business at a meeting of the Trismegistus Club. Kraken slipped away into a rear chamber. Godall shoved a hand beneath his coat, an act which startled St. Ives.

At the newly opened door stood a young man who was, largely because of a disastrous complexion, of indeterminate age. He might have been thirty, but was more likely twenty-five: of medium height, paunchy, brooding, and slightly stooped. The smile that played across the corners of his mouth was evidently false and served in no way to animate his cold eyes – eyes ringed and dark from an excess of study under inadequate light. He seemed to St. Ives to be a student. Not a student of anything identifiable or practical, but a student of dark arts, or of the sort who wags his head morosely and knowingly over cynical and woeful poetry and who has ingested opiates and stalked through midnight streets, without destination, but out of an excess of morbidity and bile. His cheeks seemed almost to be sucked inward, as if he were consuming himself or were metamorphosing into a particularly picturesque fish. He needed a pint of good ale, a kidney pie, and a half-dozen jolly companions.

"I am addressing a meeting of the Trismegistus Club," said he, bowing almost imperceptibly. No one answered, perhaps because he had addressed no one or perhaps because it seemed as if he expected no response. The wind whistled behind him, trifling with the tattered hem of his coat.

"Come in, mate," said the Captain after a long pause. "Pour yourself a glass of brandy and state your business. This is a private club, you see, and no one with a full deck would want to join, if you follow me. We're all idle and we have little regard for hands, you might say, looking for a sail to mend."

The Captain's speech didn't wrinkle the man in the least. He introduced himself as Willis Pule, an acquaintance of Dorothy Keeble. Jack's eyes narrowed. He was certain the claim was a lie.

He was familiar with Dorothy's friends, and even more, he was familiar with the sorts of people who could likely *be* Dorothy's friends. Pule wasn't one of them. He hesitated to say so only out of a spirit of hospitality – it was the Captain's shop, after all – but the man's very presence became an immediate affront.

Godall, his hand yet in his coat, addressed Pule, who hadn't touched a glass despite the Captain's offer. "What do *you* suppose we are?" he asked.

The question seemed to take Pule aback. "A club," he stammered, looking at Godall, then glancing quickly away. "A scientific organization. I'm a student of alchemy and phrenology. I've read of Sebastian Owlesby. Very interesting matter."

Pule chattered on nervously in an unfortunately high voice. Jack was doubly insulted – first at the mention of Dorothy, now at the mention of his father. He'd have to pitch this Pule into the road. But Godall got in before him, waving his free hand and thanking Pule for his interest. The Trismegistus Club, he said, was an organization devoted to biology, to lepidoptery, in fact. They were compiling a field guide to the moths of Wales. Their discussions could be of no use to a student of alchemy. Or of phrenology, for that matter, which, insisted Godall, was a fascinating study. They were awfully sorry. The Captain echoed Godall's general sorrow, and Hasbro instinctively arose and showed Pule the door, bowing graciously as he did so. A silent moment passed after Pule's ejection. Then Godall stood, pulled his coat from its hook, and hurried out.

St. Ives was astonished at Godall's so quickly and handily ejecting Pule, who was, to be sure, not at all the right sort, but who might have been well intentioned. There could be little harm, after all, in his praising Owlesby, though Owlesby's experimentation was not entirely praiseworthy. In fact, when he considered it,

St. Ives wasn't sure what part of Owlesby's work Pule had such admiration for. None of the rest of them could enlighten him. No one, apparently, knew this Pule.

Kraken peeked out of the rear chamber, and Captain Powers waved him into the room. Godall and Pule were forgotten for the moment as Kraken, at the Captain's bidding, spouted the story of his months as a hireling of Kelso Drake, the millionaire, punctuating it with accounts of his readings into scientific and metaphysical matters, the deep waters of which he sailed on a daily basis. And what he found there, he could assure them, would astonish the lot of them. But Kelso Drake – nothing about Kelso Drake would astonish Bill Kraken. Kraken wouldn't put up with the likes of Drake, not for all the money the man possessed. He gulped at his Scotch. His face grew red. He'd been fired by Drake, threatened with a thrashing. He'd see who was thrashed. Drake was a coward, a pimp, a cheat. Let Drake get in his way. Drake would reel from it. Kraken would show him.

Had Kraken news of the machine, asked St. Ives delicately. Not exactly, came the answer, it was in the West End, in one of Drake's several brothels. Was St. Ives aware of that? St. Ives was. Did Kraken know which of the brothels it might be in? Kraken did not. Kraken wouldn't go into Drake's brothels. They wouldn't hold Drake and him at once. They'd explode. Bits of Drake would fall on London like a blighted rain.

St. Ives nodded. The evening would reveal nothing about the alien craft. He might have guessed it. Kraken was proud of himself, of the stuff he was made of. He launched suddenly into a vague dissertation on the backward spinning of a spoked wheel, then broke off abruptly to address Keeble. "Billy Deener," he seemed to say.

"What?" asked Keeble, taken by surprise.

"I say, Billy Deener. The chap who broke in at the window."

"Do you know him?" asked Keeble, startled. The Captain sat up and ceased drumming his fingers on the countertop.

"Know him!" cried the slumping Kraken. "Know him!" But he didn't bother to elaborate. "Billy Deener is who it was, I tell you. And if you're sharp, you won't get within a mile of him. Works for Drake. So did I, once. But no more. Not for the likes of him." And with that Kraken reached once again for the Scotch. "A man needs a drink," he said, meaning, St. Ives supposed, men in general and intending to do right by all men who weren't there to satisfy that particular need. Moments later he slid into a chair and began to snore so loudly that Jack Owlesby and Hasbro hauled him into the back room on the Captain's orders and arrayed him on a bed, shutting the door behind them on their return.

"Billy Deener," said St. Ives to Keeble. "Does it mean anything to you?"

"Not a blessed thing. But it's Drake. That much is clear. Godall was right."

Keeble seemed to pale at the idea, as if he'd rather it weren't Drake. A common garret thief was far preferable. Keeble poured out a draught of the Scotch left in the bottle, then clacked the bottle down onto the tray just as Theophilus Godall slipped back in out of the night, easing the door shut behind him.

"I'll apologize," he said straightaway, "for my behavior – hardly the sort one would expect from a gentleman, which, I profess, is what I heartily wish myself to be considered." The Captain waved his hand. Hasbro tut-tutted. Godall continued, "I hurried Mr. Pule on his way only because I knew him. He is, I'm sure, ignorant of that. He meant us no good, I can assure you. He was in the company, day before yesterday, of your man Narbondo." He nodded at the surprised Captain. "The two struck me as being passing familiar with each other, and although we might have led this Pule along a bit to see what stuff he was made of, I thought the idea rather a dangerous one, in the light of what I perceive as a situation of growing seriousness. Forgive me if I acted in haste. My rushing away was merely a matter of desiring to confirm my suspicions. I followed him to Haymarket where he met our hunchback. The two of them climbed into a hansom cab and I returned with as much haste as propriety allowed."

St. Ives was stunned. Here was a fresh mystery. "Hunchback?" he asked, swiveling his head from Godall to the Captain, who squinted grimly at him and nodded. "Ignacio Narbondo?" Again the Captain nodded. St. Ives fell silent. The woods, apparently, had thickened. And as mysterious as the rest of it was the mere fact that Captain Powers was so well acquainted with Narbondo, quite apparently had an eye on the machinations of the evil doctor. But why? How? It wasn't a question that could be asked outright.

And Langdon St. Ives wasn't the only one mystified. Jack Owlesby, perhaps, was the one among them most seething with angry curiosity. He hardly knew the Captain, who, it seemed to Jack, carried on a strange sort of business for a tobacconist. He knew Godall not a bit. He was certain of only one thing – that he would marry Dorothy Keeble or blow his brains out. The slightest hint that she was being swept unwittingly into a maelstrom of intrigue made him fairly burst with anger. The idea of Willis Pule flattened him with irrational jealousy. His window, he reminded himself, overlooked the Captain's shop. He'd be a bit more attentive in the future; that was certain.

It was almost one in the morning, and nothing had been

accomplished. Like a good poem, the night's doings had aroused more questions, had unveiled more mysteries, than they had solved.

The seven of them agreed to meet in a week – sooner if something telling occurred – and they departed, Keeble and Jack across the road, Hasbro and St. Ives toward Pimlico, Theophilus Godall toward Soho. Kraken stayed on with the Captain, unlikely to awaken before morning, despite the shrieks of the wind rattling at the shutters and whistling under the eaves.

THREE

A ROOM WITH A VIEW

The open doors of the public and lodging houses along Buckeridge Street were wreathed with smoke, which wandered out to be consumed by the London fog, yellow and acrid in the still air. A gaunt man could be seen through one such door, sitting at a table in a dim corner, half a glass of claret before him, boldly clipping the gats off counterfeit half crowns and filing the edges smooth with a tiny, triangular iron. He'd been at the work all evening, tirelessly tossing cleaned blue coin into a basket and covering the heap with a scattering of religious tracts that prophesied the coming doom.

He employed no agents to sell the coin, preferring to distribute it at greater profit and peril through the faithful – his lambs, who understood that they did the work of Shiloh, the New Messiah. They'd be very pretty coins, once they'd been plated, and would further the work of God. The time approached when such work would be at an end. The Reverend Shiloh had honed the coming of the apocalyptic dirigible to the day. Twice it had passed in the early morning, and the last time, more than four long years ago, it had appeared to him out of the west, emblazoned by a dying moon, its impossibly animate pilot peering down out of the heavens.

Historically speaking, the current years should have been fraught with disaster and portent, but recent months had little to recommend themselves beyond the crowning of the Queen as Empress of India and a spate of lackluster scuffling in Turkestan. The next month would see changes, though – that was certain – changes that would knock the Earth askew of its axis and which, Shiloh knew, would reveal the truth of his monumental birth and the identity of his natural, or unnatural, father. It had been twelve years since he'd confronted Nelvina Owlesby on a balcony in Kingston, a blooming trumpet flower vine behind her, shading the two of them from a noon sun. She, in a passion of momentary spiritual remorse, had confessed to him the existence and the fate of the tiny creature in the box. But she was unfaithful. She had recanted, and disappeared into the Leeward Islands that night, and for a dozen years he had waited to see if she had cheated him. The day was nigh. And in the long night to come no end of people would pay. In fact, it was easier to count the few who wouldn't, scattered here and there about London, passing out tracts, doing his work. Bless the lot of them, thought Shiloh, tossing another coin into the heap. "As ye sow," he said, half aloud.

More than anything he would have liked to see the ruination of those who had condemned his mother, who had diagnosed her dropsical when she knew that she carried within her the messiah; those who had denied his very existence, who scoffed at the notion of the union of woman and god. But they were dead, the filth, long years since – beyond his grasp. And so he carried out his father's work. He was certain that the tiny man in the box, the homunculus possessed by Sebastian Owlesby, *had* been his father. Let the doubting Thomases doubt. There was no end of gibbets in hell.

Idly he snipped a gat with a scissors, rubbing the slick coin with his fingers and gazing out toward the street at the hovering fog. If there was the slightest chance, the remotest chance, that the hunchback could resurrect his mother, Joanna Southcote, whose body lay beneath the loam of Hammersmith Cemetery – if the vanished flesh could be regained, revitalized… Shiloh clutched at his basket, overwhelmed at the thought. The act would be worth a thousand of Narbondo's animated corpses, a million of them. They weren't, after all, ideal converts, but they worked without protest, demanded nothing, and thought not at all. Perhaps they *were* ideal converts. Shiloh sighed. The last of his coins was clean.

He arose, wrapped himself in a dark and tattered cloak, drained the lees of his claret, and strode toward the tilting stairs, glaring into the eyes of anyone who dared to look at him. The floor above was dark save for the light of a single tallow candle that burned in a greasy wall niche. The smoke-blackened triangle that fanned away on the wall above it was the least of the filth that stained the plaster.

Shiloh kicked loose the stuck door, lifted the edge by the latch, and pushed it in a foot where it stuck fast, wedged against the floor. The room beyond was bare but for a heap of bedclothes in one corner, a tilted wooden chair, and a little gate-leg table leaning against the wall.

He stepped across to the street end of the room and pulled aside a bit of curtain. Beyond were the artifacts of a little shrine: a silver crucifix, a miniature portrait of his mother's noble face, and a sketch of the man Shiloh knew to he his father, a man who might have danced in the palm of the evangelist's hand, had Shiloh less an aversion to dancing and had the homunculus not been spirited away and set adrift these last fourteen years. The sketch had been done by James Clerk Maxwell, who, in the months he'd possessed the so-called demon, hadn't the vaguest notion what it was, no more than did the Abyssinian, dying of some inexplicable wasting disease, who had sold it to Joanna Southcote eighty-two years ago and had set into motion the creaking, leaden machinery of apocalypse.

Shiloh lifted the odds and ends in the shrine, raised a cleverly disguised false bottom, and dumped in the coin. Then he retrieved from the space a bag of finished, plated coin, replaced the floor and the relics, wrapped himself once again in his cloak, and left. He spoke to no one as he made his way toward the street, where a biting wind whistled across the cobbles and persuaded almost everyone to stay indoors. A single stroller, a portly man with a stick and eyepatch, limped along in his wake, his free hand pressed against his cap to stop the wind's stealing it. Shiloh paid him little heed as he hurried on into Soho.

The houses fronting the narrow stretch of Pratlow Street cramped between Old Compton and Shaftesbury Street were miserable with neglect. Whereas years and weather sometimes soften the faces of buildings, betraying some few elements of passing history, some reflection of the subtle artistry of nature, on Pratlow Street no such effects had been accomplished. Here and there shutters hung canted across windows perpetually dark, their slats held together by nails and screws that were little more than rusty powder. Some feeble attempt had been made once at enlivening a storefront with a gay color of paint, but the painter had had a singularly dull sense of harmony and had, moreover, been dead these past twenty years. His efforts lent the street an even more ghastly and barren personality, if only by contrast, and the glaucous paint, peeling and alligatored over seasons by what little sunlight penetrated the general gloom of the street, popped loose in brittle showers of chips after each rain.

It was perhaps more difficult to find a window pane that remained entire than it was to find one broken, and the only evidence of industry was in the removal of dirty glass shards from some few of the bottom-floor windows and the subsequent dumping of the broken glass onto the cobbles of the street. The effort, perhaps, was made to facilitate the sort of person who would crawl in at the window rather than step in at the door, a purely practical matter, since few of the doors hung square on their rusted hinges, and were in such appalling disrepair as to dissuade any honest man from attempting to breach them.

The effect of the place beneath the pall of smoky fog was so unutterably dismal that the man turning onto it from Shaftesbury started in spite of himself. He pulled his eyepatch down toward his nose, as if it were merely a prop and he desired to hide a fraction more of the street from view. He looked straight ahead at the broken stones of the roadway, ignoring the jabber of a ragged child and the appeals of dark shapes hunched in the shadows of ruined stoops. Halfway down the street he unlocked a bolted door and hurried through, climbing the stairs of a dark, almost vertical well. He entered a room that looked out across an empty courtyard at another house, the windows of which were lit with the glow of gaslamps. Fog drifted in the air of the courtyard, now clearing, now thickening, swirling and congealing and allowing him only occasionally a view of the room opposite – a room in which stood a particularly stooped hunchback, peering at a wall chart and holding in his hand a scalpel, the blade glowing in the lamplight.

Ignacio Narbondo pondered the corpse before him on the table. It was a sorry thing – two weeks dead, of a blow to the face that had removed its nose and eye and so mangled its jaw that yellowed teeth gaped through a wide rent, their gums shrunk back alarmingly. Animating it would accomplish little. What in the devil would it do if it could walk again, beyond horrifying the populace? It *could* beg, Narbondo supposed. There was that. It could be passed off by the charlatan Shiloh as a reformed sinner, far gone in the ravages of pox but walking upright by a miracle of God. Narbondo grunted with laughter. His limp, oily hair hung in wormy curls to his twisted shoulders, which were covered by a smock stained ocher with old blood and dirt.

Along one wall were heaps of chemical apparatus: glass coils, beakers, bell jars, and heavy glass cubes, some empty, some half-filled with amber liquid, one encasing the floating head of an enormous carp. The eyes of the fish were clear, unglazed by death, and seemed to swivel on their axes, although this last might have been an optical trick of the bubbling fluid in the jar. A human skeleton dangled by a brass chain in a corner, and above it, perched along a wide shelf, were oversize specimen bottles containing fetuses in various stages of growth.

Vast aquaria bubbled against the wall opposite, thick with elodea and foxtail and a half-dozen multi-colored koi the length of a man's arm. Narbondo gave up looking at the corpse and limped across to the aquaria, regarding the fish carefully. He reached into a tin bucket and pulled out a clot of brown, threadlike worms, knotted and wriggling, and dumped them onto the surface of the water. Five of the koi lashed about, mouths working, sucking down little clumps of worms. Narbondo watched for a moment the sixth carp, which paid no attention to the meal, but swam along the surface, gulping air, listing to one side, resting now and then until beginning to sink into the weeds, then lurching once more with a great effort toward the surface.

The hunchback snatched up a broad net from a box beneath the aquaria. He pushed back a glass top, stood atop a stool, and with a single, quick sweep, scooped up the struggling fish, tucked the middle finger of his free hand under its gill, and plucked the great fish from the water, slamming it down at once onto a cork board a foot from the head of the supine corpse and nailing its tail and head to the board with pushpins. The fish writhed helplessly for the few seconds it took Narbondo to slice it open. He paused briefly to spray it with fluid from a glass bottle, then scooped out its intestines and organs, clipping them loose and sweeping them into a box at his feet.

There was a sudden pounding at the door. Narbondo cursed aloud. The door swung open to reveal Shiloh the evangelist, cloaked and holding his leather bag. Narbondo ignored him utterly, prodding a little pulsing, bean-shaped gland out of the organ cavity of the carp. He nipped through the threads that held it, slid a thin spatula under it, and lifted it into a vial of amber liquid, corking it and setting it alongside the fetuses. He yanked the gutted carp from the cork board and dropped it into the box below, kicking it under the table. He leered up at the old man, who watched the affair with a mixture of wonder and loathing. "Cat food," said Narbondo, nodding at the dead fish.

"A tragic waste," said Shiloh. "God's children starve for want of bread."

"Feed the multitude with it, then," cried Narbondo, suddenly enraged at the old man's hypocrisy. He yanked the fish out by the tail and waved it in the air, droplets of blood spattering the floor. "A half-dozen more of these and you can feed Greater London."

Shiloh stood silent, grimacing at the blasphemy. "People hunger on this very street – hunger and die."

"And I," croaked Narbondo, "make them walk again. But you're right. It's a filthy shame. There but for fortune, and all."

He stepped across and unlatched the casement that faced the street, swung the window open, and tossed the carp onto the pavement below, the fish bursting in a shower of silver scales. Narbondo emptied the box of entrails after it, nearly onto the head of two men and an ancient old woman who had already begun to fight over the fish. Cries and curses rose from the street. Narbondo cut them short by slamming closed the window. He turned contemptuously and without warning snatched the leather bag from the old man's hand.

The evangelist cried out in surprise, caught himself, and shrugged. "Who is this poor brother?" he asked, nodding at the corpse.

"One Stephanus Biddle. Run over two weeks back by a hansom cab. Stomped to bits by the horses, poor bastard. But dead is dead, I always say. We'll enliven the slacker. He'll be passing round tracts with the best of them by midday tomorrow, if you'll kindly trot along and leave me alone." Narbondo emptied the bag onto the table, then inspected one of the coins. "You'd make money by selling these to the utterer yourself instead of making me do it. You pay dearly for my time, you know."

"I pay for the speedy recovery of God's kingdom," came the reply, "and as for selling the coin myself, I have neither the desire for risk nor the inclination to hobnob with criminals of that sort. I…"

But Narbondo cut him short with a hollow laugh. He shook his head. "Come round tomorrow noon," he said, nodding toward the door. And just as he did so, it swung to and in walked Willis Pule with an armload of books, nodding ingratiatingly at Shiloh and holding out a moist hand that had, a moment earlier, been fingering a promising boil on Pule's cheek. The evangelist strode through the open door, disregarding the proffered hand, a look of superiority and disgust on his face.

The window curtains in the second floor of the building across the courtyard slid shut, unseen by Pule and Narbondo, who bent over the still form on the table. A moment later the street door of that same building opened, and the man in the eyepatch tapped down the half-dozen stairs of the stoop and into the street, hurrying away in the wake of the receding evangelist, who pursued a course toward Wardour Street, bound for the West End.

Langdon St. Ives trudged along through the evening gloom. The enlivening effects of the oysters and champagne he'd foolishly consumed for lunch had diminished and been replaced by a general despair, magnified by his fruitless search for a brothel, of all things, that he wouldn't be able to recognize if he stumbled upon it. And he had undertaken the embarrassing errand on the advice of a man addled by years of drink, who understood the earth to wear a belt for the purpose of supporting a pair of equatorial trousers.

It was the song and dance of getting round to the nub that was most bothersome – of making the proprietor understand that it wasn't just casual satiation that he desired, that the act must somehow involve machinery – a particular machine, in fact. Lord knows what conclusions were drawn, what criminal excesses were even at that moment being heaped onto the doorstep of technology. More champagne would, perhaps, have been desirable. Halfway measures weren't doing the trick. If he were drunk, staggering, then his ears wouldn't burn quite so savagely at each theatrical and idiotic encounter. And if, in the future, he were to run across one of his would-be hosts in public, he could blame the entire sordid affair on drink. But here he was sober.

On the advice of a cabbie he approached a door with a little sliding window, knocking thrice and stepping back a foot or two so as not to seem unnaturally anxious. The door swung open ponderously and a jacketed butler peered out, slightly offended, apparently. The man looked overmuch like Hasbro, who St. Ives heartily wished were along on this adventure. The look on the man's face seemed to suggest that St. Ives, with his pipe and tweed coat, should be knocking on the rear door off the alley. "Yes?" he said, drawing the word out into a sort of monologue.

St. Ives inadvertently pushed at the false beard glued to his chin, a beard which perpetually threatened to succumb to the pull of gravity and drop ignominiously to the ground. It seemed firm enough. He smashed his eye socket around his monocle, squinting up his free eye and staring through the clear lens of the glass. He affected a look of removed and distinguished condescension.

"The cab driver," he said, "advised me that I might find some satisfaction here." He harrumphed into his fist, regretting almost at once his choice of words. What in the world would the man make of his desire for satisfaction? A challenge, perhaps, to a duel? A coarse reference to satisfied lusts?

"Satisfaction, sir?"

"That's correct," said St. Ives, brassing it out. "Not to put too fine a point on it, it was suggested to me that you could put me in the way of, shall we say, a particular machine."

"Machine, sir?" The man was maddening. With a suspicion that at once became certainty, St. Ives understood that he was being had on, either by the cabbie or by this leering, mule-faced man, whose chin appeared to have been yanked double with a tongs. The man stood silent, peering at St. Ives through the half-shut door.

"Perhaps you're unaware, my good fellow, to whom you speak." Silence followed this. "I have certain… desires, shall we say, involving mechanical apparatus. Do you grasp my meaning?" St. Ives squinted at him, losing his monocle in the process. It clanked against a coat button on his chest. He shoved at his beard.

"Ah," said the suddenly voluble man in the doorway. "If you'll use the alley door next time. Wait a moment." The door eased shut. Footsteps receded. The door once again swung open and the butler handed out a parcel. St. Ives took it, and opened it unable to think of anything else to do, and found himself possessed of an eight-hour clock sporting a pair of iron gargoyles on either side of a cracked oval glass.

"I'm not," began St. Ives, when he was struck from behind and shouldered into the street. An old man in a cloak ascended the stairs, brushed past the butler and disappeared growling into the recesses of the house. The door slammed shut.

Damn me, thought St. Ives, staring first at the clock, then at the house. He began once again to ascend the stairs, but was struck halfway up with a sudden fit of inspiration. He turned, tucked the broken clock under his arm, fixed his monocle in his eye, and set out down the road, determined to give up his quest for the moment and to seek out a clock-maker instead. In his haste he nearly collided with a round, eyepatched man tapping along with a stick in the opposite direction.

"Sorry," St. Ives mumbled.

"S'nothing," came the reply, and in moments both had turned their respective corners, two ships passing, as it were, in the afternoon.

The portly man tapped along, highly satisfied with the day's adventure. He entered Rupert Street, Soho, and disappeared into the open doorway of the Bohemian Cigar Divan, patting his pockets absentmindedly as if searching for a cigar.

FOUR
VILLAINIES

Willis Pule admired himself in the window of a bun shop on King Street. His was an intelligent face, uncoarsened by sunlight or wind and with a broad forehead that bespoke a substantial cranium. His complexion, it was true, was marred by an insidious acne, one that beggared all efforts to eradicate it. Pumice, lye, alcohol baths, nothing had diminished it. He'd abstained from eating aggravating foodstuffs, to no effect at all. The red lump on his cheek shone as if it were polished. He should have powdered it, but he sweated so fearfully that the powder might simply have dribbled away.

He pried his eyes away from his skin and regarded for a moment his profile. He'd seen the dusty storage rooms of European libraries thought to be fables by the common breed of historian, and he'd knowledge of alchemy that the likes of Ignacio Narbondo hadn't dreamed of.

It was during his studies that he first learned of the existence of the homunculus. References to it and to its craft dated into antiquity, but were tiresomely sporadic and vague, linked by the most tenuous threads of pale suggestion until its sudden appearance in London some hundred years ago. The bottle imp, maligned by the dying sea captain whose log narrated the grim story of his own decline into madness and death, was without doubt the same creature sold some few years later to Joanna Southcote by an Abyssinian merchant, who followed the sea captain into an early and unnatural grave. There had been references to the thing's having power over life and death, over motion and energy, over the transmutation of metals. It had been the source of the inspiration of Newton, of James Maxwell, the ruination of Sebastian Owlesby.

A trail of horror seemed to follow the thing. All a matter of ignorance, Pule was certain. Ignorance and bungling had squandered the thing's powers, and Narbondo's losing it was the greatest blunder of all. But the hunchback was useful. They would all be useful to Willis Pule before he was through.

And the stakes seemed to be growing. His discovery that the thing in the box had disappeared after Sebastian Owlesby's murder had led him along a clear trail to William Keeble, and, he smiled to think of it, to his fetching daughter. And then there was the matter of a second box and the very interesting transaction between Owlesby and the West African Gem Company a month before Owlesby's death. If there wasn't profit to be made here, Pule was blind. Damn Keeble and the moronic Trismegistus Club. He'd deal with the lot of them.

Around the distant corner, right on time, came Dorothy Keeble, alone. Pule's chest heaved. His days of patient observation hadn't been for naught. His hand shook in his coat pocket, and he realized that he was breathing through his mouth. Fearing vertigo, he clutched at the iron railing across the window of the bun shop and attempted to whistle a nonchalant air.

"Dorothy Keeble?" he asked when the girl was some few feet off. Her jersey dress, dark red with ivory lace, narrowed in around her waist in such a way as to make Pule light-headed. She regarded him curiously. Her skin was almost transparent it was so light, and her hair, impossibly black, fell around her shoulders in loose curls. Pule was gripped by an urge to touch it, to fondle the skin of her face, which was, compared to his own, like ivory next to wormwood. He struggled to control himself. "We have, I believe, a mutual friend."

"Have we?" she asked.

"Jack Owlesby," said Pule, reciting his prepared lie. "We were in school together. Great friends."

"I'm pleased to meet you, Mr...."

"Pule," came the reply. "Willis Pule."

"Shopping for buns, were you, Mr. Pule? I won't keep you then. I'll tell Jack I've met you." She started on her way, and Pule turned to follow, suddenly angry at her obvious indifference.

"I'm a student of arcane history," he said. "I studied at Leipzig and Munich."

"I'm sure that's very nice," said Dorothy, hurrying along. "I'll tell Jack. He'll be happy to know what you've been up to. Don't let me interfere with your errand." She nodded at him and then ignored him. Pule fumed.

"Perhaps you'd take a cup of tea with me?"

"I'm terribly sorry."

"Tomorrow, then."

"I'm afraid not. Thank you awfully."

"Why not?"

Dorothy gave him a look of surprise. “What a question! Won’t my simple refusal suffice?”

“No, it won’t,” said Pule, clutching at her arm. Dorothy jerked away, prepared to slam him with her bag. His skin seemed to be writhing as he stood gaping at her on the pavement. He sputtered, unable to speak.

“Good day to you,” said Dorothy.

“You’ll see me again,” cried Pule at her back. “And so will your father.” She walked on more quickly, not taking the bait.

“Wait until I’ve played my hand!” Pule yelled. And then he caught himself. He gasped for air and leaned against the brick of a row house. It would do no good to lose his temper now. He would wait. In time – soon – she would see reason. He glanced at a dark window. The sight of his face reflected in it didn’t compose him. His hair was awry, and his mouth, normally sensitive and aloof, was contorted in a rictus of loathing. He made a conscious effort to relax, but his face seemed to have frozen in the grip of a maniacal passion.

A scrawny, half-hairless cat wandered out just then from under a fence. Pule stared at it, hating it. He snatched the cat up by the neck and held it kicking at arm’s length. He sloughed off his jacket, letting it fall down his right arm to envelop the struggling beast, then shoved the burden under his arm and strode away in the direction of Narbondo’s cabinet, visions of the cat dismembered flickering across his mind like etchings on a copper plate.

St. Ives let himself in through the front door of the Bertasso Hotel on Belgrave and tramped up two flights of carpeted steps to his room. The red wallpaper, rampant with stylized fleursde-lis, almost made his hair stand on end. He despised the current fashion in gaudy furnishings. It was little wonder society was going to bits, surrounding itself as it did with fakery and ugliness. He was beginning to sound like his father. But it was entirely rational – empirical study would bear him out. Men were products of that with which they surrounded themselves. And men of substance could hardly spring from the cracker-box, factory-made trash they cluttered their homes and inns with. He was in a foul mood, he realized, having played the fool all afternoon. The clock gag probably wouldn't work. He'd be beaten by hired toughs. He'd have been wise to solicit the help of the Captain, who was, admittedly, far more worldly wise than he.

St. Ives himself had strayed within the confines of a house of prostitution only once, when, as a student in Heidelberg, he and a friend wandered into a questionable district after a night of revelry. He hadn't said a thing at the time. Drink had that effect on him – it thickened his tongue, made him mute. He'd merely grinned foolishly, and the grin had been correctly interpreted by an emaciated old woman in a robe who led him to a room full of painted women. "They were big girls," his artist friend had said, accurately and with an air of satisfaction as the two of them had returned to their flat near the university. "Yes," St. Ives had responded, able to add nothing to the pronouncement. Perhaps that was the key here. If he'd arrived drunk and leering on the doorstep of the house on Wardour Street he'd have been admitted. But now he'd have to depend upon masquerading as a clock repair man. The next morning would tell the tale.

He pushed his door open and discovered on a little circular table by his bed a wrapped packet, which had, apparently, just arrived by post. He tore it open and yanked out a sheaf of paper, a hundred fifty pages or so of foolscap, covered in tight handwriting – recognizable handwriting. He sat down hard on his bed. He held in his hands loose papers from the notebooks of Sebastian Owlesby, lost these fifteen years past. He looked at the envelope. It had been posted in London. But by whom? He leafed through it, page by page.

Kraken hadn't exaggerated. Not a bit. There were discussions of vivisection, of the animation of corpses. It was Owlesby's self-documented decline into madness – a day-by-day account, describing how, some few weeks before his death, he implored his sister to kill him. His experimentation had taken a nasty turn, urged on by the self-seeking Ignacio Narbondo until, in late May of 1861, his ghastly experimentation had required the brain of a living man, and Owlesby and an unnamed accomplice had clipped with a great pair of bone cutters the head from a sleeping indigent in St. James' Park and borne the bloody prize home in a sack.

Owlesby had been certain that the homunculus had the power to arrest entropy, to reverse, at least superficially, the process of decay, and had managed to make use of it at the expense of his own sanity. The reasons for his decline were vague. He himself only half understood them. St. Ives became convinced that it was the decay of Owlesby's soul, the slide into deviltry, that hammered away at the shell of sanity until it began to crumble.

Moments of rationality had staggered Owlesby. Nell must kill him if he lapsed again into madness. He had withdrawn his interests in the West African Gem Company in the form of a great emerald, his son Jack's inheritance, and had prevailed upon Keeble to build a box to house it – a box almost identical to the lead-lined cube that held the homunculus.

The notebooks rambled. Owlesby fell into irrationality. There was mention of a second murder, of a brush with Scotland Yard, of the departing of the faithful Kraken, and in the end, of the necessity of obtaining certain glands – youthful glands, and of a nightmarish journey one foggy night into Limehouse. Narbondo had been pitched into the Thames and had swum to the opposite shore. Owlesby had prayed for the hunchback's death, but fate wasn't so kind. They'd have to try again, perhaps feed a stray child opiates. The entries stopped, a day before Owlesby's death. St. Ives was aghast. He dropped the papers onto the tabletop as if they had become suddenly the dried, scaly carcass of a rat. At the end of the journal, in a different hand – a woman's hand – were the words, "I gave the box to Birdlip," and nothing more.

St. Ives was astonished. The box to Birdlip! But which box? The emerald box? Which of the two, the emerald or the homunculus, was aloft in Birdlip's blimp? And who, besides himself, was aware of the whereabouts of the box? Narbondo, certainly, would be interested. St. Ives thought about it. The hunchback would kill to know where the box lay. What had all of this to do with Narbondo's lurking in the shadows of Jermyn Street opposite the Captain's shop? Nothing? Impossible. St. Ives knuckled his brow. Strange things were afoot – that was sure. But as compelling as the mystery of Birdlip's descent and of the blimp's alien passenger might be, St. Ives was doubly determined to find the thing's spacecraft. Failing that, he'd return to Harrogate straightaway to outfit his own craft with the oxygenator box that Keeble was even then working away on. First things first, after all. For fifteen years Birdlip had taken care of himself, and apparently, one of the boxes. He could be trusted to carry on. But it was a damnable and enticing mystery nonetheless. St. Ives packed tobacco into his pipe, held a match to it, and puffed away, the rising clouds of smoke bumping against the low ceiling and flattening in a general haze.

* * *

"Peas here!" shouted Bill Kraken, thumping along down Haymarket toward Orange Street. It was nearing midnight, and Haymarket and Regent Street were mobbed with an assortment of revelers, made up in a large part by prostitutes on the arms of newly met gentlemen, strolling out of the Argyle Rooms and the Alhambra Music Hall. The weather was startlingly warm. A sort of trade wind had blown for three days and the air was tropical and clean. A wash of stars shone overhead, and the effect of the weather and the night sky and the coming of summer seemed to lend the city a breezy spirit.

Kraken could feel it himself. He was almost jaunty with it, and had sat into the morning reading metaphysics in a tuppenny copy of Ashbless' *Account of London Philosophers* that he'd bought at Seven Dials. The bugs that infested its spine had reduced a good portion of the Morocco cover to dust, but had, apparently, failed to reduce the philosophers themselves. Kraken had the volume in his coat pocket. There was no telling how many idle hours he would spend before he discovered what he sought.

An enormous full moon, harvest orange in the warm sky, hung directly overhead, grinning down on the throng and illuminating the white satin bonnets and silk coats of courtesans and the grimed faces of shoe blacks and crossing sweepers. Music tumbled out of cafes as if it were blood coursing through the arteries and veins of the West End, and even Kraken, tired from a day that had added miles to his wanderings about London, felt as if his own blood pulsed to the heat and noise of the moonlit street. The scent of coffee whirled past him in a rush, and four French girls, wide-eyed and chattering among themselves, stepped gaily from the door of a Turkish divan, nearly treading on his toes. For a moment he considered addressing them. But the moment passed, and just as well. What would they say to a pea pod man? Nothing he'd want to hear; that was certain. But the night was warm and almost magic with suggestion, and his mission on behalf of Langdon St. Ives and Captain Powers had been faithfully if unsuccessfully executed since eight that same morning.

He leered momentarily at his reflection in the unlit window of a hatter's shop and pulled the bill of his cap down over his left eye, considered it, then cocked it back onto his head with the air of a man satisfied with himself and faintly contemptuous of the rest of the populace.

Beside him materialized the face of a grinning woman. She'd been there for a bit, he was certain, but he'd just that moment focused on her. He winked. In his coat pocket, such as it was, lay a tin flask of gin he'd bought from a river vendor under Blackfriars Bridge. It was two thirds empty – or one third full, from the long view. It was a good night for optimism. Kraken winked at the reflection again and held the bottle aloft, raising his eyebrows in a silent query.

The woman nodded and smiled. She hadn't, Kraken noticed, any front teeth. He poured a warm, juniper-tinged trickle down his throat, smacked his lips, and turned, handing across the flask. What were a few teeth? Several of his own were gone. She wasn't, taken altogether, utterly unappealing. That is to say, there was something about her, in the pleasant pudding of her cheeks, perhaps, or in the way she fleshed out the tattered merino gown she wore so thoroughly – almost as if she'd been poured into it from a bucket. A large bucket, to be sure. She'd seen better days in some distant time. But haven't we all, thought Kraken, buoyed by the Socratic wisdom of the London Philosophers.

The woman handed the tin back empty. She had a nose like a peach. She caught Kraken's forearm in the crook of her meaty elbow, pinioned it, and hauled him away down Regent toward Leicester Square in a fit of romantic cackling, lifting the lid from the peapot and plunging her free right hand in among the peas. Let her eat, thought Kraken generously. He patted her arm.

"Do you know anything about the stars?" he asked, settling on an appropriate subject.

"Heaps," she replied, dipping once again into the peas.

"There aren't but a few," said Kraken, gazing heavenward. "Sixty or eighty. The heavens are a great mirror, you see. It's a matter of atmosphere, is what it is, of the reflected light of the sun, which..."

"A looking glass, is it? Heaven?"

"In a manner of speaking, miss. The sun, you see, and the moon..."

"A bleedin' looking glass? The moon? You've been sufferin', love, haven't you?" She steered him down Coventry past a line of cafes. Kraken searched for the right words. The concept was a broad one for someone less schooled in the scientific and metaphysical arts than he. "It's astronomy is what it is."

"The moon's nothing but astronomy," agreed the woman, prying among her remaining teeth for a peapod string. "Drives them all mad." And she indicated with a sweep of her hand the entire street.

"The '*spiritus vitae cerebri*,'" intoned Kraken agreeably, "is attracted to the moon in the same manner as the needle of the compass is attracted toward the Pole." He was proud of his storehouse of quotations from Paracelsus, although they were quite likely wasted here. The woman gave his arm a squeeze, screwed her face up awfully so that her eyes seemed to disappear behind the flesh of her nose. She gouged Kraken playfully with a bent finger.

Before them was a lit house, on the door of which hung a sign reading, "Beds to be had within." Kraken found himself in a state of mingled desire and regret, being dragged up the stoop and finally into a darkened room little bigger than a pair of end to end closets. He stumbled against a disheveled bed and collapsed onto his face, hunched over his peapot, the lid of which sailed off and clattered into the opposite wall.

The bedclothes wanted perfume – a tubful. He pushed himself up. "Miss," he said, peering around him in the dark. A hand shoved him roughly down again. She was frolicsome, Kraken had to admit. "If you've a drop of something," he began, wondering if he were reading aright the heavy breathing and shuffling behind him. A warm hand grasped the thong round his neck, and, as he once again began to clamber onto his elbows, yanked the peapot from under him – rather roughly, he thought. He collapsed sideways when his right hand flopped up to allow the pot to travel beneath it. He'd have to be a bit more forward. That was the ticket.

He rolled over to have a look at his companion in the moonlight that illuminated the room. A woman of that stature... He anticipated a monumental revelation. But standing over him was a man, slowly chewing at his own tongue. He wore a black chimney pipe hat, smashed in and perched atop his head like a carton. Raised above it was the peapot. "Deener!" shouted Kraken. The peapot smashed down at him. There was a grunt of effort from the man in the hat. Kraken lurched aside, his left hand shielding his face. His wrist snapped down as the peapot glanced off it, smashing against his cheek. Kraken rolled into a wall. There seemed to be nothing in the tiny room but the villainous bed – nowhere to retreat.

The man swung the pot by its thong, bouncing it off Kraken's forehead and hauling it back for another blow. He seemed to be growling through his gaping mouth, and Kraken noticed in a moment of frozen clarity the droplets of spittle that flew in a little arc as the man's head was tossed backward with the momentum of his next swing.

Kraken regretted in a mist that his own head seemed to have stopped the peapot very handily, and through eyes suddenly blurred behind a wash of gore from his forehead, he watched with removed wonder as Billy Deener very slowly hauled a pistol from his coat, cocked it, and aimed it.

The being confronting a sleepy William Keeble chewed at the end of an ostentatious cigar. Keeble didn't half like his looks. He liked them less, in fact, than he had when the man had visited him once before. It was his moneyed air that was so annoying – an air that betrayed a sort of Benthamite smugness and superiority, that exclaimed its own satisfaction with itself and its faint dissatisfaction with, in this case, William Keeble, who had been surprised in his nightshirt and cloth cap and so was automatically one down.

Kelso Drake hauled his cigar from his mouth and pried his lips apart into an oily, condescending smile. He wore a MacFarlane coat and a silk hat, both of which had left Bond Street, it was reasonably certain, not more than a week or so earlier. Keeble felt a fool in his cloth pointy-hat – doubly so, for he was wearing the one onto which Dorothy had embroidered a comical face, one eye of which was closer to the sideways nose than was the other, an eccentricity which gave the stitched countenance a look of cockeyed lunacy. Drake wouldn't understand such a thing. Keeble could see that in a glance.

The industrialist's desires hadn't changed. He was prepared to offer Keeble a sum of money – a substantial sum for the plans to the engine, for the patent. Keeble wasn't at all interested. Drake's eyes narrowed. He doubled the sum. Keeble didn't care for sums. Damn all sums. He was suddenly powerfully thirsty. On the hall table sat a walrus tusk, carved into the semblance of the beast that had sprouted it. Keeble imagined twisting its foolish head off and draining the peaty contents. But he'd have to offer Drake a glass, and he wasn't about to. Damn Drake and all of his affairs. He and his notion of textile mills run by perpetual motion engines made Keeble sick. The idea of a textile mill alone – a mill of any sort – made Keeble sick. Practicality in general made him sick, and the contrived practicality of Drake's utilitarian vision instilled in him an inexplicable mixture of indifference and loathing that made him long for his bed and a glass with which to chase Drake into nonexistence.

Drake champed at his cigar, rolling it in his mouth, his eyes squinting up into tight little slits. This wasn't, insisted Drake, merely a casual offer. He had certain methods. He had vast resources. He could exert pressure. He could buy and sell Keeble a dozen times. He could ruin him. He could this; he could that; he could the other. Keeble shrugged in his ridiculous cap. The clock on the wall opposite the hall table suddenly went off, pealing in a sort of doleful, leaden tone, utterly out of keeping with the little clockwork apes who charged grinning out of their lair in the interior and banged away with mallets at a bell-shaped iron octopus.

Drake frowned at it, recoiling slightly. The door opened behind him, and Dorothy, a troubled look on her face, stepped through, stopping in sudden surprise at the sight of the stranger's back. Keeble motioned with his eyes toward the stairway, but Dorothy hadn't taken a half step toward them when Drake turned, a broad smile betraying splayed yellow teeth. He clamped his mouth shut at the sight of Dorothy's involuntary grimace, and bowed slightly, flourishing his hat. "Kelso Drake, ma'am," he said, rolling his chewed cigar from one side of his mouth to the other. "Very happy to make your acquaintance."

Dorothy nodded and proceeded toward the stairs, saying, "Pleased, I'm sure," over her shoulder, impolite as it seemed. Her father nodded his head toward the stairs in quick little jerks, stopping abruptly when Drake turned and looked at him quizzically. The questioning look turned once again into a leer, as if Drake's face naturally molded itself that way out of long practice. "What was I saying?" he asked the toymaker. "I was momentarily," he paused and pretended to search for a word, then said theatrically, "distracted."

"You were just saying good day," Keeble stated flatly. "You've got my answer. There isn't any room for discussion."

"No, I suppose there isn't. I'm averse to discussion anyway. A waste of time. Very pretty daughter, that one. Fetching, you might say. You have three days."

"I don't need three days."

"Thursday, let's say. And do stay sober. This business will require all of your efforts, regardless of the outcome." And with that, Drake raised his stick and neatly flipped Keeble's nightcap from his head, turned, and strode through the yawning door. He climbed into the interior of a waiting brougham and was gone.

Keeble stood still for a moment, as if his blood had solidified. His neck and face were hot. Without turning his head he plucked up the cap from where it had fallen on the hall table. A door shut with a bang upstairs. Had Dorothy listened? Had she witnessed Drake's departure? Keeble peered up the stairwell, a forced grin stretching his mouth. The stairs were empty. He pulled on the cloth cap and reached for the walrus tusk. There was really nothing to think about. Drake was all bluff. He wouldn't dare come meddling round again. He'd be sorry for it if he did. Keeble's hand shook as he drained the tusk, and he set it back onto the table uncapped. What did he care for threats? He stood thinking for a moment then tottered away up the stairs to bed.

FIVE

SHADOWS ON THE WALL

The darkness of Hammersmith Cemetery was complete. Not a star shone in the clouded heavens, and the occasional gaslamps that burned in oval niches in the block wall of scattered crypts illuminated nothing but a few befuddled moths that stumbled out of the night, fluttered woodenly around the flame, then disappeared once again into darkness. A heavy river fog lay along the ground, and the old yew trees and alders whose bent branches shaded the grounds dripped moisture onto the neck and shoulders of Willis Pule, who clumsily stamped on the backside of a spade. He pulled the collar of his coat around his neck and cursed. His doeskin gloves were a ruin, and on the palm of his hand below his thumb a blister the size of a penny threatened to tear open.

He looked at his companion's face. He loathed the man – doubly so for his poverty and stupidity. His face was expressionless. No, not entirely. There was a trace of fear on it, perhaps, a shimmer of dread at the sound of the sudden creaking of a limb overhead, at the sigh of rustling leaves. Pule smiled. He raised his left foot again and brought it down sharply on the spade. It slid off, and the shovel dug in a mere inch or two and canted to the side.

There was something utterly distasteful about this sort of work, but the evening's prize couldn't be trusted to the navvy alone. Why it was Pule who wielded the second spade and not Narbondo, Pule was at a loss to say. And if they were found out, there wasn't a bit of doubt that the doctor and his dogcart would be long gone and that Pule would be left to explain himself to the constable. One day that would change. Pule stared through the gloom toward Palliser Road, but the tree trunks just ten yards hence were dark and ghostly in the fog, and the feeble light of his half-shrouded lantern seemed to make the surrounding headstones and crypts even dimmer and more obscure than they were.

The sudden chiming of a distant clock, low and sullen through the fog, startled him. He dropped his spade. A smile danced momentarily on his companion's lips and eyes, and then was gone, replaced by the heavy dull slump of stolid indifference. Pule, seething, picked up his spade, grasped it near the base of its ash handle, and thrust it into the dirt. It penetrated several inches and then jammed to a sudden arm-chattering stop against a coffin lid. Pule grunted inadvertently with a thrill of pain and dropped the shovel.

His companion, never missing a stroke, skived the dirt from atop the box, his shovel glancing against the wood and scudding across it. The noises grated unnaturally loud in the heavy silence. Pule let his shovel lie. He'd had enough.

He bent once again over the headstone, cracked to bits years earlier and half covered with moss and mud. Fragments of it were gone altogether. The largest chunk, about a foot square, was cut with deep, angular letters that spelled out half a name – COTE – and below that the number 8 and the vine-draped shoulder of a carven skeleton. The remains of Joanna Southcote lay in the coffin. Her posturing son, himself almost a corpse, would be wild with joy over the worm-gnawed bones within. To Pule, one ruined skeleton pretty much resembled another.

The coffin seemed surprisingly solid for having sat so long in the ground; only one corner, from the look of it, had succumbed to the perpetual dampness and begun to rot, the wood separating into long, mushy fragments along grain lines. Pule's companion clambered in beside the head end, dug around until he could get a purchase on the edges, and heaved it upward.

Pule grappled with it in an attempt to lever it further up out of the hole. The bottom of the coffin was wet in his hands, and his fingers smashed into clinging bits of mud and bugs. The coffin began to slide from his grasp, then gave suddenly with a sharp crack, the bottom boards splitting down the center and collapsing outward in a spray of debris, covering the face of the man in the hole. From the bottom of the coffin slid the gauze-wrapped corpse, rolling stiffly onto its side. Folds of rotten winding sheet ripped away to reveal long strands of webby hair standing away from a moldering face. Little pouchlets of flesh hung from cheekbones like fungus on a decayed tree. Ivory bone beneath shone faintly in the lamplight.

Pule stood transfixed, holding in either hand shreds of the rotted boards. The man in the open grave appeared to be strangling. His face, twisted away from the gaping countenance of the corpse, seemed about to burst. With monumental resolve, he twisted from beneath the ghastly remains, edged sideways a few precious inches, and very slowly and deliberately hoisted himself out of the hole. Then he walked calmly and stiffly away toward the lighted crypts, disappearing finally in the fog.

Pule stifled an urge to shout at him and another to shout for Narbondo. He unrolled a tarpaulin onto the ground, set his teeth, climbed into the hole and grasped the shrouded skeleton round its arms. He hauled it out and onto the canvas, folding the cloth around it, then set out toward the road, abandoning the light and dragging the tarpaulin across the wet grass, bumping over graves. The yawning black rectangle behind him vanished in mists through which glowed for a time the diffused yellow light of the veiled lantern.

Bill Kraken awoke to find himself in a strange bed. There was no confusion about it. He didn't for a moment believe himself to be in his own shabby room. He felt pleasantly elevated, as if he were floating inches above the bed, and he heard a rushing sound in his ears that reminded him of a cold night he'd spent one early spring in a riverside cannery in Limehouse. But he wasn't in Limehouse. And he was quite pleasantly warm beneath a feather comforter the likes of which he hadn't seen for upward of fifteen years.

His head felt enormous. He touched his forehead and discovered that it was wrapped like the head of an Egyptian mummy. And there was a dull ache in his chest, as if he'd been kicked by a horse. On a little table beside the bed lay a familiar book. He recognized the tattered ocher binding, a long fragment of which was curled back onto itself, as if someone had the nervous habit of rolling it between thumb and forefinger while reading. It was the *Account of London Philosophers* by William Ashbless. He picked it up happily and squinted at the cover. Dead in the center, as if it had been measured out, gaped a hole as round as the end of a finger. He opened the book, and page by page followed the little cavity down to a conical lead slug, its nose just touching the one hundred and eightieth page, stopping short of aerating a treatise on poetics. Kraken read half a page. It separated mankind into two opposing camps, like armies set to do battle – the poets, or wits, on the one side, and the men of action, or half wits, on the other. Kraken wasn't certain that the philosophy was sound, but the refusal of the bullet to damage the page seemed to signify he would have to study it further.

He knew, in a sudden rush, what bullet it was imbedded in the book. It was a miracle, the unmistakable finger of God. His peapot was gone along with his livelihood. He was sick of peapots anyway. He'd rather go back to hawking squids. If you were beaten in the head with a squid it didn't amount to so very much.

He was startled by a noise from somewhere else in the house. Through a half-open door he could see a second room, aglow with gaslight. A shadow appeared and disappeared on the wall, as if someone had stood up, perhaps from a chair, had gestured widely, and had sat back down or moved away from the lamp. The shadow belonged to a woman. There was her voice. Kraken had little interest in the woman's concerns, beyond a curiosity about the identity of his benefactors. A man spoke. Another shadow appeared, shrinking against the whitewashed wall, sharpening. A shoulder thrust into view, followed by a head – the head of Captain Powers. That explained the clay pipes, tobacco pouch, and matches next to the volume of Ashbless. The darkness beyond his window was Jermyn Street. He'd been saved by Captain Powers. And, of course, by the collected London Philosophers.

There was a sobbing in the room beyond. "I cannot!" the woman cried. The sobbing resumed. Captain Powers said nothing for moments. Then the weeping fell off, and his voice interrupted the silence. "The Indies." Kraken heard only a fragment. "St. Ives is all right." Mumbling ensued. Then, in a sudden, impassioned tone, almost shouted, came the words, "Let them try!" The woman's shadow reappeared and embraced the shadow of the Captain. Kraken picked up Ashbless and leafed through it idly, peeking up over the top of the spine.

Again the Captain hove into view, following his shadow, stumping along on his wooden leg. He fiddled with the latch of a sea chest that lay against the wall, then swung the chest open and began to haul out odds and ends: a brass spyglass, a sextant, a pair of sabers bound together with leather thongs, a carved rosewood idol, the ivory head of a pig. Then out came a false bottom built of oak plank, as if it were a piece of the floor that lay below the chest. Kraken started. Perhaps it *was* a piece of the floor. The Captain bent at the waist, and the top half of him disappeared into the box, his left hand steadying himself on the edge, his right hand groping downward. He straightened again. In his hand was a wooden box, very smooth and painted over with pictures of some sort. It was too distant and too much in shadow for Kraken to make it out.

"Is it safe here?" asked the woman.

"I've kept it these long years, haven't I?" said the Captain staunchly. "No one knows of its existence but you, now, do they? A few days, a week – and Jack will have it." The Captain bent over the chest once again, hiding the box and replacing the oak plank. He very methodically slipped the odds and ends in atop it.

Kraken goggled in wonder. He felt like crying out, but doing so would be a dangerous business. There were vast secrets afloat. He was a small fish in very deep waters – almost a dead small fish. He lay Ashbless back onto the table, pulled the bedclothes up around his chin, and closed his eyes. He was tired, and his head ached awfully. When he awoke, sun played in through the sheer curtains beside his head, and the Captain sat beside him, quietly smoking a pipe.

Wind whistled beyond the casement while St. Ives squinted into the little cheval glass atop his nightstand. The previous day's sun had, apparently, been blown out of sight, and the wind whipped the branch of a Chinese elm against the window as if the branch were rushing at him, enraged that it couldn't get into the room and warm itself at the fire. It was a disgraceful way to treat the scattering of green leaves that had just that week poked out in search of spring, only to find themselves flayed to bits by unfriendly weather.

St. Ives dabbed more glue onto the back of the mustache. It wouldn't do to have it blow off in a sudden gust. He worked his hair into a sort of willowy peak, and brushed his eyebrows upward to give himself the look of a disheveled simian, the same he'd worn the day before. Lord knew what the wind would do to it – heighten the effect, perhaps. He arose, pulled on a greatcoat, slipped Owlesby's manuscript under the carpet, picked up the newly repaired clock, and stepped out into the hall. He paused, thinking, and went back into the room. There was no use calling attention to the manuscript – better to make it seem trivial. He yanked it out from under the rug and set it atop the nightstand, shuffling the papers and laying his book and pipe atop them for good measure.

He trudged along in a foul humor with the repaired clock under his arm. It seemed as if precious little were being accomplished.

He'd been almost a month in London, and still he hadn't glimpsed the fabled ship of the alien visitor. And he wasn't at all certain what he'd do if his mission to Wardour Street were successful. The ship, by all accounts, might be prodigiously old. It might be nothing but the rusted shell of the thing's craft – nothing but the decayed shadow of a starship, good for little beyond its value as a curiosity, turned, quite likely, into some loathsome article of bodily gratification. His own ship, after all, was almost spaceworthy. The oxygenator would be done any day. Perhaps that very night Keeble would bring it to the Trismegistus meeting. If so, St. Ives would be gone in the morning. He wouldn't suffer another fog. His efforts with the clock would either be satisfactory or they wouldn't be. He was bound for home either way.

It was true that odd things were in the wind – the business with Narbondo and Kelso Drake and poor Keeble. But St. Ives was a man of science first, an amateur detective second. The Trismegistus Club would get along without him. They could always summon him from Harrogate, after all, if his assistance were required to eradicate a menace.

He walked around to the rear of the house on Wardour Street and rang the bell. The half-timbered structure gave onto a small court in which languished a granite fountain, little more than a scummed pool with a rustling, water-spitting fish in the center. From the edge of the fountain a cobbled walk led out to a muddy alley. Some few windows stared blindly out onto the court curtained with blood-red fabric. The house must be dark as a tomb inside, thought St. Ives, an odd thing on such a day, blustery and clear as it was. He rang the bell again.

The alley seemed from St. Ives' vantage point to run along for a hundred feet or so before emptying onto a thoroughfare –

Broadwick, perhaps. In the other direction it dead-ended into a stone wall, the top of which was studded with broken bottles. He heard a scuffling of feet. The door opened a crack and a meaty-looking woman peered out, white as a bled corpse. St. Ives jumped involuntarily, shaded his eyes, and realized that her face was covered in baking flour. Her nose was monumental and was somehow clean of flour, perched there like a mountaintop above a layer of cloud. She stared at him through fleshy slits, silent.

"Clock repair," said St. Ives, grinning widely at her. If there was one thing that gave him the absolute pip, it was perpetually frowning people who had no business being such. Stupidity explained it – the sort of stupidity that almost demanded a poke in the eye. The woman grunted. "I've repaired your clock," St. Ives assured her, displaying the item in question. She ran the back of her hand across her cheek, smearing the flour, then emitted a wet sniff. She reached for the clock, but St. Ives dragged it to safety. "There's the matter of the bill," he said, grinning even more widely.

She disappeared into the dark house, leaving the door ajar. It wasn't an invitation, certainly, but it was too good an opportunity to pass up. He stepped in, prepared to have a look about, but stopped abruptly, shutting the door behind him. There at a table, messing with a score of dominoes, sat a fierce-looking man, his beetling forehead spanned by a single unbroken stretch of eyebrow. There was something malevolent about him, something unwholesome, almost idiotic. A chimney pipe hat, dented and stained, sat on the table beside the dominoes. The man looked up at him slowly. St. Ives smiled woodenly, and the smile seemed to infuriate the domino player, who half rose to his feet. He was interrupted by the issuance of the mule-faced butler from whom St. Ives had received the clock. Roundabout him, filling the kitchen, hovered an atmosphere heavy with indefinable threat – a sort of pall of it that floated like a flammable gas, waiting to be set off.

"How much?" asked the butler, counting a handful of change.

St. Ives gave him a cheerful look. "Two pounds six," he said, holding on to the clock.

The man widened his eyes. "I'm sorry?"

"Two pounds six."

"A new clock wouldn't have been as much."

"The lens," said St. Ives, lying, "had to be pressed in a kiln. They aren't generally available. It's a complex process. Very complex. Involves tremendous heat and pressure. The damned things explode, often as not, and blow any number of men to bits."

"You picked up the clock yesterday," said the squinting butler, "and you're telling me this about heat and pressure and blowing up? There isn't an hour's labor here. Not half that."

"In fact," said St. Ives, brassing it out again, "that's what you're paying for. There's not another clocksmith in London who could have got it done so quick. I believe I mentioned it's a complex process. Great deal of heat. Exorbitant, really."

The butler turned in the middle of St. Ives' mumbling and stepped out of the kitchen toward the interior of the house. St. Ives followed him, hoping that the domino player would go back to his game and that the bulbous cook would abandon her diddling with meat cleavers and attend to her baking. The butler passed on into a long hallway, apparently oblivious to St. Ives having followed him. Voices drifted out from unseen rooms. A carpeted stairway angled away at his left.

St. Ives' heart thundered like a train in open country. He decided upon the stairs. He'd have a quick look and then pretend he had got lost. What would they do, shoot him? It was hardly likely. Why should they? He took the steps two at a time, still clutching the clock, and arrived at a landing illuminated by leaded windows beneath which sat a heavy, oaken Jacobean settle. A deserted hallway ran off in either direction revealing on the right a half-dozen closed doors, and on the left a stretch of plaster wall hung with brass sconces that lit, finally, a wooden balustrade that overlooked what appeared to be a broad, high-ceilinged room.

St. Ives hesitated. Would he ascend another flight, or have a look over the balustrade? A door slammed. He turned toward the stairs once again, putting a foot down silently on an immense copper-colored rose in the stair runner. Three steps farther up he paused, crouched, and, hidden by the angle of the ascending wall of the stairwell, peered between two turned posts. Along the hallway toward the landing below staggered the old man who'd elbowed him into the gutter the previous day. He seemed mesmerized, vacant, and he walked with a hesitating step. He wore a haggard, drawn expression in his eyes and in the downward curve of his mouth, as if consumed with remorse or disease – possibly both. His cloak was rumpled and stained, and his hand shook with palsy or fatigue. St. Ives at first was prompted to ask him if he needed support; he'd surely pitch down the stairs head first if he attempted to navigate them. But the atmosphere of evil and dread in the house pushed him deeper into shadow instead. This was no time for chivalry. The old man slumped against the wall, brightened a bit, and licked his lips. He wiped a hand across his face, leaving on it a feral, satisfied look.

St. Ives rose slowly to his feet, determined to see the top of the stairs. He'd left the kitchen a minute or so earlier; surely they'd be after him at any moment. Facing downward, he trod backward onto the step above, planting his heel firmly onto the top of someone's boot.

"There you are!" he half shouted, making a bluff, if idiotic, show of poise and half expecting to be precipitated down the stairs himself. He turned to look into the face of an incredibly fat man in a turban. Another man with a mangled arm stood on the stairs above. Both stared at him, or past him, St. Ives couldn't say which. He stared back, then looked over his shoulder to see if there was something ascending the staircase who was worth staring at with such fixed attention. There wasn't.

Their faces were ghostly, a lifeless white, faintly marbled with fine blue veins, and their eyes were fixed, as if made of glass. St. Ives could see a throbbing pulse beating along the neck of the turbaned man, slowly and rhythmically as if he'd been gilled in some earlier larval stage. A hand clamped onto St. Ives' arm, and the man took a step downward. Had St. Ives not stepped back himself, he would have been trodden on, and the two of them would have tumbled together down the stairs. His two companions said nothing, simply propelled him along. The old man, somewhat recovered, met them on the landing. He looked suddenly fierce, scowling at St. Ives.

"This is a nest of unspeakable sin," he croaked.

St. Ives smiled at him. "I've fixed this clock," he began, but the old man paid him little heed. He was obviously less inclined to listen than to speak.

"My children," he said to the pale men. Both of them gave him a little trilling bow, but neither spoke.

"I'm owed two pounds six for my attention to the clock here," said St. Ives, suddenly wondering if the old man weren't some sort of proprietor. He seemed far too familiar with the place to be a mere customer.

"I know nothing of that," came the reply. "What do I care

for clocks? For time? It's the infinite I pursue. The spiritual. Help me down the stairs, my child." The man with the twisted arm stepped at once out over the stairs – entirely past the first tread – and toppled forward, rolling end over end like a sack of onions, somersaulting off the bottom landing into the room below. He lay still. His companion in the turban seemed hardly to notice. The old man, however, grappled the banister with both hands and creaked down the stairs as hastily as he could, oh-oh-ohing. St. Ives and his captor followed mechanically.

The absent butler stormed into the room just then, followed by the domino player, who wore his tilted hat and carried a pistol in his right hand. The old man waved them off and bent over the still body. The injured man shook himself, rose unsteadily to his knees, then to his feet, and walked squarely into a long, drop-front desk against the wall, kicking one of the legs out from under it and going down once again, pulling the desk with him in a rattle of ink and blotters and books.

The front of the desk fell forward on its hinge and cracked him in the head. Loosed from the interior was an assortment of unidentifiable artifacts: an India rubber face with immense, yawning lips; a stupendous corset hung with whalebone stays and brass hooks; a leather halter of some inconceivable sort, attached to a block and tackle affair as if the halter and its wearer could be suspended, perhaps, from the ceiling; and finally, a brass orb the size of a grapefruit from which issued a quick spray of sparks. The butler and the old man went for the orb simultaneously, but the butler snatched it up first and pushed the other away, shoving the orb back into the fallen desk and slamming the front. What on earth, wondered St. Ives, bewildered as much by the unfathomable litter as by the flopping man it now entangled.

The butler, enraged, latched onto the back of the old man's cloak, preventing him from wading in to the injured man's assistance. "My child," the old man sobbed. "My boy! My sweet..." But the sentence was left unfinished. Chimney pipe, his face frosted with a vacant grin, shoved his pistol into his coat, bent over, and hauled the man free, dragging him out of the tangle of paraphernalia by his ears, one of which tore off in his hand. He pitched it down in disgust and kicked his victim in the side of the head. No blood flowed from the rent where the ear had been severed. Mystery upon mystery. St. Ives began to think of the alley behind the house. He'd have to remember not to run toward the walled end. No one was going to give him two pounds six for the clock. No one was going to give him anything at all for the clock. His hope was that the old man – whoever he was – and his two strange charges were of more immediate concern to the butler and his vicious accomplice, who, at that moment, was methodically beating the daylights out of the collapsed, half-earless man on the floor.

St. Ives disengaged his arm, surprisingly easily as it turned out, and edged around a chair, holding the heavy clock in both hands.

"Get these scum out of here," hissed the butler at the old man, who mewled helplessly, clinging to his turbaned friend for support. "Don't bring them here again. Your privilege doesn't extend that far."

The old man pulled himself straight, threw his cloak back theatrically, and began to rage in a hoarse voice about damnation. St. Ives disappeared into the kitchen to the sound of the butler's cursing and to shouts about who would teach whom about damnation. He sprinted for the back door, but met, halfway there, the leering figure of the toothless, befloured cook, slapping the flat edge of her cleaver onto her meaty palm.

St. Ives wasn't inclined to chat. He bowled straightaway into her, and the hastily swung cleaver rang off the iron case of the clock, dead between St. Ives' curled fingers. He shouted inadvertently, dashing the clock to the floor, and burst out into the yard, gathering the hem of his greatcoat with his right hand and leaping over the stile into the alley, loping toward its exit a hundred feet down, lost now in a swirl of fog. And as he ran, not daring to look back, thinking of the pistol in chimney pipe's coat, he understood suddenly who the bully was – could see that same malevolent face outlined in Keeble's garret window, a crack of lightning illuminating the rainy night sky around it.

SIX

BETRAYAL

Captain Powers' shop was dense with tobacco smoke – indicative, thought St. Ives, of the serious nature of the night's business. Quantity of pipe smoke, he mused, was proportionate to the nature and intensity of the thoughts of the smoker. The Captain, especially lost in deep musings, puffed so regularly at his pipe that smoke encircled his head like clouds around the moon. They were waiting for Godall, who arrived, finally, laden with beer. St. Ives had told no one of Birdlip's newly discovered manuscript. There was too much to say to have to repeat the story singly to the members. At eight o'clock, by mutual, nodded consent, the Trismegistus Club came to order.

"I've got something interesting in the post," said St. Ives, sipping from a pint glass and waving the sheaf of foolscap at his companions. "Owlesby's notebooks, or part of them."

Keeble, who until that moment had seemed peculiarly withdrawn, bent forward in anticipation. And Jack, sitting beside him, seemed to slump in his chair, fearful, perhaps, that some unwholesome revelation about his unfortunate father was in the offing. Kraken shook his bandaged head sadly. Only the Captain seemed unmoved, and St. Ives supposed that his being unacquainted with Owlesby explained his apparent indifference.

"It would be easiest," St. Ives insisted, "if I merely read a bit of it aloud. I'm not the chemist or biologist that Owlesby was, and I was unacquainted with the peculiar hold that Narbondo apparently had on him. And that, I fear, was part and parcel of Owlesby's death."

Godall closed his left eye and squinted at him at the mention of Narbondo, and St. Ives was struck of a sudden with the peculiar notion that Godall's look reminded him of something – of being elbowed into the gutter by the nameless old man in the cloak. St. Ives ignored it and went on, warming to his task. "So here it is, in Owlesby's own hand. There's too much of it altogether, but the last pages are the telling part." He cleared his throat and began:

"We've had the worst sort of luck all week: Short and Kraken brought in a fresh cadaver – took him off the gibbet themselves – and there he lies, full of fluids but stony dead despite it. If we can't find a carp and a fresh gland, he'll decompose before we have a chance at him. A terrible waste. My great fear is that all of this will come to nothing but murder and horror. But I've taken the first steps. That's a lie. First steps be damned. I'm halfway along the road by now, and it's twisted and turned so that there's no chance of finding my way back.

"We ate in Limehouse last night. I wore a disguise – a putty nose and a wig – but Narbondo laughed it to ruin. There's no hope of disguising that damned hump of his. I'm not much given to metaphor, but it seems harder by the day to disguise my own loathsome deformities. It's the thing in the

box, the bottle imp, that's caused it. If a man weren't tempted, he wouldn't fall.

"But such talk is defeatist. That's what it is. Eternal life is within my grasp. If only we hadn't bungled so badly in Limehouse. The costerlad was a jewel – wicked as they come. It was a service to dispose of him. I swear it. Damn Narbondo's bungling. We've had a tremendous pair of shears forged at Gleason's (they think me a tree surgeon) and can snip the head off..."

"And there the narrative breaks," said St. Ives.

"He was interrupted, perhaps," said the Captain.

Godall shook his head. "He couldn't bear it, gentlemen. He couldn't write the word."

St. Ives glanced up at Jack, who would have been a child himself at the time that his father had written the confessions. He might be better off not hearing this. God bless Sebastian Owlesby's doubts, thought St. Ives. They're at once the horror of this and the man's only redemption.

"Read the rest," said Jack stoutly.

St. Ives nodded and resumed the narrative:

"The lad couldn't have been above seven or eight. There was a fog, and not enough light from the streetlamps to amount to a thing. He was bound for the corner of Lead Street and Drake, I think, to buy a bucket of beer – for someone. For his father, I suppose. He had a pumpkin jack o'lantern, of all things, in his left hand, and the bucket in his right. And we walked in shadow twenty paces behind. The street was silent as it was dark. Narbondo carried the shears from Gleasons. He'd have

me along, he said, to share the glory, and would have none of my waiting in the alley off Lead Street in the dogcart, which was, I still insist, the only sensible course.

"So there we were, a musty wind cold as a fish blowing up off the Thames, and the mists swirling deeper by the moment, and the grinning face of that lit jack o'lantern swinging back and forth and back and forth, its face appearing with a dull orange glow at the top of the arc of each swing. There was a sudden gust out of an unsheltered alley, and the lad's lantern blew out. He disappeared in the night, and we could hear his bucket clank against the cobbles. Narbondo hopped forward. I grasped at his cloak to stop him – I could see the black truth in it, as that yellow, toothy light had blinked out in the pumpkin and on in my head – in my soul.

"I flew after him, and the two of us surprised the lad in the act of relighting his unlikely lantern. He stood up, a scream clipped off by those ghastly shears.

"The rest of it is a nightmare. That I fled out of Limehouse and returned in safety to my cabinet is testimony to the existence of dumb luck (if surviving that night of horror can be considered in any way lucky) and to the all-obscuring darkness and fog. It was as if evil had precipitated out of the solution of night and hid me like a veil. Narbondo wasn't so lucky, but the beating he took couldn't have been a result of his crime. If they'd known it, he wouldn't have been thrown into the river alive. Perhaps he was beaten because of what he is, like a man kills a rat or a roach or a spider.

"So the murder was for naught. And the corpse from the gibbet lies moldering on the slab. Narbondo will go out again tonight – we must have the serum."

St. Ives paused in his reading to drain half a bottle of ale. The Captain sat paralyzed in his chair, stone-faced. "Owlesby," said St. Ives hurriedly, glancing first at the Captain, then at Jack, "was out of his wits. What he accomplished – what he committed – can't be justified, but it can be explained. And in the most roundabout way can be excused – forgiven at least if you keep in mind the poison that had trickled into his soul. His discussion of the night in Limehouse is accurate – to a degree. But he dissembled throughout. That much is clear. He admits it in the pages that follow. And as I say, what he admits is all the more horrifying, but it explains a great deal. Poor Nell!"

The Captain seemed to stiffen even more at the sound of the name, and he clanked his heavy glass onto the wooden arm of his Morris chair, brown ale sloshing out onto the oak. St. Ives noted that Kraken had disappeared during the course of the narrative. Poor man, thought St. Ives, searching for his place in the journals. Even after fifteen years, the story of his master's decline is too fresh for him. But the story had to be told. There was nothing for it but to go on, now that he'd launched out:

"I'm possessed by the most evil aching of the head – such that my eyes seem to press down to the size of screwholes, so that I see as through a telescope turned wrong end to. Laudanum alone relieves it, but fills me with dreams even more evil than the pain in my forebrain. I'm certain that the pain is my due – that it is a taste of hell, and nothing less. The dreams are full of that Limehouse night, of the toothy grin of that damned pumpkin, swinging swinging swinging in the fog. And I can feel myself decay, feel my tissues drying and rotting like a beetle-eaten fungus on a stump, and my blood pounds across the

top of my skull. I can see my own eyes, wide as half crowns and black with death and decay, and Narbondo ahead with that ghastly shears. I pushed him along! That's the truth of it. I railed at him, I hissed. I'd have that gland, is what I'd have, and before the night was gone. I'd hold in my hand my salvation.

"And when he failed, when he ran down East India Dock Road in that stooped half hop, terrified, it was I who set them on him. It was I who cried out to stop him. He little knows it. He'd outdistanced me. He was certain it was the police who shouted. And when they were beating him, by God I wasn't slack. I was a ruin of failure and loathing and rot as I stamped on his hands and helped those drunken toughs drag him into the river where it splashed and roiled and slammed itself to fury below the Old Stairs, and I hoped by God to see him dead and picked by fishes.

"But there I was unlucky. Like the ghost at the feast, he came unlooked for in the night as I sat in a waking horror in the cabinet, listening to the thing in the box, staring, half expecting the tread of feet on the stair that would announce the end, the gibbet, the headsman's axe. There it came. Three in the morning it was. Deadly silent. A tramp, tramp, tramp on the wooden stairs – very heavy – and a shadow across the curtain. A hunched shadow. The door fell open on its hinge, and the hunchback stood against a scattering of lights and a clearing sky with such a look of abomination about him that his collapse onto the tiles failed to eradicate it – just as it failed to eradicate my horror of him.

"I should have killed him. I should have slit his throat. I should have cut out the toad under his fifth rib and put it in a cage. But I didn't. Fear kept me from it. Fear, perhaps, of my

own evil. It seemed to me that his face was my own, that he and I were one, that Ignacio Narbondo had somehow drawn part of me in with him, consumed the only part of me that had ever been worth a farthing, and had left a strengthless, malignant pudding, poured into the chair where I sat until half past ten the next morning.

"And it was thus that Nell found me. I begged her to kill me. I hadn't the courage to perform the deed. I pleaded. I told her of the costerlad. I swore at the same time that I was done with the pursuit – that the creation of life itself wasn't worth hell. But I lied. The thing in the box can arrest entropy. He can separate tepid water into ice and steam if he likes. He can animate the carcass of a rat dead in a wall for months and dance it about the room like a marionette. He's prodigiously old, and the only consequence of his thwarting time is his shrunken state. But he must be kept in a box.

"My fitting Keeble's clever structure with a screen through which I can communicate with him has led, I fear, to my own decay. I can't say just how I'm bartering with him – knowledge for freedom. If he could but find his craft and a pilot of sufficient stature to navigate it, he'd be lost among the stars in a moment. But that won't come to pass. Not until I have what I possess – we, *I should say, for the hunchback has recovered, and swears he'll return to Limehouse tonight if the streets are hidden by a sufficiently thick blanket of murk.*

"Shall I go with him? Will he draw me along at his heels like a shadow, a daily more fitting shadow? Or will nightfall bring an end to an unhappy and unnatural existence? I can't for the life of me imagine waking on the morrow. For the first time in my life the morning is cloaked in black."

"There's not much more," said St. Ives, putting a match to his cold pipe with a shaking hand. He'd read the manuscript earlier, but he couldn't quite get this last part straight in his mind. Nell, it was certain, was without guilt. Even more than that. She was heroic. That the act of shooting her brother, of spiriting away the damned homunculus and giving it to Birdlip to take perpetually aloft, had led to her exile and remorse, was the greatest tragedy. Kraken had been correct. St. Ives dropped the manuscript to the floor. Somehow the act of reading it aloud had emptied him of any desire to look at it again.

The Captain heaved himself to his feet and stumped across to a tobacco jar, yanking off the lid and pulling out two fingersful of curly black tobacco, wadding it into the end of his enormous pipe. "I shipped with a Portagee once," he said, "who knew of that thing – that bottle imp. He'd owned it straight out for a month and went stark staring mad in a typhoon off Zanzibar. Traded it away to a Lascar on a sloop in the Mozambique Channel." He shook his head at the enormity of the whole thing and sat back down.

"And the rest of it," asked Godall keenly. "The other hundred-odd pages – are they as wild as this part?"

"Increasingly so," said St. Ives. "The decline was swift – almost from the day he bought the thing in the box."

"In the bottle," put in Keeble, staring out the window at the street. "There wasn't any box until I built it."

St. Ives nodded. "He seemed possessed by the thing – by the idea that he could not only animate the dead, an effect, I gather, that he'd discovered without the aid of the homunculus, but that *with* it, somehow, he could perpetuate life. Indefinitely. Perhaps that he could create life. And perhaps he *could*. There's a reference to a successful experiment in which he spawned mice from a heap of old rags, and another in which he revivified an old man from Chingford, who was dying of general paresis. Sheared forty years from him, according to Owlesby. All of it fearfully alchemical, although, as I say, it's out of my province.

"He was certain that the spacecraft belonging to the homunculus was in London, and he hoped to find it in order to sell it, as it were, to the damned creature in exchange for power over death and time. Whether his decline into madness and debasement was a result of scientific greed or of slow poisoning due to contact with the homunculus is impossible to say. Even Owlesby, obviously, didn't know.

"Apparently Owlesby was jealous of owning the thing to the point of refusing to let Narbondo at it. Nell's absconding with it must have infuriated the hunchback. She snatched the secret of life out of his hands, as it were, and gave it to Birdlip..."

"Who in a matter of weeks might well drop out of the skies on us," said Godall.

The Captain frowned. St. Ives nodded.

"Well," said Keeble, topping off his glass from an open bottle of ale, "this is all a very sad business, very sad. If I were asked, I'd say meet the dirigible when it lands – and I'll bet my ape clock it touches down on Hampstead Heath where it launched – and snatch the box. Between the lot of us such a thing would be nothing. Then we tie it into a bag full of stones and drop it off the center of Westminster Bridge when the river's in flood. The box isn't tight, I can attest to that. Regardless of the thing's powers, it's got to breathe, hasn't it? It's not a fish; it's a little man. I've seen it. We'll drown it like a cat, if only to keep it out of the clutches of this humpback doctor." Keeble paused, his chin in his hand. "*And* for what it did to Sebastian. I'll kill it for that. But there's no use, really, hashing over this Limehouse business. It's water under the bridge is what it is. Nothing more than that. And murky water too. So I'll just change the subject for a moment here, gentlemen, and call your attention to the date. It's Jack's birthday is what it is, and I've got a bit of something to give him."

Jack blushed, disliking, even among friends, being the center of attention. St. Ives grimaced in spite of himself. Perhaps he shouldn't have been waving Sebastian's memoirs about so freely. On his son's birthday, for God's sake. Well, this was the Trismegistus Club, and the ends they pursued would lead them along grim paths – there was no doubt of that. There was nothing to be accomplished by pretense and timidity. Better to clear the air with the truth straightaway. Far better to do that than to hide things and make them seem even more despicable and terrifying by doing so.

St. Ives wished, though, that he had known it was Jack's birthday so as to have some trifle wrapped up. But he could remember no one's birthday – not even his own most of the time. Keeble produced a square parcel about the size and shape of a jack-in-the-box. St. Ives was fairly certain he knew what it was, that he'd witnessed the rising of its clockwork cayman not too many days past.

"A toast to young Mr. Owlesby," said Godall heartily, raising his glass. The rest of the company followed suit, giving Jack three cheers.

From the shadows of the back room, Kraken raised his own glass – or flask, rather, which was two-thirds empty of gin. It seemed to Kraken to be perpetually in that state. How it could be more often empty than full was an utter mystery. Kraken hadn't delved particularly widely into the mathematics, and so he was willing to admit that there were forces at work on his gin that he couldn't yet fathom. He'd be after them though. He'd seek them out.

Like beans in a bottle, he said to himself. Facts were nothing more. And mathematics were facts, weren't they? Numbers on a page were like bugs on a paving stone. They looked a mess, scurrying around. But they were a matter of nature. And nature had her own logic. Some of the bugs were setting about gathering supper – bits and pieces of this and that. Lord knew what they ate, elemental matter, most likely. Others were laying out trails, hauling bits of gravel to build a mound, measuring off distances, scouting out the land, all of them here and there on the pavement – a mess to the man ignorant of science, but an orchestrated bit of music to… to a man like Kraken.

He wondered if someday he couldn't write a paper on it. It was… what was it? An analogy. That's what it was. And it must, thought Kraken, explain the business of disappeared gin in a flask. The beauty of science was that it made things so clear, so logical. The cosmos, that was what science was after – the whole filthy cosmos. He smiled to think that he understood it. He'd only just run across the word in Ashbless. He'd seen it a hundred times, of course. Such were words. You were blind to them for years. Then one reached out and slammed you, and bingo, like lit candles in a dark room, it turned out they were everywhere – cosmos, cosmos, cosmos. The order of things. The secret order, hidden to most. A man had to get down on his knees and peer at the paving stones to see the bugs that hurried there, navigating about their little corner of the Earth with the certainty of a mariner setting a course by the immutable patterns of the stars.

A thrill shot up his spine. He'd rarely seen things so clearly, so… so… cosmically. That was the word. He shook his flask. There was a dram or so sloshing in the bottom. Why the devil *was* it more often empty than full? If a quantity could be poured in, the same quantity could be poured out. He'd filled it that very morning down at Whitechapel – brim full. But it hadn't stayed full for a half hour. It had been mostly empty all day. Hours of emptiness. And if it weren't for the bottle of whisky under the bed, he'd be powerfully dry by now.

Kraken grappled with the problem. It didn't seem fair to him. Like bugs, he reminded himself, screwing his eyes shut and imagining a scurrying lot of number-shaped bugs on a piece of gray slate. It didn't seem to do any good. He couldn't quite apply the bugs to the problem of the flask. He squinted through the open door into the room beyond.

He'd spent the last half hour with his hands over his ears, pressing out the sad business of Sebastian Owlesby's memoirs. He knew it all well enough – too well. He drained the flask, reached under the bed, and drew out the whisky. He was a gin man, truth to tell, but in a pinch...

Young Jack was waving some sort of box. Kraken squinted at it. He was certain he'd seen it before. But no, he hadn't. Here came some sort of business from inside – a beast of some sort, and tiny birds. The beast – a crocodile apparently tore at one of the birds, gobbled it up, then sank out of sight. Kraken puzzled over it, unsure, exactly, of the purpose of it. He sat for a moment, knuckling his brow, then got up off his bed and edged across to the open door.

Off to his left was another, dark room – the room where lay the sea chest. His heart raced. There was a tumult of talk and laughter as everyone gathered round Jack's birthday present, Keeble's engine. Kraken sidled into the dark room, drawn by bleary curiosity. He stubbed his toe into the chest before he saw it, grunting in such a way that he was certain would turn heads in the outer room. But no heads turned. Everyone, apparently, was far too keen on the marvelous toy.

Kraken bent over the chest, running his hands over the front until he found the flat, circular iron hasp. He fiddled with it, not knowing entirely how the mechanism worked and uncertain, even, what in the world he was after – certainly not the emerald. He'd have to be silent as a beetle. It wouldn't do to be heard. Lord knows what the Captain would think to see him rummaging in the chest. The hasp snapped up suddenly, rapping across Kraken's knuckles. He shoved three fingers into his mouth. They'd suppose him a common thief, of course. Or worse – they'd suppose he was in league with whomever it was they were at odds with.

Light from the rooms without lay feebly across the contents of the trunk. Kraken rummaged through them, shushing them to silence each time they rattled and swished, and shushing himself for good measure. He shoved his head amid the objects, which he'd managed to push to either side of the trunk. The cold brass of the spyglass pressed his cheek, and the smell of oak and leather and dust rose about his ears – very pleasant smells, in fact. It would be nice to remain so, his head buried like the head of an ostrich among fabulous things. He could easily have gone to sleep if he weren't standing up. He could hear blood rushing through his head – ebbing and flowing like the tides, as Aristotle would have it – and in among the general roaring of it he could just hear something else, a voice, it seemed, coming from somewhere very far away.

He puzzled over it, aware that the gash on his forehead had begun to throb. He couldn't for the life of him determine what to do next. Why am I standing here with my head in the chest, he asked himself. But only one answer was forthcoming: strong drink. Kraken smiled. "Whisky is risky," he said half aloud, listening to his voice echo up out of the chest. He was mad to drink whisky. Gin didn't do this to a man – make a fool of him. He was suddenly desperately afraid. How long had he been here, stooped over the chest? Was the room behind him filled with the faces of his friends, all of them stretched with loathing?

He extricated his head slowly, careful not to start an avalanche of nautical debris. In his hands he held the hidden box. A thrill of fear and excitement rushed along in his veins, washing away all rational thought. There it was again – the voice, tiny and distant, as if someone were trapped, perhaps, in the wall. He could understand none of it. He wasn't sure, suddenly, that he wanted to understand it, and was smitten with the wild certainty that the voice spoke from within his own head – a devil.

He was possessed. He'd read Paracelsus. It struck him at once that this was almost certainly a matter of Mumia, that the woman who'd lured him to the den where he'd been beaten was a witch. She'd used him, sensing that he was burdened with Mumia from the bodies he'd carted about London in the night. The sins of his past were rising like spectres, pointing at him. He shook with fear. It was *more* whisky he required, not less. He silenced the tiny voice, clacking his teeth to shut out the noise, then leaped in sudden horror as the noise turned into a fearful shouting.

He banged down the lid of the chest and jumped clear. The outer room was a tumult. That's where the noise had come from! Kraken peered around the doorjamb, only to lurch back into the comparative safety of the dark room. Kelso Drake stood without, in the open doorway of the shop. He'd come at last. Having Kraken beaten and shot hadn't satisfied him. He'd come to finish the job. Kraken pressed back into the room, bumping against a closed window. He unhooked the latch, swung it open, and crawled out across the sill and slid into the mud of the alley, where he lay breathing heavily. He stood up, casting a glance over his shoulder at Spode Street, then loped away toward Billingsgate. In a few hours the thronging crowd at the fishmarket would hide him and his prize from his enemies.

SEVEN

THE BLOOD PUDDING

The pounding startled the lot of them, except, perhaps, Godall, who wore on his face a look of shrewd curiosity. The Captain took a step forward as if to open the door, but it was thrown open almost at once by Kelso Drake, who smiled benignly and bowed just a bit before striding into the room. Keeble leaped up and threw his coat over Jack's lap to hide the toy.

Drake stood just inside the door, bemused in his top hat, looking about him at the shop with the air of a man half baffled that such a place could exist, and coming to the conclusion that perhaps it could, given the quality of the men whom he confronted. He swept an invisible fleck from his sleeve and rolled his cigar to the other side of his mouth.

"Light?" asked the Captain, holding a long match aloft.

Drake shook his head and squinted.

"Rather eat them, would you?" said the Captain, tossing the match into a bowl. Keeble had gone white, a peculiarity Drake seemed to relish.

He smiled at the toymaker. "You've brought it along, then," he said, nodding at the half-concealed box in Jack's lap. "It's good when a man sees reason. The world is too full of unpleasantries as it is."

"The only unpleasantry I can see," cried the Captain, reaching beneath the counter, "is you! Get out of my shop while you can still stand on yer pegs!" And with that he hauled out a braided leather cosh the length of his forearm and slapped it against his ivory leg.

Drake ignored him. "Come, come, my man," he said to Keeble. "Hand it across. The machine will do as well as the plans. My workmen can puzzle it out."

Jack was bewildered. Only Keeble and St. Ives entirely understood. St. Ives groped beside his chair for the neck of an empty ale bottle. Here was a dangerous man. It quite likely wouldn't come to blows – that wasn't Drake's way. But the man who'd tried to purloin Keeble's plans was quite clearly the domino player on Wardour Street. They'd best all be cautious. Who could say what sorts of ruffians waited in the shadows outside?

"You've had my answer," gasped Keeble, shaking visibly. "It hasn't changed."

"Then," said Drake, removing a chewed cigar from his mouth, "we'll attempt coercion." He stood silently for a moment as if lost in thought. The rest of the company was frozen, waiting for Drake's pronouncement. But instead of threatening and bribing, he merely tipped his hat and turned toward the door, saying, "*Very* pretty daughter, that Dorothy of yours. Reminds me of a girl I had once… Where was it?" He turned once again toward Keeble with a mock questioning look on his face, only to find Jack catapulting out of his chair in a fury. The box flew, Keeble caught it, and Jack punched wildly at Drake, missing the leering face by a foot and sprawling into Godall, who reached across and grasped the Captain's wrist as he brought the sap back for a swing that would have left Drake senseless.

The millionaire had feinted toward the door to avoid Jack's blow, and saw the Captain's attempt out of the edge of his eye. The look on his face changed from leering indifference and amusement to black hatred in an instant, and his hat flew off onto the floor as he checked his feint and jerked around in anticipation of the blow. But Godall still held the wrist of the furious Captain Powers, and Drake recovered, edging just a bit toward the door.

He stooped to retrieve his hat, but the Captain, stepping forward, pinned it to the floor with his peg leg, smashing the crown sideways, then, transferring the cosh to his free hand, flattened the hat utterly with three quick blows.

"That'll be your head, swabby, if I catch you around here again. You or any of your bully boys. You're filth – bilgewater, the lot o' ye, and I'd just as soon stamp you to jelly as look at ye!"

Drake's grin was palsied. He neglected the hat, turned as if to say one last thing to Keeble, but never got it out. The Captain, jerking free from Godall, struck Drake on the shoulder, sending him sprawling through the open door, then crouched, grabbed at the ruined hat and sailed it out into the night like a flying plate, banging the door shut in its wake. He opened a fresh bottle of ale and poured it into his glass with a shaking hand. Godall sat down. The Captain drained half the glass, turned to his aristocratic friend, and said, "Thanks, mate," then sat down himself.

Jack was once again possessed of the box. He stared at a spot on the floor, thoughtful or embarrassed. Keeble seemed to be staring at the same spot. St. Ives cleared his throat. "This business is growing curious," he said. "I don't half understand why we have to be embroiled in such complications – as if Narbondo's machinations aren't enough. Now we have two villains to deal with. We keep the weather eye on one of them, and all along the other one's watching us. And, I'm afraid, gentlemen, that I'll have to leave you to it – my train departs King's Cross Station tomorrow morning at ten sharp, now that the oxygenator is finished. I can't afford to put if off. Conditions are almost right."

Keeble waved his hand haphazardly. "Drake is my affair," he said, sighing, as if he were tired of the whole issue. "I'm not sure I won't sell him the plans. What difference would it make?"

"You can't!" cried Jack, half rising from his chair. And just as he shouted, lightning lit the road as if it were midday and thunder rattled the windows, rolling away for almost a minute before silence fell. Rain thudded against the panes and fell off, then thudded again in a wash of great drops that whirled and flew in the wind. The abrupt arrival of the weather seemed to furl Jack's sails, for he slumped into his chair and was silent.

"The lad is right," said Godall, knocking his pipe against the edge of a glass ashtray. "Drake mustn't have the engine. He'll have what's coming to him and no more – no less, I should say. I've come up with a bit of information myself that will, if I'm not mistaken, satisfy all of you on several points. Drake and Narbondo are in league, I mean to say. Or at least the one does business with the other. I've taken a room across from the doctor's cabinet – Drake has visited Narbondo more than once.

"I followed the two of them yesterday afternoon – not together, mind you; Drake wouldn't be seen abroad with Narbondo. They met at a public house in the Borough, a low sort of place that appears to have sprung up fairly recently. It's at the back of one of those old sprawling innyards, long ago fallen into disuse, and even the local people avoid it. There's rooms, as I say, that back up onto an alley; if there's a front entrance, I couldn't find it. Likely enough it lets out into the old inn, which is a regular warren of gables and attic rooms and hallways that seem to lead nowhere. If a man was scouting out an appropriate location for an opium den, he'd have to look no farther. There's not much else could be done with it, though.

"Anyway, these rooms – three of them with the walls broken out to connect them – let out onto the alley. There's not a window in the alley wall, and it's dark as pitch inside the pub and cold as a winding sheet. Luck for me, in fact, for I'm certain that if they'd caught a glimpse of the cut of my clothes, they'd have seen me out."

Godall paused over his pipe and studied the street, where sluicing rain was illuminated every minute or two by ragged lightning.

"Damn, but there's a draft in here," said the Captain. He pulled a plaid muffler from under the counter and wrapped it round his shoulders, then waved his pipe at Godall as if to suggest he resume his story.

"There's nothing to identify the place but a curious sign over one of the alley doors, and not a hanging sign either, but painted on and ill done: The Blood Pudding, it reads. Inside were a dozen or more men, sitting idle, not speaking, mind you, and there weren't more than two of them had anything to drink. Even those weren't interested in their glass, although one kept peering at it as if there was something in among the bubbles to see, as if he *remembered* that there was something there he liked mightily once, but couldn't quite fathom it now. The odd thing about him was that he looked as if he'd been dead for a month.

"It wasn't just lack of sun, either. There was something unwholesome about him – about all of them, for that matter, that all the fresh air wouldn't undo. One stood up after consuming a quantity of the most loathsome-looking black pudding and walked face first into the wall before he got his bearings and set a course for the door.

"Kelso Drake appeared a quarter of an hour after the doctor, who was involved, at the time, in a meal consisting entirely of live birds – sparrows if my knowledge of the science of ornithology is not amiss. He caught and consumed them beneath a drape that hung to the floor. The nature of the meal was evident, for the peeping and chirping of the poor things filled the darkened room, and the rustle of their wings against the drape played against the crush and snap of tiny bones.

"Drake was taken aback, I can tell you, when the hunchback appeared from beneath the drape, chin bloodied, and a scattering of broken meats littering the table before him."

"By God," interrupted the Captain, standing up and peering toward the rear of the shop, "there's a window open that shouldn't be, or I'm a lubber." He stumped round the counter, lit a candle, and disappeared into the room that contained, since Kraken's visit, a half-emptied sea chest. His shout brought the rest of the club to their feet.

Gaslamps were lit and the window was pulled shut and bolted. On the floor lay the spyglass, the sextant, and two bits of oak plank. The Captain leaned into the chest, hauled out the pig and the sabers, and realized almost at once that the emerald box was gone. He slammed down the lid, threw the window open once again, and leaned out into the alley in a wash of rain. There was nothing to see in either direction when lightning obliged him by brightening the otherwise dark night. He turned to his companions, dripping rain from his beard, and gestured helplessly.

"Something stolen?" asked St. Ives, a rhetorical question, given the debris on the floor and the open window.

"Aye," gasped the Captain, reeling toward a chair. But he hadn't sat for more than a few seconds before he was up and through the door, bursting into Kraken's empty room with a shout. Silence met him.

"Kraken gone!" cried St. Ives.

"The scoundrel!" shouted the Captain.

"Perhaps," said Godall passionlessly, "Kraken himself has been the *victim* of this thief. Let's not leap to conclusions."

"Of course," said St. Ives. "I'd bet on the man with the chimney pipe hat here – the one who was after the plans to the engine. I ran afoul of him myself recently. I'd bet he's sneaked in through the casement, robbed the Captain's sea chest, and done Kraken a mischief while Drake waylaid us in the shop; that's the ticket." St. Ives stroked his chin, squinting at nothing. "But why should this man *necessarily* be in league with Drake?" He addressed the question to no one, but Godall answered.

"Drake owns the house in Wardour Street – one among many. Your disguise, by the way, was a bit on the transparent side. It was me that you bumped into after you'd got hold of the clock."

The captain interrupted the exchange by raging back into the room waving the almost empty whisky bottle that he'd found under Kraken's bed. "This is all stuff!" he cried. "The man's made off with… with my property, and no mistake. There was no man in a hat – not here anyway, kidnapping and robbing and clattering about under our noses. No, sir. Kraken's made away with the goods, and there's no use making up tales."

"What goods?" asked St. Ives innocently. "Perhaps we can recover them."

The Captain fell silent and collapsed into an armchair, precipitating a little cloud of dust. He buried his face in his hands, his anger apparently having fled in the face of St. Ives' question. The Captain looked up at his congregated friends, started to speak, glanced at Jack, and shook his head. "Leave me to think," he said simply, and slouched deeper into his chair, suddenly tired and old, his face lined with a hundred thousand sea miles and the weather of countless storms and suns.

Thunder rattled the casement, and the party gathered coats and hats and silently made ready to bend out into the road, awash now with the downpour. Jack and Keeble had only to cross Jermyn Street to shelter, but St. Ives and Godall had a longer journey. The muffled chiming of a clock could be heard through the pelting rain – two doleful peals that announced, more than anything else, the certainty that hansom cabs would long since have ceased to run, and that the walk, for St. Ives at least, would be a long and sodden one. The Bohemian Cigar Divan lay some half mile to the northeast, and the Bertasso in Pimlico some three miles to the southeast, but for six blocks or so, Godall and St. Ives walked together down Jermyn toward Haymarket. Neither was satisfied with the half-finished meeting. Things were hotting up at such a rate that action of some sort seemed to be called for. Biweekly meetings over cigars and ale would avail them little.

St. Ives knew almost nothing of Godall, who was a friend, after all, of Captain Powers, and a fairly recent friend at that. But he was very apparently enmeshed in the Narbondo-Drake business, for reasons St. Ives couldn't entirely fathom. Why, in fact, was Captain Powers so thoroughly caught up? Why *had* Narbondo been seen lurking outside the smoke shop, if indeed he had? Mightn't he as easily have been watching Keeble's house, on the advice, possibly, of Kelso Drake? It was a muddle. St. Ives longed to be back in Harrogate, in among his scientific apparatus, consulting the staid and learned Hasbro, losing himself in matters of physics and astronomy. He could almost smell the steel chips and hot oil of the workshop of Peter Hall, the little Dorchester blacksmith who constructed the shell of the riveted spacecraft. There were too damned many distractions in London, all of them chattering for attention.

Just that afternoon had come a note from the Royal Academy. On the strength of his knowledge of Birdlip and his friendship with the uncommunicative William Keeble, St. Ives was invited to participate in certain programs involving the study of Birdlip's amazing craft, which had been sighted over the Denmark Strait far up into the thin air of the stratosphere, swinging toward Iceland on a course that would sweep it once again over Greater London. Balloon expeditions were being readied in Reykjavik. There was some reason to suppose that the blimp would ultimately descend, perhaps land, in the following weeks. It might – who could say? – simply fall onto London rooftops like a spent balloon. The professor's particular knowledge might be useful. And didn't he know the toymaker William Keeble? Couldn't he, perhaps, use his influence… Coercion is what it was. Here was an offer. St. Ives was to drop his work, lock the doors of his laboratory, send Hasbro to Scarborough on holiday. And in exchange, the Royal Academy would blink the ignorance and scientific prejudice out of their eyes, clean their spectacles, and agree to consider him something more than a lunatic eccentric. Why couldn't a man just go about his work? Why must he always be meddled with? Who *were* all these people and what legitimate claim had they on his time? None whatsoever. The answer was clear as Whitefriar's crystal, and yet hardly a day went by but what some new mystery, some complaint, some request arrived by post, some odd man in a chimney pipe hat peered in the window at you, or some long lost Kraken appeared from an alley and stole an unidentifiable trifle from a friend on the most rainy, miserable night imaginable – a night that had no business showing its face in the spring, for God's sake.

Water ran from the brim of his felt hat like a beaded curtain and soaked his overcoat until it hung heavy as chain mail. And just when it seemed that the rain was letting up and the shadows of recessed doorways in the houses across the street began to solidify out of the mists, there was a bang and a crash as lightning lit the rooftops and ripped to bits whatever forces had attempted to subdue the weather. Wind tore along the street, whipping the tails of St. Ives' coat and sending a chill through him that anticipated a lancing deluge from the starless heavens. The two men bounded as one into the doorway of a dark house where the wind and wet, at least, were powerless to follow.

"Deadly night," said St. Ives blackly.

"Mmm," responded his companion.

"What do you suppose Kraken stole?" asked St. Ives. "Not that it's my business entirely – although I have a sneaking suspicion it will become so. It's just that the Captain seemed so peculiarly... devastated by it. It's a side of him I hadn't seen."

Godall lit his pipe in silence, his tobacco, pipe, and equipment miraculously dry. St. Ives didn't bother to look at his own. Some day soon – after the successful launching of the starship – he'd set about developing a method to maintain the suitability of his smoking apparatus in even the most hellish weather. There would then be one thing in his life that was a certainty, a constant, that the forces of weather and chaos couldn't make a hash of.

"I'm not at all sure how you've managed to keep your tobacco and matches dry," said St. Ives, "but my own are muck."

"Here, my good fellow," responded Godall graciously, offering his open pouch. "Thank the Captain. It's his blend. Superior to any of my own, too." The two men passed matches and tampers back and forth, speaking in low tones and watching the rain roar down in an undulating, opaque curtain, looking for all the world as if the gods were shaking out a cosmic sheet in the roadway.

"I'm not certain about the theft," said Godall, when St. Ives' pipe was alight. "But you've struck it, I believe, when you said it would become our business soon enough. The next few days should clarify things a bit, though I suppose the clarification will only serve to deepen the mystery." Godall paused for a moment, contemplating, then said: "Those men at The Blood Pudding. They were dead men; I'm certain of it. And your reading Owlesby's narrative tonight is what makes me so certain. What do you think, as a man of science? *Could* Owlesby animate corpses?"

"If Sebastian said he could, he could," said St. Ives simply. "How he did it I'm not certain, but it involved enormous carp, somehow. And the homunculus, the thing in the box, wasn't required. It's apparent from the manuscript that Owlesby thought the creature would reveal the secret of perpetual life to him. Keeble thought so too. What Keeble did, or attempted to do with engines – that's what Owlesby would accomplish with human beings. That's partly the explanation of poor Keeble's decline – forgive me for speaking in such terms of a friend. But damn me, this business has been ruinous. Keeble blames himself, I think, for having put Owlesby onto the creature in the first place, for having filled Owlesby with notions of overcoming inertia."

"And so his caring for Jack these past fifteen years," said Godall.

St. Ives shrugged. "Yes and no. He'd have done so anyway. The two of them – Keeble and Owlesby – were close as brothers, and Winnifred Keeble and Nell were inseparable since childhood."

"Ah, Nell," said Godall, nodding almost imperceptibly. "Well, there it is. The men at The Blood Pudding were dead men, as I say, and I watched Narbondo through the curtain two days ago revive what was almost certainly a corpse. How Drake ties in I'm not yet sure, although it seemed to me that the two were striking some sort of bargain there – that Narbondo, perhaps, supply Drake with an army of willing workers – workers the union bosses would find unmalleable. Or, now that I listen to your story of the creature in the box, it's entirely possible that Drake hopes to purchase that which Owlesby desired, and that he believes Narbondo can deliver it. In which case the landing of this blimp might prove interesting, if, as you say, the hunchback understands the homunculus to be aboard."

"He might," said St. Ives. "But there's no certainty of it."

"And there's another party," said Godall, "a self-styled messiah with the unlikely name of Shiloh, who has a hand in the mystery. He's the one, by the by, who brushed you into the roadway moments before I appeared in front of Drake's brothel."

"The old man!" cried St. Ives, the nature of the two empty-eyed men on the stairs and of the bloodless ear suddenly revealed. St. Ives shook his head. It was a loathsome business, but none of it precluded his being on the express next morning, bound for Harrogate. He'd be only hours out of London, in terms of clock time, and could sail back in, pistol in hand, as it were, when the call came. In figurative terms, thank heaven, Harrogate was light years' distance from London, and such was the nature of reality that he'd traverse the miles in little over four hours, and eat cakes and tea in a room hung with star charts and bookshelves.

"When do you return?" asked Godall suddenly, breaking in upon St. Ives' reverie.

"I hadn't thought much along those lines," the physicist admitted.

"I rather fear for this man Kraken," said Godall. "He struck me as being a bit mad, in truth, but harmless. He'd best be found. And I'm fairly certain that none of us are man enough to see this thing through alone. It's collective spirit that will defeat them in the end."

"Of course, of course." St. Ives' pipe went dead. There was truth in Godall's statement. He could, he supposed, return to London in a few days. A week, say. Five days at most. Three. But fixing a date rather kicked the daylights out of his cakes and tea. "If anything develops," St. Ives heard himself saying, "send for me straightaway and I'll be on the next train. If I don't hear from you before, I'll see you next Thursday evening at the shop. These meetings should become a bit more regular, at least until after the appearance of Birdlip."

"Agreed," said Godall, who thrust out his hand, then hunched out into the slackening rain, striding away toward Soho, the words "Good luck" sailing back over his shoulder on the breeze. St. Ives set out down Regent, hunkering into his coat, wondering how it was that Godall seemed so damned efficient, how he wore so well his mantle of intrigue and mystery.

The lights of the Captain's shop glowed far behind them now through the rain, and just visible in the dimly lit room was the Captain himself, unmoving. The Captain's mind was empty, the dust beaten out of it by this sudden enormity. What would he say to her? To Jack? If he found Kraken… he didn't know what he would do. It was his own damned fault, waving the box around with Kraken supposedly unconscious in an adjacent room. Suddenly he stiffened. It wasn't just the box, after all, that had been waved around. He checked his pocket watch. Quarter past two. Three o'clock would tell the tale.

The hands crept round, the Captain regarding, then casting away, plan after plan. At five until three, he listened for the knock at the door. He paced from room to room, dimming lights, watching through windows. No one came. The streets were silent but for the patter of rain. Perhaps she'd forgotten, was asleep. Four o'clock passed, five. At ten next morning, when a customer rapped at the mysteriously locked door of the shop, he awakened Captain Powers, who leaped up with a shout from a dream involving dark London alleys and stooped criminals. He couldn't face the day alone; it was time to take Godall completely into his confidence.

EIGHT

AT THE OCEANARIUM

At the same time that St. Ives was reading Owlesby's manuscript to the horrified members of the Trismegistus Club at Captain Powers' shop, Dr. Ignacio Narbondo and Willis Pule were driving along Bayswater Road toward Craven Hill. The sky was a confusion of whirling clouds, and there was no moon to brighten the road, which was still dry despite little flurries of raindrops that swept along now and then, causing the two men to yank the collars of their coats tighter around their necks. The dome of the oceanarium lay like the shadow of a humped beast through the oaks, the broad branches of which shaded the road and adjacent park into utter obscurity.

The hunchback reined the horse in some twenty yards from the darkened building, keeping well back into black forest shadows. Nothing stirred but the sighing wind and the occasional patter of drops. The stone block of the oceanarium was gray with age and stained brown in long vertical streaks from the rusting iron sashes of banks of windows. Vines crept up along the wall, trimmed around windows and just beginning to leaf out in the late April spring. No lights shone from within, but the two men knew that somewhere a groundskeeper kept watch, poking around, perhaps, with a lit candle. Pule hoped the man was asleep, and his dog with him. He crept along the edge of the building, below the windows, listening and watching and trying each window in turn, ready to cut and run at the least sound.

He grasped the stile of a broad double casement and pulled, the window creaking suddenly open in a little spray of rust chips. Pule hauled himself up, scrabbling for a toe-hold against the stones and scraping the skin from his palms against the rough sill. He fell back onto the ground, cursing under his breath the night, the windows, the invisible watchman and his dog, and especially Dr. Narbondo, comfortably seated on the dogcart, ready to flee at the sound of trouble. Pule knew, though, that he'd be loath to leave without the carp, that Joanna Southcote would become nothing but a decomposed heap of dust and bone without the fish – that her doddering son wouldn't be half so anxious to part with his bag of half crowns if their attempt were a failure.

Pule struggled once again at the window – physical strength had never been his forte. He loathed it, in fact. It was beneath him. All of this intrigue was beneath him. Soon, though, when certain things were in his possession… He found himself teetering across the sill, flailing his legs to keep from tumbling back into the night. He tipped head foremost, finally, into the building. His coat caught on the hinge of the casement, yanking him sideways. Debris clattered from his pocket onto the stone floor, and he cursed as he saw dimly his half candle roll under the iron legs of an aquarium. Moments later he was on his hands and knees on the damp floor groping for it.

The air was heavy with the musty smell of aquaria and water weeds and the salt that crusted glass lids from the fine spray of aerating bubbles. Pule could hear the echoing drip of leaking tanks and the swish of bubbles on the otherwise still surface water. Thank God his matches hadn't fallen into any puddles. He crouched behind a vast, rectangular stone monolith that supported a bank of dark aquaria, and he struck a match against the rough granite in a hiss of igniting sulphur. He lit the piece of candle, shoving it securely into a brass candlestick.

He peered out into the dark room, satisfied that he was alone, then rose and stepped across toward the opposite wall.

He'd strolled about that same room a half-dozen times in the last month, familiarizing himself with the islands of aquaria, with the position and nature of closets of nets and siphons and buckets and the great rubber bladders that fed air into the tanks. He found a broad, square net and a step stool, and hauled them both back to the center of the room. He waved his candle at a long, low tank, squinting through the glare off the glass, and watching the silver bulk of the great carp that lay barely moving among the rocks and weed.

Pule stepped to the top of the stool. He pulled the glass top from the tank, then climbed down and laid it carefully onto the floor. In a moment he was up again, dipping his net into the aquarium. He'd have to be quick. If the carp were given half a chance, they'd sail to the far end of the tank and hover there, and he'd have to move the stool to get at them. That wouldn't do. He carefully yanked out clumps of weed, dropping them with a wet splat to the floor. There was no use tangling his net in them. It was a carp he wanted, not a mess of greenery. Through the dim water he could see one resting on the gravel, a mottled koi some foot and a half in length. That would suffice. Pule eased the net into the water, wiggled it to unfurl the corners, and with a sudden lunge, swept it down and over the tail of the sleeping fish, yanking it out of the water before it had a chance to awaken. He groped for its head, trying to hook a finger under a gill. Water splashed out of the aquarium, drowning the front of his coat.

The carp thrashed suddenly sideways, jerking away from Pule's hand. He lunged at it and cradled the fish in his arms, feeling the step stool canting over as he did so, aware, suddenly, of a light being trimmed behind him and of the barking of a dog.

"Here now!" came a startled voice as Pule and the fish toppled over sideways into a mess of sodden waterweeds. Trailing anacharis and ambulia, Pule wrenched at his fish, slamming it against the stone monolith as he rolled against it. The dog growled and snatched at his pantleg. Pule yelled obscenities, ululating madly at the dog and his master, hoping that the watchman – an old man with a game leg – wouldn't be quick to engage an obviously lunatic fish thief. More than that, he hoped that Narbondo would hear the ruckus and get his filthy cart under the window.

He kicked at the dog, clamped now to his pantleg, and managed only to drag it along behind him. Its master limped in, crouched and waving his arms, grappling after the dog as if worried only that Pule might make away with it as well as with the carp. Pule turned, thrusting the fish through the window – there was no way he'd clamber out holding it – and felt it snatched from his grasp. A spray and wind-driven rain stung his eyes as he boosted himself through, easily now, with the dog yammering behind him and the window sill some two feet lower now that he was inside the building rather than outside.

The distance to the ground, however, was greater than he'd

calculated, and he found himself, after a wild, thrashing tumble, twisted in the mud between the stones of the building and the wheel of the dogcart. Narbondo cursed wildly, Pule cursed him back, and the watchman clutched his little dog, staring inertly at the two from beyond the open window. The hunchback whipped up the horses as Pule grabbed the sideboard and attempted to hoist himself in, kicking furiously to keep up with the horse and falling in a heap into the bed, face first into the carcass of the great fish.

He was tempted, as he lay gasping and panting, smearing scaly ooze from his cheek with a coat sleeve, to pummel Narbondo senseless with the carp, to pitch the hunchback off the front of the dogcart into the way of the galloping horse, to run across his twisted face with the ironclad cartwheels and leave him to die in the muck of the roadway. But his time would come.

Pule picked up the heavy fish and thrust it into a half keg splashing with water barely deep enough to submerge it. He swam it back and forth to revive it, but the thing was half crushed. The water, in seconds, was a mess of blood and scales.

"He's done!" shouted Pule at the back of Narbondo's bouncing head.

The hunchback shouted something, but his words were lost in the wind. The cart bumped and clattered and raced between the shadowy oaks, careering this way and that into potholes, nearly going over into a ditch, the mud flung up from the horse's hooves spattering around Pule, who hung on with both hands now, satisfied to leave the fish to its own devices. With a suddenness that catapulted Pule into Narbondo's back, the horse reared to a stop, and in an obscuring deluge of rain, the hunchback clambered over into the back of the cart, jerking his head at Pule.

"Take the bloody reins!" he gasped, throwing open his bag

and reaching into it for a scalpel. He paused long enough to fetch Pule a shove that nearly pitched him out of the wagon, and in moments they were away again, Pule driving, the doctor laying the fish open with his blade, muttering under his breath some foul business that was swept behind them on the wind and rain and so lost entirely on Pule, who was filled with his own black thoughts of death and revenge.

There was no real reason to be fearful, quite likely. No one suspected her, yet she felt inclined toward darkness, toward venturing out at night. She prayed that the day would soon come that it would be otherwise. Captain Powers would see to it. She hurried along down Shaftesbury Street, hidden in her cloak through nearly empty streets, her umbrella slanted back to stop the wind and rain that drove in from the west. The weather was far too evil for anyone to be out and about, and the hour was late – long after midnight.

Her life of homeless wandering in the Indies, later for three years in South Carolina, and now, finally, in London – the home of her youth, but now the place in the world most laden with suspicion and fear – had been relieved by her having found a single, safe port, as it were, an island in a sea of tumult and remorse. Captain Powers was that island – a man whom nothing could unsettle, who with his peg leg could stride purposefully across heaving decks awash with seawater, could steer a course by the shadows of stars.

But what particularly suited her was the Captain's obvious regard for curious, frivolous things. In the midst of his stony practicality was a litter of oddities – his ridiculous smoking leg, a monkey-tooth necklace he'd been given by a jungle explorer in exchange for two bottles of Scotch, a pipe that burned tobacco and emitted soap bubbles simultaneously, a collection of trifles purported to yield good luck and which he carried in his pocket. "I've got my luck in my pocket," he'd say, displaying the collection to a stranger, holding in the palm of his hand a red and black bean from Peru, a red agate marble, a tiny ivory ape, and an Oriental coin with a hole drilled through it. He could tell a good deal about a man, he would say, by the nature of the man's reaction. William Keeble and Langdon St. Ives had seen the value of it all straight off.

Nell surprised herself to discover that she was only a block from the smoke shop. It was early yet, for her particular purposes; the club meeting would no doubt still be underway. If she could find some sort of shelter she would wait. It wasn't at all unpleasant watching the rain if one were safely out of it. She turned down Regent Street toward St. James' Park. She'd sit under the shelter and imagine a concert, or imagine nothing at all, but simply hide behind the darkness and the weather.

The rain diminished briefly, and the night fell silent but for her footfalls on the pavement. Behind her, clattering slowly down Regent, came a brougham, its lamp burning yellow in the misty night. It drew up apace and slowed, as if shadowing her. The driver, however, paid her no heed, but slouched on his seat looking ahead of him, the ribands slack in his hands, as if the vehicle were simply slowing down out of inertia. Nell forced herself to ignore it. She pulled her cloak around her and strode on. She debated whether to turn off down the approaching alley or simply to pursue her way toward the park.

She glanced quickly at the brougham. Two men rode within, both of them staring out at her. One was lost in shadow, the other clearly visible. He seemed to have half a face. There was something in their staring that convinced her, suddenly and completely, that they weren't casually passing in the night, that they were watching her. She stepped into the narrow alley, tall buildings tilting away above and blocking the driven rain, which ran down the wall to her left, glazing the dirty bricks and flowing into a muddy stream along the center of the alley. She lifted her skirts and ran. There was nothing to do but splash through the ankle-deep rill. She would double back when she found the end of the alley – run all the way to Jermyn Street if need be. The hour didn't matter. Better to betray herself to friends at the Trismegistus Club than to summon a constable. But better anything than to fall into the hands of whoever it was rode in the brougham. And she had a fair idea who it was.

She never reached the end of the alley. It seemed to hover there beyond a haze of rain some hundred yards distant, yellow in the glow of a gaslamp. Into the feeble light stepped a tall figure in a cloak, bent as if with age. Nell slowed, then stopped. She was suddenly certain that whoever it was stood in the mouth of the alley, it wasn't Ignacio Narbondo. She'd been wrong, but the realization didn't console her. She slowed to a walk, shrinking against the comparatively dry right wall, brushing the moist bricks with the back of her hand. She turned. Lightning cracked the sky above her, turning the two slouched figures that approached her into dense shadows against a suddenly bright backdrop. No windows, no doors presented themselves. The walls were steep and slippery. The night was one tumultuous rush of noise, and her scream was lost in a roar of thunder which threatened to collapse the sheer, crumbling bricks above her.

A hand closed over her mouth, then jerked away when she

bit it. She stumbled and kicked blindly at the man in the cloak. He cursed and stepped back in a little bent hop, as if he were infirm with age. She blinked rainwater out of her eyes, unwilling to believe what she saw. But it was so. A moment of weakness years earlier had come round to betray her.

A ruined face, the face of a corpse, loomed in front of her, and the ghoul who possessed it slammed her back into the wall, dragging a flour sack over her head. She spun around, tumbled onto her knees in the water, and was jerked upright and pushed forward.

The stumbling, blind walk back down the alley to the waiting brougham seemed endless, yet didn't afford her time for thought. Her second scream was silenced by a jerk at the sack that had been twisted round her neck. She saw two rapid lightning flashes, and automatically, out of sheer numbness, counted the six seconds that followed. The thunder still boomed in the low skies when a hand was laid against the small of her back and she was precipitated into the brougham. She remained on her knees on the floor. She heard the click of the door latch and listened as the coach careered away into the rainy night to the sound of the wheezing, rattling breath of her two strange captors. She grappled with her memory in an effort to find an explanation of her fate. There was none. What she knew, Shiloh knew. She had been, those long years past, a briefly willing convert, who had confessed thoroughly and truthfully. But the knowledge she had revealed, of her guilt and of the whereabouts of the thing in the box, hadn't altered. She could be of no further use to him. Unless it was something else they were after. Would they attempt to use her against the Captain? Was it Jack's emerald they sought? She searched her mind. Had she revealed the existence of the emerald? She almost wished she had, for if they sought to meddle with Captain Powers through her, then they made a mistake – and she heartily wished, as the brougham jerked to a stop minutes later, that it was just such a mistake they'd made.

Dr. Narbondo carried the mutilated carp up the narrow stairs toward his laboratory above Pratlow Street, Willis Pule slouching along behind. The gland he excised was a pitiful thing, itself half ruined by Pule's clumsy foolery. He'd have to mug up some sort of show to satisfy the damned missionary – have Pule hook Joanna Southcote up to the ceiling and dance her like a marionette. The old man would be loath to part with his money – worthless as it was – if he got no satisfaction at all. In fact, there was no telling what tricks the crazy old man mightn't be up to if his precious mother didn't rise from the slab.

Narbondo, his hands full of fish viscera, kicked the door open and stepped into his cabinet. The lamp above his empty aquarium was alight. Below it, his face half in shadow, stood Shiloh himself, gaunt, haggard, and dripping water onto the floor beside the slab. Dr. Narbondo could see that the old man was far from satisfied. Joanna Southcote wasn't an inspiring sight. She lay in a comfortable heap on the slab, partly disassembled, a rickety, fleshless, collapsed framework of dirt and dust and bones. Tangled wisps of hair were clotted with leaves. Her winding sheet lay in an ignominious heap beside the slab.

A dissecting board onto which was pinned an enormous, flayed toad had been swept from the slab onto the floor along with a sheaf of notes, an ink bottle, and a quill pen. The hunchback dropped the fish onto the slab and pulled off his dripping greatcoat in silence.

Shiloh, stupefied with anger, threw out his arm and shoved the fish onto the floor atop the toad. The violence of the effort jarred the slab, and the bones of his mother danced briefly, her jaws clacking shut as if she were admonishing her clumsy son.

"She speaks!" cried the evangelist, lurching forward and grasping her forearm as if to entreat her to continue. Her hand fell off onto the slab. Shiloh stepped back in horror, covering his eyes. Narbondo grunted in disgust, turned to hang his coat on a hook. He stopped, a smile spreading across his face.

"Nell Owlesby," he said. "And after so many long years. What has it been? Fifteen years now since you shot your poor brother, hasn't it?" He paused momentarily and licked his lips. "A very pretty shot, that one. Straight into his heart. Knicked a rib going in and lodged in the left ventricle. Quite a mess. I worked on him for three hours after chasing you half across London, but I couldn't save him. I animated him, though, for a week, but he wasn't worth keeping. Lost his sense. Wept the day out. I cut him to bits, finally – used a piece of him here, a piece of him there."

Nell sat tight-lipped in her corner, staring at the rainwater that beat against the window. "That's a lie," she said finally. "I saw him buried at Christchurch myself. His bones are still there. My mistake was to not shoot you instead of him. I know that now. I knew it an hour after. But the deed was done."

"You're right, of course." Narbondo stooped to pick up his toad. He lay it on a table, repinning one rubbery leg that had fallen loose. He pointed then at the ruined carp. "Your mother's soul," he said, turning to Shiloh, "resides in this carp. It's been beaten. It's a pity, really, but it couldn't be helped. My assistant here pulverized it against a window sill. But it's worlds away healthier than this, eh?" He nodded at the skeleton before frowning just a bit as if not entirely satisfied with it. He stepped slowly across to the window, flung it open, and sailed the carp out into the night.

The old missionary leaped toward him, his cloak flying behind. Narbondo flourished his right hand in front of his face, as if he were a magician uncovering a palmed coin. Between his thumb and forefinger was the little kidney-shaped gland, glistening pink. He winked at the old man, who stopped abruptly. "This is worth two hundred fifty pounds." Narbondo squinted at it, holding it to the light.

"I'll trade you the woman for it," said Shiloh, smiling for the first time that evening.

Narbondo shrugged. "What do I want with her? She's a murderess. I haven't any interest in a murderess, have I?"

"You've been asking after her around the city for a month. You've offered, in fact, nearly twice that sum for news of her. I'm prepared to let her go at a bargain."

The hunchback shrugged. He turned to Nell, who sat as before, staring into the night. She had a faint idea of what brought the two villains together – what information Narbondo craved even after fifteen years.

"Where is the box?" the doctor asked abruptly.

"Ask the old man," Nell said. "He knows."

Narbondo spun round and faced the evangelist, who stood now with a look of satisfaction on his face. He shrugged. "This is," he said slowly, as if contemplating each word, "a matter of mutual gain, is it not?"

Narbondo started to speak, apparently thought better of it, and fell silent. Then, after a pause, said: "Where is the box? I want it. Now."

The old man shook his head. "I'll pay for services rendered.

I've seen no services yet." Then, suddenly coming to himself, he gestured at the slab behind him. "Tonight," he said. "Immediately."

Pule groaned, slumping into a chair. Narbondo nodded, as if the request were simple enough, and plucked an apron from a hook, hissing at Pule to prepare for surgery.

"How...?" began Pule, but the hunchback cut him off with a curse. Shiloh backed toward a chair that sat opposite the fire, his face a mixture of reverence, satisfaction, and trepidation.

Theophilus Godall hurried along through the rainy streets, listening to the receding footfalls of Langdon St. Ives, and pondering the strange state of Captain Powers, who had evidently suffered a loss of articles unknown to the rest of them. This business was difficult enough when the bits and pieces were apparent. When they were hidden, it grew frustrating indeed – interesting certainly, but frustrating.

He'd become accustomed to staying up nights. He hadn't any business to speak of, so he could afford to nod off in pursuit of a couple of hours of sleep in the morning. It was close upon two o'clock. The night and the weather would cover his lack of disguise. He puffed thoughtfully on his pipe, tapped his stick decisively on the cobbles, and set a course toward Pratlow Street, rounding the corner as a lit window midway down the block was thrown open and a cylindrical bundle sailed out, smashing to the pavement below, followed by a shout clipped off by the shutting of the window. Godall hurried along and bent over the thing in the street. It was a dead fish of indeterminate sort – its head and most of its body having been reduced to muck by its sudden collision with the roadway. Godall turned and strode away up the stairs into his bare, rented room, arranging the curtains so as to have his usual view of the cabinet of Ignacio Narbondo.

He could see, from his curtain, three men in the room, all of whom were familiar. Shiloh, the self-proclaimed messiah, exhorted the hunchback and his assistant. He seemed to be railing at them, and now and then Godall could make out bits of shouting over the wind and rain. The hunchback squirted yellow mist at a corpse on the slab – a skeleton on the slab – from a hand-held device fed by a coiled tube. A fire roared behind him in the grate. Encased within a heavy, glass, liquid-filled jar was a tiny object of some sort – too small to identify. Herbs burned in a stone chalice. The evangelist collapsed to his knees in the semblance of prayer, and Narbondo, apparently treading on the old man's hand, stumbled and sprayed his yellow mist onto Pule, who staggered away retching. The hunchback paused to shout at the old man, who arose and stepped back a pace, out of the way of the window.

A fresh flurry of rain dimmed Godall's vision for a moment, but he squinted through it, focusing on the thing that lay on the slab. Surely, thought the tobacconist – surely the hunchback wasn't attempting to animate such a thing. But he was wrong. The machine generated mist that hovered in the air above the corpse. The chalice smoked. Narbondo fished out the business in the jar and, nodding to Pule, shoved it into something that resembled a garlic press and squeezed it into the gaping mouth of the corpse.

The old man fell back, his hands covering his face. Narbondo pumped at the machine. The thing on the slab lurched once, a scattering of debris falling from its tangle of hair, and seemed to rise as if by levitation. The shouts of Narbondo were audible but were reduced by the windy rain to gibberish.

The body jerked twice, stiffened, and very slowly began to pull itself up onto the elbow of its handless arm, as if it would slide from its slab and walk, It turned its leathery head back and forth, blind, barely animate, an unholy, rusted machine. Its other arm rose and followed the swiveling head as it rotated on its axis toward the window. For one gut-clutching moment Godall was certain the thing was looking at *him,* but the head rotated farther, settling its vacant gaze on the trembling evangelical, its pointing hand hovering in the air, as if in accusation or, just as easily, supplication. The old man clutched his robes, his hands opening and shutting in a gesture of fear and wonder. Then, like a card house tumbling, the corpse dropped straightaway to the table, and the pointing hand clacked to the floor. The old man gasped and reeled forward. Narbondo clouded the room with his vaporizer, casting it down, finally, and plucking up a fallen hand. He fought off the old man's efforts to wrestle it away, then stopped, shrugged, and tossed it onto the slab beside the heaped bones.

The mist still clouded the room. Through it, striding toward the courtyard window, came a woman who appeared to Godall to be about forty. Supposing, perhaps, that she would attempt to meddle with the corpse, the old man rushed at her, protesting. She slammed him in the side of the head with her clenched fist, burst past him, and flung open the casement, leaning out, either for a breath of air or to throw herself from the window. Godall squashed the instinctive urge to drop the curtain and duck back into his darkened room. Instead, he looked straight at her, and, as if he were passing her on the pavement at midday, he tipped his hat to her, then slid round so that he could just barely see beyond the casing.

All three of the men in the room opposite dragged her back

from the window, mortally fearful, it seemed to Godall, that she would indeed tumble out and fall the three stories to the dark stones of the courtyard below. Godall carefully slid the latch on his own window and shoved it open a crack. He was met by a rush of wet air and a cacophony of voices, accusing and shouting oaths. The men tugged on the woman as if she were a money-filled purse in the hands of thieves, until, with a lurch that threw the hunchback against his aquarium, she yanked herself free. Pule reached for her, and she kicked him in the leg.

The short, uneasy truce that followed was interrupted by the old man, who seemed to suffer a sudden fit of remorse over the state of his fallen mother. "You've ruined her!" he cried, waving at the corpse and turning suddenly on Narbondo. "You'll… you'll… *pay!*"

The hunchback shrugged, suddenly seeming calm. "No," he said, straightening his coat and winking at the woman. "*You'll* pay." And with that he jerked open the door and nodded toward the black hallway without. "I'm not done with your mother. This is something of a success. If our carp hadn't been so thoroughly dealt with, she'd be dancing us a minuet at the moment." And with that he brought his hand down onto the keys of the open piano by the door, dragging his hand along them in a rush of heightening notes.

Shiloh looked from Narbondo to Pule and from Pule to Narbondo, not moving when the hunchback jerked his head toward the door. In the hallway stood two men, one in a turban, the other with a mutilated face. The woman shrank back toward the window once again but was grasped by a frightened Pule. The man in the turban bowed to the old man and produced a pistol from his waistcoat, pointing it at the hunchback.

"Come, my dear," said the evangelist, waving a hand at the woman. Godall could barely hear his suddenly softened voice. The turbaned man leveled the gun across his upraised forearm, directly into the gaping Pule, who shoved the woman into the waiting arms of the old man. "My offer still stands. Each of us wants a particular woman alive. We haven't long, have we?" And not waiting for an answer, Shiloh, the woman, and the toughs stepped through the door and were swallowed by darkness.

Godall took the stairs two at a time and was on the street before them. St. Ives' story of the two men in the house of prostitution left little doubt in his mind of the identity and nature of Shiloh's accomplices. He hoped they were as feeble as St. Ives supposed. On the strength of the brougham parked around the corner on Old Compton Street, Godall crouched in the dark alcove of the doorway, supposing the party would pass him going out.

A door slammed, footfalls clattered on the steps of the house next door, and a moment later four dim figures hurried past, the woman dragged along unceremoniously by the old evangelical, who made a sort of unidentifiable mewling sound – something between a titter and a groan. Godall stepped silently to the walk behind them, his own footsteps lost in theirs. With no attempt at stealth, he grasped the coat of the turbaned man, jerked it back, and in the instant the man turned toward him in surprise, Godall plucked the revolver from a belt about the man's waist.

It seemed likely that threatening two walking dead men with a revolver would avail him little, so he leaped past both of them, clutched Shiloh by the front of his cloak, and shoved the revolver against the side of his head, holding his stick under his arm.

"I'll thank you to release the woman," said Godall.

The old man let her go without hesitation, waggling both hands over his head as if to demonstrate that he had no intention of arguing.

Godall released the old man's cloak and handed Nell his stick. "Theophilus Godall," he said, bowing, "at your service."

She hesitated for a moment, then said, "Nell Owlesby, sir," and watched Godall's face, which made an incomplete effort to disguise its surprise.

Turning again to the old man, who stared nervously at the gun, Godall said: "You'll accompany us for a way. Your friends will remain here."

"Of course they will. That's just what they'll do. They'll stay very well put. Won't you, my sons?"

The two were silent. Godall edged backward along the pavement, fearing suddenly that the man with the ruined face might also be armed. But he made no movement at all. They stepped from the curb and hurried along toward the end of the street. The east was gray with dawn light, and the city was awakening. Clouds overhead were breaking up, and the moon blinked through, pale as a ghost. The morning was lightening the neighborhood dangerously. If they could slip round the corner and down a block or two, they'd leave the old man to shift for himself and would make away toward Jermyn Street.

The evangelist began to utter monosyllabic spiritual doggerel about damnation and pain, and, still walking backward, he smashed his eyes shut, as if praying or as if clamping out the sight of a world too coarse and evil to be tolerated. He stumbled, nearly precipitating the three of them into the gutter. Godall, hesitating out of general chivalry to cuff an old man, said simply, "Walk, will you!" They rounded the corner and approached the parked brougham.

A horse whinnied. Godall spun toward it, surprised at the sudden noise. A curse rang out from directly over his head, and before he had time to sort the curse from the whinny, someone had dropped like an ape onto his back from the roof of the brougham.

The driver. There had been a driver, thought Godall wildly and ineffectually as he was borne down onto the wet street. His gun clattered away along the cobbles. He grappled with his attacker, striking at the man whose arms encircled his neck. But the backhand blows were worth nothing, and the man slid his forearm in beneath Godall's shoulder and around the back of his neck. Godall's head pressed against his own chest. His right foot kicked back and found the curb. He pushed, rising to his knees. His assailant was curiously light, but light or not, the pressure he exerted on Godall's neck sharpened. His hat had been shoved down half over his eyes and somehow clung there as tenaciously as the man on his back, unwilling to let go. Below the brim he could see the two thugs rounding the corner, loping toward them, and the old evangelist stooping to pick up the fallen pistol.

Godall stamped once in that direction, but accomplished nothing. He stood up, the man clinging like a bug, and ran backward into the side of the brougham. The wagon lurched on its springs; the horse bolted forward. There was a guttural shriek in Godall's ear as the man on his back twisted away, jerking Godall after him and off balance. As he fell he saw Shiloh recoiling from a blow. It was Nell with Godall's stick. She held it by the tip, and, when Shiloh made another feeble attempt to grasp the fallen pistol, she cracked him in the ear with the ivory moon handle, then turned to thrust the tip into the throat of the turbaned man, who sailed in to aid his fallen comrades.

Godall leaped on the pistol, rolled heavily onto his side, and waved it menacingly. The turbaned man kneeled in a huddle, gagging. The evangelist sat dripping blood along the line of his scalp, shaking his head slowly, casting Nell a dark look of pain and rage. The driver of the brougham lay entangled in the spokes of the rear wheel, which had caught his foot when the horse leaped forward, and had spun him from his perch on Godall's back.

The battle, clearly, was over. Godall hesitated. Should he take the old man with him? But Nell was already hurrying away, carrying his stick. The sky was clear and gray. An approaching wagon jangled in the silent morning. Godall gave the pistol a final wave, turned, and jogged after Nell Owlesby. When he passed Lexington two blocks down he looked back to see the ghouls bent over their hunched saviour.

NINE

POOR BILL KRAKEN

Willis Pule leaned against the embankment railing, looking out over the tumult of Billingsgate market. The sun was up, but not far, and it cast an orange, rippling slash along the placid waters of the Thames through parted clouds. The streets were clean and wet. Under other circumstances it would have been a pleasant enough morning, what with masts and ropes of sailing vessels rising above tiers of fishing boats against the lavender sky and hundreds of men landing fish along the docks. But Pule hadn't slept that night. Narbondo would have another carp, and he'd have it now. His were dead of swim-bladder disease. The oceanarium couldn't be attempted twice in a single day. There was the chance that breeders from fisheries in Chingford would have carp for sale at Billingsgate. And if they were fresh – if they hadn't begun to dry out – there was the chance they could restore Joanna Southcote after all.

The hunchback had been tearing his hair since the old man had left with Nell Owlesby. Narbondo was mad to suppose they could do anything with the corpse on the slab – even madder to trust Shiloh to keep his end of the bargain. The evangelist would sell them out. And his power was accumulating. Pule could see a half-dozen of his converts passing out tracts in the market, most of which were immediately put to use wrapping fish. None of the supplicants appeared to be Narbondo's animated dead men. Even the farthest-fetched, vilest sort of religious cult could develop a sort of fallacious legitimacy through numbers.

Pule wondered whether his prospects wouldn't be better if he were to throw in with Shiloh, if he were to become a convert. He could do it surreptitiously – keep a hand in with Narbondo – play the one against the other. He stared into his coffee, deaf to the whistles, cries, and shouts of the basket-laden throng around him.

The loss of sleep would play hell with his complexion. He fingered a lump on his cheek. With all the powers of ages of alchemical study at hand, he couldn't seem to prevent these damned boils and pimples. Camphor baths had nearly suffocated him. Hot towels soaked in rum, vinegar, and – he shuddered to recall it – urine, had merely activated the boils, and it had taken two solid months before he could go abroad without supposing that everyone on the street was whispering and gesturing at his expense. And they probably were, the scum. He rubbed idly at his nose, sniffing at his coffee, the acrid fumes of which just barely disguised the seaweed odors of whelk and oysters and gutted fish – odors that lay like an omnipresent shroud over the market. The smell of fish, of dead, out-of-water fish, sickened him.

Someone tapped him on the shoulder. He looked up darkly into the face of an earnest youth in a cap and neckerchief. A tract fluttered in his hand. "Excuse me," said the youth, smiling vacantly. "A wonderful morning, this." And he looked about him as if he were surrounded by evidence of it. Pule regarded his face with loathing. "I'm here to offer you salvation," said the youth. "It's easy to come by, isn't it?"

"I wouldn't know," responded Pule truthfully.

"It is, though. It's in the sunrise, in the river, in the bounty of the sea." And he waved his hand theatrically at a heap of squid laid out on a sledge below. He smiled all the while at the disheveled Pule, who absentmindedly rubbed a rising blemish on the tip of his nose. The youth, apparently satisfied with the squid illustration, rubbed his own nose, although there was no profit in it. "I'm a member of the New Church," said he, thrusting forth his tracts. "The New Church that won't have a chance to get old."

Pule blinked at him.

"Do you know why?"

"No," said Pule, rubbing at his nose once more.

As if powered by magnetism, the young man was after his own nose again, thinking, perhaps, that something clung to the side of it, a speck that eluded his previous rubbing. Pule noted his behavior and felt his face grow hot. Was the fool having him on? Pule clenched his teeth. "What the hell do you want with me?" he cried.

The violence of Pule's epithet seemed almost to catapult the youth backward. He recovered, pulled the slack out of himself, and smiled all the more widely. "The end is near," he announced, grinning. The idea of Armageddon seemed to appeal to him. "You've days to save your immortal soul. The New Church, I tell you, is the way. He, Shiloh, the New Messiah, is the way! He raiseth people from the grave! He redeemeth the dead! He..."

But Pule interrupted. "So you're saying I should become a convert to save myself? Conversion by extortion is it?"

The youth gazed at him, his smile broader, if anything. "I say," said he, having another innocent go at his nose, "that he who was born of no man can lift you out of misery, can..." and with this, the youth put his hand on Pule's forehead, as if to heal his soul there and then, in the midst of tramping men carrying baskets of shark heads and eels. The touch of a human hand on the ravaged forehead electrified Pule, but in a way other than had been intended.

Pule screamed an oath, dropped his cup and with both hands tore the tracts from the youth and flung them in a heap to the stones of the embankment. "Filthy... blathering... scum!" shrieked Pule, dancing on the tracts, scuffling and tearing at them with the soles of his shoes. He bent, grabbed a handful, and flung them over the railing, the wind sailing them merrily away like penny whirligigs. Pule cut another half-dozen capers, his eyes like saucers, his mouth twisted in rage. The youth, his smile gone with his vanishing tracts, edged backward a step at a time, until, certain that Pule was too far away to leap on him, he cut and ran toward the embankment stairs, cries of "Scum-sucking pig!" and "Damnable filth!" lending him wings. Pule grasped at the railing, oblivious to the stares of passersby, who gave him a wide berth, anxious not to set him off. He had called attention to himself, to his livid face. They would speak to each other, nudge each other, twigging him. He stared into his retrieved cup, chest heaving, until he saw, beneath his feet, a last tattered tract, smeared with gravel and rainwater footprints. He picked the thing up. On it, sketched rudely by someone whose understanding of perspective was nonsense, was an elongated dirigible, sailing among the clouds. And above it, streaming across a progressively darkening sky, a flaming comet, strangely phallic, arched in toward the flat earth. "The time is at hand!" shouted the caption below the illustration. But what time it was that was at hand wasn't at all clear, lost as it was in the unfortunate footprint. Pule folded the tract and shoved it into the pocket of his coat, then stepped away down the stairs into the interior of the market, the wooden rambling barn packed with shouting vendors and so thick with fish that it seemed impossible that the oceans hadn't been stripped clean.

A woman strung with codfish pushed past, smearing Pule with bloody slime. Directly after came a fat man leering up out of Oyster Street with a basket full of gray shells, shouting so vociferously in Pule's face that for a moment the world seemed to him nothing but a great nose, an open mouth, and a shower of spittle. Pule shrank back in disgust. Fish vendors pushed in on him from all sides. Octopi the size of bumboats seemed to be hovering over him, grasping at him with warty tentacles. Baskets of eels appeared, pushed along on a cart, wriggling out over the sides of their prison only to be ignominiously shoved back in and buried beneath a ballast of cabbage leaves.

Pule gagged. It was close as a tanyard. He'd faint if he didn't have air. "Carp! Carp! Carp!" came a sudden cry. "Who'll have these ha-a-an-some carp! All alive! Alive O! Prime carp! Carp o' the gods!" Pule steered toward the voice, groping for his purse. He wouldn't haggle. This was no time for haggling. He'd have his carp and away. He stumbled, slipped on the carcass of a fish trod to slime by a hundred shoes. In front of him was a plank piled with enormous reddish shrimp, like impossible bugs, their eyes staring on stalks from out of brittle carapaces, huge feelers waving like antennae. Pule rocked against a wagon of squid, nearly upsetting it. "'Ere now!" came a cry, and he was shoved along. There were the carp – seven of them, submerged in a trough of water.

"Fresh as any daisy!" cried the vendor, noting Pule's evident interest.

"How much?"

"Two pounds buys the lot."

Pule produced the money and waved it blindly at the man, who snatched it away and winked at a seller of dried herring beside him. "Want them all, then?"

"I gave you enough, didn't I?"

"No," said the vendor, "you were a pound shy. What're you up to? Precious sort of fellow, aren't you, trying to cheat a poor carp man like me."

Pule looked up at him, astonished, far too tired and frightened to argue. The man dangled a single pound note from his fingers. Pule gave him a look and got another look in return. "How many for a pound?" he whispered.

"What's that?"

"For a pound? What do I get for a pound?"

"One bleeding fish, is what. We had an agreement. Me mate here heard it from your very face, and an unnatural sort of pocky face it is, if I says so myself." And with that he leered across at the herring dealer, who nodded widely and finally.

Pule dug out another pound. "I want the trough too," he said weakly.

"That'll cost you another, carbuncle," said the carp vendor. Pule nodded, his fear and embarrassment metamorphosing into anger. "Here, you!" he cried, gesturing to a costerlad who sat in an empty barrow. "Five shillings to transport this tub of carp out to Soho."

The boy leaped up and grappled with the heavy trough, spilling water. Pule cuffed him on the side of the head.

"Here's a brave one!" shouted the carp man, pocketing the most recent pound note. "Look at moony beat this here lad!" And he burst into laughter, reached across the trough, and jerked Pule's cap off, dipping it full of squid from a passing basket. He shoved the cap back onto the head of the fleeing and humiliated Pule, who, with the barrow at his heels, burst out into the chilly morning sunlight and pitched the cap, squids and all, into the Thames.

"Say!" cried the lad with the barrow. For a moment he looked as if he were going to leap in after them. "That were a good hat, weren't it?" he asked innocently, marveling, perhaps, at the apparent wealth of a man who would throw such a hat into the river. "And they was prime squid too." He shook his head and sloshed along in Pule's wake.

Some hundred yards down the embankment, the cries and odors of Billingsgate market having receded behind him, Pule noticed a sleeping figure, hunched out of the wind beneath a little stony outcropping that had been, before it crumbled, a decorative granite buttress on an ancient bit of river wall. It wasn't the reclining figure that caught his eye so much as the half-exposed object that protruded from a pillowcase which the sleeper cradled in his arms.

Pule slowed and squinted at it. He looked at the man's face. It appeared to be Bill Kraken. And the box? It was a Keeble box. He'd seen Narbondo's sketches. There wasn't any question about it: the grinning face of the clothed hippo that peered out from the folds of the pillowcase, the dancing apes carved into the exposed lid. What rare piece of serendipity *was* this, he asked himself. Could this be heavenly repayment for his recent ill-use?

He studied the sleeping Kraken. He was unacquainted with the man, literally speaking, but perhaps knew enough about him to turn the happenstance of their meeting to profit. He addressed the costerlad: "Run along down the way," he said, "and buy me a bottle of brandy, heated, will you? And two glasses." He gave the boy three shillings. "There's another for you if you come back." He realized as he watched the boy run off that he hadn't had to offer him a bribe to return. He'd have come back after his barrow sure enough. Perhaps he could cheat him of it somehow. Pule turned his attention to Kraken, who snored volubly and held on to his prize.

The sun peeked over the treetops below London Bridge, casting its rays full into Kraken's face. He recoiled in the glare of it, blinking and squinting, then seemed to realize what it was he clutched to his chest, and clutched it all the more tightly, as if it were a beast of some sort that might leap from his arms and run. In an instant he pushed it away, hoping, it seemed, that it would run, then yanked it to him again. He stopped his odd tug of war, however, when he noted Pule, bent over the barrow of carp.

"Good morning to you," said Pule pleasantly, one eye cocked for the approach of the lad with his brandy. Kraken sat in silence. "Cold enough this morning."

"That it is," said Kraken suspiciously.

"Bit of hot brandy would be the ticket."

Kraken swallowed hard. He ran a dry tongue over his lips and regarded Pule. "Have a bit of fish there, have you?"

"That's it. Fish. Carp, actually."

"Carp is it? They say carp is… What do they say? Immortal. That's it."

"Do they?" asked Pule, feigning deep interest.

"Science does. They've studied 'em. In China mainly. Live forever and grow as big as the pool they're kept in. That's a fact. Read up your Bible – it's all there. Loads of talk about the leviathan – the devil's own fish. Shows up as a serpent here, a crocodile there

– they can't keep him straight. But he's a carp, sure enough, with his tail in his own mouth. And soon – weeks they say – he's going to let loose and come up out of the sea like one of them monsoons. I'm a man of science and the spirit both, but I don't trust to neither one entirely. There's no affidavit you can sign. That's my thinking."

Pule was momentarily awash. He nodded vehement agreement. "Spirit, is it?" he asked, seeing that the brandy bottle approached at a run from up the embankment. The brandy was delivered, Pule was relieved of another shilling, and the boy pushed the barrow twenty yards farther along and waited.

"Glass of Old Pope?" asked Pule, pouring half a tumbler full for Kraken before he had an answer.

"I am dry, thank you. And I haven't had breakfast yet. What did you say you were?" Kraken sipped at the brandy. Then, as if in rushing relief, he drained half of it, gasping and coughing.

"I'm a naturalist."

"Are you?"

"That's right. I'm an associate of the noted Professor Langdon St. Ives."

Kraken gasped again, without the help of the brandy, then his face dropped into a melancholy scowl of self-pity. Pule poured another dollop into his glass. Kraken drank. The brandy seemed to run the morning chill away. Kraken suddenly thought of the box, which lay on his lap like a coiled serpent. Why had he taken it? What use had he for it? He didn't at all want it. He'd sunk very low. That was certainly the truth. Another glass wouldn't sink him any lower. He wiped a tear from his eye and let go a heaving sigh.

"Interested in the scientific arts, you say?" said Pule.

Kraken nodded morosely, gazing into his empty glass. Pule filled it.

"Of what branch of the sciences are you an aficionado?"

Kraken shook his head, unable to utter a response. Pule loomed in at him, proffering the bottle, stretching his countenance into an expression both pitying and interested. "You seem," said Pule, "if you'll excuse my meddling in your affairs, to be a student of the turnings of the human heart, which, if I'm correct, is as often broken as it is whole." And Pule heaved a sigh, as if he too saw the sad end of things.

Kraken nodded a rubbery head. The brandy rallied him a bit. "You're a philosopher, sir," he said. "Have you read Ashbless?"

"I read little else," Pule lied, "unless, of course, it's scientific arcana. One is forever learning from reading the philosophers. It's nothing more nor less than a study of the human soul. And we're living, I fear, in a world too negligent of that part of man's anatomy."

"There's truth in that," cried Kraken, rising unsteadily to his feet. "Some of us have souls the rag man wouldn't touch. Not with a toasting fork." And with that, Kraken began to cry aloud.

Pule placed a comforting hand on his shoulder. He hadn't any idea where the conversation was leading, but was reasonably certain that he couldn't just relieve Kraken of the box and walk away. He'd have to trust to the fates, who if not positively smiling upon him, were at least grinning in his direction. He poured Kraken another two inches of brandy, wondering if he hadn't ought to have bought two bottles when he had the chance. The effects of the warm liquor, however, seemed to have been somehow cumulative, for Kraken suddenly slumped heavily against the stones of the low wall that fronted the embankment, and it occurred to Pule that it might be possible simply to wait until Kraken was blind drunk and then walk away with his box. "Do you..." asked Kraken, "do you suppose there's a bit of hope?"

"Surely," said Pule, to be safe. Kraken appeared to be satisfied. "You've a great burden."

"That's a fact," muttered Kraken.

"I can help you. Trust me. This talk about toasting forks is unhealthy, doubly so: I won't believe it of you on the one hand, and it denies the very root of salvation on the other. There is no better time than this to round the bend, to draw a course for home."

"Do you think so, guv'nor? Would they have me?" Kraken drained his glass.

"What have you done that's so awful? Stolen your master's goods? Checked the missus?"

Kraken heaved another sigh and looked inadvertently at the box.

"What can that be," Pule asked, "but a toy for a child? Stride back in and lay it at the feet of your employer. Brass it out. Admit your guilt."

"Oh no," lamented Kraken. "It's a bit more than a toy. It's the gallows, is what it is for Bill Kraken. It's the gibbet. This here ain't no toy."

"Come, come. What can it be that's so valuable as that? The world loves a man who confesses his sins."

"Then they hang him." Kraken lapsed into silence.

Pule, unspeakably irritated but grinning broadly, filled his glass and cast the empty bottle end over end into the river. "Come now," he said, "tell us what it is you've got off with there and I'll see if I can't make it right."

"Can you, guv'nor?" asked the befuddled Kraken, suddenly animated.

"I'm the nephew of the Lord Mayor."

"Ah," said Kraken, considering this. "The Lord Mayor. The Lord Mayor hisself. It's a precious great emerald, is what it is.

Poor Jacky's inheritance in a lump. And I've gone and pinched it. It's drink that did it, and that's the truth. Drink and this bonk on the conk." And with that he fingered the freshly healed cut along his forehead.

Pule's mind wrenched and clanked like a broken engine. The emerald. If Narbondo got hold of it, Pule could whistle for a share. Damn the homunculus. Damn the rotten Joanna Southcote and her doddering son. The emerald was worth more than all the hunchback's scientific maundering. And it would be worth twice as much to see Owlesby deprived of it. Dorothy Keeble would regret snubbing him. He'd lure Kraken into an alley and bash him to pieces. But the lad with the barrow. There he stood, waiting stupidly. He would send the lad ahead with the carp. Narbondo had paid for them, after all. Give him his due.

"I think I see a way out of this entanglement," said Pule.

"Eh?"

"I say, come along with me and I'll put this right. Straightaway. You'll be back in tune in no time. And for the love of God, don't let go the box there. There's villains in this city would murder you over it soon as tip their hat to you. Look sharp now."

"There's truth in that," said Kraken half to himself, stumbling along behind Pule, who advanced toward the boy with the barrow.

"Look here, lad," said Pule. "Haul these carp to two-sixty-six Pratlow Street, off Old Compton, and be quick as you can about it without sloshing the things onto the road. There'll be a half crown for you there from Mr. Narbondo if the fish are breathing when you get there. Tell him Mr. Pule says he can eat these, with Mr. Pule's regards for salt. Now go along with you." And away the lad went innocently about his task. Pule shook with anticipation, following along the embankment toward Blackfriars. He'd have to act before Kraken sobered up. He played in his mind scenes of Kraken's demise, of the telling blow, the glinting knife, the gasp of drunken surprise.

"What the devil do you here!" came a startling cry from behind him. Pule leaped. A wagon rattled up, and in it sat Ignacio Narbondo in a fury. Pule's stomach felt suddenly empty. "It's coming on ten o'clock! Does it take you half a morning to buy a stinking carp? That damned skeleton is dropping to dust before us and you're out taking the sun. Shiloh the bloody messiah has us by the nub!" He paused in his tirade and looked Pule up and down. "Where's my carp?"

"I sent them ahead with a boy. You'll get your stinking carp."

"And they *will* be stinking at this rate. What's this?" He squinted at Kraken. "It's Bill Kraken, by God! Old Bill Kraken. Diggin' up any corpses, Bill?"

Kraken looked from Pule to Narbondo, then back at Pule, suspicions revolving in his sodden mind.

"By God!" said Narbondo under his breath, noting the box for the first time. He turned on Pule. "So that's your game, is it? Going to slip it to an old rummy like Bill and make away with the box. Leave the poor doctor to fend for himself." He shook his head as if out of sympathy with the idea. "And after all I've taught you."

"That's a lie," said Pule hotly. "I was leading him back to Pratlow Street. The woman on the slab would profit from… *reorganizing*." Pule winked hugely at Narbondo, inwardly fuming, berating himself for taking so monumentally long about the business.

Narbondo frowned at Pule's punning, but his humor seemed instantly to improve. "I can see that he's a man of parts," he said, then burst into momentary laughter, cut off as suddenly as it began. "What's in the Keeble box? Does he know?"

"The emerald," said Pule. There was no reason to dissemble here. He'd either have the emerald or he wouldn't. No, that wasn't so. He'd *have* the emerald, period. Even if he had to feed Narbondo to the carp. He'd wait it out. This simply hadn't been the right moment. One can't get greedy with the fates. One has simply to wait.

Kraken looked sick, whether over his mounting suspicions or over the excess of warm brandy it was impossible to say, but it could be seen at a glance that he was no longer the docile, repentant Kraken who moments before had been following Pule like an obedient dog. A look of resolve flickered across his face. He stepped back a pace and started to speak. But the sight of a suddenly appearing revolver in the hand of the hunchback silenced him. The look of resolve collapsed.

"Into the wagon with you, Bill," said the doctor, gesturing with the pistol. Kraken attempted to climb in and stumbled against the side. "Help the sod, numbskull!" roared Narbondo at Pule. "Heave him in and let's be gone. We've got a day's work ahead. In you go, Bill!" And Pule, hauling on Kraken's legs, tumbled him into the wagon as Kraken clutched the box, doubly certain now of his own damnation. Pule climbed in beside him and took the pistol from Narbondo. The wagon rattled away up the road, passing some half mile down the costerlad wheeling his barrow.

"There's the carp!" cried Pule, pointing.

But Narbondo drove past without slackening his pace. "They'll come along right enough," he said over his shoulder. "We'll just get poor Bill home safe while we're at it. No detours now. Not with the box riding along beside us!" And with that he whipped up the horses, careening around onto the Victoria Embankment and away.

TEN

TROUBLE AT HARROGATE

Langdon St. Ives marveled at the sunny skies over Harrogate. The clouds that shaded London were invisible beyond the horizon, and the pall that overhung Leeds could only dimly be seen, blown away west and south by chill winds off green Scottish hillsides. The weather was brisk – sunny and brisk – and it fitted St. Ives to a tee.

He'd collected the oxygenator from Keeble at King's Cross Station, the toymaker fearful that he'd been followed, perhaps by his nemesis in the chimney pipe hat – the man Kraken had referred to as Billy Deener. But no such villain showed himself. Nothing at all suspicious occurred until the train was an hour north of London. And that little business, thought St. Ives with a certain amount of satisfaction, he'd dealt with handily enough.

He poured another cup of tea and sank his teeth into a scone. A hammering at a closet door behind him and the muffled grunts of someone apparently locked inside gave him no pause. Hasbro walked in just then, nodding to St. Ives. "Shall I just clear these away, sir?"

"By all means."

"He's still thumping, sir."

"And the other one?"

"Quiet, sir, these last two hours."

St. Ives nodded, satisfied, but saddened in spite of himself. "Dead, do you suppose?"

"From his countenance – as well as I can perceive it through the peephole – I would answer in the affirmative. Dead as a herring, I'd say, sir, to quote the populace."

St. Ives arose, walked into his laboratory, and peered in through a door fixed with a porthole window. On the floor of a tiny room beyond lay a man who appeared to have been dead for a week. On a plate beside him was a quantity of fruit. A pitcher of water stood on a window sill behind. His moldery clothes fit loosely, as if he'd worn the same suit for a month or two of a starvation diet, and his face was the face of a ghoul. The long, open scar of a bullet wound mutilated his cheek, and through it showed three yellowed teeth.

"Didn't touch the food?"

"Not a bite, sir."

"And dead in a day's time. Very interesting. We'll bury him on the grounds, poor sod. This is a sad business, Hasbro, a sad business. But he was a dead man before we starved him. I could see that when they sat down behind me on the express. They had the odor of death and dust on them. What they were up to I can't say, or even whether they belong to Narbondo or to the old man. Filthy pity, really. Let's have a look at the other."

Back into the library they went, where Hasbro stacked a cup and plate onto a tea tray, dusting with a little horsehair brush the table crumbs onto a tray. St. Ives peered in at the second prisoner. The blood pudding they'd left in the closet was gone, the plate, apparently, licked clean. The prisoner thumped morosely at the door, as if the pounding were something he were doing out of necessity but had no real interest in.

"What does a zombie care about lodgings?" asked St. Ives over his shoulder. "A closet or a hillside, it must be immaterial."

"I rather suppose, sir," said Hasbro, "that the animated dead man might fancy a closet more than a hillside. A closet, if you follow me, is something more like home to him."

"Perhaps he's thumping for another pan of pudding," said St. Ives. "I'm half inclined to give it to him. Reminds me of Mr. Dick – do you recall? – up at Bingley. He built that clever device for trapping roaches and then hadn't the heart to do them in. Fed a small family of them for a week until the cat ate them and destroyed the device. Do you remember that?"

"Very well, sir."

"Damned curious cat, if you ask me. But we won't feed this roach. Not a drop of blood, not a slice of pudding. We'll give him back to the infinite."

The next morning, when St. Ives peered in at the window once again, the second ghoul was dead. Shards of the crockery bowl that had contained the pudding protruded from his mouth like teeth.

St. Ives spent the day testing the aerating device and readying his ship, a spherical iron shell crosshatched with lines of rivets, atop what would appear to the untutored eye to be an enormous Chinese rocket, pointed toward the domed roof of the silo in which it sat. A series of pulleys and chains allowed for the drawing-back of the dome and, St. Ives prayed, for the issuance of the craft. Along either side of the vehicle were arched wings, batlike and close to the hull. And from the base of the wings protruded exhaust and motivator tubes. Windows, heavy with glass, encircled the craft beneath the conical locking mechanism of the hatch. The sight of the ship satisfied St. Ives entirely. He climbed the wooden stairway that spiraled up and around to the hatch, rapping the iron skin of the ship, peering in at the little cluster of potted orchids and begonias that would aid Keeble's box in supplying oxygen. He puffed a lungful of air onto the sensing device that would record prevailing levels of gases in the cabin. It was a frightful risk, sending the craft into the heavens unmanned. He might quite easily lose it in the sea, or watch horror-struck as it smashed down into the suburbs. But it was preferable, all in all, to being *aboard* an untested craft that suffered such a fate. The needle on the gas detection gauge swung briefly beneath its crystal.

The Keeble box was anchored firmly, the ridiculous hippos and apes carved into the rosewood top grinning out at St. Ives, absolute Keeble trademarks. He pushed the tester button with his finger and a little spray of green chlorophyll dust shot out, carried on a mixture of helium and oxygen. The gauge once again gave a brief leap, then settled as the oxygen dissipated in the general atmosphere of the cabin. St. Ives nodded.

As he clumped back down the stairs, he noted with satisfaction that there wasn't a single compelling reason to return to London. No word had come regarding the endeavors of the Trismegistus Club. Certainly they could carry on without him for a week. It was entirely likely that the wayward Kraken had been found, that Kelso Drake had heeded the Captain's warning and scuttled like a beetle into his dark satanic mills. Godall was a marvel – inscrutable, capable. Captain Powers was a rock. The two alone could defend London against a siege of zombies and millionaires. What were they all fooling about with, anyway? What dreary machinations were worth St. Ives' abandoning the spacecraft, which would, early next morning, angle out through the heavens above West Yorkshire, above the astonished populace of Wetherby and Leeds, to describe its flaming halo in the thin air of the twilit sky and plummet homeward that same evening, already the stuff of legend, to its berth on the moor beyond Robb's Head?

London could wait for him. They'd have him soon enough. But for the moment they'd play second fiddle. It was the consequence of the scientific fates, and – he thought to himself while regarding from the open doorway of the silo the finny sweep of the wings and the brass and silver of the polished hull – of the scientific muses. He set out across the lawn. It was three in the afternoon by his pocketwatch. Late enough by any reckoning for a glass of Double Diamond. Two, perhaps.

But he wasn't halfway to the house when, from the direction of the River Nidd, two shots rang out, echoing against the afternoon stillness. St. Ives began to run, redoubling his pace at the sight of Hasbro, a rifle smoking in his hands, standing among the willows. Hasbro threw the rifle to his shoulder, and settled his cheek against the stock. He jerked just a bit with the recoil, then crouched and peered away east into the foliage along the river.

"What the devil!" cried St. Ives, racing up. He could see nothing among the willows and shrubs.

"A prowler, sir," replied Hasbro, ready, it seemed, to let fly another round if given the least opportunity. "I caught him in the study, and he was out the open window before I could have a go at him. My fetching the rifle, I fear, gave him time to make away along the riverbank. He'd been at your papers, sir – strewed them across the floor, emptied drawers in the press. He was still at it when I happened in – and a lucky circumstance that was – so I'm in hopes he hadn't found what it was he was after."

St. Ives was loping across the lawn when these last words were uttered, leaving Hasbro to poke among the riverside shrubs for the prowler. He burst in through the open front door, past the disheveled study and into the library. He hauled out his copy of *Squires' Complications* and thrust his hand into the broad hiatus left by the stout volume. Behind was the familiar bulk of Owlesby's manuscript, undiscovered.

He sighed with relief, wondering at the same time who it was had been after it. For it had to be Owlesby's manuscript the prowler sought. Like it or not, he thought despairingly, London would have him. Mohammed had refused to go the mountain, so here was the mountain, dragging round to Harrogate to kick apart his personal effects. He couldn't shake the machinations after all. He returned *Squires'* to its niche and walked into the study where Hasbro, having lost his man on the riverbank, was just then stepping in through an open French window.

The study, as Hasbro had promised, was ransacked. What had been heaps of paper were no longer heaped, but were scattered across the plank floor. Books lay higgledy-piggledy. Drawers were yanked from chests, their contents flung and kicked. A plaster bust of Kepler lay split in two, clubbed, apparently, with a heavy Waterford decanter, shards of which glistened in the afternoon sunlight that poured through the windows. Half the destruction was clearly a matter of a wild and hasty search for the manuscript; half of it was pure, irrational villainy.

St. Ives rolled Kepler's broken head with his toe. "Did you get a good look at this man?"

"Tolerably, sir, but he was clothed so strangely that his features were effectively hidden."

"Disguise was it?"

Hasbro shrugged, then shook his head. "Bandages, it seemed to me, swaddling his head. He peered at me through eyeslits, for all the world like one of the Pharaohs at the museum in Cairo. And he reeked of some chemical – carbon tetrachloride, if I'm not mistaken, and something that very much resembled anchovy paste."

"Was it, do you suppose, one of our ghouls?"

"I'd hesitate to say so, sir. He was far too energetic – in the act of beating poor Kepler so altogether viciously that I took him at once for a madman. The rifle, I could see straightaway, was the ticket."

St. Ives nodded. It certainly seemed so, given the mess. Damned foolish way to go about thievery – smashing things up for sport in the middle of the afternoon. St. Ives stiffened, the sudden picture of the man with the chimney pipe hat flickering unbidden into his mind. "Did he wear a hat?"

"No, sir."

"Fairly short, was he? Lank, oily hair? Yellow shirt, perhaps, and a leather coat with the sleeves out at the elbows?"

Hasbro shook his head. "On the stout side, sir, running to fat. Blondish hair in curls."

St. Ives was relieved. He didn't at all *want* it to have been Keeble's garret thief. And what on earth would the man have been after? *Keeble* had the plans to the engine, after all. Blond, curly hair – the description was maddeningly familiar somehow. A face swaddled in chemical-soaked bandages. St. Ives snapped his fingers, then slammed his hand into his open fist. Narbondo's assistant! What was his name? Pigby… Peebles… Publes. St. Ives rooted through his mind. Pule! That was it. Willis Pule. Of course it was he. Narbondo had set him to it. But how in the world, he wondered, did the doctor know that St. Ives possessed the papers? "Let's have a look along the river, shall we? Lock the house up and tell Mrs. Langley to shriek like a banshee from the kitchen window if she hears so much as a floorboard creak."

And in moments the two men, each carrying a rifle loaded with birdshot, thrashed among shore grasses and willows, following Pule's evident footprints northwest along the Nidd until, some mile down, they disappeared into the waters of the river itself, their quarry having, apparently, swum for it. A man named Binger ferried the two across in a little rowboat, promising, on the strength of a half crown's reward, to return to the manor and keep Mrs. Langley company in the kitchen, and to retrieve the two of them from the opposite shore when they'd worked their way back down.

But across the Nidd there were no footprints at all, and their chances of success declined with the settling dusk. Pule, apparently, had sloshed along in the shallows, perhaps doubled back upriver to confuse them. There were endless boats swirling past and here and there one anchored along shore. He might easily have clambered into one and rowed away downriver to Kirk Hammerton. And who was to say he had no accomplices? Narbondo himself might have been waiting beyond the hill in a wagon. Narbondo! The thought of him sobered St. Ives, who had been caught up in the idea of pursuing Pule, of running him down and delivering the scoundrel to the magistrate.

He'd taken a bit for granted, leaving his cook alone in the manor and merely sending an old man along to her when none of them had any idea what sort of foe it was they hunted. He'd been rash. Pule, after all, hadn't got away with a thing. The threat of future danger certainly outweighed the necessity of pursuit.

Stars had flickered on in the evening sky. The lights of Harrogate shown in the west. St. Ives shouldered his rifle, and the two men set out apace for the manor, St. Ives breaking into a jog at the idea of poor Mrs. Langley confronting the hunchbacked doctor or a band of his blood-eating zombies. He and Hasbro were scouring along the last quarter-mile of riverside when the sky beyond the willows changed without warning from deep twilight purple to bright yellow, and a thunderous explosion rocked the meadows.

The man in the chimney pipe hat sat in the branches of a willow, squinting in wondering assessment at the fleeing figure whose head was a mess of loose rags. Through an open window stepped a tall, balding man in a dark suit, a rifle over his shoulder. Billy Deener hadn't any liking for guns if they were in someone else's hands – and here was one in the hands of a man who quite apparently knew what he was about. He threw the weapon to his shoulder and emptied both barrels at the retreating figure, who stumbled, rolled back to his feet, and ran all the faster, weaving back and forth through knee-high grass, white filaments of loosening bandages trailing behind him as if he were an unraveling mummy.

Deener wondered who this interloper was – a common thief? Not at all likely, not with a head wrapped in rags. Countryside thieves wouldn't go abroad dressed so. It was easier by far simply to wear a mask. Whoever the man was, he hadn't been carrying the box, more's the pity. It would have been an easy thing to strangle him with his own loose bandages.

Deener climbed out of his willow and sprinted toward the silo recently vacated by St. Ives. In a moment he was in at the door, out of sight of the two on the riverbank. Luck was with him. They'd be caught up in the pursuit of the bandaged man. It was a perfect diversion. He couldn't have planned a better one.

Before him sat the rocket, the space vehicle perched atop it, almost lost in the shadows of the windowless upper reaches of the silo. Deener climbed the stairway toward the domed ceiling. A rare smile flickered along the set line of his lips. Here was something worth meddling with. Worth smashing up. Worth destroying. He'd have the box for Drake and some fun besides, at the expense of the tweed-coated phony with the idiot false mustache. He was tired of the man and his showy friends. He'd fix the filthy lot of them if he could, starting now. He fiddled with the hatch, twisting at the cone with both hands until, with a sigh of escaping air, it clicked counter clockwise half a turn and the circular hatch popped open like the lid of a jack-in-the-box, narrowly missing his outthrust chin. All was dark inside. He fumbled in his coat pocket for a match, struck it against his shoe, and thrust it into the interior. The light illuminated the cabin briefly, and when it flickered out, Deener lowered himself in, struck a second match, and lit a pair of little gaslamps, one on either side of the cabin.

The interior of the craft was a gothic wonder of potted plants and machinery. Deener scratched his head at it, not knowing where to begin. Best to start at the start, he thought wisely. That had always been his way. It was the box he was after first, or at least it was the box that Drake was after. And there it was, affixed to the wall next to his left ear.

He patted his pantleg, feeling beneath the fabric the flat surface of a prybar and the round bulk of a ballpeen hammer. In a moment he had them out and tapped the prybar under the edge of the box with the hammer. A grinning hippo watched him from the front of the box. He raised the hammer in a sudden rage; he'd beat the thing from the wall. Smash the offending hippo. Reduce the thing beside it to splinters. What the hell was it anyway? A sea monster? An octopod? He'd beat it to bits. He'd… but Drake. What would Drake do to him? He lowered the hammer and breathed heavily for a moment, staring at the loathsome box. Then once again he shoved his bar in under it, gave it a heave, and caught the box as it fell to the floor. He shook it, but nothing rattled inside. He searched for a latch, but there was none. All six sides of the box were identical, aside from the carvings and a cigar-shaped brass pipe issuing from the mouth of a winking basilisk seated on a divan, a tiny book open on a table beside him. A brass crank thrust out from the ear of the basilisk.

Deener shrugged in momentary resignation, shoved through the hatch, and lay the box on the landing outside, then lowered himself back in. Drooping spikes of orchid flowers caught his eye. Flowers offended him almost as much as the hippo foolery of the box. He slashed at a stem, severing it. Then he hacked at another. They were astonishingly brittle. He swept his arm back and slashed at the little forest of stems. Blossoms flew. He stamped at them, danced on them, pummeling the broad leaves of begonias until they sailed like scattered paper in an autumn wind.

The reflection of his face in a porthole window caught his eye, and he lashed out at it, smashing the curved end of the bar against the heavy glass, which thudded with the blow but refused to shatter. That wouldn't do. He smashed at it again and then again, cursing it, wheezing for breath. He threw down the bar and plucked up the hammer. Indestructible, was it? He'd see about that. He grabbed an iron rung on the curved wall of the ship and edged in around a cushioned seat. He couldn't seem to get the right angle. Glancing blows wouldn't do. The damned seat was square in the way. He beat at the chair, the hammerhead ripping into the soft leather. He kicked at it, shrieking, whipping around as if to surprise the window and delivering against it one final blow. The handle of the hammer split as a spider web of cracks sprang into the heavy glass, breaking the reflection of his sweating face into fragments. He threw down the rest of the handle and pulled himself through the hatch, losing his hat in the process. It bounced once on the landing, rolled onto the stairs, and sailed into the diminishing light of the silo, tumbling groundward end over end.

In a rage, he threw his prybar after it, then stooped, grabbed the box, and raised it over his head as if to smash it down too, to reduce it to rubble on the cobbled floor forty feet below. He stood just so, heaving with exertion, animal noises issuing past his teeth, and then slowly lowered the box, visions of Kelso Drake winking into focus across the tangled confusion of his mind. He turned and leaped wildly down the stairs, three at a time, his breath escaping in mewling grunts with each jolt.

He jerked to a stop at the base of the stairs, crouching before a bank of levers on the smooth side of the rocket. He dropped the box and grasped first one and then another of the levers, wrenching them this way and that. One snapped off in his hand and he slammed it against the others, then cast it with such force against the clapboard wall of the silo that it impaled itself, vibrating audibly.

He reached for another lever, but stopped dead. A humming noise, growing louder by the moment, filled the silo. A low rush followed, building toward a roar. Billy Deener leaped back at a quick surge of heat from the base of the rocket. He grinned with sudden anticipation, and in a stooping run, grabbed the box from the stones with one hand, his fallen hat with the other, and was out the door, pounding across the green toward a distant copse that lay like a shadow against the evening sky.

A blast behind threw him onto his face in the grass, and the darkness suddenly evaporated. He crouched, turned his shaded eyes toward the silo, and watched in amazement the domed roof burst outward in a spray of shingles and shards of wood, the debris spinning slowly in the air roundabout the shattered roof. Through the airborne debris rose the rocket, a pinwheel of sparks showering down like bursting fireworks. It seemed hardly to make headway, but angled jerkily, its nose threatening to dip groundward.

Deener was struck with the sudden thought that the entire thing was going nowhere, that it might teeter over and plummet onto the green, onto his head, in fact. He rose slowly to all fours, ready to throw himself flat, then dashed once more for the trees, watching the struggling rocket over his shoulder.

The thing stopped abruptly and hung for a moment in the air. It shuddered, like a dog shaking water from its coat, and the dark little sphere at the top popped off in another wash of sparks, soaring like a champagne cork northward, over the tops of the willows along the River Nidd, whistling as it flew like a rubberized, inflated bat slowly losing air through a tiny hole. The whistling diminished, momentary silence fell, then the remains of the rocket smashed full length onto the meadow, flickering with sparkling little fires before snuffing out into darkness. Deener watched with evident satisfaction from the edge of the wood. He clapped his hat onto his head, tossed his box skyward, caught it, and strode away through the trees toward the village of Kirk Hammerton.

"Holy Mother of God," whispered St. Ives, staring in horror across the tops of the willows. A nebula of sparks whirled from the burst top of the distant silo, lighting a rain of shingles. The suddenly appearing rocket edged skyward, visible above the trees, threatening to soar into the heavens, to shoot away toward the winking stars. But it didn't. It was almost stationary, as if it hung by a sky hook, and just before its nose dipped and the thing fell lifeless to the meadow, the spacecraft, the product of years of work, jumped from the end of the rocket as if shot from a child's pop gun, and arched through the air over their heads, its gaslamps curiously lit within, its hatch flung back on its hinges.

It sailed several hundred yards toward town, stuttering out little jets of smoke and fire through motivator tubes, and making a foolish whistling noise that died out even as the two men watched the craft disappear beyond distant trees. A short, far-off crash sounded. St. Ives lurched. A wave of fear washed through him – fear that some local manor house had been destroyed by his craft, or worse, that people had been hurt, killed perhaps. The fear turned almost at once to anger, and he shouldered his rifle and fired both rounds at the moon, imagining briefly that it was the loathsome, pocked face of Willis Pule, who had, obviously, doubled back on them and launched St. Ives' rocket out of spite.

Well *he'd* see. If it was a fight the bastards wanted, St. Ives would jolly well give it to them. Tomorrow. It was too late to get an evening train; the seven a.m. express would do nicely. London would regret his return. The Trismegistus Club had set out to fight villainy, and here was villainy in spades.

He shouted across the river, but had hardly begun when he noticed that the rowboat was already halfway across, skimming along behind a bow lantern that illuminated the astonished face of old Binger.

"Did you see it!" he cried, slamming up against the grassy bank. St. Ives said nothing, but merely clambered aboard. Hasbro followed, respectfully silent, considering, perhaps, that there was little but cliché to offer when a man's work had gone up, literally, in smoke.

The old man carried on wildly. He'd seen the explosion, the tired flight of the rocket. And it had burst out of a silo too, that anyone would think would be filled with corn. Bang, out the top it came like some kind of bird. It gave a man a start, with all the talk of burglars and such. Did St. Ives suppose it was his man in the river that did it, that set it off? St. Ives did. That beat all, said the old man. He'd seen the little ball pop off and sail away. It was the damnedest thing. He and Mrs. Langley went up to the attic, and there the damned thing went over the trees like a duck and smashed Lord Kelvin's barn to splinters. Right through the roof.

The old man dropped an oar in order to illustrate his story with helpful gestures, sailing his hand in a little arch while he whistled through the gap in his front teeth, then disappearing the hand between his knees, which, St. Ives supposed darkly, represented Lord Kelvin's barn. "Pow!" shouted old Binger, throwing his knees apart to demonstrate the barn's going to bits. He wheezed out a sort of laugh and had another go at his knees. Meanwhile the little rowboat rocked dangerously and slipped downstream. St. Ives gritted his teeth. It *would* be Lord Kelvin, secretary of the Royal Academy. Pule had reduced his spacecraft and his reputation to rubble in a single, fell yank of a lever. Why the devil hadn't he locked the door to the silo?

St. Ives lurched forward as the rowboat ran up onto the bank, nearly dumping his fowling piece into the river. Off to the north, coming along the highroad, was a scattering of waving lights, flickering against the dark night. They bounced and flared – torches, evidently, carried by any number of people. A murmuring reached them on the breeze. St. Ives was struck suddenly by the ominous implication of the approaching people – a mob, perhaps. What were they about? Did they carry hay forks? Guns?

He'd never seen any profit in advertising his experimentations. Rumors filtered out now and again. He'd been suspected of vivisection and of the building of infernal devices. Men from the metalworks no doubt alerted the populace to his having contracted for the shell of the craft and odd parts. But no one, certainly, besides Hasbro and certain friends – the Trismegistus Club specifically – knew that an hour earlier a launchable space vehicle had been moored in the silo.

He climbed the little rise atop which sat his house, lit, now, like Christmas, Mrs. Langley having apparently decided that an abundance of lights would frighten off villains. Perhaps she was right. The blasted silo sat dark and silent on its meadow, lit only by a little sliver of moon that slipped in a low arc above the horizon. It was impossible at the moment to see that the silo was roofless – a relief, certainly.

The torchbearers approached. St. Ives recognized an old farmer – McNally, it was, and his two pudding-faced sons. And there behind them was Stooton from the post office, and Brinsing, the Scandinavian baker. There were a dozen more, generally speaking, and the lot of them seemed to be in a collective terror; they didn't at all bear accusatory looks. Old Binger, seeing that he had lucked upon a comparatively vast audience, started in on the subject of the sailing bat thing, using hand gestures and grimaces to good effect.

St. Ives was in a sweat to shut him up. It mustn't be known that the imbroglio was sponsored by St. Ives. Hasbro, anticipating as much, silently and unheeded, shoved Binger's rowboat out into the current with his foot, then stepped forward and shouted, "The boat!" in such a commanding and inflammatory tone that Binger stopped in midsentence, his hand having completed only half its customary flight, and bolted through the ferns along the riverbank, shouting at his mutinous boat.

St. Ives nodded appreciatively at Hasbro, and decided to give Binger twice what he owed him when he returned, for the old man would without a doubt be wet through before he found his way home that night to work the space vehicle gestures on his tired wife.

The mob – not one of whom was carrying a hayfork, to St. Ives' immense relief – was full of an undefined fear. The spacecraft, apparently, played second fiddle to a more nefarious threat. An alien had been sighted. It bore, insisted Mr. Stooton, the rag headgear of Islam, and was taken to be a member of that tribe by Mrs. Stooton, who hadn't, as yet, been apprised of the spacecraft that had just pulverized Lord Kelvin's barn and smokehouse.

More sightings had occurred, always the same. A man wound with rags was abroad, a creature, surely, from a distant sun. Wasn't the thing in Lord Kelvin's barn a spacecraft? Could there be any doubt that this wrapped man had driven it? Mightn't he be a very dangerous alien?

No doubt whatsoever, assented St. Ives. He was surely a dangerous villain, this rag man from a far-off galaxy. Beat him into submission first, suggested St. Ives; question him afterward – when he was malleable. The man had been sighted, went the rumor, on the road into Harrogate, fleeing the general area of Lord Kelvin's manor. Two farmers had given chase, one of them managing to hit him in the back of the head with a hastily thrown rock, but the alien made away into the fields and disappeared.

"Toward Harrogate, did you say?" asked St. Ives.

"Right you are, sir," said McNally. "Hoofing it into town like the devil was after him. And he was a bad 'un, too, I can tell you. He beat a dog, he did, on the road. Chased him with a stick long as your arm. A vicious thing, your space man. That was when old Dyke hit him with the rock – slam on the noodle, and away he went. And they'd have had him too, if it weren't for the dog, poor beast. It's thought this alien was going to eat it, raw, right there on the road."

"I wouldn't at all doubt it," said St. Ives grimly, trudging up to the manor with Hasbro beside him and the crowd of men behind. "If I were you," he said, "I'd set out after him with dogs. Run him down. I'm a man of science, you know. What we face here is a threat, and there's no gainsaying it. Dogs are your man for tracking aliens of this sort. They have a distinct smell. Comes from travel through space. And they're prodigious liars. I've studied it out. The first thing he'll do is deny the whole business. But there's his craft, isn't it? And there he is wound up in lord knows what sort of filthy rags. Don't let the creature deny his rotten origins; that's the word from the scientific end. Loosen his tongue for him."

St. Ives' speech worked the mob up thoroughly. Along the road two hundred yards off came another dozen men, and St. Ives could see, in the direction of Kirk Hammerton, a procession of torchlights. By God, he thought, they'd have Pule yet! And if the populace made it warm for the scoundrel, fine. There was, apparently, no end to the man's villainy. Beating a dog on the road! St. Ives fumed. He was suddenly anxious, however, to diminish his role in the night's proceedings. He wondered if there were any identifying marks about the ruinous spacecraft that would give him away before he had a chance to think of something to do. He looked at Hasbro, who stood silently holding both rifles. Hasbro raised his eyebrows and nodded toward the house. This was, he seemed to indicate, no time to be chatting with local vigilantes.

"I'd like to know," St. Ives said to McNally, "if you run this man down. Don't kill him, mind you. Science will need to have a go at him – to study him. This sort of thing doesn't happen every day, you know."

The growing crowd of men agreed that it didn't. They seemed to be waiting for some further word from St. Ives. He could sense that they looked to him for advice, he being the one among them who most understood such strange transpirings. "Keep at it, then!" he said in a stout voice. And he turned on his heel and clumped up the stairs.

"Look there!" cried someone directly behind him. It was a familiar voice – Hasbro's voice. St. Ives spun round, expecting to see some revelation – perhaps Pule being dragged across the meadow by his heels. What he saw was Hasbro pointing in theatrical horror at the blasted silo, clearly visible now in the thin moonlight. A simultaneous murmur of surprise issued from the crowd.

St. Ives flinched. Had Hasbro gone mad? Had he been bought off by Narbondo? He squinted at his otherwise capable gentleman's gentleman with a face which he hoped betrayed nothing to the several dozen onlookers, but which would be an open book to Hasbro.

"The spacecraft, sir, appears to have shorn off the silo roof – blew it to bits, if I'm any judge."

"So it has!" cried McNally.

"The scoundrel!" shouted Brinsing the baker, shaking a fist over his head to illustrate the enormity of the act.

"The filthy dog!" cried St. Ives, echoing the general sentiment and relieved that Hasbro hadn't, after all, gone mad. They'd eventually have seen the silo, after all. It was far safer to explain it away so simply and logically. The ship had destroyed *his* property too – had narrowly missed the house, had strewed all sorts of debris about the meadow. Poor Mrs. Langley! He glanced down and there was old Binger, returned, standing agog, scratching his head. Hasbro's suggestion that the craft had simply ripped the lid from the silo as it passed along overhead ran counter to his memory.

"Binger!" shouted St. Ives suddenly, descending the stairs and collaring the old man. "There's that business of the half pound I owe you. Step along with me now, and I'll pay up. Mrs. Langley has a pie, too, unless I'm mistaken, and we've bottles of ale to wash it down with. Come along, then." And he stepped across the threshold, dragging Binger with him, Hasbro closing in behind.

"Half a pound, sir?" asked the innocent Binger, thoroughly befuddled.

"That's right," said St. Ives. "Step along here now." He turned to the crowd on the meadow, tipping his hat. "Keep at it, lads," he cried, shutting the door behind him and precipitating the old man down the hallway toward the kitchen. "We'll just have a go at that pie now." He smiled and drew a half pound from his pocket. "It'll be in the pantry, I should think. Cool as a cellar in here." The pantry door swung back to reveal two prone corpses on the stone floor – the remains of Narbondo's ghouls. "No pies here," rattled St. Ives, slamming the door shut. "Take care of this, will you?" he whispered to Hasbro.

"Certainly, sir. And I'll just take the wagon along to Lord Kelvin's afterward, don't you think? If I can… collect the spacecraft, sir, we could study it at our leisure."

St. Ives nodded hugely. Hasbro's talk of "studying" the spacecraft was lost on Binger, though, for the man stared open-mouthed at the shut pantry door.

"A five-pound note was it?" asked St. Ives evenly.

"Beg pardon, sir, but..."

"No buts, Mr. Binger," cried St. Ives. "You've rendered us a service, man. And I intend to reward you. Disregard the dead men in the pantry; they're not what you suppose. Sent along by the undertaker, they were. Victims of a wasting disease. Quite conceivably virulent. Here's the note, eh? And here, by heaven, is a bottle of ale. Join me? Of course you will!" He hauled Mr. Binger along toward the parlor. "I was just set to have a go at one of these when that damned alien appeared. Tore the roof right off the silo. You saw that, did you?"

"Aye, sir. What was he doing inside it, sir? I'd swear he come out through the roof."

"Optical illusion, I should think. Difficult scientific matter. These men from the stars aren't like you and me. Not a bit. Liable to do anything, aren't they?"

"But wasn't he down on the river..."

"I don't at all wonder that he was," said St. Ives. "He's been high and low tonight, hasn't he? Smashing my silo, beating dogs up and down the highroad, tearing into Lord Kelvin's barn – you witnessed that, didn't you, Mr. Binger. Quite a sight, I don't doubt. From the attic window, you say, after it beat the devil out of my silo?"

"Yes, sir," said Binger, livening up. He balled his hand into a fist and sailed it along from one side of his chair to the other, burying it between the arm and the cushion.

St. Ives sat transfixed. "Just like that, was it? Remarkable narrative powers you have, Mr. Binger. Really remarkable. Quite an explosion when it struck, was there?" St. Ives opened two more bottles of ale. He needed them every bit as much as he needed to pour them down the confused Binger.

Out of the corner of his eye he could see Hasbro dragging a

body down the hallway toward the rear door – the second ghoul, from the look of the checked trousers. Mr. Binger's back was to the hall. St. Ives blinked and grimaced at him, hoping that his evident satisfaction with the man's brief but gesture-ridden tale would encourage him to generate some really colorful, time-consuming detail. The next corpse followed the first out the back door, which slammed after it. And in a moment St. Ives heard the wagon rattle away out of the carriage house. He looked out through the window to see Hasbro driving along toward the river through moonlit dust, the two corpses flung into the wagon behind him.

St. Ives was relieved. It wouldn't do to bury the creatures on the grounds – not with the night's complications. They'd be miles down the Nidd by morning. And if they were discovered, their deaths would be laid to the alien, to Willis Pule. Damn Pule, thought St. Ives. Willis Pule! His very name sounded almost like an obscenity. The spacecraft gone! If Hasbro could retrieve it, he'd put in to have the man declared a saint. He pulled out his pocketwatch. It was coming onto ten o'clock. He'd have to pack. There was no telling when Hasbro would return. They'd be on their way into Harrogate by four in the morning.

"Astonishing business!" cried St. Ives heartily, interrupting the old man's by now oft-told story. "Come round and see us again, my good fellow. That's right. Here's a bottle for the road. Give Mrs. Binger our best. And what of young Binger? Working at the mill is he? Capital, capital." With that Mr. Binger found himself on the front porch, a bottle of ale in each hand, trying to answer all of the professor's questions at once, but finding himself in conversation, all of a sudden, with an oak slab door. He set off down the drive, richer by five pounds, two bottles of ale, and a story that would last him years.

St. Ives tumbled halfway up out of sleep three hours later at the sound of the wagon rolling along the drive. He pulled himself up in bed and peered out into the night. The wagon drove past, the dark bulk of the spacecraft atop the bed. Into the carriage house it went. A door slammed. St. Ives dropped away again and awakened before dawn the next morning to the sound of Hasbro hauling suitcases out the front door.

The two of them drove along toward Harrogate and the London express a half hour later, the sun just peering up over the trees in the east. What strange activities lay before them St. Ives could only guess at, but the set of his mouth and the squint of his eye promised that he was ready for them, that he'd breakfast on them. His error had been that he'd thought himself apart from the villainies of the London underworld. But he saw things more clearly now, much more clearly.

ELEVEN

BACK TO LONDON

Willis Pule shivered in the undergrowth that choked the empty streambed of a little tributary to the River Nidd. The willow and bracken was thick enough to keep out searching eyes – he'd lie low there until the train was a moment from pulling away toward London. The station was a five-minute dash to the south. He'd been a genius to buy his return ticket the day before. His goose would be cooked otherwise. They were scouring the countryside for him. But why, for the love of God? Surely not because of the affair at St. Ives' manor. That would hardly have loosed such a lunatic mob. Perhaps it had something to do with the explosions that had followed his retreat. But for heaven's sake, *he* had had nothing to do with that. Damn these country clowns, he thought to himself, peering above the foliage roundabout him. If he could manage it, he'd exterminate the lot of them. Some sort of infectious disease, perhaps – animated rats that fed on blood and were hopping with plague fleas.

He patted his nose gingerly, arranging the sagging bandages. He'd have torn them off, thrown them into a ditch, but the chemicals they'd been soaked in had lent his face an amber-blue tint that was startling and inexplicable. The bandages were less so. And more than that, they seemed to be having a positive effect. The skin on his face felt drawn and tight, and he'd long ago overcome his compulsion to retch at the smell of the anchovy paste. He tugged at the knots in the end of the bandages, loosened them, and pulled the whole works taut, tying it off once again.

He checked his pocketwatch. It was time to go. He'd simply have to brass it out – there was nothing else to be done, He could hardly sit in the bushes forever, and he'd be caught for sure if he set out down the road. He'd have liked to steal a cart – garrote the owner and make away with the man's goods, but he was in a deep enough mire as it was. The cost of further mayhem might perhaps be greater than the profit.

He peered again over the bushes. Surely the mob had tired itself out long since. No one, apparently, was about, save a thin man in knee breeches who cleaned cod at a trough behind a fish shop. Pule stepped through a gap in the shrubbery and strode away purposefully, not at all, he fancied, like a man fearful of pursuit. The cod man slashed away at his fish, oblivious to him. Pule rounded the corner of the fish shop, saw that the street before him was empty, and bolted for the train station, one hand pressed to his head to keep the bandages from flying apart.

A block from the station he slowed to a walk. He had enough time. It was dangerous to call attention to himself so. There was the open platform, the train chuffing on the track. Some few people climbed aboard. A tired-looking man in a mustache sold scones and coffee through the windows. Pule would kill for a scone – literally, he thought to himself. He was in a regrettable mood, and hunger put an edge on it.

There were the steel steps into the second-class car, ten feet ahead of him. No one shouted. No one menaced him. He snatched a newspaper from a boy idling on the platform, sprang into the car, found an empty compartment, and hid behind the newspaper. He'd stay there, he decided, until they were at least halfway to London.

The train edged forward in a hiss of escaping steam, then lurched to a stop. Footsteps rang on the platform. Pule peeked past the edge of his newspaper, horrified to see Langdon St. Ives and his manservant climbing into the train car. Damn! He raised the newspaper. If the door to his compartment opened he'd go out through the window. What else could he do? He hadn't any weapons. Next time he wouldn't be caught weaponless. And there *would* be a next time.

Narbondo would rail at him for having failed to find the papers. It had taken hours to wring Kraken clean of information. Liquor had done it far more neatly than had torture – although Pule rather preferred the latter; since they had no idea whether Kraken had anything to offer them anyway, torture seemed pretty much an end in itself. He'd been a determined old sod, though, and a sorry one, but he'd divulged it all in the end, weeping into his cups. Pule smiled behind his newspaper. He wondered idly whether St. Ives had taken a compartment on his car or had gone along to the next. What did it matter?

Pule was overcome by a sudden idea. He could slip off the train, return to St. Ives' estate, and in the master's absence, ransack it. Torch the place, if it came to it. He'd been hasty – was on the edge of missing his chance. He arose, casting down his paper, when the train lurched forward again, dumping him backward onto the seat. It seemed certain that the train was at last underway. Pule thrust open the compartment door and shoved out his head, only to see some few yards before him the back of St. Ives' servant, who stood in the aisle, speaking to his employer through an open door. Pule slid back in as the train lurched once again to a stop. Was he fated to stay on the damned train? To be robbed of a second chance? He shrugged. What did it matter, after all? It was Narbondo who would profit from his returning to the manor. It was always Narbondo who profited.

"Hot scones!" came a cry from out the window. "Coffee and tea!"

Pule reached out a shilling. The flour-speckled scone seller shrieked and dropped his pastries, tray and all, onto the platform. Coffee flew. The man shrieked again. "The halien!" he cried, falling backward. "The bloody halien!"

A window slid open in the next compartment. "Brinsing!" shouted a voice. A head shoved out into the morning. Pule, casting secrecy onto the scrapheap, peered out at it. Langdon St. Ives stared back, aghast, speechless. The train bolted. Pule jumped for the door. The scone seller continued to shriek. Hasbro rushed at Pule. Pule grabbed the knob of a compartment door and flung it open into the face of his attacker, throwing his shoulder into it in an effort to knock the man down. Behind him in yet another compartment sat a frail old woman, wide-eyed with terror at the sight of the wrapped Pule. Her feet were propped on a steamer trunk, too heavy, no doubt, to be hefted onto the rack.

Pule set his feet against the doorjamb, his back against the door open in the aisle, and dragged the trunk from beneath the woman's feet, cursing it, cursing her, cursing St. Ives. He wedged the trunk against the open door, realizing as he did so that his efforts weren't worth the time he was wasting. Shouting a parting curse, he leaped out the end of the car and into the next, slowing a bit, wondering where on earth a man could hide on a train.

Trees and meadows shot past along the tracks. If it came to it, he thought, he'd leap for it. Perhaps he should jump now, before they disentangled themselves from the door and trunk. They'd never suppose him rash enough to attempt such a thing. But the countryside was flying by wonderfully quickly – dangerously so. Pule strode along through the next car and the next, into a third-class car comprising two parallel rows of wooden benches facing the front of the train. The car was empty but for a single man in a chimney pipe hat who dozed in a seat on the aisle.

In his lap was a Keeble box. Pule nearly strangled. He grabbed a seat for support, gripped by vertigo. What did this mean? What weird offspring of fate had come to meet him so peculiarly here? A shouting arose behind him, along with the splintering sound of wood tearing. If he wasn't quick he'd fail. And the fault would be his own. He looked about him, barely breathing. Beneath the seats were metal baggage racks in various states of disrepair. He grasped a section of iron bar that had come unbolted and wrenched at it. He waited for the sound of the door slamming open behind, for the shouting to commence, for the man with the box – quite possibly in league with St. Ives – to awaken and cut off his escape. The bar clanked to the floor. Pule seized it as the sleeper stirred. The man opened one eye as Pule flailed at him, a cry wrenching out of his lungs. The iron bar struck the man's forehead and seemed to settle into it, as if he'd hit a pudding with a wooden spoon. Pule dropped the bar and caught the box as the man fell forward. The door burst in behind him. He was out in a trice, leaping in great hopping strides through a succession of cars, out, finally, into the morning air with no place left to flee. He braced his back against the door, holding it tight. His pursuers clattered hollering up behind. Sheep winked by on a sailing meadow.

The train tipped into a curve, slowing a bit, and Pule, shutting his eyes, catapulted from the moving car, howling and flailing into high grass and rolling down to the edge of a pond to the astonishment of the chewing sheep. He lay for a moment, imagining the damage he'd done to his spleen or his liver. He jiggled his extremities and pronounced himself fit. Inordinately proud of himself, he stood up and strode away across the pasture with the air of a man who'd done a day's work. He fancied, as he limped along the highway, his bandages finally relinquished, what St. Ives' reaction would be if he *did* slip back up to Harrogate and have another go at the house. It would be what an artist would call a finishing touch. But it would also, he could see at a glance, be unwise. He had a good deal to lose by such heroics all of a sudden, and he was determined that no one – not Narbondo, not St. Ives, not revenge – nothing would deny him the prize he'd so handily won. A moment's serendipity had turned the disastrous trip into a victory. He stopped to look at the box. It was the same sort they'd wrested from Kraken the day before. All of Keeble's damned boxes were the same. Was there a second emerald? Was this the fabled homunculus itself?

Pule considered the brass tube and what appeared to be a little crank device on the side. Kraken's box hadn't had any such accoutrements – although their presence certainly didn't reveal the contents of the box. They could, quite conceivably, be a breathing mechanism of some sort for a creature housed within. Had Owlesby's manuscript revealed the whereabouts of the creature? Had St. Ives recovered it? Pule's head swan with unanswerable questions. Only one thing seemed certain – that here was a Keeble box that contained a mystery, quite possibly a valuable mystery. Pule possessed it and would continue to possess it. If worse came to worst, if all of Narbondo's plans came to naught, Pule would have the box, a much-needed wild card in a game in which Narbondo held the aces. A wagon clattered toward him along the road, and Pule stepped out to meet it, the morning sun shining down on him in an altogether friendly way.

Bill Kraken had never before felt so low. He'd done some vile things in his life – robbed graves, pinched carp from the aquarium, been drunk more often than he'd been sober. He'd been a merchant of overripe squid, a failed purl man, a reasonably successful pea pod man, and for a two-month period a year or so after his separation from Owlesby, he'd taken up the pure trade, selling dog waste to the tanyards for enough money to keep himself fed – if cabbage broth and black bread were food. But his worst moments since poor Sebastian had fallen were mere nothings compared to the depths to which he had sunk in the last forty-eight hours. He had betrayed everyone who had befriended him. He'd sold them all. And for what? Nothing. Not a farthing. Not even a handful of beans.

He knuckled his brow and immersed himself in self-loathing. It was drink that did it – strong drink. It made a man mad. There was no way round that truth. But then so did the absence of drink, didn't it? He licked his dry lips. His tongue felt feathered. His hands shook uncontrollably when he held them in front of him. So he sat on them, perched on a stool in a corner of Narbondo's laboratory. He saw things, too, out of the corner of his eye – things he oughtn't to see. It was the horrors, is what it was. And if it wasn't, it would lead to them sure enough, to the gibbering horrors. He hadn't been so dry in a week, a month.

Now, watching out of the edge of his left eye the thing on the slab that lay not fifteen feet distant, he wondered what in the world it would look like to him if he were drunk. Given half a chance, he'd set out to discover the truth of the matter. He patted his coat pocket and there was Ashbless, bullet hole and all. The problem with the philosophers was that they were short on practical advice. They could reveal little to him about his present circumstance. Better the book were hollow and held a pint of gin.

He mashed his eyes closed and held them so. Time passed fearfully slowly. He remembered, fifteen long years past, having wrestled out of open coffins dead men not much prettier than the thing on the slab. Better his eyes had been plucked out. They quite likely would be. They'd beaten him, but he could stand that. He'd been beaten before. And he'd had the horrors before, too. But those he didn't want again. He'd given up squid merchanting when he'd found that the creatures inhabited his dreams, all leggy and cold.

For the hundredth time he looked roundabout him for something to consume – spirits of any sort – but saw nothing but the empty wine glass left with diabolical purpose on a tabletop by the fat boy in curls, along with the carcass of a fowl. The breadth of the glass magnified the depth of the little crimson circle settled in the bottom. In truth there wasn't enough in it to dribble to the edge when the glass was upturned.

Kraken had tried, to be sure. He'd mopped up the dregs with his fingers, but little of substance was accomplished by it. There was even less in the way of food on the plate – nothing but broken bones – just the gristly burnt carcass of a peculiar game bird, a pea hen with the head on, eyeless and charred.

Pule and Narbondo had gone out, locking the doors and

windows. They'd abandoned him hours earlier, before night had fallen. The ghostly light of the gaslamps did nothing to enliven the general gloom of the cabinet – simply cast unpleasant shadows on the walls and floor, like the shadow, thought Kraken, barely able to look at it, of the humped, skeletal pea hen across the edge of the piano. They'd left him a pitcher of water. Perhaps if he got desperate enough...

They'd return, he knew, with a body. Pule's trip to Harrogate in search of poor Sebastian's manuscript had ended in a general rage. Curses flew. The doctor had cuffed Pule across the chin, destroyed the pot of carbolic and stewed horsehide that Pule was cooking as a facial treatment. It had smelled awful. Then they'd gone out. The thing on the slab must be vivified, that's what Narbondo had said. Tonight. They would find a donor. If not, hinted the doctor, Kraken would do nicely. Kraken or Pule, either one of them. Pule had smiled through his tirade, like a cat full of milk.

The gaslamps flickered. Shadows danced. The game bird rattled suddenly on its plate as if it were trying to drag itself away. Kraken started in horror. Silence fell once again. Across the room on a small table beside the fishless aquarium sat the Keeble box. What could Kraken do with it? He could smash out the window and pitch it into the street, then dive out after it. But what would it profit him? He was a hunted man. There could be no doubt about that. Newgate was too good for him. It would mean the gibbet if he were caught.

Outside the window swirled a thick fog, most of it river fog off the Thames. Dirty little rivulets dripped down the panes, pooling up along the mullions and dripping off, one by one, onto the pavement below. The street outside was silent. It was the silence, dense as the fog, that bothered him. He'd tried singing and whistling, but in the dim, shadow-haunted room the noise had merely been unnatural. It seemed to him, in fact, that the slightest sound would awaken the thing on the slab.

Its head was twisted toward him, dropped crookedly across its chest. Flesh hung beneath its eyesockets like parchment. It seemed as if a breeze through a broken window pane would turn it to dust. Or perhaps the thing would rise in the draft like a kite to twitch and gibber at him, to lurch along toward him, silhouetted against the light that shone dimly through the curtained window of the room across the courtyard. Earlier he'd seen the shadow of a face peer past the curtain – watching him, perhaps; perhaps one of Narbondo's agents.

Kraken shut his eyes, but through the lids he could see the dancing shadows animated by gaslight. He pressed his eyes with his hands, but the horrors that swirled into view against the back of his eyelids were worse than the thing on the table. What had Paracelsus said about such emanations? He couldn't quite recall. Paracelsus was mist in his memory, a product of another age, an age that had ended when he'd stolen the damned emerald from the Captain, the emerald that the smug Narbondo had left so casually beside the aquarium.

On the edge of the slab, as if they had crawled there of their own power, were two skeletal hands, obviously fallen from the hunched corpse behind them. Kraken avoided looking at them. He had been certain an hour earlier that for an instant the things had moved, rattled their fingers atop the table, inched inexorably toward him, and that the ruined pea hen had sighed on its plate, rustling among cold potatoes.

But all had fallen silent. It was the wind through the broken panes, carrying on it the sharp, sooty odor of fog. There lay the hands, almost grasping the edge of the lamplit table, ready, perhaps, to lunge at him. Why in the devil weren't they attached to the corpse? What unholy thing did their separation betoken?

Kraken peered at them, and was certain for one rigid moment that the index finger of the left hand twitched. Beckoning. He glanced away toward the fogbound window and gasped in horror at his own reflection, hovering in the glass, staring in at him. He edged farther into his corner. If the hands crept from the slab would they shatter when they hit the floor? Or would they fall into shadow, pausing for a moment before scuttling out like crabs toward his feet? Kraken was suddenly fearfully cold. Narbondo, perhaps, wouldn't return at all. Perhaps they'd gone out, knowing that Kraken would die in horror during the night, that the thing in the shroud would rush at him like a sheet hauled along a clothesline, would envelop him in dust and rot and clacking bones and suffocate him in horror.

On the wall behind him hung a collection of instruments, but there was nothing with which to defend himself against animated corpses. His eyes settled on a pair of elongated tongs, the jaws of which were wrapped in a rubber casing. He stood up slowly, barely breathing, understanding that the thing on the slab was watching, trying, perhaps, to fathom his fear, his intent.

He very slowly removed the tongs and stepped across toward the slab, wheezing with fear, waiting for the hands to fly at him like papery bugs, like leather-winged bats, to clutch at his throat, to reach into his mouth. At the touch of the tongs, surely they'd leap at him as if spring-driven. He knew they would.

But they didn't. He plucked one of the hands up and very gingerly turned, took a step toward the open piano, and shoved the thing onto the silent keys, banging out a wild note with the edge of the tongs and leaping backward, a shriek lodged in his throat. The other hand lay as before. Or did it? Was it turned now? Had it crept about to face him? He clamped the tongs around it, whirled, and dumped it onto the piano keys along with its grisly counterpart, then slammed down the key cover, locking it with a little triangular brass key that lay atop the piano.

Could he bear to do the same with the thing's head – yank it loose and hide it somewhere? Perhaps shove the top of the piano aside and toss it in? He forced himself to look at it, to imagine clamping the tongs against the ivory cheekbones and twisting the head until it snapped. The thought paralyzed him, but he had to do it. He steeled himself. He couldn't be stared at any longer. He stepped toward it, reaching out with the tongs, slowly drawing the jaws apart. He daren't get the tongs in the thing's mouth; it would snap the steel rods like twigs.

The tongs inched closer. Kraken shook so that the loose rivet about which the tongs swiveled rattled like a locust. He gasped for breath. The horrible eye sockets seemed to stare through him – through his forehead beaded with cold sweat, a great salty drop of which rolled into his right eye, nearly blinding him. The tongs settled in against the cheekbones, and, with a thrum of settling bones, the thing on the table gave a quick lurch, as if shaking off the rubber clamp.

Kraken hooted in fear, dropped the tongs onto the top of the slab, and trod backward toward his corner, slamming into the game bird's table with his right foot. The spindly table leg buckled, and the skeletal bird rolled from the plate in a little cascade of peas and fell to the floor. Kraken watched it in horror, half expecting the thin gray bones of the wings to vibrate and the bird to sail off like a great moth toward the flame of the gaslamp. The tongs banged down on the floor beside it.

This wouldn't do. He couldn't abide the idea of the bird out of sight on the floor behind the table. He must know its movements, if there were any. If it flew out of nowhere at him, he'd simply drop dead. He bent suddenly, summoning his strength. He grasped the tongs, plucked the bird from the floor, and tossed it, tongs and all, into a coal bucket on the hearth next to the piano. The bird whumped into the bucket in a cloud of coal dust; the tongs banged against the wall and dropped onto the hearth tiles. Kraken whirled around at the sound of a sudden scuffling behind him, expecting to find himself confronted by the handless skeleton. But there it sat, unmoving. The scuffling issued from beyond the wall across the room. Something pawed at the wall, trying to get in at him. Kraken slumped backward toward his stool in the corner.

TWELVE

THE ANIMATION OF JOANNA SOUTHCOTE

A panel in the oak wainscot slid abruptly open, and beyond it, tugging weirdly at a pair of shoes, was a bent Willis Pule. He backed into the room, grunting with effort, and Dr. Narbondo appeared behind him, holding up the opposite end of a corpse. Pule dropped it as soon as it was entirely past the wall, as if he were immensely tired. Narbondo kicked the corner of the panel, and it slid shut, cutting off the entrance to what looked to Kraken to be a dark, low hallway. Kraken shrank into his corner, wondering in horror at this new act of villainy, half relieved, however, that it wasn't him that was being dragged down tunnels.

The panel had just slid shut when there came a fearful pounding at the conventional door. Pule swung it open, and there stood Shiloh the messiah with a look on his face that seemed to imply that he would brook no nonsense, that he'd come for his mother and there would be hell to pay, perhaps literally, if he wasn't satisfied. Narbondo scowled back at him. "Where is Nell Owlesby?" he asked suddenly.

"She's safe – safer by far with my flock than with you."

"Half your flock is *my* flock," said Narbondo, "and they'd as soon eat her as give her a tract. Get her."

"Quite impossible, I assure you." Shiloh stepped in and closed the door, frowning at the littered room and at Bill Kraken, who, it seemed, was at least as offensive to him as was the corpse on the floor. "I'll keep my end of the bargain. You don't need the woman for that. *I* know where the box is hidden, and have these ten years. If you do as I say, you'll know too. It's as simple as that. But you needn't worry about the woman. She's worth nothing to you beyond that single bit of knowledge. And *that,* as we both know, is worth an enormous amount, isn't it?"

The old man slouched on a stool, obviously enjoying the advantage he held over Narbondo. He removed a snuffbox from his pocket, pinched out a frightful quantity, and inhaled hugely, surrounding his head in a momentary brown cloud. He sneezed voluminously six times in rapid, deflating succession until he was reduced to a bent, wheezing ruin, his face a mask of mixed pain and satisfaction. Dr. Narbondo shook his head in disgust. Shiloh groped for his pocket, replacing the snuffbox, and wiped his eyes with the hem of his robe. His wrinkled forehead alternately relaxed and contracted like an irritated slug, as if he were experiencing after-tremors of his recent snuff-inspired earthquake.

He pulled himself erect and looked straightaway at the Keeble box atop the aquarium; then, before Narbondo could stop him, he stepped across and picked it up. "Very nice article, this."

The hunchback jerked toward him, snatching the box away. The old man put on a theatrically offended face and then looked in mock surprise at his empty hands. Narbondo scowled and set the box gingerly atop the piano.

The heap of bones and winding sheet on the slab seemed to slump just a bit in response to the box having been moved, and the wisp of settling debris struck the grin from Shiloh's face. He seemed to recall suddenly that it was his mother that lay before him. Narbondo wheeled his misting device past on a tea cart, brushing the old man out of the way. Then he hauled out of a cupboard a low gurney. He and Pule tugged the fresh cadaver onto the gurney and cranked it up level with the slab. From a wooden trough beneath the jar of yellow fluid he pulled a dripping, desultory carp, alive but sluggish, and slapped it onto the gurney beside the corpse. He worked quickly and deftly, but with a contracted brow and sweat-beaded forehead, as if he knew precisely what he was about and knew equally well that what he was about was not at all a simple business.

Pule stood silently by, spurred now and then to grudging action when Narbondo snarled out orders, then falling into inactivity, either out of a lack of comprehension or a general unwillingness to be ordered about. The old man twittered near the window like a bird – the approaching experiment having eliminated any veneer of detached coolness. He gasped suddenly and clutched his breast. "Where," he cried, pointing. "Her hands… where are her hands? I swear to heaven, Narbondo, if you've made a hash of this, if you've…"

"Shut up, old man!" cried Narbondo, clipping him off in midsentence. "Where are Lady Southcote's beautiful hands?" he asked Pule. Pule stared at him, then looked around, bending to peer under the slab. Kraken quaked in silence on his stool.

"You foul…!" cried the evangelist, unable to think of a word sufficiently foul to express his indignity. "I'll…" he began again, but this time a wild clattering arose from the direction of the hearth, and a chunk of coal the size of a walnut popped out of the coal bucket onto the floor.

"A rat," whispered Narbondo, reaching for the poker at the far side of the hearth and raising it over his head.

"Damn me!" shouted the old man, enraged that Narbondo had abandoned his mother to chase a rat. Narbondo hunched toward the coal bucket, a finger to his lips. A wild rattling issued from it. Coal dust rose in a cloud. The bucket tipped over with a clang, cascading a little delta of clinkers onto the hearth, atop which rode the blackened remains of the pea hen, its broken wings working furiously, its head swiveling from side to side. And, as if in accompaniment, the piano erupted into discordant play, as if someone were beating randomly on the concealed keys. Kraken crossed himself. Shiloh threw open the window over the courtyard and perched one foot onto the sill, ready to leap. Narbondo swung the poker wildly at the hopping pea hen, slamming it into the piano leg. The bird rose into the air, a thin whistling sound chirping from its stretched throat where ragged, charred skin still clung in patches. The box atop the piano danced in tune to the wild playing, and the pea hen shot off like a stone out of a sling, straight into the wall above the aquarium, smearing coal dust and grease onto the yellowed plaster, then dropping with a splash into the water, sinking slowly to the gravel and staring out at them mournfully before collapsing onto its side.

The piano, meanwhile, banged away. Narbondo, emboldened by the demise of the pea hen and certain that a properly objective attitude would explain away the phenomenon of the mysterious piano, lunged at the instrument and pushed back the lid. He picked up his poker, raised it ceilingward, and peered in to find nothing but flying hammers. Squinting at Pule, who had retreated toward Kraken's end of the room, he pulled gingerly on the key cover. It was locked. Mystified, he found the key, unlocked the cover, threw it back, and shouted in surprise at the weird scene before him – the crabbed, skeletal hands of Joanna Southcote, thumping pointlessly on the keys. They flailed across the keyboard in an agitated whirl, hopping onto the floor where they twitched and danced.

"Her hands!" Shiloh shouted, repeating himself, more horrified at their spectacular reappearance than he had been at their absence.

Narbondo lunged for Kraken's fallen tongs, grappling each hand in turn, flopping them onto the slab. The first leaped off immediately, and Narbondo was on it at once, avidly now, slamming it back beside its mate. The two, finally, lay still.

"This is an outrage!" sputtered Shiloh, his mouth working spasmodically.

"This is powerful alchemy!" whispered Narbondo, as much to himself as to anyone else, and he immediately trained his sprayer onto the corpse. She seemed to stretch. Joints crackled. Her neck swiveled and rose a half inch off her chest. "Damn!" cried Narbondo, remembering her hands. He yanked out a roll of thin, braided wire from a box on his desk and affixed her wayward hands to her wrists. Her jaws clacked as if in satisfaction. Kraken was stupefied with terror. He grabbed suddenly for the water pitcher, swallowed a great draught, choked, and collapsed onto the floor, coughing and sputtering. Pule kicked him out of a lack of anything else to do, and Kraken scuttled in behind the stool, holding it in front of him to ward off the detested Pule.

Yellow mist clouded the room, swirling round in the draft as Narbondo excised the carp gland. "Her hands!" cried Shiloh again. "You've got them on backward!"

"Silence!" shouted the hunchback, beside himself with success. He capered back and forth beside the slab, dancing round the edge of the gurney, spraying mist, affixing coiled tubing into a slit cut in the trachea of the dead man that Pule and he had dragged in through the secret door. He shoved it into his lungs, crying out to Pule to hold the sprayer, to prop up Joanna Southcote, to measure out a beaker of fluids.

"Her thumbs point outward!" whined the evangelist tiresomely, obsessed with Narbondo's mistake.

"She's lucky to have hands at all," responded the doctor, leaping and jigging. "I'll put the hands of an ape on her!"

And as if in response to this last threat, the corpse of Lady Southcote loomed up out of the mist like a marionette in a fever dream, jaws clacking, wavering there atop the slab as if she were adrift on a current of air.

"Mother!" cried Shiloh, collapsing onto his knees. From his robe he produced a stoppered bottle. He twisted it open and shook it liberally at the creature which slouched down the slab toward him. He intoned a nasal prayer, crossing himself, waving and gesturing. Narbondo sprayed on, stamping at a bladder on the ground that pumped something – Lord knew what – from the lungs of the dead man into the shrouded chest cavity of Joanna Southcote. The escaping gases whistled eerily, like wind through the gap under a door.

"Speak!" implored the evangelist.

"Whee, whee, whee!" hooted the creeping skeleton before dropping off the end of the slab in a clatter of bones.

"Christ!" shouted Narbondo, genuinely dismayed at this new turn. A loose foot slid past him, out of sight under the piano, and a leg, severed from its pelvis, wobbled storklike in the settling mist before collapsing slowly forward, bouncing just a bit when it hit the ground, then clattering into silence. Only the skull, its toothy mouth working, remained animate, chattering round and round in a tight little circle on the slab.

"Command me, Mother!" cried the evangelist, grabbing for it, then stopping suddenly in mid-grab, as if he were reconsidering his actions. "She's a ruin!" he wept, hitting tiredly at Narbondo, who stood nearby, breathing heavily.

Shiloh looked around suddenly, wildly. "She'll come with me!" he cried.

"Gladly," said the doctor, pulling down one of the cast glass cubes. "This is spade work." He turned, humped across to a closet, flung it open, grabbed a dirty spade from among a half-dozen of the things, and turned to see Kraken, eyes whirling with fear, reaching for the box atop the piano.

Narbondo swung the spade at Kraken, who fended it off with his arm, howling in pain and hopping away from the piano. The hunchback spun around, recovered, and set himself to bash Kraken once again, but his quarry had abandoned the box and bolted toward the stairs. Narbondo leaped after him, paused at the top of the dark landing, listening to Kraken pound in wild steps toward the street. He turned once again into the room, where Pule crawled on his hands and knees, scuttling into the path of the skull, which jabbered along toward the street wall. The evangelist leaped back and forth, shouting orders.

"Get out of the way!" shouted Narbondo, storming past both of them and shoveling the head into the glass jar. In a moment Joanna Southcote was captive, the gibbering evangelist snatching a broad volume from a bookshelf and slamming it atop the square mouth of the jar, fearful, perhaps, that the skull, giddy with animation, would clamber out to resume its skittering journey across the oak plank of the floor.

The old man sat wheezing, cradling the prize in his lap. He stared mournfully at the heap of disconnected bone that had, for some few moments, shown such promise. With her he could have astonished the populace of London. Converts would have flocked in. The eyes of kings and dukes would have shot open. The doors of treasuries would have swung to. And here it was, a ruin.

Then again… He peered in at the head, considering. Its mouth worked silently. Without the aid of the air-filled bladder it could say nothing. But what would it take, he wondered, to provide it with a voice, from offstage, perhaps. It seemed like a blasphemy, to trump up a voice for the holy article, but the work mustn't languish. It must go on at any cost. She would have been the first to agree. It looked to him as if she were nodding agreement from within her box, voicing her approval.

He stood up and moved toward the door. Narbondo and Pule stood talking in low tones near the courtyard window, but on perceiving Shiloh's intent, they stepped along after him.

"It's useless," said Narbondo, reaching the door ahead of the tired evangelist. "I've done what I could. No man alive could have done more. If I had the box, there's no telling what sort of restoration we could accomplish. Where is it?"

The old man glared at him. "You can hardly be serious. You've purposely made a mess of this. Out of spite. Out of evil and nothing else. I owe you nothing at all, nothing."

"Then you're a dead man," replied the doctor, drawing his pistol. "Take the head," he snapped at Pule.

"Wait!" cried Shiloh. "This is no time for haste, my son. Perhaps we can reach an agreement – twenty-five converts, shall we say, in recompense for the damage you've done tonight."

"I'll graft her head onto a carp – or better yet, a pig – and show her in carnivals. Take the head!" He waved with the pistol at Pule.

Shiloh glared at the hunchback. "You leave me no choice," he said.

Narbondo nodded, rolling his eyes. "That's correct. No choice at all. Not a bit. There's nothing I'd like more than to shoot you and turn the both of you into some sort of instructive sideshow attraction. Where is the box?"

"Aboard the blimp of Dr. Birdlip. Nell Owlesby gave it to him the night of her brother's death. There's your accursed information – fat lot of good it will do you. When the blimp..."

But Narbondo turned his back and walked toward the courtyard window, stroking his chin. "Of course it is," he muttered.

"Let me say," began the evangelist, catching sight of Willis Pule as if for the first time. He stopped, gazing with sudden astonishment at the sight of Pule's ravaged and discolored face. "My son," he began again, "your countenance is as an open book, the pages recounting a life of degradation. It is not too late. It is..." But what it was, finally, was left unsaid, for Pule lashed out at the proselytizing evangelist with his open palm, swatting him on the forehead and sending him sprawling through the doorway waving the bottled head. The door slammed shut between them.

THIRTEEN

THE ROYAL ACADEMY

"I've just witnessed the most amazing spectacle," said Theophilus Godall with uncharacteristic enthusiasm. Captain Powers hunched forward in his chair to encourage his friend. But he held up his right hand as if to signal for a brief pause and picked up a decanter of port, offering it to Nell Owlesby, who shook her head and smiled at him.

Godall related the story of the animation of the thing on the slab: how he'd watched through the window the sad antics of Bill Kraken; how he'd seen Narbondo enliven a skeleton, dance it about the laboratory; how the thing had gone to bits and Shiloh the evangelist had sunk from view, he and Willis Pule banging about the floor while Narbondo flailed at Kraken with a shovel. Atop the piano had sat the Captain's box, or one very much like it, and Godall had been in a quandary about how to retrieve it. But his well-laid plan had gone awry when Kraken, obviously a prisoner, had fled, and Godall had gone after him, chasing him half across London only to lose him in Limehouse and come away empty-handed.

The Captain nodded over his pipe, clenching and unclenching his fists so that corded muscles danced along his forearms. "We'll go in after it, then," he said finally, squinting across at Godall.

His friend nodded. It seemed, certainly, the only clear course – an emerald, after all, big as a fist. It was Jack and Dorothy's livelihood – Jack's inheritance.

Contacting the police would avail them little. Nell would be exposed. And where, they would ask, did this emerald come from? If it was Jack Owlesby's inheritance, why didn't he have it? Why all the secrecy, the convolutions? How, in fact, did Dr. Narbondo come to possess it? Were they accusing *him* of stealing it? No, they weren't. He took it from the man who stole it. And where was this fellow, this Kraken? No one knew. Somewhere in London, maybe. The police would scratch their chins and give each other looks, and in the end, not only would suspicion fall upon the innocent, but no end of skeletons would be dragged, perhaps literally, from dusty old closets.

No, said the Captain, shaking his head with determination, in for a penny, in for a pound. They'd act tomorrow. Godall produced a pen and paper, poured himself a brandy and water, and began to sketch out a plan of Narbondo's cabinet, the building it occupied on Pratwell, his own room opposite, and the courtyard between. Nell filled in elements of the laboratory itself that Godall could only speculate on, much of the room being invisible from his curtain slit.

If Narbondo were out, they'd force the door, walk in, and take the box – reduce the room to rubble, if need be, to find it. Narbondo would have to be watched. He might, after all, remove the box to another location. But why should he? Then, if the doctor was in, Godall could resort to disguise to gain entrance – an official from social welfare, a seller of scientific apparatus – that would do nicely. They'd hold him up like burglars. What would he do? Call the authorities? Shout through the windows? It was hardly likely. He'd know, then, what sort of men he'd fallen out with, said the Captain. He'd find that he'd made a mistake.

There was a slamming of a street door opposite, and the Captain broke off his speculating to look out, in the hope that it was William Keeble coming across to chat. It was high time, he realized now, that the Keebles knew of the presence of Nell Owlesby. They would all have to fall together in this thing. There could be no more secrets, no disconnected pieces of the puzzle. No more boxes hidden under floors. It would quite likely take the vigilance of the lot of them and to spare if they weren't to be borne down by the collective forces of evil.

But it wasn't William Keeble; it was Jack and Dorothy, setting out hand in hand through the murky morning, the fog swirling round the streetlamps, their shoes clumping on the pavement. Jack held a box beneath his free arm. Nell watched over the Captain's shoulder. "I'd give anything to call out to them," she said in a low voice. "Or to run ahead and step out of a doorway and utter his name." She stopped, watching the pair turn up Spode Street and disappear, and she stood silently for a moment, as if lost in thought. "He'd hate me, I suppose," she said finally, "for what happened to his father."

"I think you'd be surprised," the Captain said, squeezing her hand. "He knows what happened to his father. His death wasn't the worst of it, not by a sea mile, and he wouldn't be the lad I know he is if he was blind to what you did, for the reason of it."

Nell remained silent, watching the door of the Keeble house. Godall pretended to be fiddling intently with his pipe, oblivious to the conversation going on three or four feet away. The Captain slapped his ivory leg and said, "First things first, that's my way. We'll pay a visit to this hunchback sawbones first. Get the fun out of the way. There's time enough for work afterward." And he turned back to the map and to Godall, gesturing at the open courtyard and reaching for his cold pipe.

St. James' Square lay torpid beneath the fog and the chill, as if waiting languidly for the murk to lift. But the fog hovered through the morning, shot through now and again with rays of feeble sunlight that faltered and faded almost as soon as they appeared, rays that thinned the murk momentarily, then abandoned any hope of success and fled. Cabs rattled apace along Pall Mall, pale ghosts with lamps glowing fitfully through the gloom, then winking out, making it seem as if they had been nothing but disembodied rattle and clatter that sprang into and then out of muted clarity.

The man in the chimney pipe hat stood in the darkness of the very alley in which Bill Kraken had caught St. Ives' discarded cigar. His hat perched atop a blood-spotted bandage wrapped around his forehead, and threatened to topple at any moment onto the dirt of the pavement. He yawned, deciding that he'd risk stepping across to a tavern in a court opposite for a quick pint. The girl wouldn't be out on such a day anyway. Her schedule, after all, hadn't been unvaried. There was some chance that he'd spend another two hours waiting in vain, perhaps be questioned by a constable and sent on his way.

But if he packed it in and she *was* true to her Thursday

morning schedule, what then? Time was short. Drake was in no mood for failure. His returning from Harrogate without the box had almost cost him… he didn't know what. It didn't bear thinking about. Time, somehow, was growing short, and Drake's patience with it. The pint could wait. He'd need it all the more desperately in two hours' time anyway.

A distant bell chimed eleven o'clock. Footfalls sounded out of the murk, which had suddenly swirled into such obscurity that the tree in the center of the square was blotted out. Two shapes approached. Billy Deener squinted into the gloom. It was she. But who was this with her? Her young man. This was unexpected.

What was even less expected was the thing he held under his arm – a box, one that Deener recognized even through the gloom. A vivid picture of a bandage-wrapped figure flailing at him with an iron rod leaped into his mind, a figure that stole the box and fled. And here, apparently, he was, come round to give the box up. Here were two birds, hand in hand. Deener smiled malignly. He hefted the sap in his right hand, stepped out of the shadows behind the loitering, chattering couple, grasped the girl's arm, and slammed the sap against Jack's head, chortling through his nose as his prey fell forward onto his face like a toppled tree.

Dorothy screamed at the sudden clutching hand from the shadows, then screamed again at the solid whump of the cosh and Jack's collapse onto the roadway. But her second scream was cut off instantaneously by a rough hand. She bit at it, kicking backward and scraping her heel down the shin of the man who twisted her arm around behind her. An almost simultaneous scream broke forth from the lips of a woman who herded a covey of children through the square and who stood open-mouthed, pointing, her children cringing horrorstruck beside her, not so much at the sight of Dorothy being dragged into the alley or of Jack lying senseless on the pavement, as at the sound of their horrified mother's shriek. Sporadic crying and screaming broke out, one shriek igniting another, the collective squealing fueling itself. Deener backed down the alley. The hue and cry would mean the end of him. In a moment he'd have to abandon the struggling girl and flee. He had only to drag her forty feet down the alley to freedom through a door left purposely ajar. But there on the ground, beside the meddling youth, lay the box he'd been cheated of once. He was damned if he'd be cheated again. He raised his hand, allowing the struggling girl to pull her right hand free and bury her nails into his bruised forehead. A thrill of pain shot along his scalp, and he yelped in rage, swinging the cosh hard enough to end the struggle there and then. He shoved his hand into his mouth, blew through two fingers, and scuttled out of the alley, picking up the fallen box. A head popped out of the open door. Deener shouted a curse at it, and a man, the owner of the head, loped along the alley toward him.

"Murder! Murder!" cried the woman with the howling children. The cry was followed close on by the sound of stamping feet and the shrill blast of a police whistle. As Deener and his companion – a beefy, lard-faced man in shirtsleeves – dragged the inert girl through the yawning door, the mouth of the alley was filled with a growing crowd of dim spirits, peering in, unwilling to follow two seeming murderers into the dim shadows.

Billy Deener eased the door shut, knowing that the general darkness of the alley obscured almost entirely by the fog would serve to hide their movements, and that a subsequent search would reveal nothing more than a crumbled hole below the street, a hole that led into the filthy darkness of the London sewers.

The cellar wall was a tumbled heap of ancient brick some

three feet thick, beyond which ran the upper level of the Kermit Street sewer. Mortar had cracked and fallen for a hundred years from hastily pointed joints, and the continual wet of the sewer had caused the wall to slump and the bricks one by one to fall out, until some final bit of mortar or the corner of an ancient brick had decomposed, precipitating the collapse of a long section of sewer wall in a foul-smelling heap of muck.

The sewer was running at low water, but even so, Deener and his accomplice were hard pressed to make headway. They felt their way along planks slimy and rotten with sewage, kicking into the soft surface of the wood with the hobnails of their hoots. A lit candle flickered in a tin holder wrapped around the head of Deener's companion, and the light danced and shrank, was snuffed out and had to be relit time and time again, both men half expecting the flame to set off an explosion in the dense air. Deener, wary of choke damp, breathed through a kerchief tied over his nose and mouth. They stooped along beneath the low ceiling, watching for the mark that would signal their arrival at the house on Wardour Street.

The Kermit Street sewer was badly in need of leveling, for the general sinking of the ground had created long cesspools, the settling water further decomposing what solid ground remained, so that the foundations of houses above cracked and pitched and loathsome sewer gases drifted up into courtyards. But the cesspools which so hampered leveling and flushing had their own value, were the resting place, in fact, for murdered men, not a few of whom had found their way into the sewers with the help of Billy Deener. Their bodies lay mired in offal and garbage and road sweepings emptied down gulley grates, until the corpses swirled at high water into the Thames where, bloated and faceless, they were declared drowned for lack of any sensible alternative.

But the unconscious girl was a different sort of victim. She should, Deener knew, be the one among them to wear the kerchief over her face, but his service to Kelso Drake only stretched so far. The score of minutes she spent below ground wouldn't hurt her. She wasn't even conscious of their passing.

When Dorothy awoke, a tearing pain pounding in her head, the cigar-chewing face of the man who had stood in the entry hall of her house arguing with her father smiled down at her, the cigar rolling from side to side as if it were alive. His smile, however, was void of humor or concern for anything but Kelso Drake. She was certain, even in her fuddled state, that it was a smile of loathsome self-satisfaction, empty of anything but falsehood.

It swam out of focus and then back in. She felt awful. There was a horrible stench in the room, the smell of an open sewer, and it seemed to her as Drake materialized before her that it was he who smelled so foul, he or the bent man who stood beside him, squinting at her as if she were some sort of interesting specimen. Then she lost interest in either of the two men, drifting away into herself and the pain in her head. She moved her arm, intent upon touching the hair beside her ear, which, pressed against a pillow, felt clotted with dried blood. She'd been hit on the head. She remembered part of it. Surely, though, this was no hospital. Bits and pieces of memory filtered in, scrabbling around in her mind until they joined like interlocking pieces of a puzzle to form the picture of Jack lying senseless on the pavement of St. James' Square, of her struggling with a man in a hat, of a woman screaming over and over, of gaping children, of nothing at all after that.

She tried to push herself up onto her left elbow, to swing her right hand at the face before her. But something got in the way. She couldn't move, was fastened, somehow, secured to the bed by a sheet tied across her shoulders. The cigar face laughed. A hand removed the cigar. The mouth said, "She'll do nicely – pay us twice over," and the face laughed again. "Sedate her," it said, and disappeared from view.

The hunchback loomed over her, a cup full of violet liquid in his hand. The sheet was loosed briefly, and she was yanked onto her elbows by a balding man in a black coat. She hadn't the strength to fight. She drank the thin, bitter draught, and very soon swam away into darkness.

Langdon St. Ives sawed away at a grilled cutlet that had the consistency of shoe leather. The gray meat lay like a curled bit of tanned hide between a boiled potato and a collection of thumb-sized peas. A sauce – "*Andalouse aux fines herbes*," as the hastily drawn menu had called it – was dribbled stingily over the cutlet, the chef careful not to be so liberal as to allow the liquid to pollute the boiled potato. This last, cold as the plate it sat on, sorely needed the sauce, and St. Ives tried with limited success to spoon a bit onto it. But most of what he scraped from the surface of the cutlet merely glued itself to the spoon in a scum of tomato and pepper, leading St. Ives to curse both the quality and the quantity of it. Rationally, he supposed, he should count himself lucky to be faced with such a meager plateful of the wretched stuff, but eating, like anything else, wasn't a particularly rational business.

He pushed the tiresome plate away, listening to the droning

voice of an equally tiresome bespectacled gentleman who sat opposite, tearing into his own cutlet indifferently, as if the act of eating were merely a matter of satisfying bodily processes. He might as well consume a plateful of leaves and twigs. The man spoke to St. Ives as he masticated his veal and peas, chomp chomp chomp, over and over like a machine grinding rock into cement.

"The digestion," he said, waggling his jaw, "is a tricky business. Gastric juices and all that. It takes a vast quantity of stomach-produced chemicals to break down a lump of sustenance like this pea." And he held a pea aloft for St. Ives' benefit, as if the thing were a fascinating little world which the two of them could examine.

"Biology has never been my forte," admitted St. Ives, who couldn't abide peas under any circumstances.

The man popped the pea into his mouth and ground it up. "Gallons of bodily fluids," he said, "produced, mind you, at great expense to the system. Now this same pea reduced to pulp can be readied for evacuation by a tenth amount of gastro-intestinal juices…"

St. Ives stared out the window, unable to look at his plate. He couldn't work up much enthusiasm for bodily talk. He had nothing against physiology; some of his best friends were physiologists. But it was hardly supper conversation – was it? – all this business about fluids and evacuation. And what was it leading to here? It constituted the friendly sort of banter that preceded really serious discussion – the reason he was once again being fed at the Bayswater Club owned by the Royal Academy of Sciences. With all their powers of scientific perception, thought St. Ives, they ought to be able to see that the supposed veal they were served was in fact a slab of old dairy cow – or worse, a paring of horseflesh, bled pale and bleached with chemicals by the knacker.

No one, however, seemed to be eating save he and old Parsons, whose fellow Academist Lord Kelvin owned a barn in Harrogate alongside his summer house, a barn that, since the debacle of the alien starship, hadn't any roof. He also, according to Hasbro, owned two dead cows, which had suffered the misfortune of having strayed into the barn minutes before the ship caved in the roof.

And now St. Ives would pay the price. He was in a foul humor – he realized that. First the launching of the craft, then the escape of Willis Pule from the train. The man must have been desperate. It was entirely conceivable that he had leaped to his death in the ditch, an unsatisfying thought altogether. Villains, St. Ives considered, ought to be made to account for themselves. Their demise should be both spectacular and humiliating.

"And the molars of a horse can reduce the most surprising weeds to fortifying pulp in moments," his host intoned, working at a mouthful of his own surprising foodstuffs. "Now, like a human being, a horse has only a single stomach, but his intestine is phenomenally elongated, adapted to the digestion of coarse forages. This is all a fascinating subject, this business of eating. I've spent a lifetime studying it. And I've found few things more interesting in the eating line than a workhorse – and of the right sort, mind you. Some sorts of hay are superior due to their effects on the bowel." He waved his fork proudly, as if to illustrate this last statement, and speared up a row of peas.

St. Ives took advantage of the man's pausing to yank out his pocketwatch, widening his eyes in alarm, as if he'd just now become conscious of the prodigious passage of time. But his intended attempt to hurry the end of the engagement disappeared into a lecture on the bacterial manifestations of intestinal debris. The man paused some few minutes later to drain a great tumbler of distilled water before him, the cleansing effects of which would "leach away poisons," not at all unlike the exemplary workings of a well-constructed sewage system. He smacked his lips over the water. "Staff of life," he said.

St. Ives nodded, performing his pocketwatch activity all over again, putting on the same face filled with surprise and haste. His companion, however, wasn't so easily put off. He removed his spectacles, causing his eyes to undergo a remarkable and instantaneous shrinkage, and he wiped his face thoroughly with his napkin. "Close in here, what?"

St. Ives nodded, humoring the man. Such men, he told himself, must be humored. One had to nod continually in agreement until, when an opening presented itself, one could nod to one's feet and nod one's way down the stairs, leaving the zealot with the curious mingling of satisfaction in having been so thoroughly agreed with and wonder at being abandoned. But there was no such opportunity here.

"Dr. Birdlip, then," said Parsons suddenly. "You were a friend of his."

St. Ives steeled himself for the inevitable conversation, the same that had occurred weeks earlier, the afternoon of the night he'd been surprised by Kraken in the rain. The Royal Academy was vastly interested in Dr. Birdlip's flight and its implications in terms of technologic advance and were prevailing upon St. Ives to help elucidate the nature of the doctor's wonderful flight. Birdlip, of course, was not the real genius behind the perpetually propelled craft. They knew that. He was a sort of mystic – wasn't he? – a man who fancied himself a philosopher. More than that, he was a seeker after mysteries. He'd published, to his credit, a strange paper entitled, "The Myth of the Foggy London Night," followed by a paper speculating on the construction of spectacles through which one could see successive layers of passing time like translucent doors opening and shutting along a corridor. What was that one titled? "Time Considered as a Succession of Semi-closed Doors." Yes, said Parsons, it was all terribly – how should he put it – "theoretical," wasn't it? Poetic, almost. Perhaps he'd missed his true calling. The titles alone betrayed the peculiar bent of his mind. Genius it might he, said Parsons, but genius of a speculative and, mightn't we say, of a non-productive nature. Certainly not the sort of thing that would produce an engine such as the one that drives the dirigible. Parsons smiled up at St. Ives ingratiatingly, prodding a pea across his plate with the end of his fork, driving it into a little pool of dried sauce.

"Are you aware," he asked, squinting at St. Ives, "of the religious cult that has sprung up around the sporadic appearances of this blimp? It's rumored that there is some connection between Dr. Birdlip and this self-styled holy man who calls himself Shiloh. There's nothing more dangerous, mind you, than a religious fanatic. They presume to define morality, and their definitions are made at the expense of everyone but themselves."

"I can assure you," said St. Ives, looking first at Parsons, then glancing out the window at activities transpiring three floors below, "that Dr. Birdlip is unacquainted with the mystic. He…"

But Parsons cut him off, his spectacles dropping of their own accord to the tip of his nose. "Rumor has it, my good fellow, that Dr. Birdlip's craft carries aboard it a talisman of some sort, perhaps a device, that the cultists find sacred – a god, as they have it, that resides in a curious box. Scotland Yard has, of course, infiltrated their organization. They're a dangerous lot, and they've got an eye on the dirigible. It's generally unknown whether they wish to destroy it or make a temple of it, but I can assure you that the Academy intends to allow neither."

On the street, wading out of Kensington Gardens through Lancaster Gate, came a tremendous milling throng of people, shouting something in unison – hosannas, St. Ives decided – pushing up toward Sussex Gardens, choking the street below the club. There could be no doubt about it – at the head of the throng strode the old, robed missionary, the nemesis of the Royal Academy.

Parsons recognized him at the same time, and struck his fist upon the tabletop, the sudden appearance of the evangelist having driven home his point. "What I mean to say," he whispered, gesturing at the street, "is that this is no time for foolish misconceptions about friendships, or whatever you'd call it, to interfere with vital scientific study. You're a scientist yourself, man. The projectile that you launched into Lord Kelvin's barn was a remarkable example of heavier-than-air flight. Your purposes haven't been fully understood, perhaps, by the Academy, but I assure you that if you could prevail upon this toy-maker on Jermyn Street to cooperate with us… that's right," he said, holding up his hand to silence St. Ives, "I told you we were certain that Birdlip himself could not have built the engine. If you could prevail upon this man Keeble to communicate with us, I think you'd find us inclined to consider this last imbroglio with the spirit of scientific inquiry. Reputations are at stake here – you can see that – and much more besides. Religious lunatics gibber in the streets; rumors of blood sacrifices performed in squalid Limehouse taverns filter up from the underworld. Tales of pseudo-scientific horror, of alchemy and vivisection, are daily on the increase. And sailing into it all, like some long-awaited sign, some apocalyptic generator, comes the blimp of Dr. Birdlip.

"Two men in a balloon tracked it over the Sandwich Islands

weeks ago. There can be no doubt that it is steadily losing altitude at a rate that will soon put an end to its journey. Our mathematicians have it touching down within Greater London. But what will it do? Will it smash through the suburbs, causing great ruin, exploding in an inferno of igniting gases, ending all efforts to establish an understanding of its motivation? Will it drop into the Atlantic to be reduced by storms to sinking debris?"

Parsons grimaced through his spectacles, giving St. Ives ample opportunity to imagine the wrack and ruin the fated return of the blimp would cause if he – that is to say, if Keeble – would not turn out and share with them his knowledge of the workings of Birdlip's craft. The glory of the sciences, said Parsons, was its cold rationality, the absence of the illogical fervor that drove the crowd in the street at this very instant to inexplicable passions. Why did St. Ives hesitate? The toymaker would listen to him. What was the nature of his hesitation if not the same sort of illogical manifestations that fueled the crowds in the street? It was reason, scientific philosophy, practical reality, that must prevail at times such as these. Surely St. Ives…

But St. Ives couldn't quite see it that way. The entire subject was tedious. Keeble would do as he pleased. Birdlip's blimp would do as it pleased. St. Ives would do the same – that is to say, not the same thing as Birdlip and Keeble – what he would do was find Willis Pule and beat the dust out of him. After that, he'd hunt up the spacecraft of the homunculus. He'd find this last or find evidence that put an end to the legends of its existence. But, he said to Parsons, he would talk to Keeble, mention it all to him, feel him out. If the toymaker balked, there would be an end to it.

Parsons was delighted. Such an attitude was reason personified. And why on earth *had* St. Ives launched the projectile through the roof of Lord Kelvin's barn? The scientific community had been once again mystified.

St. Ives shrugged. It had been set off accidentally, without adjustment, without being properly motivated. Parsons nodded, understanding now, able to take the long view. He held out a limp hand, which St. Ives understood to be a signal that the lunch was at an end. There was no further need of talk, not until Keeble had been broached on the subject of his engine.

They want the engine and nothing more, thought St. Ives as he left the room. If Keeble handed it to them tomorrow they'd abandon any interest in Birdlip, about whom they were absolutely correct. Birdlip was engaged in a mission which couldn't be charted and graphed. His pursuit of truth, such as it was, had taken him on a course that paralleled, figuratively speaking, the wind-blown, haphazard course of his blimp. But by God, it *had* led him home again, hadn't it? Its means were unfathomable, inexplicable, but the ends weren't entirely so, not if you looked at it through the right pair of spectacles – which Parsons, of course, didn't own.

St. Ives trotted down the last half-dozen carpeted steps and out the entry hall into the street, where wind had blown the fog away and where a milling crowd strained to hear something. Scores of them sat in trees; some sat astride the shoulders of others; carriages were parked along the street, and atop the carriages stood what seemed to St. Ives to be a moderate portion of the citizenry of London, all of them listening, their ears cocked, to the wind that blew along the silent afternoon street.

There was a brief chattering, like a woodpecker, perhaps, striking a particularly brittle tree. A roar arose from the crowd. Silence followed, then another clacking and a fresh roar. St. Ives pushed his way toward the front, toward where he could see the head of the evangelist above the horizon of the masses. The old man stood, clearly, atop a crate.

He held something before him with both hands. St. Ives couldn't quite make out what it was – a transparent box of some sort. The sea of onlookers parted in front of him. He was struck with the pervasive religious atmosphere that lay heavily over the street. How many people were there? Enough to constitute a multitude, certainly. And here was the Red Sea, parting before him, a miraculous narrow avenue opening up for some few feet. St. Ives edged down it. A man trod on his toe. Another jabbed him in the ribs with an elbow. The wall of people behind him pressed forward suddenly, shoving him nose first into the greasy hair of a woman in what appeared to be a nightshirt. His apology went unheard. "Beg your pardon," he said, twisting through a gap an inch or so wide. Not far ahead of him stood the evangelist, peering at the sky, muttering indecipherably, perhaps speaking in tongues.

A moment later, the victim of hard looks and a pair of rapid-fire curses, St. Ives stood at the front of the crowd – no one before him but a man so short as to be negligible. The old missionary exhorted a glass cube in which sat, St. Ives was horrified to see, a partially mummified head, dusty and brown from the grave.

The thing's teeth were huge – Parsons would have admired them. What the evangelist intended to do with the head wasn't at all clear. St. Ives looked about him at the expectant faces, which seemed to betray that they, too, weren't sure of the nature of the spectacle they were about to witness.

Catcalls erupted from a gang of toughs slouching in the limbs of a great, drooping oak. "Make 'er sing!" came the shout. "Make 'er eat somethin," came another. "A bug!" shouted someone else, close on. "Ave 'er eat bugs!" After that came a roar of laughter from the tree, followed by the screaming fall of one of the toughs, who had come unseated. More laughter erupted from the tree as well as from the crowd, which seemed to be fast losing its patience with the holy man and his posturing. A handful of people passed out tracts, some of the supplicants horribly mutilated and wasted, as if from loathsome disease. Their very presence seemed to lend an air of authenticity to Shiloh's performance. It was hard to argue with people who were so obviously what they claimed to be.

Just as the laughter fell away, the woodpecker chattering resumed, very rapid, from the direction of the old man. St. Ives started. The head in the glass cube had suddenly become animated. Its jaw clacked as if they were driven by an engine. What was this but a clever bit of parlor magic? The skull hopped and bumped with the force of its clacking, stringy hair flopping in time.

"Speak, Mother!" shouted the old man. "What is it that you hear! That you see! Lift the veil that obscures the future, the scales of filth and degradation that stifle and blind us! Speak, we implore thee!" And with this last falsetto petition a hoarse voice squeaked out, as if it were carried on the breeze that whirled leaves up Bayswater Road, as if it were part of that breeze, of the natural turnings of the universe. The crowd fell instantly silent, leaning forward as one, straining to hear the words of the oracle. Silence followed. Then, shattering the silence, the cry: "Get thee to a nunnery! Go!" rang out amid screams of wild laughter, the product of a particularly educated lad in the oak tree.

Shiloh cast the laughing toughs a look of mixed venom and pity, waiting with theatrical patience for silence to descend. Again the teeth chattered, clearly taking the startled evangelist by surprise.

"Hear me… ee… ee!" came the eerie wavering voice.

"Speak!" commanded Shiloh of the dancing teeth.

"Listen to my words!" ululated the head.

"Kiss my arse!" shouted the oak tree.

The skull fell silent.

"You've ruined it!" shouted the lady in the nightshirt, directly into St. Ives' ear, obviously enraged at the crowd in the tree.

"Shut up, will you!" shouted a man at St. Ives' elbow, but it was impossible to tell whether the command was directed at the lady in the nightshirt or the laughing toughs. The head began to chatter again. St. Ives wondered exactly how the thing was supposed to be talking when it lacked flesh on its neck, when it lacked, for that matter, a neck of any sort, fleshed or otherwise. Perhaps the crowd was no more interested in physiology than St. Ives had been when sharing leather cutlets with Parsons a half hour earlier. Maybe it was the wind vibrating the bones in its chin – a sort of Aeolian harp effect.

Just as the voice started up again, the teeth gave out, seeming to take the voice by surprise, for it continued momentarily, uttering something about dread things in the sea before closing off like a faucet. Each effort by the toothy skull seemed more tired than the last. Shiloh peered in at it, shaking it just a bit as if fearing that the thing was running down – which it very apparently was, for away it went one last time, getting off a half-dozen staccato chatters before slowly playing out and, whether of its own accord or because of a misstep of the evangelist, falling over onto its side and giving up the ghost.

The crowd pressed forward to have a closer look, all of them, no doubt, feeling cheated of the show they expected, of the revelations that had a half-dozen times clearly been pending. A shower of acorns launched from the oak tree rained around the evangelist, who, St. Ives could see, was clearly puzzled and chagrined. Whatever it was he'd been attempting to accomplish hadn't entirely been a fake, and it had the unmistakable stamp on it of Ignacio Narbondo.

The old man, seeing that the head had given out, attempted to preach to the crowd from atop his crate. But the masses surged forward, anxious to get a look at the deflated prophet, and the old man's supporters rallied round, linking hands in an effort to keep the mob away from their master and his oracle. Easily two-thirds of the supplicants had eaten blood pudding in the last twenty-four hours, St. Ives determined. Parsons' fears of the growing army of cultists weren't as terrifying as they might be – it was an army that could be starved out of existence overnight.

Their linking of arms to hold back the throng was futile; St. Ives could see that at a glance. People pushed past him. Without moving he drifted toward the rear of the crowd. Shiloh, in growing dread, made away up the street, surrounded by his supporters. A brougham careered around the corner from the direction of Leinster Terrace, pulled to a halt half a block up from the charging throng, swallowed the evangelist and three of his allies, and galloped off, bearing away the chattering head, the performance of which, thought St. Ives, would not get favorable reviews.

FOURTEEN

PULE SETS OUT

The New Messiah rode along into Mayfair with his eyes clamped shut so tightly that little flickers of yellow lightning shot out across the back of his eyelids each time the brougham bounced over a dip in the road. What, he wondered, could have gone wrong? What conceivable force could be responsible for the failing of the spirit of his poor, misused mother? She'd been declining – he could see that – ever since he'd brought her away from the laboratory of the accursed Narbondo. It was as if she had fallen asleep, as if whatever animating force she'd been imbued with had drained away. Was this a sign, an indication that his own vanity had to be curbed? But he was selfless, blameless. He hadn't chosen to be what he was – the son of whom he was the son of. Had he? It had been thrust upon him, and he'd suffered for it, long years of deprivation. And here, when he had the means to sway great masses of people, when success lay within his grasp, the machinery of the spirit failed, ran down, fell mute.

He pressed his temples and looked up at the man next to him

– a droopy-eyed, pasty man, one of Narbondo's ghouls. The sight of him was tiresome, uncharitable as this might be. Shiloh couldn't suffer it, wouldn't suffer it. He pushed his head out through the curtain and railed at the driver. "Stop!" he shrieked. "Stop, you bleeding fool!"

The brougham lurched to a halt. The evangelist threw open the door on the street side. "Out!" he said tiredly. "All of you." They stared at him stupidly. He picked up a heap of tracts on the floor and pitched them out into the dirt. "Fetch those." The man beside him rose obediently, stepping out through the open door. The others followed, the last sailing face first into the road on the heel of the evangelist's boot. The old man reached out and pulled the door shut. "Drive on!" he cried, and away the brougham raced, the old man alone now, contemplating his failure.

There was simply no accounting for it. Or rather there was, but he simply couldn't see it. Something nagged at him – something about the business at Narbondo's: the hands pounding on the piano, the ill-fated flight of the skeletal bird, his mother's brief revitalization. What explained it? Surely not the capering hunchback with his yellow vapors. Something more had been in evidence. A spirit – that was it. Some presence had charged the room, had launched the bird. The explanation of it all lay just out of sight around a turning of his memory.

The box. Had that been it? Of course it had. Narbondo had set the box atop the piano, and straightaway had set off the playing, had stirred the corpse of the bird. What if, wondered Shiloh, squirming in his seat in the glare of sudden illumination, what if the box in Narbondo's hands were the homunculus?

Had the hunchback left the thing in sight to mock him? Knowing that the creature in the box was, in fact, Shiloh's father?

A creature with power over life and death? The stinking swine! He'd known all along, hadn't he? Or had he? Why was he so anxious to get hold of Nell Owlesby? And what *of* Nell Owlesby? Had she lied to him those long years ago in Jamaica? Impossible. She'd been too sincere, too much a product of her momentary passions. She could, of course, have been mistaken. There had, after all, been two boxes.

The evangelist stroked his chin. He'd been played, perhaps, for a fool by any number of people. But he'd have the box. That much Narbondo owed him.

Pratlow Street was silent. No one was about, not even a stray dog or cat. The moon, which had shone for an hour or so between the tilting buildings that lined the street, had long since drifted away. No light burned in Narbondo's cabinet, the hunchback having departed for the night. His relative success with the remains of Joanna Southcote and knowledge of the whereabouts of the homunculus box had improved his mood, which had suffered from Pule's failure to obtain Owlesby's manuscript. Narbondo's house call at Drake's Wardour Street address had given him certain ideas, excited certain passions, and he dallied there into the evening.

The lights of Westminster Bridge were ample to read by; Bill Kraken had read in worse light. And the night sounds – the Thames rushing along beneath the bridge, hurrying toward the sea, the low murmur of conversation from the men who lounged against lampposts – all of it seemed to Kraken to mean something, taken collectively. Especially the river. There was a great deal of talk in Ashbless about rivers. He seemed particularly fond of them, and it was a restful chapter that didn't call on the river to serve as an illustration for an abstraction which, without the tea-dark, swirling waters of the Thames to color it, would have been a lifeless and pale reflection of the world.

Kraken had wandered fitfully along the Thames all that day and most of the preceding night, after he'd failed to retrieve the box from the odious doctor. His life seemed to him to be played out. It was empty of substance – hollow. Most of his teeth were gone. His only possession beyond his clothes was the bullet-ridden copy of Ashbless, whose philosophers, try as they might to pour substance into the cavity of his soul, were powerless to help him. He was adrift, and would soon enough float out onto a gray sea.

He had speculated his way through Holborn and the City and Whitechapel, plodding along, lost in thought, finding himself late in the afternoon below Limehouse, looking out over the London docks. It was unimaginable that such commerce existed, that so many thousands of people labored to some particular end, that the basket of tobacco they hauled out of the hold at midday had to be hauled out just then, because at quarter till midday there had been twenty-five baskets atop it – one leading to another sensibly, each pulled off in turn, by design, according, it seemed, to an unwritten script.

But what pattern was it, he wondered while watching it all, governed the shambling life of Bill Kraken, squid man, pea pod man, thief. He'd been beaten senseless by criminals and then had become one himself. It didn't stand to reason.

He'd ambled back upriver, past St. Katharine Docks and London Bridge and the Old Swan Pier, and everywhere people hurried along about their business, as if their lives were read out of a book, with a second page that followed a first, a twenty-fifth page that followed a twenty-fourth. But the pages of Kraken's life had somewhere been dumped onto the road. The wind had caught them and blown them hither and thither over the rooftops. He'd tramped around, ever on the watch for them, but they were scattered and flown, and here he was, at the end of his tramp, leaning over the parapet in the center of Westminster Bridge and watching the black water of the Thames roil below.

He opened Ashbless at random. "Least of all the sins," he read, "is gluttony." That didn't help him a bit. He closed his eyes and pointed. "The stone that the builder refused," promised the text, quoting the Bible, "shall be the cornerstone." He put the book down and thought about it. What was he, if not that very stone? Here were thousands – millions – of people chiseled just so, fit into a vast and sensible order, while he, wandering through London, could find no niche into which he could wedge himself. He hadn't been chiseled so.

But how, he wondered practically, could old Bill Kraken be the cornerstone? What was it that would lend him a ticket to enter Captain Powers' shop by the door when he'd gone out once by the window? The emerald, of course. That was the only route. But recovering it would almost certainly mean destruction, wouldn't it? Kraken shoved Ashbless into his coat and set out apace. Destruction, perhaps, was less odious than other fates. His journey that day had made him weary, but his sudden resolution, his discerning purpose, no matter how fleeting or mistaken, drove him on with a steady gait, north up Whitehall toward Soho and Pratlow Street where he would settle a score with himself.

* * *

The cramped room in the Bailey Hotel was sufficient to hold an iron bed, but the bed, unfortunately, wasn't sufficient to hold Willis Pule. He was sick and tired of kicking the bedstead all night, of jamming his ankle between iron posts. And the gaslamp at the head was always fizzling and sputtering and smelled so overwhelmingly of leaked gas that he had to keep one window jammed open with a pile of books. He longed for the day when he could unbox his library, arrange the volumes along shelves. That's when his really serious study would begin. He would accomplish something then – exercise his genius.

He peered at himself in a glass tipped against another little heap of books. The bandage wrap hadn't accomplished a thing beyond, perhaps, disguising him a bit. His face appeared even in the wan light of the faltering gaslamp to be enflamed. It seemed stretched, almost oily. He picked up a stained copy of Euglena's *Chemical Cures* and studied a long discourse on the application of facial washes. He could see nothing in it. He had tried Lord knows how many plasters. At best they seemed to dry him up. That was the problem; he was certain of it. His cranial capacity, his abundant mental activity, drew fluids from other parts of his body – hence his perpetually dry and scaly hands. Perhaps a loathsome complexion was the price of genius.

He sighed and flopped back onto the creaking bed, cracking his elbow against the wall and cursing. It was his fate to be contained within a body that betrayed him. He felt at times as if he were attached to an enormous vermin – a corrupt physical bag that contained a pure, sensitive, intelligent soul. It was an attitude that might easily produce envy, but in Pule, of course, it didn't. He saw through the world too clearly. There was little in it to attract him.

Pule had often lamented the problem inherent to genius: genius simply wasn't self-evident. It was evident in works, and yet Pule was certain that works were condescending. One hadn't ought to soil one's hands. And what was there in the productions of time that wasn't transparent? That wasn't pretense? When one possessed – was cursed with – genius, with vision, then one saw too clearly the emptiness of it all. One was aware of the shallowness of it, the false and brittle face of things. Even the stuff of poets was, when one ridded oneself of their romantic foolery, nothing but cleverly painted backdrops hung roundabout to veil a gray and empty world.

Pule heaved a sigh and rubbed at the end of his nose. If only he didn't see things with such insight. And Narbondo! Pule had been tormented by the hunchback on the promise of… of what? Who had waylaid Kraken and got the box? Pule had. Who had organized and carried off the recovery of Joanna Southcote? Pule had. Who was it that fetched the carp from the oceanarium? Pule. Narbondo was one of those officious inferior, self-serving braggarts who had attained a position of imagined power. And he would profit by it too. He'd muddle along, appropriating that which belonged to Willis Pule, using him, and would, in the end, stroll away with the emerald, leaving Willis Pule to explain their activities to the judge. Or so thought the hunchback.

Pule bent over and groped under the bed, hauling out the Keeble box he'd retrieved from the man on the train. He shook it for the hundredth time, but the box was silent. What in the world, wondered Pule, could be in it? There was apparently no lid to the thing. It was possible, even, that the box was designed in such a way as to foil uninstructed attempts to open it. Perhaps it would explode. It had the look about it, with its spout and crank mechanism, of an infernal device. The clothed animals painted over it argued against such a thing; but mightn't that be just a clever sort of ruse?

In the laboratory lay the emerald box, or so Kraken had insisted – drunk, to be sure. Who was to say that *this* wasn't the emerald box? The crank, in fact, might be the means of opening the thing. It might, on the other hand, be a detonator – a timed detonator. No one would build a device which would explode in one's hands. It was no doubt a clock-spring mechanism that could be wound with the crank to a desired tension, then wind down of its own to set off the explosion. Or was it? Who could say? Pule's mind drifted, converting the clock-spring mechanism of the box to an analog of his life – a life which had, it seemed to him, run down. It was a consequence of growing awareness, of intellect. As one's understanding of things grew, the things themselves paled, ceased to exist almost. The world hadn't so much wound down as he had wound up, so to speak, become taut through perception to the point at which he'd shed the world – stood alone, as it were, upon an empty hilltop, the common people scurrying below like bugs, like worms, with little or no consciousness.

The way, suddenly, was clear. He'd come to a sort of crossroad, to a point at which a choice was required – an action. To act would save him. He plucked up the box, held it in front of him, and began slowly to wind the crank. If the result was the springing open of the box, then he'd know, wouldn't he, what lay within? If no such result occurred, then he would assume it was a bomb – dynamite perhaps – and he'd simply haul it along the dark streets to Narbondo's laboratory. Once he got there – *if* he got there; the thing might easily explode on the street – he'd leave it atop the piano in exchange for Kraken's box. And if the result was that Narbondo's cabinet and all of Narbondo's works were blown to hell, the entire transaction would be eminently satisfactory.

It would require tremendous will, he mused, to stroll across Soho with a live bomb under his arm. Its detonation would likely cost the lives of any number of people, but so what? In the long run of things, what were their lives worth? Hadn't he already established that they were worms? There was no crime in stepping on a few of them. And what was crime to him anyway? It was, perhaps, more to the point to pity them the loss of Willis Pule.

He looked at himself in the mirror one last time, arching his eyebrows to heighten the look of natural intelligence and wit. His mind was set. The effort of will that would crush a lesser being had been summoned in the space of moments, and once it was called into existence, no power on earth could gainsay it.

Pule spun the crank more rapidly. He could feel tension within the box – a mechanism winding tight. It was as he thought. A grim smile stretched his lips. Would the lid fly up like a jack-in-the-box to betray the existence of the emerald? Was Kraken's box merely a clever ploy to throw them off the scent? He listened at the spout that thrust out of the front of the box. He could hear the ratchet turnings of the clockworks. He held the box in front of his face so that the light from the gaslamp illuminated the spout. He closed one eye and squinted, following the thread of illumination up the spout and into the interior of the box. There was a click, a whir; Pule jerked back in sudden tenor. *Was* it a suicide device?

A jet of gas wheezed out, spraying over his face. Spitting and coughing, he cast the box onto the bed. He'd been poisoned. He knew it. The box wheezed again, and a great cloud of green dust blew out of the spout with such force that although he threw himself over backward onto the floor, the gas enveloped him utterly.

He rolled, smashing into the wall beneath the open window.

The tower of books that propped the window cascaded into the street, and the window crashed down, sealing the room. Pule shrieked, a high, frightful, elflike ululation that reinforced his fear that he'd been poisoned. The air had been suddenly dyed a livid green. He would choke on poison gas! He'd been tricked. It had been a plot to eliminate the hunchback, and his betrayal of the monster had brought about his own ruin.

He yanked on the window, batting at the frame. It wouldn't budge. He looked wildly about him and lunged for the door, catching sight of his coat on a nail driven into the jamb. Lunging for it, he tore the coat free and flung it over the still-spouting box, smothering the escaping gases. He picked up the mirror and the books in a single heap and flung the lot of them through the closed window, shoving his head out into the night air, breathing great gulps of it and watching books and glass shards cascade onto the street four stories below.

His chest heaved; his head cleared; his equilibrium and sense of proportion returned. Of course it wasn't a poisoned gas device. There would have been no conceivable way to have calculated the odd events that had led him to board that train in Harrogate. His enemies weren't half that clever. This was something else. It was just possible that he'd been a victim of his own zealous actions. What if, he wondered, the box *had* contained an emerald, and was designed so that uninformed tampering would destroy the gem? Was it emerald dust that filled the room? But why in the devil would a man build such a box, or have it built? Had Owlesby been a lunatic who would rather the emerald be destroyed than profit a thief? Or was there more to it? Had Owlesby been a smuggler?

Of course he had. And here, it seemed certain, was a way by which to utterly destroy and disperse evidence that had fallen into the wrong hands. It was frightfully ingenious if it was so.

Pule bent back into the room. Idle speculation was getting him nowhere. One way or another, the box was worth nothing to him. It might, however, give Narbondo a few trying moments. And Narbondo's box – Pule would have that. He tucked the coat around the still-whirring box and stepped out through the door, passing on the stairs his hurrying landlord who began to address him, then fell silent, staring at him in horror.

"Damn you!" cried Pule, pushing the man out of the way and drawing himself up as if to flail at him. Pule stood heaving with wrath, the man cowering against the banister, his countenance frozen. "What are you staring at, idiot!" shrieked Pule. "You soulless halfwit!" Pule choked. He couldn't breathe. The man's face seemed to be inflating like a balloon, the shocked look in his eyes testimony to Pule's condition. Blood rushed in Pule's ears. His heart smashed in his chest. His face burned.

With a snarl of released rage he kicked the man in the ribs, possessed by the desire to beat him senseless, to flail at him with the heavy box, to bash him through the tilted railing and watch him fall down the vortex between the spiraling stairs the thirty-odd feet to the distant floor below.

The man's face loosened. He screamed, and the sound of it propelled Pule down the stairs in great leaping strides, hollering curses over his shoulder. An old man stepped out from a door onto a landing as if to detain Pule. He gasped and fled back inside, slamming the door behind him. A bolt rattled into place. At the ground floor Pule crashed through the street door, surprising two women who were just that moment stepping in. They shrieked in unison, one fainting, one leaping across toward a half-open closet as if to hide.

Pule gritted his teeth. His foes were falling before him. And they'd continue to fall. There'd be no stopping him. On the street he took to his heels, fleeing through the black night, neither running from anything nor toward anything, just running, holding the box beneath his arm, beset, it seemed to him, by no end of devils. He slowed, finally, gasping and sweating, outside a low tavern on Drury Lane. A group of men lounged in the gutter, tossing coins at a target chalked on the street. They paid him little heed. As he walked past, a coin rebounded off his heel.

"Hey, mate!" shouted an exasperated, accusing voice.

Pule turned on him. The man blanched, croaked out a halfmouthed curse, and fled into the open door of the tavern. His companions, themselves looking up, shouted, rose in a body, and followed the first man, the door of the tavern sailing shut with such force that rust from the hinges sprayed out into the lamplit road. The sound of scraping tables and benches could be heard from within, clunking against the door.

Pule turned slowly and resumed his journey, pondering darkly the revenge he'd have on them all – the well-placed anarchist bomb blowing to shreds the likes of such idlers along with the leering carp dealers of the world. He set a course for Pratlow Street.

FIFTEEN

TURMOIL ON PRATLOW STREET

Shiloh the New Messiah leaned against the wall in a straight-backed oak chair, all of the joints of which were loose, the glue having dried to dust years before. He sat in silent meditation – hadn't moved for half an hour. The curtain had been pulled back from the little shrine across the room, and in it, sitting beside the miniature portrait of Joanna Southcote, was the head of the lady herself in its aquarium.

The crosses we bear... thought Shiloh. He shook his head over it. The afternoon's meeting in Kensington Gardens had been a disaster. It wouldn't stand thinking about. It would have to be righted; there was no getting round it. One owed as much to one's mother.

A brief chattering ensued from the glass box – three or four tentative clacks, then silence. The spark hadn't entirely departed the head. There were elements of it left, apparently, that awakened at odd intervals like bubbles on the side of a glass, released suddenly for no apparent reason to sail surfaceward and burst. It would be the greatest miracle of all, he thought to himself, if during one of her sojourns into consciousness she would speak – give him a sign of some sort. Utter a telling phrase. Refer, perhaps, to the drawing nigh of the dirigible. But there was nothing, alas, save the random click-clacking of dry molars.

In an hour the moon would be down. Darkness would serve him well. The hunchback, he knew, was engaged at the house on Wardour Street, and would be until morning or until his filthy habits burst his pea-sized heart.

There was a chance, of course, that Narbondo had removed the box from his cabinet – an action that would make its recovery infinitely more complicated. But even so, there were the bones of his mother to consider – bones that he'd foolishly abandoned to the hunchback and his base experimentation. Shiloh remembered the confused hands and shuddered. He'd take the bones and the shroud out in a Gladstone bag. The shroud could be enshrined in its own glass case, not unlike the shroud of Turin. Enthusiasts were eager for the sort of circumstantial evidence inherent in such relics.

There had been the case of the woman on the Normandy coast who possessed a felt cap into which was indelibly stained the image of the Bambino of Aracoeli. A shrine had been built for it in the little village of Combray, and fully ten thousand people a year paraded through to view it – or, for two francs, to touch it. A drunken sailor from Toulouse had snatched it from its perch and clapped it onto his head, which promptly burst into flame, reducing the sailor and the cap simultaneously to ash. Not surprisingly, the urn of mixed ashes drew half again as many pilgrims yearly at double the price. The evangelist, laughing to himself, contemplated the fact that thus even the most vile sinners are put to work for the church. They rot in hell, of course, despite their works.

He arose, closed the curtain, and found the street. Outside, pasty and silent, stood an obedient convert, who in a moment trotted away up Buckeridge Street to summon the brougham. Shiloh was impatient. Eternity lay before him, just a few short days away, and he was itching to get at it. And he was itching, at the same time, to hasten Narbondo's decline into the pit. He grinned to think of the cursing and gnashing of teeth that would ensue on the morrow when the hunchback dragged himself home, worn and degraded, wondering at his own sanity, perhaps injured from some ill-advised acrobatics, to find that he'd been relieved of the bones and the box in a single evening, that his smug posing hadn't been worth a penny toot. The brougham swung round the distant corner, stopped before the tavern, and waited, as Shiloh climbed in beside the man in the turban.

"Wipe your disgusting face!" shouted the evangelist, watching in horror as the man smeared at his blood-caked lips. The old man shuddered involuntarily, looked straight ahead, and sank into himself as the brougham clattered along into Soho, bound for Pratlow Street.

"I don't intend to sue them," said St. Ives heatedly, "I intend to beat them senseless. What would a lawsuit avail us? What, for God's sake, would we claim?"

"It bears contemplation, sir, if you'll pardon my saying so. Breaking into a man's house is ill advised, regardless of its location or the motivation of the burglar. The law, I'm afraid, sir, is adamant on that point. Your own argument is solid. What *would* we claim, sir, if we were apprehended as common thieves?"

St. Ives strode on without speaking. They'd taken a cab to Charing Cross Road – far enough away, thought St. Ives, so that not even the most scrupulous detective would connect them to any ill doings on Pratlow Street – supposing, that is, that the authorities were concerned with what was happening on Pratlow Street, which they almost certainly weren't.

He wished heartily that either Godall or the Captain had been in that evening, but neither had – off on some mutual business, no doubt. Scouring Limehouse, perhaps, for the absconded Bill Kraken. St. Ives would have to act without them. This wasn't their affair anyway, this aerator business. It was his – his and Keeble's, who would be imposed upon to build another if St. Ives failed. He could hardly, though, drag the toymaker into it. It had been St. Ives' own idiotic fault that the silo door had been left unbolted, that Pule had been allowed to escape them twice, first at the manor, then later on the train. They must strike while the proverbial iron was still hot. Peculiar events were fast sliding toward possibly dangerous conclusions. Narbondo and Pule sailed in the current of some sort of hellish, swiftly moving stream, which would carry the villains out of reach if St. Ives weren't brisk.

"Toynbee and Koontz would accomplish little," he said to Hasbro, repealing his disinclination to carry the issue to the authorities.

"There aren't a sharper pair of investigators in the Yard," insisted Hasbro. "Koontz is a legend – feared in the London underworld. It's the peculiar look in his eye, if you ask me, that throws the fear into them. That and the cut of his suit. If he can't come it across this Pule, then no one can. He was involved in the

Isadora Persano affair, do you recall – the business with the worm and the inside-out pouch of tobacco. His aunt is a fast friend of my sister. We could look him up tonight, I don't doubt. Lay the case before him."

The dim corner of Old Compton Street loomed ahead of them, the sorry buildings disguised by darkness, the pavements in utter shadow. St. Ives slowed his pace and asked himself for the first time exactly what it was he intended to do. And the more he thought on it, the more he recalled the faith he held in the remarkable Hasbro, a faith which his headstrong determination to retrieve the aerating device and deal with Pule had momentarily effaced. Hasbro, in fact, was not altogether wrong. If this man Koontz could be prevailed upon to take the case…

He stopped altogether and stepped back into the darkness of an overhanging gable that shadowed a ruined front stoop. This is decidedly unwise, thought St. Ives. The least he should do was wait for Godall and the Captain. The aerator box was their affair in a roundabout way. What was it Godall had said three nights ago in the rain? "The collective spirit," or some such thing. There was truth in that. No good would come from them each hacking out his own path, only to go blundering into one another in some secret, foliage-obscured crossroad.

"Hasbro," whispered St. Ives, the very atmosphere of the dilapidated neighborhood dampening his voice.

"Sir?"

"You're quite right, of course. This man Koontz – can we find him?"

"He's said to have an almost legendary passion for crustaceans, sir, and might conceivably be engaged even now in a late supper in the environs of Regent Street, at a club with the unlikely appellation of Bistro Shrimp-o-Dandy. He's infamous, I'm afraid, for keeping cooks and waiters up until dawn."

"We'll have a look in, then, at this Shrimp-o-Dandy. I've seen reason, Hasbro."

But at that moment, St. Ives saw something more – the running shadow of a man that slipped in and out of darkness across the street, crossing toward the laboratory of Dr. Ignacio Narbondo.

St. Ives and Hasbro stepped as one into a dim corner, the Shrimp-o-Dandy forgotten, and crept along up the pavement toward where the mysterious figure had vanished into a doorway. Neither of them spoke. There was no use pointing out that something was afoot, or that they were duty-bound to follow. They'd gone out that evening on the trail of mystery, and here it was, wearing a placard. There was nothing to do but investigate.

Bill Kraken, trembling with fear and animated by determination. found himself alone within the dark confines of the cabinet of Dr. Narbondo. Odd noises assailed him – the languid splashing of lazy carp in the tank on the floor, the sound of his own labored breathing, and the tremendous pounding of his heart which might, it seemed, burst like a piece of ripe fruit before he found what it was he sought. And at random intervals came the brief clatter of what sounded like a handful of ivory dominoes being dropped into a sack.

There was nothing either on the slab or on the table – no corpses to leap up or pea hens to dash at him. And there, atop the piano, lay the Keeble box; he could just see the outline of it in the faint light of the flickering candle he carried. He slipped across toward it, walking on tiptoe. This was no time to dillydally. There was nothing in the accursed laboratory that attracted him. He'd just pluck up the box and nip out the way he'd come. If he heard the doctor or Pule ascending the stairs, he'd simply backtrack to an upper floor and wait for them to enter the laboratory, then bolt for the street.

He squinted into the darkness, fearful that Narbondo would surprise him again by entering through the passage in the wainscot. It wouldn't do to actually confront the doctor or, for that matter, his loathsome accomplice. He hauled a chair from beneath the table of the pea hen and jammed it under the door latch, wiggling it for good measure.

Waving the candle in the direction of the box, he sent shadows leaping and flickering up the walls in the yellow light. Before him, lying in the pile where they'd fallen, were the grisly, skull-less remains of Joanna Southcote. The sight of them petrified Kraken, froze him into a wide-eyed, half-bent statue. For while he watched, the bones seemed to shudder and collect themselves, half rise, and then collapse again into a disordered pile, making the clacking sound of dominoes.

Quaking, Kraken groped inside his coat for a flask of gin, half of which he poured down his open throat in a hot, leafy rush. The bones made another effort, no more successful than the last, one of the backward hands skittering around the floor like a crab before the whole loose business went limp.

Kraken vowed not to look at it. That was best. If it managed to stand, he could outrun it, or beat it to pieces with the poker that lay now atop the hearth. He was damned if he would allow a heap of bones to frighten him off. He took a last, healthy gulp of the gin, grimaced, and snatched the box from atop the piano. He turned, took a step toward the door, and discovered in horror that the door latch, very softly and slowly, was turning. He heard a shuffling of feet, and saw the faint orange glow of a hooded lantern cast across the threshold.

Kraken backed slowly toward the far wall. What if it were Willis Pule? What if it were Narbondo himself? It would mean the end of him, sure enough, and of any attempt to restore himself in the eyes of Captain Powers and poor Jack Owlesby. Whoever stood without wrestled with the stubborn handle, giving off any attempt at secrecy and wrenching at the thing. Curses rang out in the peculiar, high voice of Willis Pule. There was the sound of a foot kicking the bottom of the door.

Kraken jabbed desperately at the wainscot with his free hand, searching for the moving panel. He pummeled the panels up and down either side, sobbing for breath, listening to the thudding on the door behind him and the sudden scrape of the chair as it pushed across the floor.

With a startling suddenness the smooth panel lurched inward, paused, then slowly swung to. Kraken threw his shoulder against it in desperation. His candle tipped and drowned in its own melted wax as he tumbled into a cold and dusty passage, the panel closing behind him. He lay on the musty floor, stifling his wheezing breath, watching through the diminishing crack the chair with which he'd wedged the door tumble inward, followed by the headlong rush of Willis Pule. Utter darkness followed, but through the wainscot came a sudden raging voice, then Pule's voice even louder, maniacal. A crashing of chairs, the shouting of curses, and the sudden firing of a pistol gave way to silence. Kraken beat his pockets for a match.

* * *

At the sound of the pistol shot, Langdon St. Ives and Hasbro froze on the stairs. They had determined to remain in the street. The alley door of the house was nailed shut. Any thieves – whoever they might be – in the house above would have to exit through the street door. There was precious little to be gained in yammering up the stairs after them, bursting unarmed into a room full of desperate men. They'd simply wait at the bottom of the stairs and confront anyone who came out with the box. Whatever odd machinations had brought about the appearance of the evangelist were none of their business.

But the pistol shot put an edge on the mystery. It was possible that Godall had been too concerned with the collection of villains; they seemed bent on exterminating each other. A door slammed above. Another shot banged out, followed by a howl of pain. A door crashed open. Wild shouting ensued. St. Ives bolted down the few stairs they'd ascended, leaping along at Hasbro's heels. At the bottom landing, just inside the street door, Hasbro ripped open the door of a tiny room – an oversize closet from the look of it – and the two men tumbled in, closing the door but for a crack through which they had a tolerably good view of the stairs. Down those same stairs tumbled, head over heels, a howling Willis Pule, who whumped down onto the landing and lay still. St. Ives could just see Pule's face. There was something peculiarly wrong with it. In the feeble light that shone through the open street door, Pule's face appeared to be a ghastly shade of pallid green, as if he were the victim, perhaps, of a tropical disease.

"What on earth…" began St. Ives, staring at the ruined face in horror, when behind him, against the paneled wall of the closet, came such a fearful banging and moaning that Hasbro leaped with a shout against St. Ives' back, and the two of them would have catapulted out onto the landing if Pule's body hadn't blocked the door.

St. Ives gripped the shoulder of the frightened Hasbro and found himself shrieking involuntarily into his ear as the oaken panel slid back slowly to reveal the ghastly, inhuman, eyeless face of a tottering corpse, dank, clotted hair thrusting out around it like a hideous aura. A fetid odor of decay blew out, and another face peered over the shoulder of the first ghoul – the mouths of both working and smacking like cattle chewing cud.

A light glowed behind the things, revealing, impossibly, a dancing collection of the grim apparitions, in the middle of which stood a wild-eyed Bill Kraken, looking mightily like a corpse himself, frozen in mid-stride, a piercing, inhuman shriek issuing from his open mouth. The first of the ghouls, heaving breaths rattling from his throat, his hands clutching, utterly blind, lurched forward into Hasbro. St. Ives was propelled against the door, pinned by Pule, who flopped a bit farther out onto the landing. St. Ives pushed, the ghoul howling in his ear. Hasbro reached past St. Ives, pounding with both fists on the door. Pule budged farther; St. Ives shoved again – threw his shoulder into it; and Shiloh the evangelist, flanked by the turbaned man on the one side and the earless man on the other, appeared suddenly on the stairs, the old man carrying a Keeble box in one hand and an open Gladstone bag stuffed with bones in the other. The evangelist paused, squinted with obvious amazement at the trapped St. Ives, who was pressed against the door jamb by a closetful of gibbering ghouls, and shouted at his two companions. The two hurled themselves against the door, forcing it shut in the face of St. Ives' protestations. The whump of Pule being rolled once more against the door followed, and St. Ives turned to see Hasbro fending off a score of shambling ghouls in various states of decomposition, the lot of them jigging and jibbering pointlessly as if they were marionettes dangled by a lunatic puppeteer. St. Ives smashed against the door, fighting for footing, and inch by inch once again shoved an inert Pule across the landing. He squeezed out, tripping over Pule's legs, and stumbled against the far wall. In a nonce, Hasbro was out beside him, wheezing and doubled up.

Two arms shot through the hiatus. A shoulder followed along with a foot, two ghouls trying simultaneously to squeeze out through the door. St. Ives placed his foot beneath the knob and shoved, thinking to trap the struggling creatures within the closet. But he suddenly remembered poor Kraken, and heard, it seemed to him, a smothered, purposeful cry from within. He abandoned his efforts, turning instead to the supine Pule. In a trice, St. Ives hauled him away. St. Ives and Hasbro sprang onto the stairs, and a veritable rush of ghouls hobbled, leaped, and crawled through the open closet door, the lot of them fleeing into the open night. Among them, slit-eyed and gibbering like a ghoul himself, strode Bill Kraken.

"Stop him!" shouted St. Ives, but Hasbro could do no more than his master to intercept the determined student of philosophy, who, shielded by ghouls, raced into the street and away, clutching in his arms a Keeble box. Hasbro and St. Ives followed, caught up in a tangle of animated corpses, some few of which had already begun to wind down and collapse – one on the stoop, one across the curb, another on the pavement, his legs splayed out like scissors as if they had tried to walk two directions at once.

Around the corner, kicking up sparks from the pavement and clattering like an express train in the still night, drove the evangelist's brougham, dead away down the center of the street, bowling through a little knot of ghouls that flew like ninepins. One door hung open, and the turbaned ghoul, his cap knocked back off his head but hanging yet by a chin strap, dangled out the door. He bounced along until the brougham canted round the distant corner, where he sailed out onto the roadway and rolled to a stop in the gutter. St. Ives could do nothing but watch the coach race away, carrying within it his aerator box. Lord knew what the old man thought he had.

A shout sounded from behind them, down the street in the direction from which the brougham had just appeared. And there, limping along slowly, were Theophilus Godall and Captain Powers, the Captain clutching a bloody shoulder.

"Shot, by God!" shouted St. Ives to no one, and not stopping to wonder why it was that his two stalwart friends should have suddenly appeared out of the night. He and Hasbro reached them simultaneously, and found, happily, that the Captain's shoulder had merely been creased by a bullet fired haphazardly by the old evangelist when the two had sought to grab the reins and stop the brougham's escape.

It was an hour later. The company slumped in chairs in Captain Powers' shop, before the general furor of the night's doings drained out of them and it was revealed to St. Ives what the second Keeble box had contained. St. Ives, in turn, related how in the tumult Kraken had fled once again into the City, seemingly deranged by his bout with the ghouls.

"So that," muttered St. Ives, "is what the man stole." He shook his head. "Do you suppose he was trapped in the passage with the ghouls ever since? No wonder he was gibbering mad."

Godall shook his head and related to St. Ives some few of the intrigues of the past three days. "I knew," said Godall, "that a good number of bodies had been brought to the house. Narbondo must have used the passage as a sort of storehouse. Fancy them all coming round together like that. This is a strange business."

"Cut and run; that's my motto," said the Captain, poking gingerly at his shoulder.

Hasbro shook his head. "The papers will be full of this," he said. "We've stirred up a curious nest of bugs, and not a single gain was made in the process."

No one in the shop could deny it as they sat tired and hungry and watching the early morning sky pale with the dawn. The entire business had become woefully complicated, and the Pratlow Street failure took some of the pleasure out of St. Ives' meeting, after fifteen long years, Nell Owlesby.

The arrival of Parsons, pounding on the door hours later, did little to enliven St. Ives' mood. He cursed himself for having told the man that he could be contacted through Powers' shop, and it took a half hour of lying before the scientist could be dissuaded from knocking up Keeble himself. Even Parsons' revelation that the blimp had been sighted over Limerick, looping over the Irish west coast in a long half elipse that would aim it, they were certain, toward London – even that merely added to the general confusion and early morning muddle. Somehow, it seemed to them, the arrival of Birdlip would be the natural culmination of the tangle of plots they'd become involved in, that the appearance of the blimp, a dot in the distant sky, would place a period, an end mark, to their confused and fruitless efforts to slay the various dragons.

It was hours after dawn, the streets long since awake, when there came a new and furious pounding on the door, startling St. Ives, who dozed in a stuffed chair. His companions were awake, making and discarding plans. Hasbro threw the door open, and there stood Winnifred Keeble, disheveled and tired. "Jack's coming round," she said, then turned and hurried back across the street, the collected members of the Trismegistus Club hauling on coats and following in her wake.

SIXTEEN

THE RETURN OF BILL KRAKEN

Willis Pule rushed up out of unconsciousness all in a moment, becoming aware suddenly of the sound of dripping water and of an almost numbing, clammy cold. He lay, it seemed to him, on a stone slab, or on pavement, and lying there had apparently made him overwhelmingly stiff and sore, for when he moved, his joints and muscles shrieked at him.

He opened his eyes. Far above him was a vaulted, cathedral-like ceiling of gray stone. Gaslamps hissed, each throwing out a diffused yellow radiance in a circle around it, precious little of the light drifting down toward the floor below. The room at first seemed to be enormous – a huge subterranean chamber hewn, possibly, out of rock. Pule craned his neck, wincing at a throbbing headache. The room wasn't, he determined, as big as all that. It was built of cut stone. Vast porcelain sinks lined one wall, and beneath them sat rows of glass and wood cabinets, several of their doors standing ajar to reveal boxes of surgical instruments – bone saws and knives and clamps. I'm in a hospital, thought Pule groggily.

But what sort of a hospital is it that freezes its patients and requires them to sleep on granite mattresses?

Another wall was nothing but great drawers like oversize file cabinets, one of which was pulled open. A foot thrust out sporting a broad paper tag tied to its big toe with a string. This was no hospital, Pule realized with sudden certainty. He was in a morgue. He was dead. But he couldn't be dead, could he? He was cold as an oyster boat, something a dead man might be, but wouldn't be conscious of. It occurred to him with a shock of horror that perhaps he'd died and somehow been reanimated by Dr. Narbondo for some despicable purpose.

He could remember the fight with the old evangelist: the pistol shot, grappling at the top of the stairs, being pushed headlong down them. He had no recollection at all of having landed, only of sailing through the air. But he must have landed, mustn't he? Landed and worse. He was lying on a slab in the morgue, in among what appeared to be an army of corpses, most of which were laid out in a long line on the floor.

How desperate, he wondered, was his situation? On what grounds could he be arrested? None. He had, it's true, booted his landlord in the ribs and broken the window in his room. But he had no identifying papers on his person. No one here would confront him with that. He was alive and free – that much was clear. But how in the world had he got into the morgue, and what sort of débâcle had occurred to bring about the death of so many people? And why, for God's sake, did his hands seem to be tinted green?

On a nearby slab lay a man who was turned toward Pule. His mouth hung open and his eyes stared, as if in accusation. Pule stared back at him. It seemed as if he knew the man, as if he'd seen the face before, looking at him in much the same way. Of course he had – not two weeks before in Westminster Cemetery. Pule sat up, began to pass out, and lay back down, breathing heavily, one hand on his cold brow. He tried again, swinging his legs over the edge of the slab, slumping forward with his head between his knees until the rushing and pounding settled.

He squinted at the row of corpses, which waited as if in line to file back into the grave. All of them, every one, had come from Narbondo's storeroom. There was the woman pulled drowned from the Thames; there was the child run down in the street by a wagon; there was the freshly hanged forger, his neck broken and twisted, stolen from the gibbet by the navvy who had deserted Pule on the night of the recovery of Joanna Southcote. But how on earth? Had the passageway been discovered? That would put an end to Narbondo's freedom – to his life if they caught him. And what of himself? What of Willis Pule? If Narbondo were jailed, Pule would follow.

The room was empty. Pule slid from his slab and stood erect, swaying, faint. He bent over, resting his head for a moment on the cool slab before turning and shuffling toward the door. If he had to run, his goose was cooked. The line of corpses gaped at him – half of them deprived of the dubious joys of becoming members of the Church of the New Messiah, the other half of going into the unremunerative employ of Kelso Drake. Better, perhaps, to be returned to the ground. It was a far more restful business, anyway, was death.

Pule stopped inside the door, peering through into an ill-lit antechamber beyond, where a lone man sat at a desk, facing away. Pule backed off softly, slipping across to the cabinets and rooting quietly among the debris for a weapon – anything. A bone saw would do. In a moment he was back at the door, which creaked as he pushed it farther open and crept through. The man at the desk turned lazily, expecting, perhaps, a fellow worker back from dinner, but not, certainly, the grimacing corpse that confronted him, green and lurching and waving a bone saw – a corpse fresh from the slab, lately of the London streets, which were rife with rumors of the walking dead. The man arose, a shriek on his lips, and Pule was upon him. He slashed with the saw, the blade snapping almost immediately against the edge of the chair. Pule cast it to the floor, grasping a crystal paperweight from atop a heap of papers, leaping after the bloodied man who was halfway through the door, shrieking down a dark hallway. Pule clubbed at him blindly with the paperweight again and again. The man stumbled and fell. Pule found himself holding half the weight, the thing having cracked neatly in two against the man's crushed skull.

Pule dropped the chunk of glass onto the floor, stepped across the dead man, and found himself afoot in the London night, heading for Wardour Street where Ignacio Narbondo awaited his fate. He had been promised Dorothy Keeble as a prize if his sojourn to Harrogate were successful. Well, success was a relative business at best. He'd been swindled of the emerald, swindled of his dreams. But before the day was out, he'd have what was his.

William Keeble sat in the corner of the room, his brandy untouched on a table beside him, his head in his hands. He looks done in, thought St. Ives, condemning himself for having been sporting in Harrogate while Dorothy Keeble was being kidnapped in London. The sun was high in the sky, lightening the shadowy room. Keeble rose to draw the drapes tighter, to dim the room, but Winnifred followed behind, pulling them entirely apart, flooding the room with spring sunlight.

"We've enough gloom," she said simply. "We can study this out as easily in the light of day as we can in darkness."

"There's nothing to study out!" cried poor Keeble, gripped by a despair which was deepened by two sleepless nights. "If I hadn't been so damned pig-headed with the engine, if I'd given it over, she'd be here now, wouldn't she? And Jack's head wouldn't be split like a melon, would it? Drake would have pocketed another fortune – so what? Would I be any the worse off for another man's fortune?"

"We all would..." began Theophilus Godall, rising out of a deep, tobacco-enshrouded study. But Keeble, it was clear, wasn't keen on reason, on thrashing it out. He seemed to spiral down into himself and sat poking at the end of a sort of brass grapefruit, each poke precipitating from out of the opposite end the grinning rubber head of a man with enormous ears. Smoke and spark accompanied each issuance.

The device reminded St. Ives, somehow shamefully, of the strange pornographic debris that had fallen out of the drop-front desk at the house on Wardour Street. He found himself wondering how on earth it could – whether this wasn't evidence of some deformity in his own rusted moral apparatus. He needed sleep. He could blame peculiarities of intellect on the lack of it. Then he remembered. The thing Keeble toyed innocently with was the odd device the old man had scrambled after and which had been snatched away from him by the butler. "What is that business?" he asked idly, pointing at the orb and the idiotic rubber man that shot from it.

"Some piece of rot left last night by that man Drake," said

Winnifred Keeble. "Heaven knows what it signifies. I would have thrown it in his face if I knew then what Jack has told us since. But I didn't."

"Kelso Drake?" muttered Godall, standing up. "He left this, did he?"

"He asked if William could build him a hundred of the same, then laughed like a man insane. He's utterly daft, if you want my opinion. I wouldn't wonder, though, if there's not some darker purpose in this that I don't see." With that she left the room, up the stairs to the second floor where Jack lay, ministered by his aunt, Nell Owlesby.

Godall bent over St. Ives. "I don't like the look of this at all." he said.

"Of the device there?" asked St. Ives.

"Yes. It's imported, of course, from France."

"I didn't know that," said St. Ives. "What, exactly, is it used for?"

Godall shook his head darkly, as if the Queen's English hadn't the sorts of syllables necessary to reveal the grim truth of the matter. "We've got to get it away from Keeble. If Captain Powers awakens and sees it... well, he's too good a man, too simple and uncorrupted to stand for it. He'll want to beat the stuffing out of someone, and he'll do it too, shoulder or no shoulder."

"What in the world..." began St. Ives, looking once again at the curious device, which was covered, he could see, with nodules of some sort and a little porthole door that opened on either side to reveal what looked for all the world to be glass eyes, staring out from within the ball. Keeble stabbed at the end of it and out popped the rubber man, a puff of smoke and sparks erupting from extended, elephantine ears. A whistle of air poofed from rubber lips. The thing's eyes whirled crazily, and in an instant he was gone, swallowed by the orb. The portholes clamped shut; the sparking stopped; and the thing sat silent and treacherous.

Godall shook his head again grimly. "It's called a Marseilles Pinkle. You can imagine, I'm sure, what the thing is. Only the excesses of a southern climate could have produced it."

"Ah," said St. Ives, wondering at his own unworldliness.

"Keeble, blessedly, hasn't a notion. It was widely used in the last century, after the abduction of young French and Italian noblewomen into white slavery. It was sent to their homes – an announcement, I fear, that no ransom would suffice to return them. Even the most coldhearted royalty have been known to fly head foremost into lunacy at the receiving of one, and, tragically, to disgrace themselves utterly with the device despite their grief. The gesture is wasted here, of course. It's merely a sign of Drake's monumental wantonness and conceit, probably intended in some roundabout and perverse way to parody poor Keeble's attraction to toys. It's also, perhaps, a mistake. It tells us something, I believe, of Dorothy's whereabouts."

Before the conversation had gone forward another inch, there came a terrible knocking at the door, which, when thrown back by a surprised Theophilus Godall, revealed Bill Kraken tottering on the stoop. "Kraken!" cried St. Ives from his chair, but the man had no opportunity to reply – he pitched forward like a dead man onto the carpet.

St. Ives and Godall sprang to his assistance, and even Captain Powers, who was startled out of sleep by St. Ives' shout, bent in to help. It seemed entirely possible that Kraken's sudden appearance betokened his return to right-mindedness.

"Give him air, mates," said the Captain, loosening the dirty kerchief round Kraken's neck. Then, with Godall supporting

Kraken's head, Captain Powers poured a thin stream of brandy into his mouth, which St. Ives contrived to open by pinching Kraken's cheeks. "Damn me," said the Captain in a low voice, and wrinkling his nose. "He's covered with sewer muck, isn't he? Get them shoes off him and pitch 'em out the door."

The effects of the brandy were such, though, that Kraken awoke of his own accord as St. Ives wrestled with his shoes. Braced by a mouthful of the elixir, he managed to wave St. Ives away and remove the shoes himself. The result was a small improvement in his general odor, and he was obliged to remove one by one the rest of his outer garments and to suffer the Captain's pouring a bucket of water over his head as he sat in a galvanized tub. Wrapped finally in shawls, he was recovered enough to be fit company. His clothes were sent out to be burnt.

"And so," he was saying to the collected party – including Winnifred Keeble, who had come downstairs for news of her daughter – "I come around at last. It was them ghouls what set it off, is what I think – a state o' shock is what it's called. If you ain't in one, then such a sight puts you there. If you're already sufferin' some sort of brain fever, then the particular sight of all them dead men has the opposite effect. A cure is what it is then.

"I studied it out myself when I come out of the George and Pigmy up in Soho. I'd been shouting, they tell me, about dead men slouched in the walls, when I was hit from behind by a pint mug that fell off the shelf. It was like I woke up – like I been out o' my mind since bein' beat on the head a week past, kind of in a mist, you know. Liquor didn't help – sober was worse. And then I went and fetched away the Captain's box – don't ask me why. I don't know. I been through hell, gentlemen, but I've come back now. That crack on the noggin in the Pigmy, comin' on top o' the corpses, was like a bracer. 'Let me out,' says I. 'Show me the road!' And off I went, straight as a die, and didn't stop neither, till I drew up at Wardour Street – you know the house, sir."

And with that he nodded at St. Ives, who did, indeed, know the house. They tried to waken Keeble, who snored in his chair, oblivious to Kraken's timely return. He slept so profoundly, however, that their efforts were in vain. Kraken was in a state – much more the old Kraken, thought St. Ives, than the tired, morose Kraken who had drifted in and out of the front room in Captain Powers' shop Thursday last. St. Ives listened in astonishment to Kraken's strange tale – how when crouched in the passage off Narbondo's laboratory he had overheard Pule and Shiloh exchanging words, Pule offering to give up his Keeble box if the old evangelist would see him right in the business of Dorothy Keeble – would use his influence to get Pule an audience with her, so to speak, at Drake's house on Wardour Street. The old man had raged about sin and damnation. Shots had been fired and Shiloh had said that he'd just *take* the box, thank you. Then out Kraken had gone, into the depths of the passage where there was no end of dead men, dirt from the grave in their hair, and the lot of them stirring there in the candlelight and rising up and starting for him until he'd just about gone mad, and…

"And wait just a minute," cried St. Ives, furrowing his brow. "These corpses were just lying about until you came in?"

"That's it, guv'nor. Dead as herrings, then all of them jumped to it like they heard the last trumpet. Damn me if they didn't."

"And this business of the dancing skeleton," asked St. Ives of Godall, "and the piano playing and the chicken bones or whatever sort of bird it was…"

"How'd yer know about that?" asked Kraken, amazed.

St. Ives nodded at Godall by way of explanation, as if to indicate that there was little or nothing that the man didn't know. "Where was this box when all of that business was transpiring?"

"On the piano," put in Kraken. "I tried for it, too, but the humpback nearly killed me with a spade."

"By Christ!" whispered St. Ives, striking the table before him with his fist. "What if... what if... Wake up Keeble! Straightaway."

Waking the toymaker took a full minute, either because he was so enormously fatigued or because the very spark of life within him had begun to fade, but in time he was conscious and listening to St. Ives. Yes, he said, the emerald box and the homunculus box were identical, beyond the eccentricities of carving and painting that went with that sort of handiwork. Might Nell Owlesby, in her agitated state, have crossed them up? Of course she might. Nell was summoned. She admitted that such an error was possible. Birdlip, she said, might indeed have the emerald. She paused, frowning. "I beg of you," she said, looking particularly at Captain Powers, "not to think me mad for asking this. But could the little man speak?"

"Absolutely," said St. Ives immediately. "According to your brother's manuscript, it was rarely silent – kept up a night and day harangue, an utterly tiresome performance, in any of a number of languages, not all of them of earthly origin."

Nell nodded. "I never read his papers," she said simply, assuming that her reasoning would be apparent. "I only ask because I suffered in Jamaica the certainty that the emerald spoke to me – the fear, that is, that I was going mad. I was feverish. I'd hidden the box in a table beside my bed. And in the night I awoke in a sweat, tossing, certain that a voice had issued from the box in the darkness, and had uttered the name of the false prophet that we're daily more familiar with. I sought this man out, revealed that I'd heard his name in a dream, and, I fear, confessed all, going so far as to tell him that the homunculus – a creature he took an unwarranted interest in – was with Dr. Birdlip. I've told no one of this but Captain Powers. It was part of those shameful and dreadful early years. And I'm afraid, dear," she said, addressing the Captain particularly, "that I omitted any reference to the box having spoken. It seemed those long months later to be a product of fever."

Kraken had sat stony-faced through Nell's speech, but he could sit still no longer. "If it please your honor," he said to St. Ives, "I've heard the blasted thing speak too. I'm damned if I haven't. Last Thursday night, it was. Lord knows what it said, buried in the floor there while you gentlemen carried on in the next room. Yes, sir, I've heard it talk, and I didn't have the horrors neither."

"I rather believe, gentlemen," said St. Ives, "that this plays a new light over the page. We're in a less dangerous fix than we thought, barring, of course, the problem of Dorothy. The box, then, what did you do with it?"

"Well, sir," said Kraken, peering into the bottom of a snifter gone empty. "I made straight off for Wardour Street when I left the George and Pigmy, aiming to do my part. I could see, there at Narbondo's, that you lads didn't have what they call the upper hand."

"Right you are there," interrupted Godall, who poured Kraken a generous dollop of spirit.

"Thankee, sir, I'm sure. So I… Well… The long and short of it is, I ain't got the box. I had it, to be sure, but I ain't got it now."

"Where is it, man!" cried St. Ives.

"Billy Deener with the chimney pot hat's got it. Leastways he *had* it. Murderous villain, too, is what I'm telling you. If I'd have been sharp, I'd have left it with a pal o' mine in Farthing Alley, but I warn't sharp. I was uncommon dull from that bonk on the conk – I could see straight, you understand, but I couldn't hardly see clear.

"Well, chimney pot cleared me right out. I seen him before. And pardon me, yer honors, that I didn't care to see him again. So when he 'costed me with that 'ere pistol of his, why I give him the box and run, assumin', in my haste, you see, that he'd let me slide and make away with the prize. And so he did. I blushes to tell it, too. But we can fetch it back, and the girl with it, if you'll give me a chance to say on."

And with that he inhaled hugely and drained his glass again, trusting to the element of suspense to keep the rest of them listening.

"Fetch it back!" cried the Captain. "How, lad? Oil yourself, for the love of God! Don't dry out on us now."

"Don't mind if I do," agreed Kraken, tilting the handy bottle. St. Ives poured an ounce for himself, noting that it was past noon. It was close to the truth to say that it was smack in the middle of a long damned day, a day that would grow a good sight longer before it was played out.

Kraken set in again: "Sewers, is what I said to myself. I worked for Drake; you know that. What I did I daren't say. It don't make no difference now. After the last year with the poor master, Drake's little jobs looked uncommon genteel. We used the sewers, is what we did, for the delicate operations – and not a few of them there is too, when you're in that line o' business."

With that Kraken appeared to see for the first time the instrument that lay beside Keeble's chair, fallen from the toy-maker's fingers when he'd once again drifted off to sleep. "Holy Mother of God," uttered Kraken, turning pale. "Where did that infernal contraption appear from?"

"Drake," said Godall simply, tossing a shawl over the thing.

Kraken shook his head slowly and took a conscientious sip of brandy, cut, now, with water. "If you've seen what Lord Bingley done to himself with such an article up on Wardour Street..." Kraken paused in his shaking and shut his eyes, trying, perhaps, to crush out the memory of Lord Bingley's demise. He didn't speak for thirty seconds by the clock.

"Lord Bingley?" asked St. Ives, exercising his scientific curiosity.

Godall shook his head at St. Ives and held a finger across pursed lips, as if to say that the Lord Bingley business hadn't ought to be brought to light – that some few of the antics of humankind, when illuminated, were all the darker for the light cast upon them.

Kraken failed to acknowledge St. Ives' question anyway, but resumed his story instead. "I cut down the Stilton Lane Sewer and popped in through the trap, clean as a baby, speakin' figural, of course. You seen what the sewer does to a man's boots. And didn't I see some visions." Kraken paused and looked closely at the sleeping Keeble. "Dorothy Keeble's safe, I can tell you again, though what makes her so ain't what a man might choose. She's got a fever, or such like, and Drake won't let nobody near her, excepting, of course, the doctor." With this last utterance Kraken waggled his eyes at the men around him, to let them know, perhaps, which doctor it was who looked on at Dorothy's bedside.

"The filthy scoundrel!" cried the Captain, heaving to his feet as if he were intending to thrash the hunchback there and then.

Kraken held up his hand. "It ain't like that, gentlemen. Drake won't stand for it, for reasons of his own, if you follow me. He aims to clarify her of fever, or so he lets on. I was in a closet, top o' the second-floor landing. Pule come in not a nickel's worth after I slipped in unseen. Raging after the girl, he was. Had himself wound with sticking plaster, too. Another of his 'cures' as he called it that night when him and the hunchback was twisting the business of the master's papers out of me. Anyway, there was Pule smelling to high heaven of chemical and his hands painted green. I never hope to see such a thing again. Well, they pitched him out – the bum's rush. He swore he'd kill Narbondo. Then he swore he'd kill Drake. Then he swore he'd kill the whole blessed city. Then they showed him the road. Narbondo left directly, worried, if you ask me, gentlemen, that Pule would make trouble up on Pratlow. But little enough trouble it would be, alongside o' what's been done last night. The doctor was in for a peeper, I can tell you."

Kraken grinned at that, fancying Narbondo's reaction when he witnessed the carnage at the Pratlow Street laboratory, Scotland Yard, perhaps, awaiting him on the stairs, the Keeble box long gone, Narbondo discovering that while he frolicked at Drake's the slats were being generally kicked out of his best-laid plans.

St. Ives struck his fist onto his open palm and leaped to his feet. "It's through the sewer then!" he cried. "Can you take me there? We may as well get on with it. They've had the advantage of us since this business began. We'll turn it round now."

"Whoa on," said Kraken, grinning just a bit. "There's more."

St. Ives stared at him. "What more?"

"Your vehicle, guv'nor, it's in the hall."

St. Ives was baffled. "My space vehicle is in Harrogate, locked away."

"The one you been looking about town for, is the one."

"The alien craft!"

"Aye, that's the one. Polished like a mirror, it is, lookin' out at the dome o' St. Paul's like the two of them was cousins."

St. Ives was in a state. Here was news indeed. Was it possible that within the house on Wardour Street lay the cumulative ends of their search? That they could wade in, pistols drawn, and in minutes take back weeks worth of defeat? Well, by God they'd try. St. Ives clapped his hand onto the arm of the couch in a show of determination. "The report from Swansea forecast the blimp at mid-afternoon. How long for it to make London?"

Kraken sneezed voluminously, waking Keeble up again. They put the question to him. "A few hours, I suppose," he said. "Not longer. This evening, to be sure."

"Can we assume, then, that the fourth box will be aboard?"

Keeble nodded. They might, of course, be fooled again, but it was odds on that when the ubiquitous Dr. Birdlip appeared in the sky overhead, he'd be carrying with him Jack Owlesby's inheritance.

"We've got to be on hand, of course," said Godall.

St. Ives nodded. There was no denying that. Jack's emerald, after all. Unless they snatched it at the first crack, they'd likely lose it. They'd never wrestle it away from the authorities – that much was certain, not without compromising Nell.

"There's a half-dozen of us," said Godall. "We'll break into parties. There's too much risk otherwise – we've too much ground to cover."

Godall was interrupted by a sound on the stairs. There stood Jack Owlesby, leaning on the banister. "Jack!" cried the Captain, limping over and offering the lad his arm.

"Afternoon," said Jack, grinning and stepping gamely but slowly down into the room. He took the Captain's arm for the trip across the rug to the couch, and he sat down gingerly when he got there, grimacing just a bit. Nell Owlesby and Winnifred Keeble followed. "I'm going with you to Drake's," said Jack.

There was a general silence in the room. It was a heroic offer, under the circumstances, but of course was out of the question. No one, however, wanted to deny Jack his part.

Captain Powers, having just that moment sat down, lay down his pipe with exaggerated care and stood up once again.

"Now see here," he said, looking at each one of them in turn. "I sailed a bit in my day – forty years of it, in truth, and commanded who knows how many lads from the Straits o' Magellan to the China Sea. It seems natural to me then to step lively here. We got too many officers and not enough hands, and that's been the long and short of her these last weeks, me bein' guiltier than the rest of you."

St. Ives' protest to this last statement was cut short. "Hear me out," said the Captain, poking his pipe stem in the scientist's direction. "Don't buck me, lad. I'm an old man, but I know what I'm about. Time's drawin' on. That 'ere blimp's got to be circumvented, as they say. And the hunchback doctor – we'll go for him straightaway. There's going to be half o' London out on Hampstead Heath tonight, blow me if there ain't, and it won't do to have any more scuffle than we can avoid, if you see my point. We square things away with the doctor now, is what I mean. Tie him up fast and lay him out in that there closet o' his. We can fetch him out in a week or so if we recalls it. So here's what I say, mates:

"I'm the blasted Captain here, so I'll point and you'll jump, and we'll all run aground out on the Heath when the sun goes down, for that's when we'll need the lot of us and to spare. For now, Professor, you and Keeble here will slide into Drakes' through the sewer. I'd get hold of a couple pair o' India rubber boots for the job."

St. Ives looked at Keeble. Did he have the stuff for it? It was clear he had to be given the chance. Keeble seemed to make a visible effort to pull himself together, to haul in loose limbs and slap some color into his face. He picked up his glass, thought better of it, and set it down hard on the table.

"I'm going with them," said Jack staunchly.

"You're going with *me*," cried the Captain, puffing like an engine on his pipe.

"I'm…" began Jack.

"Enough! You'll take orders or by heaven you'll stay home and scrub the slime out o' Kraken's boots! You and Nell, as I was saying, will lie low outside o' Wardour Street with a wagon. We'll be ready to fly when the Professor and Keeble steps out wi' the girl. It's action enough you'll see then, my lad. Can you fire a pistol?"

Jack nodded silently.

"One thing," interrupted St. Ives. He considered for a moment, his face brightening, his eyes gleaming. "In the event," he said, "that I don't come out – through the door that is – look sharp for me in the sky. I mean to get the starship out of Drake's just as soon as we've got Dorothy safe. Be ready, then, to make for Hampstead without me."

The Captain shrugged. That was St. Ives' affair. Certainly there would be no way of going back in after the ship, not after the confrontation that would likely occur that afternoon. "And we'll leave ye too, mate. Don't think we won't. I aim to be on hand when Birdlip heaves to. The em'rald's been in my hands these long years, if you follow me, whether it's been in my sea chest or aboard that 'ere blimp. Yes, sir, starship or no, I'm for Hampstead when I see the black of that girl's hair."

St. Ives nodded.

"And you two," he said, nodding first to Hasbro and then to Kraken. "You swabs will take care of this here doctor, like I said."

Kraken chortled and rubbed his hands. "That we will," he said.

Hasbro was more eloquent. "Since his ruffians," said the starchy gentleman's gentleman, "tore the manor to bits and shattered the visage of poor Kepler, I've wanted nothing more than to have words with the good doctor, strong words, perhaps."

"Aye," cried Kraken, leaping up in a rush and whirling away with his fists at phantoms, then sitting down in a rush when he remembered that he wasn't wearing trousers. "Mighty strong words," he said squinting.

"That's the spirit," said the Captain. "Don't take no."

"Not us, sir," replied Hasbro, nodding obediently. "Am I to understand, then, that Mr. Kraken and myself are to rendezvous with the rest of you on the green at Hampstead?"

The Captain nodded vigorously. "That's it in a nut. And mind you, it's the blimp we want. This ain't no social affair. First one in grabs the box. Don't be shy. Don't wait for slackards. Lord knows which of us will get in first."

"Well it won't be me," said Winnifred Keeble, frowning at the Captain. "Apparently I'm to stay home, am I? Well I'm not, and you, sir, can smoke that if you'd like. I'm going in after Dorothy."

"As you say, ma'am," replied the Captain humbly. "The more hands the better when foul weather blows up."

"And I, gentlemen," said Godall, rising and picking up his stick, "intend to confront our evangelist. He has, if I'm not mistaken, one of the boxes in question. Which might it be again?"

St. Ives looked at Hasbro for help. "That would be the aerator box, sir, if I remember aright, which Pule possessed when he leaped from the train. And there will be two of the boxes at Drake's, sir, if you'll allow a gentle reminder – the little man inhabiting the one and the clockwork alligator in the other – both, I believe, of some value to us."

"Quite," said St. Ives, itching to be off. "What detains us then?"

The Captain knocked his ashes out into a glass ashtray. He blew through his pipe, shoved it into his coat pocket, and stood up. "Not a blessed thing," he said.

SEVENTEEN

THE FLIGHT OF NARBONDO

It was very little presence of mind that Willis Pule had left. Outrage after outrage had been heaped upon him. And now this last business at Drake's… He strode along down alleys and byways out of the way of the London populace, grimacing at each jarring step at the pain of the chemical bath that heated his face beneath the sticking plaster. There was a good chance that the mixture would quite simply explode, reducing his head to rubble. Well so be it. He grinned at the thought of him strolling with a will into the presence of his collected enemies and, in the midst of a fine speech, detonating, as if his head were a bomb. It would have been a very nice effect, taken altogether. He laughed outright. He hadn't lost his sense of humor, had he? It was a sign that he would prevail. He was a man who could keep his head, he thought, while everyone else was… no, that wouldn't work. He giggled through his bandages, thinking about it, unable to stop giggling. Finally he was whooping and reeling, as if in a drunken passion, laughing down on the occasional loiterer like a madman, sending people scurrying for open doorways.

A mile of shouting and laughing, however, took it out of him, and he fell into a deepening despair, intermittent giggles turning to sobs until, wretched, homeless, and corroded by active chemicals, he stumbled into the dark public house for which he'd been bound.

Some few morose and shifty-eyed customers drank at long tables, looking as if they were ready to rise and flee at the slightest provocation. Pule was enough provocation to cause three unrelated loungers to drop their cups and start up, but upon seeing that he was obviously bound for the curtained doorway that communicated with a rear room, they slid back down onto their benches and simply regarded him with hostility.

The head of a newsboy, just then, was thrust in through the open street door, shouting incoherently the latest horrors that littered the front page of the *Times* and the *Morning Herald*. "Corpses!" he yelled. "Viversuction in Soho."

Pule slipped beneath the curtain, thinking darkly of corpses and vivisection. If it was corpses the public called for, then by God it was corpses they'd have. He descended a steep, broad stairs into a sub-street shop lit only by sunlight through high transom windows around the perimeter. An enormous man with a beard like that of a Nordic berserker pounded away with a hammer at what looked like an iron sausage casing. Dismantled clocks cluttered the bench around him. He wore on his face such a look of loathing and cynical contempt for the world in general that he was immediately recognizable as a revolutionary of the sort with no fixed philosophy beyond explosions. He built, however, what Pule sought – a dynamite bomb, of the spherical sort, cast of iron and with a short fuse. A "roll 'n' run" as they were called by the purveyors of such things. It took a little less than ten minutes before Pule strode along once again, a box under his arm, he and his device bound for Pratlow Street where, if he was lucky, he'd find Narbondo in among his instruments.

Pule stared at the pavement as he walked, his nostrils flaring, his eyes squinting, counting the bits and pieces of abuse he'd countenanced in the months he'd known Narbondo, raging within at the demise of the well-laid plans he'd carried into London. It wouldn't do, he thought, to be careless. He must have his revenge on all of them – there wasn't a one among them who wouldn't feel his wrath. He would settle Narbondo first, and Drake if he were able. And if he weren't, then he'd be on hand when the precious blimp landed, and he'd have his pickings then, wouldn't he? Somehow the chemical preparation vaporized beneath the bandages, and the rising fumes smarted his eyes, generating a steady stream of tears. He mopped at his face. The bandages were loose, unraveling even as he walked along.

Another newsboy chanted past. Rarely had there been as much news. The headlines were wild with it. "Blimp to land!" shouted the boy, waving a newspaper as if it were a banner. "Man from Mars inside! Alien threat! Harmergideon!"

Here, thought Pule, what's this? In a moment he owned a paper, the front page of which was given over equally to the story of the Pratlow Street corpses and the story of the approaching blimp, this last replete with predictions from the Royal Academy itself that the blimp would touch down in Hampstead. The minister of a popular religious sect insisted that aboard the blimp flew an alien creature who would "usher in Armageddon."

There was some confusion as to whether the two stories – the ghouls and the blimp – weren't somehow connected, the ghouls themselves perhaps amounting to aliens in some particularly opaque way. Or, it was equally likely, the ghouls were the first of millions of what Cicero had called the silent majority to rise bodily from their earthly resting place and shake off their shrouds. So said the man called Shiloh, the self-proclaimed messianic figure so common of recent date on London streets, and connected with the recent gatherings at Hyde Park. Why the newly enraptured crowd had chosen to wander down to Pratlow Street and pitch over into the gutter wasn't made at all clear.

Pule read while he walked, paying less attention to direction, perhaps, than would under the circumstances have been wise. His bandages were in full mutiny, his face half-exposed when he stumbled out into the sunlight of Charing Cross Road. He neglected the safer byways and alleys out of interest in the newspaper. Indeed, half the street seemed to have the same interest, for papers, it was clear, were in short demand. People read over each other's shoulders. A great knot of men and women stood in the center of the road, so engrossed in the communal reading of a paper that they were nearly trampled by a hansom cab, the driver of which grappled with a fluttering paper.

The populace, all in all, wore a fairly horrified look on their collective faces – news of aliens and ghouls being, apparently, the sort of ill wind that blew no one any good. Pule, sobbing out of a green malodorous face, dripping unwound sticking plaster, and slouching into the midst of such an assemblage of fear and suspicion, had a predictable effect. A woman shrieked and pointed. Others joined her. People turned where they stood, gaping at Pule, who was, for a moment, oblivious to the developing turmoil. Looking up, though, he saw at once that he'd been mistaken for something awful. For what, no one could immediately determine, neither Pule nor the horrified populace who fell back shrieking and pointing. Could *this* perhaps be the alien? A ghoul? Both? Who could say? Something unnatural it very clearly was.

"It's running!" squeaked a man in a waistcoat several sizes too small for him. And the cry was taken up by the street, Pule's flight seeming to be clear evidence that he was, somehow, what they thought him to be.

He pounded along, ridding himself of newspapers and bandages. If he could have pitched the bomb among them, silenced most of them and given the rest something substantial to shriek about, he would have done so gladly. But they would have been on him before he could act, and he would have been deprived the pleasure of demonstrating the device to Narbondo. The shouts, finally, were fading; no one on the street had been terribly keen on pursuit. It was enough, perhaps, merely to have been a party to the strange events of the day.

He could see very clearly what he had to do. It was a simple business: slip into the passage through the downstairs closet, climb to the laboratory, slide back the panel, and, without a word, roll the lit bomb into the room. Pule prayed that Narbondo would be there. It would almost be worth extinction to stay, to whisper something to the hunchback just as the bomb detonated, to see the look of futility and fear wash across his face, watch him scramble, perhaps, for the device, only to be blown to evil bits, weeping and shouting for mercy. Pule smiled at the thought. It *was* almost worth it, except that Narbondo was only one of a half score of people who sorely required comeuppance. And there was, of course, the matter of Dorothy Keeble. He wouldn't be deprived entirely of her company. That wouldn't do at all. He angled along down Pratlow, keeping well in toward the dilapidated façades so that an anxious Narbondo wouldn't catch sight of him through the casement. He slid through the street door at the base of the stairs, nipped into the closet, and punched the corner of the panel behind which was hidden the spring latch.

It was unlikely that there had ever before been such a crowd in Regent's Park. A continual stream of people trudged along either side of the Parkway and up Seven Sisters Road. Between the human rivers rattled no end of dogcarts and cabrioles and hackney coaches and chaises, clattering and hopping across potholes and ruts, their drivers cursing the masses of people that seemed to flow out into the center of the road on a whim, clogging traffic. Wagons full of people jerked along, then stopped dead for the space of a half dozen minutes, then jerked along again, only to stop almost at once to avoid running down three score of travelers who, because of a mud puddle, perhaps, had drifted again into the roadway, oblivious to the wagons clamoring to get through. If half of London *isn't* on the march, thought Theophilus Godall as he handed a tract to a gaunt man in a pince nez, then I'm a corpse. He certainly did his best to look like one – in a hastily donned suit bought in Houndsditch for a shilling.

He'd had to do little to authenticate it; it was almost dirty enough to suffice. A bit of shredding, an energetically executed dance on the heaped garments in the street, some smearing on of mud – all in all it was an effective costume. A putty scar down the center of his forehead and running under his right eye made it seem probable that he'd had a rough-and-tumble life, which, when paired with the once-ostentatious suit, advertised him, perhaps, as a reformed gambler or other sort of rakehell.

At first he supposed that his fellow ghouls were utterly speechless, but that didn't seem to be the case. Those who had a comparatively fresh look about them, who, perhaps, had lain in the grave only a day or two before being liberated, could utter some few syllables through rusted vocal cords. They hadn't, however, any elasticity to them, and the croaking of the ghouls was, like the production of any unnatural sound, difficult for a healthy man to imitate. Godall did his best, remaining mute for the most part.

The evangelist was inflamed with his usual false spirit, fired by the bellows of approaching apocalypse. Part of him gnashed and cursed the loss of the homunculus box – if that's what it was. That there was another box of inestimable value aboard the blimp was certain. And he had Pule's wonderful device – hadn't he? – the use of which a half hour earlier had brought about a miracle, and a very useful miracle at that. He'd been imbued with the powers of fertility, with the spirit of the Garden, even to the extent of his visage having turned a mysterious pale green, as if he were the incarnation, perhaps, of a vegetable deity. He'd become a walking illustration of the paradox of rebirth – the wrinkles of age giving way to the budding of a new spring, the age of lead wheezing into extinction as the age of gold clambered up out of the wings. And he'd spoken in a curious voice, squeaky and birdlike – frightening at first; there was no denying it.

But being a vehicle of such cataclysmic change wasn't, to be sure, an easy business and had never been such. The power that had assumed control of his larynx was quite clearly the spirit of his departed mother, hovering in the London aether like a waiting dove. He could remember the particular timbre of her voice, whispering through the dusty halls of memory. When he'd whirled the crank on the device and been sprayed, as it were, by the curious green dust, he'd been gripped by her spirit; he'd spoken for the space of a long moment in his mother's sweet voice. He'd been overwhelmed, amazed. He'd doubted, even. But doubt was everywhere; he knew that. Flesh was weak, vilely weak. It had, often, to be satiated. Give it some harmless trifle to placate it, and by so doing beat it down so that the spirit could go on about its business. "Let the filthy yet be filthy," he said half aloud.

His mind wandered, from the curious box to the crowds surging behind and around him to a young lady in a muslin dress – one of his particular favorites among the live converts. She reminded him of Dorothy Keeble, a prisoner in Drake's establishment. He squinted a bit, as if diminishing the scene roundabout him in order to call up a more immediately pleasurable picture.

His face writhed into something idiotic, a facsimile of a smile. His hands shook and he was gripped by the immediacy of his unspent passion. His chest heaved as he struggled to catch his breath. He reached surreptitiously into his cloak and groped for a flask of medicine – gin and laudanum – the combined wonders of which had a distinctly calming effect. He shuddered and looked round him wondering if, perhaps, he hadn't ought to crank up the device and treat the captive audience around him to the first of the evening's bountiful collection of miracles. There before him, smiling benignly, stood one of Narbondo's animations, bless his enlivened heart. His comparatively uncorrupted countenance suggested that he wasn't one of the mutes, one of the recovered long-dead.

"I can see from the cut of your suit that you were of genteel breeding," said the evangelist benevolently to the man he supposed to be a corpse.

Godall continued to smile at him with the same vacant,

empty-headed smile that resided on the faces of the faithful, both living and dead, who milled through the crowds. He decided to respond, having little to lose, even if he were found out. "I was indeed, master," said Godall thickly.

The evangelist gawked at him, surprised. Here was a lively ghoul indeed. Could such a miracle be possible? Of course it could. The end, after all, was drawing nigh. The sea would give up its dead and all would be given tongues so that they might, like lawyers, argue their cases before a holy tribunal. He was fired with the idea. "My son!" he exclaimed into the face of Theophilus Godall. And with that he began to blubber and wheeze, carried away by the sight of London on the march, hurrying toward they knew not what. "Stand beside me, my child! You'll be called upon to testify!"

With that admonition, the old man grasped the Keeble box – St. Ives' aerator – and whirled away at the crank, launching a cloud of green vapors that brought forth, as he had hoped, torrents of exclamation from the pressing crowd. A flat-bed wagon sat abandoned in the road before them, its driver having grown impatient and tramped away toward Hampstead Heath on foot.

"Kneel, my son," commanded Shiloh. Godall kneeled. Shiloh placed a foot on his back and boosted himself onto the wagon, waving the spirit box.

The crowd roundabout fell silent. The press was so thick that the audience, for the moment anyway, was literally captive, and there were no oak trees nearby, thank heaven, to provide shelter for mocking sinners. The evangelist gave the box another crank, bathing his face in the dust of fecundity. "Hear me!" he squeaked in a voice weirdly reminiscent of pipid frogs. He motioned wildly at an attendant who lifted above his head the glass case in which rested the skull of Joanna Southcote. The teeth seemed to hop and chatter just a bit, but the effect was negligible. It was impossible to tell whether the result was a matter of the head's sudden animation or of the attendant's having given it a shake.

Shiloh twisted the crank, shoving the tube into his mouth so as to get the full effect of the emitted holy gases. He staggered under the power of it just as the horse in front of the cart lurched. "The hour," piped the old man, "hath come! We hasten toward the gate. Outside are the dogs and sorcerers and fornicators and murderers and idolators..." and halfway through idolators the effects of the gases diminished and with a frightening burst the piping voice gave way to the old man's creaking shout. He whirled away at the crank with a passion, squirting himself down with vapors, playing the green spray on the multitude who stood in silent wonder. "Come!" he resumed. "Come!" he shrieked.

Godall realized suddenly that the old man was shouting particularly at him. "Me?" mouthed Godall, looking up questioningly.

"Yes, my child! Come hither. Leap aboard this chariot!"

Godall complied. Before them, the road had cleared, part of the crowd having moved along. Those that hadn't clustered round the rear of the wagon, watching the prophet in expectation of further miracle. The attendant lay the skull on the wagon, heaving the Gladstone bone-bag up beside it. Godall waved at the crowd, put his foot against the forehead of the erstwhile attendant, and pushed the man down onto the road.

"Here now!" cried the evangelist turning in surprise upon Godall. But the tobacconist grabbed the flapping cloth of the old man's robe and, giving it a jerk, hauled him over backward. Shouts arose from the baffled masses. Godall whirled, grabbed the reins, and whipped up the anxious horses. The cart leaped ahead. A handful of the faithful raced after it as if to climb aboard, but the effort was wasted. The horses tore away up the road while Shiloh the evangelist, flopping and shrieking on the wagon, held onto his collected props as the jigging skull of Joanna Southcote chattered and clattered accusingly into his ear.

Godall raced up Camden Town Road and angled along a narrow, deserted street into comparatively empty countryside, and for ten minutes he rattled along farther and farther from the environs of Hampstead Heath. He reined in the horses, finally, amid the shadows of a scattering of trees and turned on the scrambling missionary, who quaked in fear at the sight of the pistol in Godall's hand. He squinted into his captor's face, slow recognition appearing in his own. "You!" he cried.

Godall nodded. "I should, I suppose, put a bullet into you, mad dog that you are…"

"On the contrary, sir," began Shiloh, interrupting.

"Silence!" cried Godall. "Now, sir. As I say, I'd just as soon drill a hole in your forehead with this pistol as shake your hand. In fact, I'd gladly do the one and wouldn't consider the other. But it's not my place to judge another man…"

"Judge not!" cried the evangelist, waving both hands about his head as if suffering a fit, "lest ye be judged!"

Godall eyed him coolly. "Don't press me, villain, or you'll find yourself respiring through the top of your head. Hear me out. And save your breath; you have a trek before you, carrying all that gear along. You may, I suppose, be mad – I've no reason to believe otherwise – and a madman, though he might commit vile acts, can hardly be held entirely accountable for them. The extent of your crimes, moreover, can only be measured by an examination of the damage done in the infection of innocent people with your dubious proclamations. Such people, perhaps, would have fallen prey to someone else had you not been handy. The judging of the thing, then, is beyond my powers. It will have to be the unpleasant duty of a higher authority.

"But hear me, sir. I have very powerful acquaintances. Your perversions at the house on Wardour Street haven't gone unnoticed, and the coin you so liberally sprinkle about on your own behalf is transparent, to speak figuratively. If you continue, then, to practice your chicanery publicly, to delude the London innocent, then, sir, you'll be called out, the disparity between our ages notwithstanding."

The evangelist stood rigid as a post, his face purple, his eyes squeezed almost shut. Had he been a jack-in-the-box his lid would have blown off in the next moment. "D-d-do you!" he cried, breathing heavily thereafter and scooping up from the leaves on the ground the foolish head. "Do you know, sir, that you've unalterably called down upon you your own vile damnation!" And this last syllable was uttered with such ferocity that Theophilus Godall was certain for a moment that the old man's tongue would fly out, like the poisonous tongue of a newt. The display, all in all, confirmed Godall's suspicion that the old man was the most deluded of his entire flock, if the shepherd can be said to occupy such a position.

Time was wasting. Light was failing. He was an hour and a half out of Hampstead in the borrowed wagon. And if the roads were clogged yet with sightseers, then it would be odds on that the blimp would descend without him. He'd had enough of the old man, and was tempted to tie him to the tree to prevent the possibility of his following along to the Heath. But such a course might well burst the man's head. So without another word, Godall took up the ribands, flicked at the horses with the whip, and set off up the road at a canter followed by the receding figure of Shiloh the New Messiah, who struggled cursing along, toting in one hand the Gladstone coffin and in the other the encased skull, and hoping heartily that some few of his congregation might have followed them out of the city.

The partly shaded lantern threw an amazingly bright shaft of light across the floor of the cupboard. Hasbro and Kraken had carried it up the passage from the street, finding themselves, finally, beyond the wall of Narbondo's laboratory. The lantern did nothing, however, to generally illuminate the close quarters, and Kraken, bending across to whisper into his companion's ear, smashed his nose against Hasbro's shoulder in the process. "Ugh," whispered Kraken, putting a hand to his face.

"Ssshh!" said Hasbro, who made an effort to peer through a wire-thin crack that ran along the edge of the moving panel. Lamplight shone from beyond, and every now and then someone – the hunchback surely – passed across in front of the crack.

"Shall we clip it open and throttle him, then?" whispered Kraken.

"Patience, sir."

"He's a bad'n, is the doctor. Not a man o' science, mind you. A different sort. A devil. I'm agoing to pummel him," whispered Kraken, jolting around for a moment, perhaps practicing his pummeling. Hasbro peered through the crack, undisturbed. "Science don't slice up dead men," insisted Kraken in a stage whisper of increasing vehemence. "Science don't..." he began, but a noise on the stairs behind interrupted him.

"Sh!" whispered Hasbro, jiggling the covered lamp so that the cloth fell and nipped off the light altogether. The two held their breath. A tramp, scrape, tramp sounded on the stairs. Someone, something approached, ascended toward them. Hasbro squeezed Kraken's shoulder twice, as if signaling that action was imminent. "As silent as possible," he murmured into Kraken's ear.

"Aye," breathed Kraken.

A sputtering light appeared, preceding low giggling and a muffled cough. The light flickered across the landing at the top of the narrow stairs. Both men half expected the appearance on the landing of a ghoul, of one of the walking dead who would shuffle round to face them up the dark corridor. With a last scrape and thud, a knee and a foot appeared; then a head bent into view – the grinning, open-mouthed head of Willis Pule, lit by the unnaturally white light of a sputtering fuse that curled up out of the bowels of an infernal device. He turned and crept toward them, the circle of light cast by the fuse approaching along the floor.

Hasbro crouched there, waiting, ready to spring the moment they were revealed. Kraken shook beside him, his teeth rattling audibly. Pule stopped, canted his head, squinting through the gloom, suspicious.

"Lord!" howled Kraken. "He'll blow us to flinders!" And with that he launched himself at the horrified Pule, who made as if to heave the bomb full into Kraken's face. The two went down in a heap of arms and legs, both shouting, Kraken rolling astride Pule and flailing away at him with both fists. The bomb bounced on the wooden floorboards, Hasbro scooping it up and pinching at the fuse, which, despite his efforts, sputtered continually to life.

"This won't do," he said aloud, and he pitched the bomb along the corridor. It bounced, rolled, caromed off the wall and down the stairs, bump, bump, humping along. The corridor was cast into sudden darkness.

"Ow!" cried Kraken. "Filthy animal!"

Hasbro whipped the cloth from atop the lamp and punched at the oak panel before him. Expecting an explosion that would literally bring the house down, he stepped through into an empty laboratory, the door standing ajar. Kraken sprang in beside him, blood pouring down his arm.

"You've been injured, sir," said Hasbro as he strode toward the gaping door.

"Filthy blighter bit me," heaved Kraken, laboring for breath. "So I kicked him down the well."

"Bravo!" cried Hasbro, leaping up the stairs two at a time toward the upper floors.

"He went up, did he?"

"I haven't the foggiest," shouted Hasbro over his shoulder. "But the house might, if it's going up you want."

"Oh Lord, yes!" hooted Kraken, close at Hasbro's heels. In a trice they found the door to the roof, and without slackening pace, leaped across to the next roof, neither pausing to question the possibility of slowing up, but leaping instead to a third just as the expected explosion boomed up from the street. Both men dropped instinctively; then, realizing that the roof they stood on was yet solid, they crept across and peered between chimney pots. In the center of Pratlow Street was a smoking crater. Half a block down, high-stepping toward Holborn as if pursued by goblins, flew a desperate Willis Pule, foiled once again.

"It must ha' gone out the door," observed Kraken.

"I believe you're correct. A pity, really, that it didn't destroy the laboratory."

"We can have a go at that one ourselves," Kraken shouted, the idea clearly appealing to him. "We can smash it and smash it and smash it!"

Hasbro considered Kraken's suggestion, recalling, perhaps, the broken Kepler. "It's growing a bit late," he began, only to cut himself off and shout, for there, half a dozen rooftops away, springing suddenly out of hiding, leaped Dr. Ignacio Narbondo, a satchel in either hand.

Without a word the two were after him, neither knowing what it was they intended to do with him if they caught him, but remarkably keen on the catching.

It was clear, though, before the chase was six minutes old, that the doctor had taken to those same rooftops more than once in the past, for it seemed that he gained two each time the two pursuers crossed one, sliding along gables, clattering across copper sheathing, skidding on the scree of decomposing chimneys and all the time falling farther behind.

They paused, finally, some two blocks from Old Compton Street, listening to what sounded for all the world like distant laughter ring over the rooftops. For the slice of a moment the doctor appeared at what seemed to be an impossible distance, standing before the brick front of a steep garret, an orange sun beyond him dropping across the afternoon sky. Then he was gone.

EIGHTEEN

ON WARDOUR STREET

Langdon St. Ives and William Keeble crouched in the darkness of an ill-lit hallway on the second floor of the house on Wardour Street. Their short journey through the sewers had been both unpleasant and uneventful. It had been such an easy business gaining access to the house, in fact, that last week's song and dance with the clock crystal seemed an idiotically bad idea. Where they were to go now that they were inside, however, remained to be seen.

The air was almost unnaturally still and quiet. There had to have been any number of people within earshot, but in the heavy, somnolent atmosphere, it seemed as if most were asleep – not at all an unlikely thing, given that most of their business was transacted during the night. There was some stirring and banging downstairs, from the kitchen, possibly. Muted voices could be heard, one of which sounded as if it might be the voice of Winnifred Keeble, who, dressed as a washerwoman, might well have gained entrance through the back door. The thought of her confronting the flour-faced cook was bothersome, but Winnifred had insisted. And cleaver or no cleaver, the cook would find Winnifred Keeble a difficult case.

St. Ives and Keeble tiptoed down the hallway, half wondering which room to peer into. Opening the wrong door would be disastrous. Kraken had supposed that Dorothy was somewhere on the third floor, guarded, no doubt, by Drake's toughs, perhaps by Drake himself. So there was no real need to start peeking into doorways on the second floor, except that the doors presented themselves. Who could say what lay behind them?

They approached the wooden balustrade that fronted the great open hall which St. Ives had been deprived of seeing on his previous visit. There, Kraken had said, lay the starship. Would it be merely an empty hull, stripped and rusted by the centuries? And what purpose did Drake put it to? Was it enough just to possess it, or was there, as rumor had it, some darker, foul purpose? St. Ives thought momentarily of the dreaded Marseilles Pinkle, wrapped in a shawl, lying in the Captain's wagon on the street. There were, apparently, no limits to the perversions concocted by desperate men. What might such men do with the space vehicle of the homunculus? St. Ives couldn't imagine.

A sudden sobbing erupted from beyond the door to their right, followed by the utterance of a low laugh. Keeble straightened, his eyes wide. "Dorothy," he called, half aloud, reaching for the door handle.

St. Ives' attempt to stop him was in vain. He grabbed the back of Keeble's coat, whispered, "Wait!" and was pulled into the room along with the toymaker. On a narrow, unmade bed sat a pasty-faced woman wearing what appeared to be a fruit bowl for a hat. Crawling on his hands and knees on the floor was a man in kneebreeches and a striped topcoat, this last being hauled up over his head, the tails caught up and tied with a broad strip of dotted ribbon. On his feet were pointed, women's shoes, turned around backward and wedged on awkwardly. It was the man on the floor who sobbed in girlish tones.

At the raging issuance of Keeble and St. Ives, the woman on the bed shrieked, and without a second's hesitation, plucked up a glass vase full of wilted roses and pitched the entire affair at the horrorstruck Keeble. The man on the floor stopped his capering at the sound of the shriek and shouted: "What? Who is it!" He struggled, pinioned helplessly in his coat and shoes and bombarded by the fruit that cascaded from the woman's hat. She shrieked again, even though her first shriek had driven Keeble halfway back out into the hallway.

Looking desperately for concealment, St. Ives hauled the toymaker along. Doors slammed on the floor below. Two half-dressed, bearded men thrust their heads through a suddenly opened door, then fled toward the stairs, perhaps assuming that St. Ives and Keeble, rushing at them along the hallway, were police officers. Another door shot open and out dashed an enormous gentleman in ventilated rubber trousers, a sheet of newspaper in front of his face. He too bowled away down the stairs toward the street.

Within moments, it seemed, the cry had gone round the house, and the air was full of shouts and pounding feet and the slamming of doors. Behind St. Ives raged the man with the coat over his head, shouting curses, threatening through a mouthful of tweed. His ridiculous twisted shoes lay on the carpet behind. A head, shouting a fearful string of venomous oaths, shot through the gathered coat, the dotted ribbon and coattails encircling his neck like a clown's collar, his arms cocked up, trapped and thrashing as if he wore a makeshift straightjacket. It was Kelso Drake.

At the sight of Keeble and St. Ives, Drake blanched. His

mouth writhed. He flailed away within the confines of his woolen prison. Keeble stopped, dumbstruck. He hesitated a quarter of a second, pondering Drake's bound state, then slid past St. Ives in a rush and struck the industrialist on the nose. Drake was propelled backward, struggling in his coat, in fear now as well as anger. Keeble struck him again. He grasped a handful of coat front, slapped Drake three or four times on the cheek, then tweaked both his ears. Keeble capered and yodeled before his helpless victim as St. Ives, anxious to conclude their business and be away, hauled at the toymaker's collar.

With a rip of rending material, Drake was suddenly free of the restricting garment, and, with the cry of a madman, he launched himself at Keeble, punching and flailing at the toymaker, who, with a deliberation and sobriety that startled St. Ives, pulled from his coat a leather truncheon, and slammed the industrialist on the side of the head, felling him to the carpet. Keeble replaced the truncheon, apparently satisfied, and turned toward St. Ives a face pale and beaded with sweat. "I don't suppose I should kill him," he said slowly.

"No!" cried St. Ives, hauling Keeble once again along the hallway toward the stairs. Jolting up from the ground floor raged two men, obviously not customers. One, St. Ives realized with a shock of horror, was the man with the chimney pot hat, who held in his hand a carving knife. His companion scrabbled in his coat, perhaps after a gun.

"The bench!" cried St. Ives, grappling with the end of the carved Jacobean trestle bench that sat on the landing. Keeble went for the opposite end. The two men swung it in a quick arch, then let it go, Keeble a second or so ahead of St. Ives. Chimney pot flattened himself against the balustrade as Keeble's end of the heavy bench swung round, grazing his forehead, plowing into the neck and chest of his companion, who had, to his own great misfortune, been peering into his coat. The man screamed and pitched over backward, he and the bench skidding together down the stairs. Chimney pot was after them, waving the knife.

St. Ives skipped up the stairs, Keeble beside him, both men running headlong into a surprised Winnifred Keeble who supported Dorothy around the shoulders with her left arm. In her right hand she clutched a revolver. "Where on earth…" she began before catching sight of the murderous chimney-pipe. "I have your gun!" she cried, pointing the weapon in his general direction.

He slowed momentarily, cocked his head as if debating the extent of the threat, then rushed heedlessly on. Winnifred pushed Dorothy in William's direction, grasped the revolver with both hands, and fired off three or four shots, one after the other, eyes closed. St. Ives dove onto his chest, rolling against the wall of the stairwell, as he watched Billy Deener sail over backward and tumble to the floor below, then roll six feet toward the center of the room, his hands over his head, before scrambling away toward the kitchen. The back door slammed in his wake. Kelso Drake staggered into the room below, then abruptly disappeared after he looked up to see the smoking pistol in the hands of Winnifred Keeble.

The Keebles ushered a stumbling and bewildered Dorothy along to the now empty room, all of them intent only on reaching the street. Fearful that they wouldn't be quick enough, Keeble bent over and scooped the drugged girl into his arms, tilting dangerously for a moment before tossing her just a bit so that she settled in and balanced. St. Ives crouched halfway up the second-floor stairs, watching the toymaker and his wife disappear below. He turned, bolted for the top landing, and burst out onto a deserted corridor, lit dimly by gaslamps in the shape of brass cupids, clinging at intervals along the wall.

Twenty feet along, the corridor opened onto the great hall that St. Ives had been denied a look at ten days earlier. He stepped toward it, wafering himself against the wall to peer out over the high, open room, fearful that he'd be seen from below. No one, however, was in the room save Kelso Drake, who limped along across the floor, his head now swathed in bandages. A low murmur arose, as if he were cursing under his breath. Then he shouted at someone unseen about bringing the brougham around. There sounded an answering shout, then a grunt from Drake, then another shout about Deener having "taken the other box."

"Good!" cried Drake, struggling to open a leather bag, the clasp of which refused to cooperate. The millionaire flung it against the back of a velvet couch with a fury that astonished St. Ives, and set to kicking the bag about the room like a football, dancing atop it until he'd stomped the clasp into submission. Then, yanking open the bag, he tore apart the doors of a broad, mirrored buffet, and yanked out a Keeble box, dropping it into the bag and hurrying out of sight. A moment later the front door banged shut and silence reigned. The house, no doubt, contained any number of people, hidden away from daylight and activity like bats in caves.

St. Ives wasted no time. He had no desire to confront murderers or to hide behind potted plants. He would find a way into the strange ship that sat toadlike in the center of the room below. It was apparently nothing more than a curious ornament, like a china vase or a marble cupid, the peculiar bric-a-brac of a millionaire, polished, no doubt, by a cleaning woman with a rag, who assumed it to be some sort of inexplicable and filthy contrivance for the gratification of the abhorrent appetites of wealthy customers. It was thought to be a sort of giant Pinkle, perhaps, the uses of which were veiled from the sight of the uncorrupted.

St. Ives stared at the machine for a long minute, peering at the little crenelations along its fins, its emerald-tinted ports, the silver sheen of its globular bulk. All in all it wasn't vastly different in character from his own ship – they weren't brothers, to be sure, but they bore each other an unmistakable family resemblance. Curious, thought St. Ives, how two vehicles that hailed from galaxies so immensely distant from each other should have such an obvious affinity. There was a metaphysic there that bore contemplation, but it seemed a good idea to wait until later to contemplate it. He turned and made off down the stairs, pushing through two doors and under a tremendous arch into the hall.

He grasped the rope that hung behind the drawn curtains and gave it a yank, the curtains swinging back and the room flooding with midafternoon sunlight. The vast, unshuttered window looked out onto Wardour Street, obscured partly from view by a scattering of junipers and boxwoods that grew up close along the walls of the house, entangled in the creeping tendrils of climbing fig. It might easily have been years since the foliage had been trimmed, and easily as long since the drape had been drawn to illuminate the dim and unwholesome room with sunlight.

At the sound of a crashing upstairs and what sounded like the whispering of furtive voices, St. Ives hastily manipulated what seemed to him to be the hatch – a circular panel that popped open like the stone door of Aladdin's cave, emitting a little airy chirp as if startled, perhaps, by the touch of the scientist's hand.

At the sudden sight of the interior of the ship, St. Ives found himself trembling so that he could hardly command his hands and feet. He attempted to scale the side, but his foot slid from a protruding bit of polished metal and his hands could find no purchase on the slippery arched edge of the open hatch. His breath whooshed out by the lungful. He felt suddenly giddy and faint, faced, as he was, by the object of a long and sometimes desperate search and fired by the fear that at any moment he'd hear the click of a pistol hammer drawn back or the rough shout of one of Drake's men. He hauled on the arm of a nearby upholstered chair, drawing it up next to the spacecraft, climbing up onto the seat and nearly sinking at once to the level of the floor in the soft, lack-springed cushion. He stepped up onto an arm, teetered back and forth, and slid head first in at the hatch. After yanking the hatch shut, he settled into a cushioned seat and surveyed the interior of the ship.

Before him were a plethora of dials and gauges. He'd wage a sum on his being able to guess out the nature of half a dozen of them, but others were a mystery. The dials were mounted under clock crystals, filled, it seemed, with violet liquid. Scattered in between and roundabout were buttons that one might push, fabricated of what appeared to be ivory and ebony. St. Ives had the sudden urge to jab away at them, like a man with no musical training might poke at the keys of a piano. But the discordant result might easily mean his doom – probably *would* mean his doom. He calculated, trusting to his earlier conclusions about the peculiar but telling affinity of related objects in the universe. His fingers wandered from one switch to the next. Nothing ventured… he told himself, stopping before an ivory button beside which was a sort of hieroglyphic depiction of a sun. He stabbed at it. The dials glowed suddenly through the violet liquid. Emboldened, he pushed another, this one next to a little picture of an aeolus-faced puff of wind. A humming ensued. St. Ives braced himself, then felt, against the back of his neck, a little rush of air. An oxygenator, he thought, smiling at his pair of successes. He jabbed another button and the hatch opened.

"Damn," he said, half aloud. He stooped up through the hiatus, grasped the hatch in order to haul it back down, and looked straight into the ruined face of a ghoul, who stood precariously on the upholstered chair. St. Ives shrieked at it, dropping into the craft, bounding up again to clutch at the hatch, the ghoul meanwhile endeavoring to hoist itself in. Its gaping face, hair tumbling over its forehead, loomed in above St. Ives, who pressed his right hand against the thing's nose and forehead, shoving with all his strength, his feet braced against the deck of the craft. The ghoul stared out stupidly from beneath St. Ives' fingers, its own hands stubbornly clutching the edges of the circular hatch opening. St. Ives banged at the fingers with the fist of his free hand, then reached past, grasped the hatch, and slammed it down on the back of the thing's head.

It lurched forward, eyes widening, then jerked its head out, throwing the hatch open with it. A third hand joined the pair still clutching the ship – another ghoul endeavoring to clamber in. St. Ives banged the hatch down onto the fingers, mashing at them once, then twice, then a third time, grimacing at each blow, expecting a rain of severed fingers. He shut his eyes and slammed the hatch again. It settled into place. Outside were the two ghouls, examining their hands with looks of wonder on their faces, as if having already forgotten how they'd come to be in such a state. Beyond them was another ghoul. Two more slumped in through the door.

St. Ives gritted his teeth and poked an ebony button. The ship lurched and lay still. He poked another. Nothing at all happened. Two ghouls pushed a sofa toward the craft. Another hauled at an oak secretary. Three more wandered into the room and tugged at a piano, inching it forward, intent upon… what? Scuttling St. Ives' ship by burying it in furniture? The scientist settled to his work. A heavy rope end flicked past the window. They were tying the craft to the leg of the upholstered chair, then winding it around the leg of the piano. He'd been wrong about the cleaning woman again. Apparently it was common knowledge, even among ghouls, that the craft was a ship of some sort – not at all a bad thing, thought St. Ives. It argued that the craft worked, that Drake had given orders to prevent its being hijacked.

At the pressing of a button next to the drawing of a spiralling arrow, the ship spun suddenly on its axis, dragging with it the stuffed chair and tearing the rope from the hands of a bent and ragged zombie that crept about under the piano. St. Ives pressed the same button and the movement stopped. He pressed again and the craft resumed its revolution. When he faced the window straight on, he pushed it once again. Then, throwing caution onto the dust heap, he stabbed away at a succession of buttons.

The ship shuddered, lurched, slid forward a foot. The chair in which he sat tilted back, nearly dumping him onto the floor. A wild hum erupted as the craft lurched again, skittered across the floor, and, in an avalanche of cascading glass and tearing vines, rose in a sudden escalating rush, hauling with it the stuffed chair and a single dangling ghoul whose face, smitten with wonder and confusion, pressed against one of the starboard ports for a quick second or so before sliding away and disappearing.

St. Ives, hands flying over the controls in a wild effort to steady the craft, had no time to be concerned with attached zombies. The ship cartwheeled. St. Ives watched in a whirling rush the topsy turvy dome of St. Paul's spin past, followed by a brief glimpse of the spiraling armchair, lost almost immediately to sight and giving way to what was almost certainly a split-second view of the Kennington Oval. The ship shot away to the south and west, bound, it seemed, for the Channel.

He was moving prodigiously fast in an utterly uncontrolled flight, pinned to his seat by the laws of physics on a voyage that, he was suddenly certain, was making him sick at his stomach. It would end in disaster. He knew it. He could picture himself catapulting out of hand into the sea. He couldn't, in fact, picture anything else. It was evident that the slightest manipulation of a pair of curved levers at dead center in front of him would cause the ship to tumble or swerve or skip or in some way run mad. Hesitantly, he prodded one. But he succeeded only in once again cavorting along end over end. There was the sea, the lying chair, what appeared briefly to be a pantleg with a shoeless foot dangling from it, this last entangled in the swinging rope. A prod at the other lever sent him plummeting breathlessly toward the sea, his stomach at once in his throat, the chair rising weirdly past the ports followed by the staring face of the zombie, whose ankle was fouled in the line. The gray swell of the Channel hurtled toward him as he edged the lever back, ever so slowly. The craft swung round in a slow arc, leveling off, then rising once again. It was slow deliberation that was called for – the mere consideration of pressure on a lever was nearly sufficient for a change of course.

His stomach returned to its rightful position, the blood in his veins ceased its racing and settled in apace, and with a keen-minded deliberation, tempered by a vision of the collected, astonished visages of the Royal Academy when he swept in among them at prodigious speeds, and encouraged by the vast canvas of the deepening evening sky, St. Ives eased the lever forward with a subtle pressure from his right hand. He steadied the ship with his left, satisfied with the controlled response. He dipped suddenly, evened her out, and smiled, angling in an increasing rush toward the Dover Strait. The ship slanted upward through thinning atmosphere into the purple heavens. The sky above darkened, brimming suddenly with flickering emerald lamps through the tinted ports, as if he stared into a deep, stellar well, half full of dark water and reflected stars.

NINETEEN

ON THE HEATH

From Hampstead Heath, the lights of London winked and glittered in the darkness, an earthbound counterpoint to the stars amid which St. Ives raced in his borrowed ship miles and miles above. Theophilus Godall stood with Captain Powers and Hasbro, alternately watching the wash of lights and the heavens, the first for no practical reason save beauty, the latter for the appearance of the dark bulk of Birdlip's blimp.

The village of Hampstead was choked with people, slogging in the mud of the streets, jamming the taverns, perching in trees. Pots of ale and cups of gin and rum were carried around by hustling children, who got no farther than a dozen feet from their doors before their wares were snatched away and consumed and a hundred voices called for more of the same. Half the populace of Greater London seemed to have found itself in the vicinity of Hampstead, although a good part of them got no farther than Hampstead Village or Camden Town before encamping, either having little interest in approaching blimps, or, more likely, having little idea what it was that approached, satisfied to be afoot on a warm evening in the carnival atmosphere.

Godall professed to Captain Powers that he hoped the ale and spirits would hold up. And just when he finished the sentence, a great crash sounded from across the green on which they stood, and a low building collapsed in a heap of flying debris. Screams and moaning erupted from a score of people who had moments before been perched atop it and had been singing a tumultuous hymn. A band of robed faithful, two of whom supported a worn but animated Shiloh between them, hurried toward the wrecked shack, pitching handfuls of tracts to the enthusiastic crowds they passed along the way.

The Royal Academy clustered within the confines of a roped-off rectangle on the green onto which had been arranged lawn chairs. The perimeter of the rectangle was threatened roundabout by the pressing multitude. Parsons, a powdered wig canted across the top of his head, shouted over a sheaf of foolscap at his fellows, but his words were one with the general mélée, and not a scientist among them had his eyes on anything but the stars.

Godall was faintly surprised to see the evangelist. There seemed to be no end to the perspicacity of a zealot. The old man appeared, however, to be deflated, to have had the wind taken out of his sails. In the glass cube, still clutched under his arm, lay the head of Joanna Southcote, mute now and toppled over onto its side. It was hard to imagine that the evangelist would cause them trouble. It was the blimp he was interested in. When it landed, *then* they'd have to look sharp. But he'd hardly risk attacking them outright, despite the affront of being manhandled by Godall hours earlier.

Kelso Drake, though, was a different proposition. He'd ridden up minutes after the arrival of the Captain's wagon, then had vanished immediately – an ominous thing, all in all. Godall would far sooner keep him in sight. It was impossible to say whose ghouls lurched about the Heath, Shiloh's or Drake's – quite conceivably both. Kraken was crouched in the upper limbs of a particularly tall alder fifty meters away, a whistle in his teeth. He was on the watch, especially, for the man in the chimney pipe hat. The Keebles were ensconced in the wagon, neither Jack nor Dorothy being in condition to venture out among the multitude. Dorothy, however, was coming round, the haste of their retreat from Wardour Street having chased off some of the effects of the drugs. William Keeble looked about furtively, his right hand on the pistol in his coat, utterly certain that Drake would attempt to repay him for the pummeling in the hallway. Wrapped in a shawl beneath his feet lay the notorious Marseilles Pinkle.

Once, as the wagon had banged and rattled up the hill from Hampstead, they'd rounded a corner, pressing through a mob of trudging merrymakers, and among them, a broad-brimmed hat yanked across his eyes, Willis Pule had bent along slowly. He had glanced up, as if to join the bulk of the mob in cursing the wagon, and his eyes might as well have been pinwheels. If ever Keeble had seen a madman, Pule was it, and no mistake. His face was awash with a deadly, green pallor, as if his head were a pocked and cratered ball of green cheese gouged from the moon.

At the sight of the wagon pushing past, the spinning rear wheels sluicing mud onto Pule's trousers and Pule himself understanding in a rush who it was that rode in the wagon, his mouth twitched open spasmodically, and his suddenly whirling eyes rolled back up under the brim of his hat. He'd lurched forward to grab the wheel, as if to yank the wagon to a stop. But the crowd, finally, had thinned, and the horses leaped forward onto the clear quarter mile of road appearing ahead. Pule was dragged along in a sudden head-over-heels tumble, onto his back like a roach in the mud and moaning unrepeatable curses.

The episode had mystified Keeble. What on earth, he wondered, had befallen Pule to have brought him to such a pass, and why had the sight of the wagon so enraged him? There was much, clearly, in the world that Keeble didn't understand – much that he didn't care to understand.

Parsons strode back and forth across the green – ten steps this way, ten steps that. He paused in mid-stride coming and going to address comments to his fellows, remarking on the direction of prevailing winds, the possibility of warm valley air rushing in a dangerous updraft and pushing the blimp along to Chingford or Southgate or farther. Winds, after all, were treacherous things. Like teeth, actually. But if one knew their peculiarities, their habits, they would reveal monumental knowledge and could be read and deciphered, much like the interior winds of the human organism could be relied upon to betray gastrointestinal peculiarities. If only Birdlip, Parsons lamented, had been a different breed of scientist – what the man mightn't have learned, adrift on the skytides for close onto fifteen years! Ah, but they could hope for little, expect even less. Wish for the worst, he insisted, and one was rarely disappointed. He strode up and down, hauling out his pocketwatch at intervals, then shoving it back into his vest pocket.

A dozen gray beards wagged behind him, and no end of brass telescopes were trained on the empty heavens – empty, that is, but for a wash of stars and a crescent moon risen to the top of the sky. A cry arose, and a finger or two pointed briefly at the ivory slice of moon, but whatever it was that had prompted the cry had disappeared. Something, apparently, had for a brief moment been silhouetted there, but had sailed at once into darkness. Parsons pronounced the mystery a bat, whose nocturnal eating habits accounted for its astonishingly proficient digestive system. Still there was no sign of the blimp.

Parsons wished heartily that the populace would go home. The shouting and singing and general drunkenness were at best a distraction, and certainly had no place at a function of this magnitude. Their presence was due solely to the idiotic posing of the charlatan evangelist, whose apocalyptic tracts had stirred a million Londoners into unwholesome exodus. The man should be in a madhouse. There he stood, one foot planted squarely on the back of each of two kneeling parishioners. What he shouted into the night air was lost in the general cacophony, and Parsons couldn't fathom a bit of it. The few phrases that blew across the green were tangles of hellfire, final trumpets, avenging angels, and – remarkably – creatures from the stars. This last, under calmer circumstances, would have appealed to Parsons, but it was such utter blather here that to attend to it for ten seconds running was a tiresome business.

The hands of the old evangelist rose slowly over his head, and in them, held for the crowd to appreciate, was a cube of some sort. It was far too dark, despite burning clumps of brush scattered round the green, for Parsons to see clearly what it was – a holy object, no doubt. People pressed in around the evangelist, listening. The starry sky and the distant lights of London winking and glittering on the plain below enlivened the night with a spirit of mysticism.

The evangelist exhorted the crowd. There was an answering shout, a confirmation, it seemed. A scream followed. Hands pointed heavenward. A general shouting arose. Spyglasses were aimed toward where a tiny pinprick of light arced out of the sky, falling toward the Heath and brightening as it fell. The general tumult gave way to an awed silence, broken by the shouting evangelist. "And the name of the star," he cried, "is Wormwood!"

But the utterance of the last syllable was followed by a sudden shriek as the evangelist catapulted forward off the backs of his supplicants. The box he held over his head sailed some few feet above the green until it was snatched out of the air by a running figure in a broad-brimmed hat, who dashed among the multitude, knocking people aside like billiard balls and racing as a man possessed toward where Parsons stood before the assembled scientists.

"What in the devil is *this*?" cried Parsons, an utterance that might easily have applied to either mystery – to the glowing orb that plummeted earthward, or to the gibbering, fright-masked lunatic who capered up, yowling at the thing in his hands and lurched to a stop not ten feet in front of the collected Royal Academy. He regarded the cube as if stupefied, betrayed. Parsons could see now that it was built of glass and contained some rattling object. The madman's mouth worked, gibbering silently. With a sobbing heave, as if the strange cube were perhaps the most inconceivably disheartening thing he'd run across in recent years, he dashed it to the ground, then slumped off unpursued. For the minions of the evangelist, along with the old man himself, watched in growing wonder the thing in the sky – a glowing, spheroid ship, fallen from the stars.

Parsons blinked. He looked at the receding madman. He looked at the approaching starship. He looked at the decayed head, toothy and brown, that rolled to a stop at his feet, peering up at him through empty sockets. Its jaws clacked once, as if in a tired attempt to bite his shoes or to utter some final lamentation. Then it lay still. "What on earth…" murmured Parsons.

* * *

St. Ives could once again see Greater London spread out below him, but this time it wasn't spinning like a top. It lay below like jeweled pinpoints flung along the winding dark ribbon of the Thames. To the west the sky was tinged red with dying sunlight, which quickly deepened to purple then blue-black as his craft dropped toward Hampstead Heath. Behind him lay the uncharted oceans of deep space – oceans traversed by comets and moons and planets and asteroids, the vast and lonely sailing ships that plied the trade lanes among the stars, and among which, for a few brief minutes. St. Ives had maneuvered his little coracle of a star vessel.

But he was destined now for Hampstead Heath. The wonders of the heavens would wait for him, of that there could be little doubt. But the machinations of earthbound villainy would not. His friends at that moment were embroiled in God knew what sorts of dangers and intrigues. St. Ives smiled as he diminished the speed of the craft sliding in toward the fires that dotted the hillsides like beacons above the lights of Hampstead.

The great oval green was thick with people who swirled and parted and fell back. There, he could see, was a knot of people on chairs in a cordoned area – the Royal Academy, without a doubt. And before them – that had to be Parsons. St. Ives angled in toward him, looking in vain for his own companions. But there were horse carts aplenty, and one looked pretty much like another from such lofty heights. The ground sailed up at him. Upturned faces, mouths agape, swam into clarity. St. Ives fingered the levers, toyed with them, eased them this way and that, settling, finally, onto the green, dead center between two roaring fires, with no more jarring than if he'd sailed in on a feather.

He arose, flipped open the hatch, thrust out his head, and was amazed to see, sitting directly in front of the ship, its back turned toward him, the upholstered chair from the house on Wardour Street, still tethered to the ship, the luckless ghoul bound into it by three turns of hempen rope. The thing's hair stood on end – elevated by the spate of rapid travel through space – and its face was pulpy and bent, as if shoved and pummeled by atmospheric pressures. The ghoul seemed to be staring straightaway toward an open-mouthed Parsons, who held in his right hand, of all things, the severed, diminished head of Joanna Southcote.

St. Ives smiled and nodded at Parsons, who, quite apparently, was going to weep. He'd clearly been affected by the glorious issuance of the craft. St. Ives had underestimated Parsons; that much was certain. What was even more certain was that the members had underestimated St. Ives. Their countenances betrayed them.

"Gentlemen!" cried Langdon St. Ives, having prepared a small speech while cavorting through the upper reaches of the atmosphere. But his speech ended as abruptly as it began, for there arose immediately a furious shouting from the direction of the village of Hampstead, a shouting that climbed the hill like an approaching giant. And there, hovering out of the starry distances, sailed the blimp of Dr. Birdlip, swinging slowly on the breeze, making for Hampstead Heath.

As wonderful as St. Ives' arrival had been, the approach of the wonderful dirigible diminished it. The Royal Academy pushed past the star vessel in a rush, leaving St. Ives to address the back of the head of the thing in the chair. Duty, thought St. Ives, recalling the point of his journey to the Heath. His friends were somewhere nearby, as were his enemies. Birdlip approached, carrying with him the inheritance of Jack Owlesby – independence for Jack and Dorothy, Sebastian Owlesby's only respectable legacy. And there would be no end of villains afoot with an eye toward it.

St. Ives was torn. He dared not leave the craft unattended. Who could say what deviltry might be perpetrated against it? Drake, certainly, would attempt to repossess it, Pule to blow it to bits, Shiloh to claim it as a chariot of some peculiar god or another. Still, what could he do? Sit in it? Let the same crowd overrun the blimp, pluck the jewel from their grasp? He bent through the hatch, overbalancing and sliding out onto the riveted shell of the craft, grabbing at a pair of brass protrusions to haul himself free.

The shouting increased in volume. St. Ives slid head first onto the dewy grass of the Heath, then scrambled onto his feet, yanking at his rumpled clothes. A loud crack sounded behind him along with the snap and zing of something ricocheting off the hull of the ship. Another crack rang out, and St. Ives was once again in the grass, scuttling like a lobster around the ship, peering out beneath the lower curve of the thing at a man in the chimney pipe hat – Billy Deener – crouched beneath the spreading limbs of a shadowy oak. A pistol smoked in his hands. Beside him was a horse and wagon, empty, tethered to the tree. Deener took aim with his pistol and stepped forward, as if to stride toward St. Ives in order to flush him out. There could be no doubt that it was murder he intended. And there in the tumult on the Heath he'd get away with it too. They'd find St. Ives stiff as a gaffed fish on the green and half a million Londoners suspect.

St. Ives edged round the far side of the ship. Would it be wise to run, trusting the increasing distance to confound Deener's aim? He peeked out and a shot banged off the hull of the ship, the bullet singing past his ear. St. Ives contracted like a startled snail. He could, perhaps, clamber into the ship, shut the hatch, and sail away, but the man would be on him like a dog – St. Ives would be found murdered, dangling from the hatch, exterminated in a sorry effort to flee. It was run or nothing. Zigzag – that was the ticket. He'd dash away toward a far stand of trees. He'd keep the ship between them so that Deener would have to fire past it.

St. Ives leaped up and ran for it. "Hey! Hey! Hey!" he shouted, for no purpose other than to alert the night to the ensuing mayhem. He glanced over his shoulder as soon as he was underway, unable to stand the idea of not knowing where the assassin stood.

But there was no assassin – not standing, anyway. A man leaned out of the tree like an ape above Deener, and even as St. Ives watched, he slammed the chimney pipe hat cockeyed with what appeared to be a cricket bat. The hat sailed off end over end as Deener collapsed forward onto his knees. The man dropped from the tree, his own hat tumbling to the ground, and gripping the club with both hands smashed Deener again. Drake's hireling fell poleaxed onto his face in the weeds.

The man with the bat raised it aloft for another blow. St. Ives set out cautiously toward the ship. This is thick, he thought. There was, after all, such a thing as common decency, even toward a would-be murderer. The cricket bat descended, cracking against Deener's skull, then again and again, as if the man who wielded it was wild with fury. "Here now!" cried St. Ives, setting off at a run. The man cast the bat haphazardly into the air, turned toward the approaching St. Ives, and bent to pick something up out of the grass. It was the pistol. He leveled it at St. Ives, who lurched to a skipping halt, reversed direction, and weaved away across the green, tempted to run downhill toward the assembled masses below, but fearful that some innocent Londoner might take a bullet intended for him.

St. Ives ducked in once again behind the ship, wondering

wildly at the strange course of events that had led Willis Pule to save him from the murderous Billy Deener, for it had been Pule, gibbering mad, who had leaned out of the tree with the cricket bat to pulverize Deener. But why? In order, apparently, to have the pleasure of killing St. Ives himself. But Pule had given up the idea. He strode across to the tethered horse and wagon, rummaged among Deener's effects, and hauled something out – a Keeble box. Even from a distance there could be no doubting it.

The gun forgotten, St. Ives leaped from his cover and raced toward Pule. Which of the boxes it was that Pule was even then making away with, St. Ives couldn't say. But visions of the spark-throwing rocket bursting through the silo roof and of Willis Pule smashing about in his study, beating poor Kepler's bust into pieces, leant St. Ives a sudden disregard for danger. Madness, however, had given the student of alchemy wings, for he paid the advancing St. Ives no heed at all, but raced away into the night, gabbling to himself as he ran, half sobbing, his words utterly indecipherable. Billy Deener, St. Ives discovered, was dead.

The blimp swayed in the night sky on winds which seemed to be blowing into the stars. The moon rode at anchor, heaving on a heavenly groundswell, encircled by a radiant halo of stellar light, as if the stars themselves were ship's lamps that illuminated the invisible avenue down which rode Birdlip's craft, its gondola creaking to and fro in practiced rhythms. St. Ives wondered how many people were mesmerized there on the green; how many were perched in the treetops, peered skyward through unshuttered windows, or stood craning their necks along the dark and muddy roads that led up out of smoky London. Hundreds of thousands? And all of them still – not even the peep of a slanting bat or the chirp of a cricket in the nearby wood broke the silence. There was simply the shrub-scented night, heavy, quiet, expectant, and the slow creak, creak, creak of the swaying gondola, lit now by the sliver of moon. There at the helm stood the skeletal Birdlip, the indomitable pilot, his coat a tatter of webby lace, wisping 'round the ivory swerve of his ribcage. The moon showed straight through the coat like lamplight through muslin – seemed magnified, if that were possible, as if the coat were a wonderful bit of glass spun of silk and silver that drew through it the accumulated light of the heavens.

St. Ives couldn't move. What did it mean, this humming dirigible that had, after years of circuitous wanderings in the atmosphere, decided to wend its way homeward at last? What did it signify? Birdlip knew. He'd pursued something – a demon, a will o' the wisp, the reflection of a phantom moon that beckoned on the night wind and receded toward unimagined horizons. Had Birdlip caught it? Had it eluded him? And what, in the name of all that was holy, would poor Parsons make of it? He'd shortly be faced with yet another fleshless visage. What, wondered St. Ives, did it all mean?

The blimp hovered fifty feet above the Heath, seeming actually to rise now, following the natural curve of the hill, intent upon landing not just anywhere, but at some predetermined spot, an utterly necessary spot, as if it were indeed piloted yet by the straddle-legged doctor. His French cocked hat was settled low over his forehead, shading his empty eye sockets, the jellied orbs within having long since been burned by a remorseless sun and picked away by seabirds. What strange eyesight did Birdlip retain? How clearly did he see?

TWENTY

BIRDLIP

Bill Kraken, sitting astride the limb of an oak some five feet above the heads of the crowd below, wondered much the same thing. In none of Kraken's investigations into science was there anything as grand, as majestic, as the homeward-bound Birdlip and his astonishing craft. Something, Kraken was certain, was pending. He could feel it in the air – a static charge that shivered through the masses who stood mute with anticipation.

The descending blimp swung low overhead. People leaned out of the uppermost branches of trees, endeavoring to touch it. It seemed to Kraken as if the sky was nothing but blimp. He glanced back over his shoulder, looking proudly at Langdon St. Ives who stood before his own incredible ship. The night, indeed, was full of marvels. And he, Bill Kraken, squid merchant, pea pod man, had a hand in them. The man beside him in the branches, an unshaven pinch-faced man in a stocking cap, hadn't. Kraken smiled at him good-naturedly. It wasn't his fault, after all, that he didn't hobnob with geniuses. The man gave him a dark look, disliking the familiarity. Someone above trod on the top of Kraken's head in an effort to boost himself even higher. Below him on the green, stumbling from shadow to shadow as if working his way surreptitiously toward where the blimp seemed destined to land, lurched a man who appeared to be sick or drunk. Kraken squinted at him, disbelieving. It was Willis Pule.

Kraken dangled one leg down along the trunk, feeling for the crotch of two great limbs that forked up some six feet from the ground. Things, apparently, were hotting up. Pule disappeared into the shadows, then reappeared again beyond a heaped bonfire, the dancing orange light of which seemed to intensify the darkness behind it.

Not twenty paces behind Pule, possessed by a determination that belied his age, Shiloh the New Messiah limped along, accompanied by a straggling covey of converts strung along like quail, half intent on catching up to the disappeared Pule, half intent on Birdlip's craft. The blimp hung now over the green, suspended by the magic, perhaps, of its Keeble engine. The evangelist was lit for a moment by the same firelight which had illuminated Pule and which now betrayed on the old man a face twisted slantwise in a rictus of loathing, the messiah pursuing the worm, the devil who had made away with the head of his mother, and who now carried one of the fabulous boxes, quite conceivably the same box stolen hours ago by the imposter in the wagon.

And there, sliding along down the edge of the crowd, came Theophilus Godall, carrying with *him,* Kraken was horrified to see, a round, metallic object that could be nothing other than the Marseilles Pinkle, glinting in the firelight. He was clearly unseen either by Pule or the old man. But Bill Kraken saw him, and so did St. Ives. The tune had begun to be called, and it was time for

Kraken to dance to it. He slid to the ground and set out, running straight on into Kelso Drake, an inch and a half of cigar protruding from Drake's mouth like a blackened tongue.

If he'd had time to think, Kraken would have sailed back into his tree, scaled the slippery trunk like an ape. But he had no such time. He launched himself at the millionaire. "Here's for Ashbless!" he cried, an obtuse reference to the bullet Billy Deener had drilled into his treasured volume. And he struck Drake squarely on the chin, snatching the Keeble box from his hands as Drake fell sputtering, stupefied with surprise, his hat sailing off to reveal a bandaged head.

Kraken turned and ran, holding the box before him as if it were a pitcher of water he daren't spill. Drake pounded along behind, filling the suddenly tumultuous night with curses, drowned out when a hundred thousand voices arose in a sudden monumental cheer. The blimp, its time come round at last, shot forward and settled in onto the green, not twenty-five feet from St. Ives' space vehicle. The bulk of the crowd surged up the hill behind it. The ghoul in the stuffed chair sat placid as a man at tea in front of it. The Royal Academy, directed by the indomitable Parsons, clustered around it, eager to have a look at the skeletal sailor, home at last from the sea.

Kraken angled away into the rushing crowd. There was the Captain, stumping along, and William Keeble at the heels of his stalwart wife, all of them charging toward the blimp, toward the fourth and final box that rode within. "Cap'n!" shouted Kraken, capering along behind them, carried in a rush by the swarming masses, A sea of heads cut off his view. Someone trod on his toe. He stumbled. A dozen people smashed past him. He was pushed from his knees onto his face, nearly trampled, lying atop the Keeble box.

"Filthy piece of dirt!" hissed a voice in his ear, and as he hunched forward in an effort to stand, he was borne down again by the weight of Kelso Drake, his cigar gone, his jaws working as if he were full of speeches too vile to utter.

Kraken plowed his elbow into Drake's nose. A hand closed over his face, tugging his head back. He clamped his scattered teeth onto a finger and chewed away until the teeth closed against bone. A shriek erupted in his ear, and the hand was jerked away, nearly tearing the precious tooth away with it.

Kraken stumbled forward, half rose, and was elbowed sideways into a host of people, slowing now in the press. He was on his feet, though. Indeed, it would be difficult to fall, closed in as he was by the throng. Over his shoulder he could see Kelso Drake, cursing at the people around him – people who were in no mood to be cursed. A fist shot out and clipped Drake in the ear. He lurched aside. Kraken grinned. Drake was obviously possessed by the thought that millionaires ought not to be treated so. He railed at the man who he supposed had hit him – the wrong man, as it turned out, a man who had the general shape of a hogshead and the facial consistency of a bag of stones.

"Here now!" shouted the man, not wasting words, and he slammed Drake on the nose to the general encouragement of the crowd. Kraken pushed toward the erupting mêlée, shouting happily to see the color of Drake's blood. The industrialist flailed like a windmill, utterly ineffectively, so far gone was he in his anger and loathing.

Kraken hoped to get in a blow or two of his own, but his hopes were dashed when, with sudden inspiration, he shouted: "That's the man who murdered the child!" at the top of his lungs, pointing past the circle of Drake's tormenters into the millionaire's face. A cry of disgust and abandonment arose, and before Kraken could have a go at him, Drake disappeared beneath a monsoon of whirling fists. "Get him!" cried Kraken, but the suggestion, he quickly saw, was unnecessary. He pushed along toward the blimp, hugging his box.

Ahead of him, two dozen or so men scrambled to string ropes around the craft, cordoning it off against the possible rush of the masses. But the London populace, apparently, harbored suspicions, fears, and perhaps reverence, for they hovered round the perimeter of an oblong patch of ground on which sat the blimp, the corpse in the chair, and the starship. Parsons directed the roping efforts, arguing all the while with both the Captain and St. Ives. Captain Powers grew more heated by the moment, shouting that Parsons had no "jurisdiction." Parsons attempted to ignore him, but cast meaningful glances at St. Ives, as if to encourage the scientist to calm his bellowing friend.

St. Ives, however, was distracted by a scuffling and shouting off to his right, beyond the bonfire, which blazed now with increased ferocity, fed by a hail of limbs and forest debris tossed by the enthusiastic mob. St. Ives stepped along toward the scuffle when he saw amid it the head and shoulders of Theophilus Godall. Bill Kraken sprang into view just then, hurrying toward St. Ives, carrying his Keeble box like a trophy.

Willis Pule writhed and grunted, heaving in a tangle of grasping fanatics that included Shiloh the New Messiah. Godall circled round, intent on the box that Pule clutched. Jack Owlesby circled gamely beside him, looking for an opportunity. Pule shrieked; the box jumped out of his hands and was snatched by a beefy young man in a soiled robe. Shiloh hauled the box away from the man and lurched toward clear ground, jabbering excitedly, having no earthly idea which of the many strange boxes he possessed, but certain that the lot of them were somehow holy and somehow rightfully his.

Jack Owlesby strode along after him. The several parishioners who made as if to stop Jack found themselves peering at the business end of Godall's pistol. Jack reached past the old man and snatched the box, leaping away toward the blimp. Shiloh turned, an unuttered shriek stretching his mouth. Godall, smiling calmly, thrust the Pinkle into the old man's outstretched hands.

"What!" cried the evangelist, setting in to pitch the thing away. He saw it clearly for the first time even as he threw it. His eyes, yellow in the light of the fire, seemed to expand like balloons. He checked his throw, warbling out a little deflating cry. But it was too late. The Pinkle threw out a spoonful of sparks that whirled around the thrusting rubber head and flew in a wheeling arc into a stand of shadowy bracken and broom that muffled the strange noises and lights emitted by the orb.

The evangelist stiffened, his mouth going suddenly slack. Jack was beyond his reach. The bird he'd had momentarily in hand had flown. But here was another in the bush. He turned, ignoring Godall, who made no move to stop him. In a second he was gone, creeping through the dark shrubs on his hands and knees, as unheeding of the apocalyptic gyrations on the Heath roundabout him as if he'd been one of Narbondo's ghouls.

The evening, in the space of five minutes, had begun to look very satisfactory to St. Ives. Here was Jack Owlesby, toting a recovered Keeble box. Here was Bill Kraken, toting another. There was Theophilus Godall with yet another. St. Ives smiled at Jack and reached out to shake the lad's hand. Evil, it was clear, was fairly literally being pummeled. Jack grinned, the flames roared, the

Captain shouted, and Bill Kraken, with an alarming suddenness, pitched forward toward the edge of the fire.

Behind him, his face bleeding, his right eye shut, his left arm dangling uselessly, crouched a lunatic Kelso Drake. Kraken shouted and threw out his hands. The Keeble box set sail as if shot from a catapult. St. Ives leaped for it, knocking it askew in its flight, saving it from the fire but sending it cartwheeling toward where the enigmatic ghoul reclined in his chair. The box struck him on the chin, snapped his head down onto his chest, and landed in his lap.

With an oath, Drake limped forward, grimacing murderously. But there was Godall, smiling in the circle of firelight, his pistol drawn and mimed at Drake's chest. The millionaire lurched to a stop, raising his bands.

A cry arose from the crowd. St. Ives turned toward the blimp, expecting a revelation. But the blimp sat silent and dark on the Heath, surrounded by scientists scribbling in notepads, casting looks at the insistent Captain who held the sputtering Parsons by the collar.

Another cry. Hands pointed. It was the corpse in the chair, stirring. His back straightened; his fists clenched; air gasped through his closed teeth. The Captain released Parsons, who goggled at the corpse as it stood upright, dragging the ropes loose from where they were entangled among the springs of the chair. It held the box aloft, almost with reverence.

"Lord have mercy," muttered Kraken. Jack stood mute. The ghoul shuffled forward, bearing the Keeble box.

"Homunculus!" whispered St. Ives. Godall nodded beside him, his pistol disappeared. In his right hand now was St. Ives' aerator, in his left was a handful of Pule's jacket, the murderous student of alchemy slouching beside him like a man stuffed with rags, his mouth agape. Thousands of pairs of eyes watched the dumb show on the Heath.

The ghoul hunched toward Parsons, who stepped back, regretting suddenly that he'd got rid of the severed head he'd been given earlier. Would this ghoul demand it? Or would it hand Parsons yet another inexplicable item? What, for God's sake, was in the damned box?

But the ghoul strode past him unhindered, toward the gondola where stood the strident Birdlip. Only Captain Powers had the temerity to follow him. Parsons said nothing. The Captain fell in behind, hearing as he did the incessant demanding voice that jabbered from the Keeble box in the ghoul's hand.

Dr. Birdlip, suddenly, seemed to shake himself. Those on the edge of the crowd gasped. Was it the wind? A trick of moonlight? Birdlip released his hold on the wheel – a grip he'd maintained without pause for a decade. Finger bones picked at the rotted cords that lashed him to the gondola. The cords fell. Birdlip turned, jerking forward toward the little swinging stile door fallen back on its hinge. Firelight danced and leaped. Parsons gaped. St. Ives barely breathed. Godall stood bemused. The Captain nodded politely to the skeleton of Dr. Birdlip, then bent suddenly and picked something up from the floor of the gondola. St. Ives knew what it was. Birdlip seemed to heed nothing – nothing but the proferred box, which the ghoul relinquished, seeming to deflate almost and stagger just a bit, backward, stepping toward the stuffed chair as if suddenly fatigued to the point of collapse. Parsons began to step along after him, wondering at the nature of the animate corpse that gaped at him, opening and shutting its mouth like a conger eel.

"Speak, man!" cried the biologist.

The corpse dropped dead into the chair.

Birdlip jerked down onto the green in quick little lurching, stiff-jointed steps, holding the Keeble box, his skull canted sideways as if in perplexity. The dead silence was broken by the utterance of an immense sob, as Willis Pule, taking the startled Godall by surprise, twisted out of his coat in a rush. Pule sailed down on Birdlip, ducking under a murderous blow aimed at him by the stalwart Captain. But Pule, apparently, hadn't theft in mind as a motive. All such practical pursuits had been abandoned; it was mayhem and ruin he coveted, gibbering destruction, the mindless, drooling desire to tear the weary world to bits.

In an instant he snatched the box from Birdlip, who tottered there on the green, suddenly enervated. Pule raised the box overhead and smashed it to the green. The clever joinery of the Keeble box flew asunder as the thing cracked against a stone. The lid wheeled away into the astonished crowd. Ten thousand mouths gaped in wide wonder to see a tiny man tumble forth – the fabled homunculus – and leap to his feet on the green free of his prison at long last. Even though he wore a hat he couldn't have been eight inches tall.

What, wondered the treetop crowds and the staring masses on the Heath, what thing was this that ran dead away toward the skeletal Birdlip, past the goggling Parsons, through spring grasses that waved round his ears, step by tiny step? It clearly had a destination in mind. What, conceivably, could it desire?

Willis Pule clutched at his head, his wild loathing played out. He was reduced to a thing as empty as the airy gondola sitting like the bleached bones of a dinosaur on the green behind the teetering Birdlip. Theophilus Godall watched Pule creep away into shadow. He'd allow the spent thing to wander away unpursued, to take up a life, perhaps, of begging or of geeking in some low sideshow. A great wind blew up out of the south, buffeting the dark dirigible, which swayed on its makeshift moorings, threatening to tumble over onto its side like a wounded beast. The crowd gasped and surged away, fearful of being crushed. The homunculus confronted Dr. Birdlip, spoke to him, pointed, it seemed, toward the heavens. It doffed its clever little hat and gestured animatedly with it. Then, with a startling alacrity, it leaped onto the swaying skeleton, grappling its way into the doctor's ribcage, peering out as if through the bars of Newgate Prison. Birdlip took a tentative step forward, animate once again, and, to the degree that a skull can reflect emotion, he seemed smitten with sudden elation, perhaps a flowering of the sense of wanderlust that had motivated his journey through the heavens.

A cheer arose from those close enough to perceive this sudden illumination. Jack Owlesby, perhaps, cheered most loudly of all, but his cheer was cut short when, with a sudden whump, he was struck in the small of the back, and the box that he carried flew from his hands. Kelso Drake, having gone down the same twisted road as Willis Pule, shrieked past Godall into the firelight and endeavored to dance on the box, to smash it up. He was stopped cold, however, by the simultaneous effort of Godall and St. Ives, and by the curious behavior of the fallen box.

It shuddered there in front of the teetering Birdlip, in front of the astonished Parsons, clearly illuminated in the fireglow. Dr. Birdlip jerked round and stood still. Kelso Drake stepped a pace back toward the fire. The top of the box sprang away with a suddenness that brought a cry from any of a number of treetops. And very slowly and majestically there arose from the depths of the box the bird-eating cayman, snatching up one then another and another and another of the little fowl before sinking again into his tomb.

"Hooray!" shouted a hundred voices, a thousand. The cheer was taken up by the multitude, who could have no earthly idea what it was they cheered. And with the salutory cries fueling his departure, Dr. Randal Birdlip, himself piloted now by the little man within him, clacked jerkily over the grass, Parsons at his heels. He stopped at the side of the starship, turned and gazed one last long moment at the jeweled lights of London, bent over and unknotted the rope from round one of the little feet of the starship and clambered woodenly into the open hatch. The hatch slammed shut. Emerald lights burned suddenly within the ship. The ground seemed to shudder momentarily, and in the wink of an eye the ship was nothing but a speck of fire in the vast heavens, the intrepid Dr. Birdlip piloting the craft of the homunculus among the countless stars that hung suspended above the streetcorners of space like gaslamps.

EPILOGUE

St. Ives didn't rue the loss of the ship for a moment. He'd had his voyage. And the future, he was certain, held the promise of more. Here was Dorothy Keeble, recovered, clutching Jack's arm, the two of them smiling at the Captain, who held before them an open Keeble box in which lay a tremendous emerald, big as a fist and seeming to burn green and immense in the firelight.

A moaning filled the night. Branches tossed on the trees. The tall grasses blew in undulating waves. The blimp canted sideways, mooring lines snapped, and people scurried like bugs, running to get out of the way. Slowly and majestically the blimp toppled over, tearing itself to bits, escaping gases whooshing through rents in the fabric of the thing. The ribby gondola, hauled onto its side, broke apart like a wooden ship beaten against rocks by high seas. And first one, then twenty, then a hundred onlookers rushed in to salvage a bit of it as a souvenir. Wood snapped. Fabric ripped. Great sheets of deflated blimp were stripped loose, clutched at by uncounted hands and rent to fragments. Within moments the once-rotund blimp was nothing but a flattened bit of wreckage that had disappeared beneath an antlike swarm of Londoners. An hour later, when the crowds, finally, abandoned their pursuit of relics and surged wearily homeward at last, not a fragment, not a scrap of Birdlip's craft remained on the Heath.

St. Ives and his companions kicked through the grass, gazing at the place where the blimp had lain. Bill Kraken said that the loss of it was shameful. William Keeble wondered at the fate of its engine, carried happily away in pieces by drunken green-grocers and costermongers and beggars who hadn't the foggiest notion of the magic it had once contained. Jack and Dorothy gazed at each other with an intensity of expression that seemed far removed from any wondering over disappeared blimps, an expression very like the one shared by Captain Powers and Nell Owlesby, who stood hand in hand beside Jack and Dorothy.

Ten paces away sat Parsons, astride the arm of the stuffed chair, the corpse slumped beside him, restful now and refusing to respond to Parsons' chatter. "Sheep," the biologist insisted, "aren't like you and me. They produce vast quantities of methane gas. Very inflammatory, I assure you..."

St. Ives strode across and laid a hand on the poor man's shoulder. Parsons grinned at him. "Telling this fellow about the gaseous mysteries of grass feeders."

"Fine," said St. Ives. "But he seems to have fallen asleep."

"His eyes, though..." began Parsons, glancing at the aerator box that St. Ives held in the crook of his arm. He shuddered, as if gripped by a sudden chill. "You don't mean to open that here, do you?"

St. Ives shook his head. "Not at all," he said. "Wouldn't think of it."

Parsons seemed relieved. "Tell me," he said slowly, looking askance at the head of Joanna Southcote, which lay now up to its nonexistent ears in weeds beside the stuffed chair, "does the night seem uncommonly full of dead men and severed heads to you?"

St. Ives nodded, searching for words with which to respond to Parsons' very earnest question. His search, though, came to an abrupt end with the sudden issuance of Shiloh the New Messiah, his face haggard, his cloak stained and mired, the ghastly Marseilles Pinkle tooting in his grip, its rubber head shooting in and out, throwing sparks like a pinwheel and smelling of burnt rubber and unidentifiable decay. With a mad cry the old man fell forward onto his face and lay still, his torn and soiled robes splayed out around him. Dead, apparently, he hopped once or twice as the Pinkle, trapped beneath him, continued to sputter and whir before rolling free.

St. Ives shook his head. Parsons arose and very slowly stepped across to where the Pinkle spun itself out on the green, the rubber head tooting out a final, blubbery whistle. Parsons shook his head ponderously and wandered away into the dark, weaving toward Hampstead like a rudderless boat.

St. Ives watched him in silence, wondering whether his own reputation as a scientist had in any way been cemented by the night's odd events, and determining finally that he didn't really care a rap one way or the other. The evening had taken its toll, certainly, on the good as well as the wicked. His companions trudged along toward the wagon, on the seat of which sat a placid Hasbro. St. Ives was suddenly dead tired. The morrow would see him at Harrogate. There was work ahead; that was sure. "Well," he said to Godall, "so ends the earnest endeavors of the Trismegistus Club. And with a modicum of success, too."

"For the moment," said Godall enigmatically. "We haven't, possibly, seen the last of our millionaire. But I rather believe him to be a spent force. I'll call upon him myself in a day or two."

"What ever became of Willis Pule, do you think?" asked St. Ives. "He was utterly mad there at the last."

Godall nodded. "Madness, I'm certain, is the wages of villainy. He met an old friend, in fact."

"What's that?" asked St. Ives, surprised.

"The hunchback."

"Narbondo!"

Godall nodded. "In a dogcart full of carp. Pule lay face down among them, comatose."

"Poor devil," said St. Ives. "I don't suppose Narbondo had come to his rescue."

"Not very bloody likely," said Godall darkly, and the two men hoisted themselves onto the wagon, sitting with their feet dangling over the back so that they faced the sweep of hill on which, two hours earlier, had sat the long-awaited blimp.

Ahead of them, some distance away, trudged half of London, not a man or woman among them with the least understanding of the mysteries that had supplied the evening's entertainment. What understanding have any of us, wondered St. Ives. Not a nickel's worth, not really. Not even Godall, for all the man's intellectual prowess. Intellect wouldn't answer here, wouldn't explain why the cold and measured tread of science had strayed from chartered paths and wandered unsuspecting into the curious moonlight of Hampstead Heath. Poor Parsons. What did he make of the blimp now? Would he awaken at midday having somehow clipped the evening apart and reassembled it into a more tolerable pattern, like a man who whistles his way through a dark and lonely night, then abandons his fears in the light of a noonday sun?

St. Ives gazed with sleepy wonder at the empty, receding green as the wagon bumped around a muddy swerve of road into Hampstead, the village dark now and silent. He tried to summon a picture of the blimp riding at anchor, of Dr. Birdlip visible beyond the slats of the wooden gondola, legs wide set to counter the roll of an airy swell. But the Heath lay empty above, the blimp fragmented, disappeared. And it seemed as if the strange craft had never been more than a ghostly will o' the wisp, a bit of sleepy enchantment woven out of nothing, that whirled and faded now across the back of his closed eyes until he seemed to be sailing with it above the clouded landscape of a dream.

ABOUT THE AUTHOR

James Paul Blaylock was born in Long Beach, California in 1950, and attended California State University, where he received an MA. He was befriended and mentored by Philip K. Dick, along with his contemporaries K.W. Jeter and Tim Powers, and is regarded as one of the founding fathers of the steampunk movement. Winner of two World Fantasy Awards and a Philip K. Dick Award, he is currently director of the Creative Writing Conservatory at the Orange County School of the Arts, where Tim Powers is Writer in Residence. He is also a professor at Chapman University, where he has taught for twenty years. Blaylock lives in Orange CA with his wife, they have two sons.